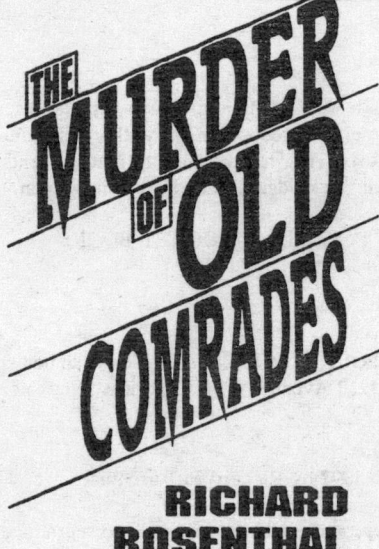

THE MURDER OF OLD COMRADES

RICHARD ROSENTHAL

POCKET BOOKS

New York   London   Toronto   Sydney   Tokyo   Singapore

This book is a work of fiction. Names, characters, places and incidents are either products of the author's imagination or are used fictitiously. Any resemblance to actual events or locales or persons, living or dead, is entirely coincidental.

An *Original* Publication of POCKET BOOKS

POCKET BOOKS, a division of Simon & Schuster Inc.
1230 Avenue of the Americas, New York, NY 10020

Copyright © 1992 by Richard P. Rosenthal

All rights reserved, including the right to reproduce
this book or portions thereof in any form whatsoever.
For information address Pocket Books, 1230 Avenue
of the Americas, New York, NY 10020

ISBN: 0-671-70732-9

First Pocket Books printing January 1992

10 9 8 7 6 5 4 3 2 1

POCKET and colophon are registered trademarks of
Simon & Schuster Inc.

Cover art by Darryl Zudeck

Printed in the U.S.A.

This was a war for export.
These were the men who fought it—

The NYPD ...

DETECTIVE JONATHAN GRAU: He's got twenty years on the force and four years with the 47th Precinct Detective Unit. For the impeccably dressed Grau, there's only one way to run a homicide investigation—the right way. He keeps meticulous notes and has a keen eye for evidence, and for a killer's mistaken moves. But in the case of this fresh double homicide he could really use a break ...

OFFICER ANTHONY TANTI: A senior man in the precinct, he drives a cherished '76 Dodge with split seats and takes the station house steps two at a time. Tanti wants out of the Patrol Bureau and into the Detective Unit. The first on the scene of the bloody double homicide, he's got his best shot at joining Grau's team ...

... Vs. The KGB

COLONEL ALEXI PROPKIN: A sharp-featured assassin, Propkin is a top man in the business with a solid, successful career behind him. A formidable threat to his enemies and a dangerous maverick to his superiors, he is on his last, most savage mission ...

THE MURDER OF OLD COMRADES

Most Pocket Books are available at special quantity discounts for bulk purchases for sales promotions, premiums or fund raising. Special books or book excerpts can also be created to fit specific needs.

For details write the office of the Vice President of Special Markets, Pocket Books, 1230 Avenue of the Americas, New York, New York 10020.

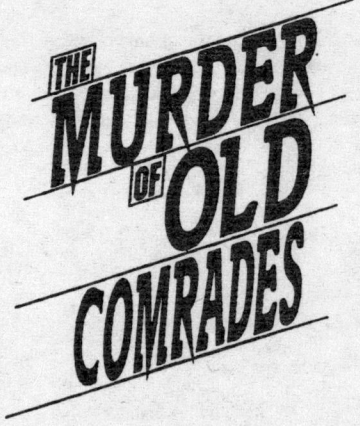

THE MURDER OF OLD COMRADES

Chapter 1

The Soviet pilot first saw New York Harbor as pinpoints of light in the early night. He adjusted the throttle and carefully trimmed up the aircraft, which now flew several hundred feet over the waves of the Atlantic, heading west toward the coast. For the previous hour he and his passenger, KGB Colonel Alexi Propkin, had skimmed the water's surface so as to avoid premature contact with American radar.

Captain Anton Brysof looked at the man on his right. The colonel had not spoken since they had begun their flight and he gave no sign now that he had any interest in conversation. During the few weeks they had been together the agent had been taciturn and cold. Brysof's attempts at conversation were almost always met with stares or grunts. He had never been particularly comfortable around members of the KGB and the continued silence of his passenger did nothing to allay his unease.

Brysof put the matter from his mind as he blotted beads of perspiration from his forehead with the sleeve of his shirt, and for the first time since the flight began, permitted himself to relax. In order to avoid American civilian air-traffic control radar near the coast he had had to fly the floatplane dangerously low, and watch the ship's flight instruments constantly. A moment of forgetfulness and they could strike the waves below at a hundred miles per hour.

His navigation equipment indicated they were already deep in airspace designated as the "exclusion" by the American government's Federal Aviation Administration. Within its boundaries there was no legal requirement for radio contact with ground controllers. The aircraft's presence on an air traffic controller's radar screen should now draw no attention.

His instructor for the mission had flown extensively in the New York area. The man had told him that each day a continuous procession of single- and twin-engine planes, helicopters and floatplanes traveled the route.

Brysof had found this difficult to believe, unable to envision such freedom of movement. He was used to the Soviet system. There, a pilot could take no action in the air without confirmation from ground controllers. But his instructor insisted it was so: that much of American airspace was unhindered by government intervention. He even said many of the American people owned their own aircraft, and they kept them at small uncontrolled airports which lay scattered around the country. How a government could permit its citizens to travel around, willy-nilly, Brysof could not comprehend. But his instructor was adamant and Brysof trusted the man's information.

Brysof was confident that his aircraft showed up on the American radar as but one speck among hundreds moving in the New York sky. To take advantage of the exclusion he would have to fly over the Hudson River, between the shores of New York and New Jersey. Flight altitude at its center, he had been instructed, could be no higher than eleven hundred feet.

Brysof had been in the Soviet Air Force for almost five years. He was a young and handsome man, with short dark hair cropped in a military style, high cheekbones and a finely shaped nose. Before they had left port he had been fitted with a set of American civilian clothes, which he now wore. He found it strange to be flying a military mission wearing tan slacks, dress shirt and a comfortable pair of loafers. On the aircraft's back seat lay a neatly folded blue blazer. There were no identifying marks on any of the items. The purpose of the clothing was obvious to Brysof, if unstated by his superiors. Should there be an untoward incident his body could not be readily identified as being that of a non-American.

The Soviet air arm was extremely selective in the personnel chosen to fly its aircraft. Of the thousands of young men who yearly volunteered for the position of military pilot, only a handful were picked. They were the best that Soviet society could produce. The rejected majority were placed in the enlisted ranks of the service, to spend the remainder of their duty as little more than brutalized slaves.

Like most of his comrades, he had hoped to be assigned to a fighter command when he had completed flight school. It was not to be. He had drawn duty in a transport squadron. While on the long sea voyage to America he had time to reflect that fate was strange. While many of his former classmates were now flying training sorties in their fighters, it was his mundane transport assignment that had permitted his superiors to chose him for this dangerous and interesting mission.

The problem as it had been explained to him during his briefing had been a simple one: Deliver an agent onto mainland America without any possibility of compromise. Because of the routine requirements for identification, passport checks and other security measures, Aeroflot and the other commercial air carriers were of no value.

Another proposal had been to have the agent enter the country by car from Canada or—better yet—Mexico. But there had been concern that the long overland trip to the East Coast could invite compromise. Additionally, this method did not solve the dilemma of how to remove the agent from the country in the event some problem developed.

Another suggestion was to use a submarine and an inflatable raft, culminating in a beach rendezvous. Still, the question of retrieval had not been answered to everyone's satisfaction.

Then one of the planners involved in the operation struck on the idea of a floatplane. The plan appealed to all. The small aircraft could deposit the agent at an upstate New York lake, for pickup by local assets. In the event a hasty removal was required, a coded radio message could be transmitted and in a few hours the floatplane could return to pick up the agent. But the most cunning part, Brysof reflected, was the Americans would never suspect such a method would be used—indeed, could be used. There was simply no place out on the ocean for such a short-range aircraft to take off from or land near.

The concept was neat, clean and above all secure. The Wilga's instruments showed that they were now within twenty-five nautical miles of the city. Brysof gently pulled back on the plane's controls and simultaneously eased the throttle forward. The floatplane slowly rose from its wave-height altitude over the dark waters of the Atlantic Ocean.

When they reached six hundred feet he reduced back pressure on the stick. As the ship's airspeed increased Brysof smoothly reduced engine power and trimmed forward pressure off the stick. The plane flew along in a state of neutral buoyancy.

Brysof saw Propkin's face, illuminated by the red glow of the instrument panel, turn toward him. He sensed the colonel wished to ask some question about his last maneuver. Seeing a chance to open communications with the man, Brysof said, "Colonel, we are now flying in the airspace designated by the American aviation officials as the exclusion."

"Who is excluded?"

Brysof smiled. "Comrade Colonel, the name comes from the fact that within this area aircraft are excluded from the control of ground radar personnel. I have been told this is due to the large number of aircraft that use this part of their airspace. Their system simply cannot handle all the traffic."

Propkin folded his arms across his chest and returned to staring out the windscreen.

Propkin was a well-built man of average height. Unlike the western European stereotype of the Slav, his features were sharp and his short-cut hair blond, although the sides were now tending to whiten. And, like the pilot's, the clothes he wore were impeccably American. With his dark woolen slacks he had on a matching dark shirt, worn open at the neck. His shoes and sport jacket were expensive, having been purchased at one of Manhattan's better stores. Except for his silver watch he had on no jewelry.

Although the night was moonless, visibility was excellent. Brysof looked up at the cloudless sky dotted with stars. Ahead the horizon glowed with a spectacular aura, caused by the brightness of the city which lay before them.

Brysof once more checked the instruments on his panel. All systems were operating normally and their gauges showed in the green. He reflected that the Wilga's reputation among pilots for dependability was well founded. The machine, although ungainly in appearance, was solidly built. It was designed to operate under primitive conditions, with minimum maintenance. The airplane was the flying single-engine equivalent of the draft horse and was used as a utility ship throughout the Eastern European countries. It had a large wing and its body narrowed sharply behind the passenger compartment. The whole effect of the design was to give the ship the appearance of being a pregnant, oversize dragonfly.

Directly ahead, Brysof could see the illuminated outline of the Verrazano Bridge. The land mass on his right he knew to be Brooklyn. To his left was Staten Island. In the night sky off his left wing he saw a line of white aircraft lights suspended over the horizon. Brysof correctly speculated that they were from the dozens of commercial jets queued up for landing at Newark Airport.

Flying over the center span of the bridge he watched as a shark-shaped Bell 222 helicopter passed off his right wing. Painted in the blue and white colors of the New York City Police Department's Aviation Unit, the ship headed south, to its base at Floyd Bennett Field in Brooklyn.

"Comrade Colonel." Brysof nodded his head in the direction of the police helicopter.

Propkin's head followed the path of the other ship. Looking back to Brysof, he asked, "How many helicopters do the American police have?"

"Three small ones and four big ones. That one that just passed us is their fastest."

"Faster than our aircraft?" Propkin asked.

"Yes, Comrade Colonel, it is a much faster ship than our floatplane," Brysof responded, enjoying the slight flicker of concern he saw on the face of the stone man next to him.

Brysof turned the Wilga north at the Verrazano. The ship's windscreen filled with a veritable cornucopia of colored lights, both on the ground and in the air. Reds, whites, greens, yellows. Some glowed steady while others flashed and blinked. The buildings of Manhattan Island, like a forest of enormous Christmas trees, loomed before them.

The plane passed the Statue of Liberty. Her torch burned brightly and the entire statue was awash in white light. The rich green color of her weathered copper body stood out from the darkness of the surrounding water. To their right the twin buildings of the World Trade Center towered over them. Several small aircraft flew by, traveling north and south. Strobe lights flashed on their tails, and reminded Brysof of fireflies as the little ships slowly moved by them.

Brysof once more attempted to elicit a human response from Propkin.

"The American city is very beautiful at night, isn't it, Colonel?"

"Perhaps, Captain. But I don't think this is the time for sightseeing," the other man coolly responded.

Brysof's face flushed with anger but he remained silent. Air Force captains did not argue with KGB colonels.

New York City moved off their right wing. The disembodied lights from a dozen cars crisscrossed Central Park. Below them a small tug moved slowly up the Hudson River. A stream of phosphorescent white water trailed in its wake.

Continuing northward, the Soviet aircraft passed over the George Washington Bridge. The massive steel structure was outlined against the black river by hundreds of intense white lamps attached to its superstructure. The white and red lights of slowly moving cars decorated its roadway. Beyond the bridge Brysof could see that the intensity of ground lighting began to diminish.

Several miles past the bridge he again increased their altitude, this time leveling off at two thousand feet. Yonkers, a miniature New York City, passed off their right and fell behind.

Reaching into a pocket on the inside of the door, Brysof removed an American aeronautical chart. He opened it and turned on an overhead light. The map confirmed what his instruments had already told him. They were now flying in a part of the exclusion where an altitude of three thousand feet was allowed. Before the night was through it would be necessary to fly over some low mountains. His new height would clear them easily.

Brysof monitored New York Approach Control on frequency 126.4. The hour was late and he heard only light radio traffic. A small aircraft asked controllers for permission to land at Westchester County Airport. Another requested a radio check. As he expected he heard no radio communication regarding the Wilga.

The floatplane passed over the Tappan Zee Bridge, one of his checkpoints. The ship's Loran C navigation unit indicated he should now turn to the left, to a heading of 320 degrees.

The evening air was calm. With no wind there was no turbulence and Brysof found the plane required minimal control input. With gentle fingertip pressure he moved the joy stick. The ship banked about and steadied itself on its new course, Brysof silently congratulating himself on his fine flying.

From out of the darkness next to him Propkin asked, "Captain, how many more miles until we reach our destination?"

The pilot looked at the navigation equipment. He calmly replied, "Twenty-five miles, Comrade Colonel," quietly hoping that Propkin was getting nervous at last.

As the big bridge fell farther behind them the ground below gradually subsided into random dots of light. Twelve miles from where they had made the last turn the first range of low mountains they would cross came into view. The glow of a town passed under them. It was Ramapo, in New York State, near the New Jersey border. Although it was less than an hour's car drive from one of the largest cities in the world, the lack of lights below showed that its steeply rising terrain inhibited sprawling suburbanization.

From out his left window Brysof saw under them an earth so black that they might well have been flying over the ocean. Without a moon the clear night sky was very dark. Beyond the windscreen of the ship the ground and horizon merged as one. He continued to fly the aircraft solely by reference to its instruments.

The ship's navigation unit told him they were now only two miles from the rendezvous point. Over the ship's glare shield the final ridge came into view. From atop its spine rose a large microwave tower. Red lights on its top flashed a warning to low-flying aircraft. As the ship's nose passed beyond the ridge a large valley spread out before them and house lights again dotted the ground.

To their left and almost directly below they saw a far more intense glow. It was a state-run prison, ringed with high-intensity sodium-vapor security lamps. The ground around it was illuminated as a large irregularly shaped circle of yellow.

"Comrade Colonel, below and to your left."

Propkin looked down. Directly off to one side lay Wickham Lake. The colonel knew from his earlier mission briefings that on the opposite side of the lake, to the southeast, but invisible now in the darkness, was a small country airport.

Brysof throttled back on the engine. The nose of the seaplane settled lower and the aircraft started a shallow descent over the water.

The Wilga had been running standard night lighting. Red on the left wing tip, green on the right and white at the tail. Brysof reached to the control panel and flicked the lights off.

The prison's intense yellow glow reflected brightly off the water's surface. Beyond the lake's boundary was nothing but blackness and the unseen airport on the far shore. Where the water met land they saw the prearranged signal: three flashes of light, two long, one short.

As the aircraft passed over the lake the pilot pulled back gently on the control stick and trimmed the ship to fly at pattern airspeed. He held her at an indicated twelve hundred feet of altitude, which he knew put them about seven hundred feet above the surface of the ground below.

He let the seaplane continue a few miles farther out, then made a thirty-degree bank to the left, back in the direction of the lake.

Brysof prepared the ship for landing. Lowering the aircraft's flaps one notch, he reduced power still further and retrimmed her so that she flew along at a low but controllable airspeed. The aircraft began to descend at a rate of 150 feet per minute.

Speaking more for himself than his passenger, the pilot said. "We will be making what is called a 'glassy water' landing, Comrade Colonel. At night I cannot visually determine our height above the water with any degree of accuracy. Thus I will permit the ship to touch down at its current rate of descent. It's a standard technique."

"How many times have you performed this maneuver before, Captain?" Propkin asked.

Brysof smiled and said, "Twice, in practice."

"Oh."

With the reduced power setting they could hear the air rush past over the sound of the ship's engine. Little dots of light quickly passed underneath them from the small homes below. Soon the bright yellow surface of the lake came up on the windscreen.

Once over the water the pilot put additional back pressure on the control stick, to further reduce his airspeed. He let the aircraft continue its descent at a shallow glide angle. The floatplane landed itself. It touched down so gently on the surface of the lake it was necessary for Brysof to look out his side window for the spray of water that would indicate the aircraft was firmly down on the lake's surface.

Brysof sighed in relief and relaxed. He turned to Propkin. "With this type of landing, because of the shallow angle at which the floats hit the water, it's possible to bounce back into the air without being aware of it."

"What happens then?" Propkin asked.

"You crash," Brysof said matter of factly, as he reduced the throttle to idle and brought the control stick fully to the rear. The Wilga's floats settled firmly into the surface of the mirror-smooth lake.

Brysof reached down by his right leg and unhooked a cable to lower the ship's water rudders. Now with directional control assured he turned the nose of the floatplane toward the shore, to a point opposite from where the prison lay. A small beam of light was aimed at them and he headed for it.

Brysof listened to the muted sound of the engine as it slowly ticked over. The little dot of light he headed for appeared suspended in midair. Aiming for it brought the

Wilga alongside a small dock that jutted twenty feet into the lake. An unseen hand grabbed the right wing and gently pulled the floats of the ship against the side of the wood structure. They bumped to a stop.

The colonel unfastened his seat belt. He reached behind and grabbed a dark rucksack. Brysof noticed that his passenger had to use a good deal of strength to pull it up and over the top of the front seat. Probably because of the awkward way he sat, Brysof decided. Even so, whatever was in the sack must be heavy.

The passenger-side door swung open. Propkin turned in his seat and gingerly felt his way out of the ship in the darkness. The invisible man on the dock said something to Propkin which Brysof couldn't hear. His passenger then slipped gracefully from the plane.

The engine still turned at idle. Brysof knew a floatplane on the water was a vulnerable target and he wished to leave as soon as his mission was accomplished and the two men stepped back.

Someone outside firmly closed and latched the right side door. A hand rapped on the plexiglass and Brysof sensed rather than felt the Wilga being pushed away from the dock and toward open water.

The men on the dock heard the floatplane's engine increase in power. The aircraft surged forward and in a moment was climbing steeply away from the lake, unseen in the night's blackness, to retrace its path home.

They walked off the dock and over to a small American sedan parked on the grass near the shore. Propkin held his rucksack firmly. The men stopped and Propkin paused a moment, took a deep breath and looked about.

The prison was clearly visible across the still lake. In the distance the ridge line he had flown over stood black against an ink-colored sky. The night air was calm and smelled of freshly cut grass and pungent lake water. A few feet away Propkin heard a bullfrog call for a mate and something small rustled in the reeds to his right.

The men climbed into the car's front seats. Propkin placed his rucksack in the back of the auto. Speaking in

The Murder of Old Comrades

Russian, he said, "Colonel Andrapovich, I haven't seen you for quite a while. How have you been?"

"I am well, comrade. I've been kept busy, so time has passed quickly. And you?"

"I also haven't had much chance for rest. And I've been told that you and I have a bit of work to do here."

Propkin settled comfortably in his seat and looked out the window. It was his first time in America and he looked forward to the ride into the city.

Andrapovich started the car. Without turning on the headlights he slowly drove across the grass runway. When they came to a macadam taxiway he stopped the car.

He looked about. The tiny airport was deserted. This was as he had expected. Andrapovich had made many previous trips to this place in preparation for the night's clandestine landing. He congratulated himself on finding the perfect location for the rendezvous. Deserted at night, with the lake illuminated by the bright prison lights, an aircraft landing or departing a small airport would be no cause for alarm.

Satisfied they were alone he turned the car left. They moved past rows of light aircraft, eventually coming to the airport's entrance.

As they drove through the open gate Propkin glanced at the hand-painted sign which hung from a thick wood post by a chain. It read Warwick Municipal Airport.

The car bumped along a narrow gravel road until they came to a small highway. Andrapovich turned the car onto it and headed in the direction of New York City.

The men had much to discuss and the hour drive would be put to good use.

Chapter 2

The blue and white patrol car glided up to the tired wood and brick house. It double-parked in front, even though the street was quite narrow. Two officers got out. The driver was short and fat, his partner was of average height and well built.

The heavier of the two looked at the cracked front window then let his eyes rest on the tiny patch of unkempt lawn. A bunch of kids' toys, most broken, lay scattered about. He sighed and made for the front door. The slimmer officer got there first. With the end of his nightstick he rapped three times on the wood and glass frame. A moment later the door cracked open. A little boy looked up at the man from the darkness of the house. He sniffled and rubbed his red eyes with the backs of his hands.

"Hi," Officer Tanti said, and smiled encouragingly. "Where's your mommy?"

The child replied by raising his arm and pointing in the general direction of the home's interior.

Without speaking Tanti gently pushed past the child and entered the house.

Over his shoulder he called to his heavyset partner, "Stay with the kid. I'll look around."

The other officer, always happy to limit his physical activity, voiced no objection.

Officer Anthony Tanti was 35 years old and had been on the force for twelve years. Due to layoffs engendered by the New York City fiscal crisis a decade earlier and the freeze on hiring for the five-year period thereafter, Tanti was a senior man in the precinct. He was a good police officer.

Moving slowly through the hallway he looked left and right as he went. The radio message that had sent him to the job had been cryptic. The caller, probably the child from what the dispatcher had told them, had said something about a possible DOA. As he walked, his right hand stayed by the butt of his revolver.

He came to an open door on his left and could hear a television cartoon character talking the gibberish that their creators have taught children to love so much. Inside the room he saw a young girl, perhaps three, sitting on an overstuffed couch. A pretty little brunette, she smiled up at Tanti, her face smeared with milk from the bowl of cold breakfast cereal that now sat empty on her lap. She was still in nightclothes and looked as if she would be happy sitting in front of that television set for the rest of her life.

He moved from the doorway and went room to room but saw nothing unusual. The residence was relatively clean but untidy. Things had been left to lie wherever they had dropped and in the kitchen there was the musty odor of stale food and unwashed dishes. Tanti had smelled it many times before, in many other homes, and he thought little of it.

Turning back to retrace his steps he stopped by the doorway which led to the basement. He considered for a moment whether he should first search the second floor of the house or go downstairs. He decided on the latter and started down the steps. The dry wood boards creaked underfoot.

Like most basements this one was only dimly lit by natural light. The narrow windows set up high along its walls were far too small for the size of the room. Homes close by on either side made any chance of direct light entering impossible. At the foot of the stairs Tanti stopped to allow his eyes to adjust to the gloom.

In a moment he saw the two forms lying on separate couches. One was a man, the other a woman. Both were on their stomachs, fully clothed even to their shoes. And both were obviously dead.

Tanti slowly approached the nearest body, the man. He

was white, about fifty years of age. There was a thick gelatinous pool of blood on the floor near the side of the couch where his head lay.

He walked over to the body of the woman. She had turned her face into the back of the couch just before she died, like a child would hide her face in the skirts of her mother when frightened.

Tanti took out his flashlight and ran its beam along her body. The woman had been in her early thirties, about five foot six with a good figure. She was wearing designer jeans and a pinkish-colored blouse, worn outside the pants. Her nails were manicured and painted a light red color. He couldn't quite make out her features but suspected she had been attractive in life. On her left wrist she wore what appeared to be an expensive watch.

He bent over to look more closely at the back of her head. With his flashlight he could make out three distinct dark-colored blotches in her hair where the bullets had entered her skull.

As with the man, Tanti observed a large pool of congealed blood by her head. He knew this was to be expected with head wounds. In his experience even a relatively minor scalp cut caused a great deal of bleeding.

The bodies were relatively fresh. That, plus the coolness of the basement, had helped delay putrefaction and Tanti was spared the sickly sweet odor of decaying human flesh.

Gingerly he backed out of the room, and returned to where he had left his partner. He found the other officer on a chair next to the children, seemingly as engrossed in the cartoon show as they were. Tanti motioned him out of the room. The heavy man grunted, struggled to his feet and walked to the hall.

In a hushed tone, Tanti explained, "Two DOAs in the basement. Looks like some sort of a hit. Find out from the kids if they have any neighbors they can stay with. I'll notify Central to send the squad."

"Okay, Tony."

Tanti's partner disappeared again into the TV room, the nightstick dangling from his belt hitting the doorjamb as he moved.

"Four seven Eddie to Central, K." Tanti transmitted over his portable radio.

"Seven Eddie, go ahead."

"Have the Four Seven detectives respond to 1157 Goodwinn Street. Confirmed homicide."

"Ten four."

He put the portable back in its plastic belt holder. Through the curtains of the front window he saw the distinctive outline of a city ambulance as it pulled up to the house. The city's emergency medical services had been notified by central radio to respond to the address at the same time the police were.

Two emergency medical technicians, dressed in their white shirts and green slacks, got out of the box-shaped van and walked into the house. Both carried large black satchels. Both held the various pieces of medical equipment used in their job. The lead technician, an olive-complexioned young woman with long black hair, stepped up to Tanti and asked, "What do you got?"

"Two DOAs, in the basement. Do me a favor and try not to move the bodies."

"No problem," she replied, understanding immediately that the officer was concerned with safeguarding whatever physical evidence was down there.

By regulation, only someone trained medically could declare a person dead. Thus, before any actual physical investigation of the bodies could take place, a technician was needed to make the determination that in fact the two people downstairs were deceased. That they had probably been dead for over twelve hours made no difference to the bureaucracy, because police officers were not deemed sufficiently well versed in the medical field to recognize a corpse when they saw one.

Most of the time the medical technicians (or EMTs) were very reasonable about preserving the integrity of a crime scene. From an investigator's standpoint the worst-case scenario would be to have a victim of a crime die, but only after having first received medical treatment.

As cold-blooded as it might appear, the detective assigned the case would prefer that the victim be left untreated. The detective would know that much forensically valuable evidence had been destroyed by the EMTs and emergency-room doctors, in their vain effort to save the life.

After a moment downstairs the two EMTs returned to the first floor. The woman technician nodded to Tanti.

"We didn't touch the bodies, officer."

"Thanks, I'll let the detectives know," Tanti said. He took out his memo book and opened it to a clean page.

Without prompting the woman EMT stated, "Harlow, number 1019."

Tanti wrote down her name and badge number. It would be part of the information he would be asked by the responding detectives.

"Thanks a lot," he said, closing his memo book. "Have a good one."

"Bye," the two EMTs said in unison and walked out the front door.

As the ambulance pulled away another car drove up in its place. Tanti recognized the men inside as two detectives from the precinct squad. With them was their sergeant. The three entered the house, the sergeant nodding to Tanti.

"What's up?"

"You got a double homicide downstairs, boss. Both shot in the head."

"Any witnesses?" asked the smaller of the two detectives, Clarence Bradford.

Detective Bradford stood five feet seven inches tall. He was a black man, neatly dressed in gray slacks and a blue blazer. His sharp features gave him the undeserved image of a hard man. But the one characteristic that most distinguished Bradford from the other men in the unit was his total lack of hair. No one knew for sure whether he shaved his head or it was naturally bald. Whatever the reason, the squad put his looks to good use. When they had a tough punk to interrogate, Bradford was invariably made to play the role of squad villain.

"Two children were in the house when we got here," Tanti replied. "They were probably here when it happened, but I didn't question them. Other than that, I don't know."

The sergeant nodded. He turned to the larger of his two men and asked, "Jon, is this one yours?"

The Murder of Old Comrades

The other detective, Jonathan Grau, replied, "Yeah, I'm catching."

Within a detective squad there was a case-catching order. Sometimes it was by crime, sometimes by the order which the case came in. If there were four detectives working they would break up the tour into four equal time periods. Each would be responsible for investigating whatever crimes came into the precinct during their allotted time. This particular case had fallen into Grau's slot.

Grau had been with the Four-Seven Precinct Detective Unit (the department liked fancy unit titles) for four years. Like Bradford he was a neat dresser. Standing over six feet tall, the detective wore a conservative light tan suit, with matching striped tie and brown wing-tip shoes. Unlike his partner he had a full head of dark hair, with some distinguished looking silver strands around his ears. Light wrinkles were visible at the corners of his eyes. They gave his face the appearance of someone who worked in the sun. In truth they were the result of his more than twenty years on the force.

Prior to his assignment to the 47 Detective Unit he had worked in a specialized homicide squad. The specialized squads had been disbanded in favor of shifting the responsibility for the investigation of unusual and criminal deaths to the precinct squads.

The current system was a poor one. In a busy precinct detective squad an investigator could catch a couple of burglaries, a petty larceny or two and a homicide, all during the same tour of duty. Being assigned the homicide did not relieve him of his other responsibilities. Thus, if the case was not solved within a reasonable period of time, it was shunted aside. As a result the city-wide clearance rate for homicides sometimes fell below 60 percent. Or stating it another way, four out of ten murders in New York City were never solved.

The fact was homicide investigation required more skill and experience than the entry-level detective possessed. A homicide detective should know law, criminology and understand how the courts function. The person assigned to a homicide investigation should be mature and not permit ego to get in the way of good decision making. In short, to include this complex type of investigation along with all the other tasks normally assigned in a precinct squad was probably the least efficient way to operate.

The three squad members walked down the stairs with Tanti close behind. Grau took from his inner jacket pocket a small spiral-bound steno pad. He favored the kind that had wide spaces between the lines as he had poor handwriting and was forced to write in large letters so that he could later decipher his own notes.

On the first few pages of the book he had already written several notations. They were there to remind him of the pieces of information he would be required to gather at the start of a homicide investigation. This prior preparation was vital, although it served no other purpose than to ensure he didn't forget which units within the department to notify and what information each would require of him.

There was a right and a wrong way to conduct a homicide investigation and detective Grau only knew how to do it the right way. The first page of his spiral book started off with the date, the complaint and case number. Then some blank spaces for a homicide log number and an aided card number. Why the latter, Grau could never understand. He figured that there was no way anyone was ever going to aid a murder victim. But an aided number was what they wanted and when he got it back at the squad it was what he would put in the report. Next came the location of the crime scene, the time he was notified and by whom. Only after he recorded the time he had arrived at the scene did his notes begin to reflect his true reason for being there. Under the caption Deceased, Grau would put both names of the victims, their dates of birth, and the physical description of the bodies as well as the clothing they wore. Next he would record the name of the first officer on the scene. That officer would be required to go to the Medical Examiner's office the next day and officially identify the corpses.

The second page of the pad still contained information required purely for the bureaucrats. Grau would jot down who in the Bronx Detective Area office had received the telephone notification of the deaths and who in the Chief of Detectives Office had received the identical information. Next to this notation came the name of the doctor who

The Murder of Old Comrades

would arrive from the Medical Examiner's office to examine the body. Until he came they could not, technically, search the corpses for identification or any other purpose.

There was a space for the name of an officer and the run number from the Crime Scene Unit team responding. Grau would also record the day's weather and perhaps the plates of any cars parked on the street near the address. After he had done all that, and only then, would Detective Second Grade Jonathan Grau put information down on his steno pad that might have some relationship to the solving of the crime.

"Watch your footing, it's damn dark," the sergeant said as he led the way to the bottom of the stairway. Once in the basement it took a moment for their eyes to adjust to the poor lighting and the three investigators were at first uncertain of the scene before them.

Grau removed a small but powerful flashlight from his inside jacket pocket. Since he had discovered the light in a sporting goods store the detective always carried it with him when he worked. It was one of the new thin-bodied aluminum variety, powered by two triple A-size batteries. Its bulb was no larger than a grain of wheat. Grau thought it was probably filled with some exotic gas as the intensity of its light went far beyond what a bulb its size should be capable of.

Grau played its narrow beam first on the man, then the woman. The detective viewed the scene as an art critic might take in an unfamiliar painting.

"Clarence, the light," Grau said, and pointed to one end of the room with the beam of his flashlight.

On a table at the far corner of the basement stood a small lamp. The other detective stepped over and flicked the light on. A shadowy brightness illuminated the scene.

Bradford asked his sergeant, "Can we search the bodies?"

Sergeant Carrol turned to Tanti to confirm what he already knew. "Has Crime Scene been here yet?"

"Negative, boss," Tanti replied.

The Medical Examiner, although important and serving a vital function in the investigation process, was of less concern at the moment than the lack of the Crime Scene Unit personnel. The investigators knew from experience that the doctor would simply make a cursory examination of the bodies, take down a few notes and be on his way. His job would really start once the bodies were on the autopsy table.

It was the lack of the Crime Scene Unit people that held them back. The investigators knew the value of first taking photographs of a homicide scene before moving or disturbing any of the physical evidence. There was no way a person could remember every nuance and detail of such a scene. Photos taken by Crime Scene now might later prove to be invaluable. The men therefore made only a visual examination of the victims.

The sergeant turned to Detective Bradford. "Call the squad. Have Timpkins and Schwartzman get over here. You and Timpkins will start on a canvas of the neighbors. Tell Schwartzman I want him to get all the plate numbers on the street."

"Right, boss," Bradford said and headed for the stairs. Speaking to the detective's departing back the sergeant added, "And don't use the phone in the house to make the call! Go to the neighbors and con them into letting you use theirs."

Bradford acknowledged the order with a wave of his hand and was gone.

Proper procedure should have made the sergeant's last order unnecessary. A telephone handset was an ideal location for latent fingerprints to be found. Permitting officers to use a phone located at a crime scene would surely destroy any such evidence.

But people are lazy. The sergeant had been to enough homicide scenes to know that unless he said something about the telephone upstairs it would be the one the detective would head for.

Grau squatted and took a close look at the bullet wounds in the man's head. The victim wore his hair short. By brushing aside a few of the strands the entrance holes became clearly visible.

"Sarge, looks like he was hit three times," Grau said.

"The woman, too," Tanti quietly offered, standing off to the side.

The Murder of Old Comrades

The holes in the scalp had been made by a very small-caliber weapon. They looked almost like needle marks. Grau was not surprised at this. Bullet entrance wounds in living tissue almost always appeared smaller than the diameter of the projectiles which created them. What did strike Grau as odd was the bulging of the man's eyes. It was as if some great pressure had been inside the skull. Such bulging shouldn't occur with the kind of small-caliber handgun that was obviously used here.

He stood up, looked around the floor, and saw a number of spent cartridge casings. From where everyone was standing it was clear their feet had already displaced many from where they first fell. Grau picked one up. It was a small rimfire case from a .22-caliber weapon. The markings on its back showed it to be a common brand of American ammunition. As Grau bent to put it back on the floor he noticed a different shell which lay a few feet away. He picked it up.

"Unusual shape, don't you think?" he asked Carrol, the casing lying exposed in his open palm.

The sergeant looked and nodded.

Grau was fairly familiar with firearms, but this particular shell looked strange to him. It was more narrow at its mouth, where the bullet had once been seated, than at its base. He knew this type of round was referred to as a bottleneck cartridge and was commonly seen in rifle calibers. But this shell was far too small to be from any rifle. Shining his light on it, he turned the casing over. The headstamp markings imprinted in the rear of the case were no help. Straddling the primer were the indentations of two stars. Above and below the primer were the numbers 270 and 79. The inscriptions were meaningless to Grau. Just as he had done with the other shell, he put the casing back exactly where he had found it on the floor.

Footsteps sounded above them. Grau, Tanti and the sergeant turned toward the foot of the stairs. In a neat procession came the Medical Examiner followed closely by two detectives from the Crime Scene Unit.

"Hi, fellas, what do we have here?" the doctor asked, shaking the hands of the three officers.

"The usual. A couple of DOAs, shot in the head," Grau

said. It was more a way of exchanging pleasantries than a serious attempt at imparting useful information.

The doctor began to examine the two victims while Grau hovered over his shoulder.

"Doc, those entrance wounds on the male, they seem damn small, especially considering the bulging of the eyeballs. I've only seen that when someone is hit with a .357 magnum or something."

The doctor looked again at the head of the male victim. "Hard to say, detective. We'll have to wait until he's opened up at the autopsy."

Grau hadn't expected much information from the doctor. The man was a medical expert not a ballistician. Only rarely had Grau met someone who was knowledgeable in both fields.

The Medical Examiner put on a pair of thin translucent gloves and began probing the man's body with his fingers. He gently moved the head back and forth. Then he did the same for the arms and legs. He grasped the victim first by the wrist, then the ankle. Moving over to the woman, he performed the same ritual on her.

The doctor remembered that photos of the scene had not yet been taken and was careful not to disturb the positioning of the bodies. Without lifting his head from his task, he asked, "Anyone got the time?"

A voice replied, "9:20."

The doctor stood up and removed his gloves. Speaking to anyone who cared to listen, he announced, "My guess is, they died last night. Around midnight. Could have been an hour or two either way." Then he moved off to the side and repacked his bag.

"Good luck with the case," he said and headed back up the stairs.

The detectives from the Crime Scene Unit took over. They photographed the room from all angles using a large Horseman camera loaded with Tri-X, black and white high-speed film.

The sergeant said to one of the technicians, "Can you give me a sketch of the scene?"

The technician nodded and continued with his work. He took the right hand of the woman and carefully examined the fingernails. Satisfied, he went over to his attaché case and removed a small metal tool that appeared similar to a common nail file. He also took back to the body several small flat twist-top aluminum cans used for storing minute particles of evidence.

He knelt by the body and picked up the woman's hand. Placing one of her fingers at a time in the now open can, he gently scraped out from under each fingernail whatever was there.

Upon completing the chore he sealed the can and carefully marked on its label the day's date, the time, the run number of the job and his initials.

"Sarge, I'm going upstairs to start my paper work," Grau said and moved toward the stairs.

Sergeant Carrol nodded, intent on the work the Crime Scene investigators were performing.

On the first floor Grau stepped into the kitchen. The table still held the carton of milk and box of cereal from the children's breakfast. That reminded him that he would have to speak to the children soon. He pushed the mess to one side and sat down to work.

This was no novel, where homicide investigators engaged in assorted adventures while they solved their cases. Grau prepared to act as the central recipient for the various pieces of information that would be brought to him by the other members of the squad. He was the man responsible for the case and his primary duty would be to act as the hub of an information-gathering wheel. Other members of the squad would be the spokes. During this period in the investigation it would be their responsibility to see that Grau received whatever facts they could gather, in order for him to have the tools needed to successfully work the case.

He opened his steno pad and began to fill in the times, names and relevant numbers he had gotten from the different people who had been to the crime scene that morning. Looking through his rough notes he saw that he had yet to get the single most important information he needed: the names of the deceased.

As a general rule, as long as the victim of a homicide

remains unidentified the case cannot be investigated. Certainly, as in the investigation in which Grau was now involved, some preliminary work could be done. The same people and units would be called and would respond. Pictures of the scene would be taken and the Medical Examiner's office would perform the standard autopsy. All the right pieces of paper would be filled out. But once that was completed there would be nothing further for the detectives to do.

Without a name to go on, how does one inquire of others what the victim had been doing just prior to his death? Who he was with? What his friends had to say, his boss, his wife, his lover? Without a name, the victim has no history. And without a history there could be no investigation.

Detective Bradford walked into the kitchen. In his hand he held a steno pad similar to Grau's.

Bradford pulled up a chair and cleared his throat. "I spoke with the people next door. They've got the two kids that came from here. The dead woman's name is Judith Bartlett. She's been living in the house for about eight months or so. They weren't sure. Kinda kept to herself, although they said she was friendly enough."

Grau wrote down the name silently, waiting for more.

"The man they described as staying here a lot fits the description of the DOA downstairs pretty well. The guy is probably her boyfriend. She wasn't married. They knew even less about him than about her."

Grau asked the obvious question, "Did they hear anything last night?"

"Nope."

"What about the children?"

"Schwartzman and Tanti's partner are still over there trying to get what they can out of the two kids, but it don't look good. Both kids went to bed before 9 P.M. Neither one heard anything. They still really don't know what's going on. And one last thing. Have you taken a look upstairs yet?"

Grau shook his head.

"Well I did. Someone gave the place a good toss. All the drawers were turned upside-down in the bedroom and the mattresses were ripped from the frames. Even the clothes in the closet were tossed on the floor. Same thing with the kids' rooms. They must've slept through it."

"Sounds like whoever did the homicide wanted something pretty bad," Grau offered.

At that moment Sergeant Carrol looked in on the two detectives. "Come on downstairs. We can search the bodies now."

The two men got up and followed their supervisor back down to the basement. The Crime Scene Unit people were just tidying up their equipment as the three walked in.

One of the technicians walked up to Grau. "I've got all the empty shell casings. One is a strange looking thing. You want me to voucher them for you?"

"Thanks anyway, I'll take them," responded Grau. The officer handed over a little plastic bag. Inside were the five small, empty casings and one that was larger than the rest. Grau put the bag in his jacket pocket and walked over to the body of the male. He reached into the man's left rear pocket and removed the victim's wallet. Inside were the usual items of identification: driver's license, social security card, a vehicle registration and assorted credit cards. He put the wallet down on the lamp table in the corner.

"Give me a hand," Grau asked the three men standing around him.

A dead body is a difficult thing to move. Even a live person who resisted movement unconsciously helped the people he sought to hinder. A dead body had no such consideration. The corpse's two hundred pounds felt like three hundred to the detectives.

Grau pulled on the man's right arm. Bradford and Tanti helped by grabbing and tugging at the legs. Between them they managed to get the body on its back. Nature was having its way and an unpleasant odor, like meat left overnight on the table, rose from the deceased.

The man was wearing expensive gray woolen slacks. His shirt also looked to be of high quality. In his pockets Grau found two sets of keys including one set for a car. There were also several hundred dollars rolled in a wad of tens and twenties as well as some loose change.

So much for robbery being the motive, Grau mused silently.

Except for a watch the victim wore no jewelry. He had been powerfully built in life and Grau wondered why there was no sign of a struggle.

Grau noted that the man's shoes somehow did not match the rest of his attire. They were brown leather and, although fairly new, had an indifference of style that made them look somewhat peculiar. He couldn't quite put his finger on it, then guessed the shoes were European.

Grau looked closely at the dead man's head. He saw that only one of the three slugs had completely penetrated the skull and had continued on into the body of the couch. He said, "Let's get him off here. I'd like to find that bullet."

Again the three pulled on the body, this time laying it on the floor next to the couch.

Grau and the sergeant turned the couch over. They ripped the bottom lining out as they searched for the track of the slug. One of the Crime Scene detectives brought over a large powerful light. He shone the beam on the underside of the upturned sofa while Grau started to hack away at the cloth and stuffing with a pocket penknife he carried for such purposes. In a few moments the detective uncovered what he was after. Imbedded deeply in the foam was a tiny projectile.

Grau held the bullet between his thumb and forefinger and examined it closely. The other men in the room crowded around the detective to view his prize.

"Hardly larger than a .22," Grau said, examining the slug.

One of the Crime Scene men extended his open palm and Grau placed the bullet in it.

The man shook his head and quietly observed, "I've never seen one of these before."

The bullet was shaped like a miniature rifle slug. It appeared to have a dull, silvery metal jacket and its nose came to a point. Although it had gone through the man's head and continued several feet into the furniture under him the slug remained intact, almost pristine in condition.

The other officer handed it back to Grau, who again looked it over closely. Etched into the side of the projectile were six clearly visible grooves, created when the bullet traveled down the bore of the weapon. Grau knew that if he could come up with the right gun, ballistics could make the match. He wrapped the bullet up in his handkerchief and put it in his jacket pocket. Grau wondered why the killer used two guns for the killings. Perhaps there were two people involved. Still, it would have made more sense if one victim had been shot with one weapon and the other with a second. He turned to the other men and said, "Let's see if we can find any other slugs. Maybe he missed a couple of times."

The detectives, having once tasted success, vigorously dug at the disemboweled sofa, searching for any other projectiles. After a few minutes they gave up on the effort, accepting the fact that indeed only one had gotten through the man and the shooter hadn't missed.

They then turned their attention to the woman. She had no identification on her. This was no cause for comment as the detectives knew that most women carry such things in a purse or pocketbook.

At the woman's side Grau said, "Well, let's do it again."

The other men grunted in acknowledgment and grabbed her arms and legs. Upon turning her over they saw that, unlike the man, there had been no complete penetration of the skull. Still, they repeated the drill performed with the other victim. They removed her from the couch and searched for any possible spent projectiles. As they had expected this time they found none.

Tanti stepped over to the wall to give the investigators room to work. As he walked he noticed a brass-colored object just under the edge of a small throw rug. The rug had been in the middle of the room. During the shifting of the bodies it had been kicked off to the side. The officer bent down and saw it was a live round of ammunition.

"Hey, you guys. Look at this." Tanti held the newly discovered treasure out for the others to appreciate. Grau walked over and took it from the officer.

"It's unfired but damaged," Grau said as he examined the round. A Crime Scene man came over and Grau handed it to him.

The other man nodded and said, "Okay, I think I understand why we got two different guns here." He pointed to the dark gray lead bullet of the small-caliber round. The lead was smeared and the bullet bent at an angle to the case.

"The killer's gun jammed. See how deformed the bullet is? While he was pumping shots into this guy his gun failed to chamber the round properly. So he hit him a third time with his second piece."

"And the woman?" Grau asked.

The technician shrugged. "My guess is he cleared the .22 pistol and finished her with it. Stands to reason he'd do the guy first. The DOA was a big boy. There'd be less chance of a hassle once he was dead." He handed the damaged round back to Grau who put it in his pocket with the other evidence.

While the other detectives went back to their work Grau picked up the wallet from the table and went upstairs. He pulled up the same chair in the kitchen, sat down, and methodically dissected the brown leather pouch.

First he removed the driver's license. It read Sergi Gorkin, of 79 Brighton First Street, Brooklyn. Grau had been to that borough only a few times and was unfamiliar with the neighborhood. He put the license to one side.

He removed a vehicle registration next. It was in Gorkin's name. The car it described was an older Dodge Colt, an inexpensive compact.

Grau opened the part of the wallet where money would normally be kept, to see if there was any inside that had to be vouchered. All he found was a folded-up bill of some foreign currency. He laid it flat on the table. It had words in French, Italian, German and English. Whatever it was it was worth five hundred of them, as that was the number printed on its face. Grau tossed it on the table.

The rest of the wallet contained some credit cards, mostly from gasoline companies, and a black-and-white photograph of a woman, definitely not the one downstairs. This photo was that of a twenty year old, with full but pleasant features. He removed the picture from the plastic holder and turned it over. There was no inscription and Grau noted that the photographic paper was rather thin. Either it was an old photo, which he didn't believe, or it was foreign. He put it back in the wallet and placed everything else he had found in a small plastic bag.

By now the other detectives who had been called to the homicide scene by Bradford had completed their jobs and were wandering into the house. Grau's sergeant, just up from the basement, entered the kitchen and asked, "Anything else you need?"

Grau thought for a moment, then shook his head. "No, there's nothing more to do here. I want to get back to the squad and run their names and DOBs. Maybe I'll come up with something."

Grau knew that by checking the victims' names and dates of birth through a number of different sources he might get an overview of the kind of people he was dealing with.

The detectives collected their various bits of paraphernalia and left the house. It was 2:10 in the afternoon. As Grau stepped from the house the bright sun momentarily blinded him. He threw up his hands to shield his eyes from the glare. The detectives walked down the front path, got into their respective cars and drove back to the precinct.

Once Grau was back at the squad he began to put together a homicide case folder. He also had to ensure that all notifications had been properly made and he had to type up an "unusual" report, standard procedure in all murder cases. The report was a short narrative of the crime and it would be sent to half a dozen different units within the department. He also had to type out the opening "DD-5," the standard snap-out investigative report form used throughout the bureau. By the end of a homicide investigation a detective might have well over a hundred such forms in a case folder.

Grau was in a hurry. He had to do all this before his tour ended. Recently, in an effort to economize, the department did not permit detectives, even when working a fresh homicide investigation, to continue past their normal tour of duty. The rationale behind this was that the team coming on duty for the next shift could continue the investigation. This of course was nonsense. Even if the other detectives had some interest in another's case, which they didn't, they had more than enough work of their own to concern them.

Besides which, the fresh detectives hadn't been to the scene and had no feel for the case. A ten-minute briefing by a tired detective would be of little value to them.

Grau rushed through with his work and at the end of his tour signed out and left for the day.

On the way home he stopped at a small newsstand and picked up the *Post* and the *Daily News,* curious to see if the double homicide would be mentioned. It wasn't.

Chapter 3

Tanti arrived at the Four-Seven Precinct at quarter to seven the next morning. He managed to find parking close to the building, which he thought was a nice way to start the day. Sliding out of his blue '76 Dodge he stepped back and looked the car over. She was a two-hundred-dollar purchase made three years earlier. Her seats were split, the paint was faded, and rust showed through the metal along the lower body panel. The car's odometer showed 37,450 miles only because the manufacturer hadn't made provision for more than five digits. The car was kept alive because of Tanti's preference for spending a hundred and forty dollars a month on gas rather than a hundred dollars on new-car payments and forty dollars a month on gas.

Tanti crossed the street and headed for the precinct. He wore his normal off-duty attire: a pair of dungarees purchased at a local army-navy store, old brown loafers that hadn't seen shoe polish for a very long time and a multicolored polyester short-sleeve shirt of uncertain lineage. His off-duty gun bulged underneath the shirt, which was as close to concealing the weapon as Tanti got when the weather was warm.

The Murder of Old Comrades

It was his third day tour, which meant he was scheduled to work the second platoon from 0705 until 1535 hours.

He took the front steps of the precinct two at a time. The building had been constructed during the 1970s when there had been a flurry of capital improvements of the department's aging infrastructure. The outside was of a reddish-colored brick and the structure was modern in style. Its walls and windows jutted at some places and were set angled in at others.

As he made his way up the steps Tanti looked at the cracks which ran through the cement work. They had been there since he could remember and he had begun to work out of the building shortly after it was built.

The weather was going to be hot and humid. Just like the day before, he thought as he pushed open the large glass front doors of the station house. Once inside, the precinct's tepid air-conditioning did little to allay the outside temperature.

"Hi, Fred," Tanti said to the weary-eyed officer stationed at the precinct telephone which was set off to the right of the main desk.

"Hi, Tony," Fred replied, pleased to see that the day tour was arriving and he could soon go home and get some sleep.

Sam Coyne, also in for the day tour, came up to Tanti. Coyne was a tall thin man, with sparse gray hair and a dark moustache that defied department regulations by extending below the top of his lip. Like Tanti he was dressed in a dungaree outfit that would have looked more in place at a construction site.

"Hey, Tony, what you been up to? I was looking for you yesterday."

The two officers had come on the force together. Although about the same age Tanti was in much better physical condition than Coyne, working out regularly as he did. The other man's idea of exercise was to lift a couple of bottles of Heineken beer after work.

"I got stuck with a double homicide, Sam. I was off the clock all tour."

Coyne smiled. "Well, in this weather anything beats bein' out on the streets."

"You got that right. It sure beats patrol," Tanti replied. He watched Coyne walk away. What Tanti would have had trouble explaining to Officer Coyne, or to himself for that matter, was that he hadn't really believed his answer to the other man's innocent banter. Seeing the two bodies and newly orphaned children hadn't been a pleasant experience for Tanti. But it was just one more small nick taken off the man's psyche, and his deeply ingrained "cop" need was to show those around him how little he thought of such things.

The fact was, Anthony Tanti had been very troubled by what he had seen yesterday. He had been troubled by what he had seen on many of his tours of duty. And, as with most officers, Tanti was wholly incapable of discussing these feelings with other people. Especially with other cops.

A combination of factors mitigated most police officers' ability to express their feelings about what was in their heads. Certainly part of the problem was the macho self-image which most officers had. This false bravado hindered real communication. Both the men and women on the force believed they knew what was expected of them—by the public as well as their peers. They strove to live up to an artificial hardness, the image of the unflappable cop who in time of trouble could deal with any situation.

The officers tried to be like the make-believe police they saw on television and in the movies. They swaggered, spoke from the sides of their mouths, cursed at each other and the street people they dealt with, and generally tried to live out the fantasy image.

In the *New York Daily News* they saw the political cartoonist's caricature of city officers as large and burly white men. Irish names were inscribed under their shields. They came to subconsciously believe those were the "real" police, that this melting pot of men and women from different nationalities and ethnic groups, ranging in size from four foot ten up, was somehow an aberration.

The public was also to blame. People had a stereotyped view of police officers molded by the same media images. The police were either heroes or bums, saviors of society or corrupt incompetents who violated honest citizens' constitutional rights.

At any nonpolice social function an officer came to

expect either to be insulted about his occupation, harangued about a traffic ticket unjustly received, or prodded by expectant listeners for exciting tales of adventure.

When at the scene of some true emergency, when others around them were hysterical with panic and confusion, officers had to be above the emotional tumult. Of necessity they trained themselves to be aloof and detached during periods of crisis.

It was this complex combination of factors that explained why officers walked around in hardened emotional shells. It protected them from psychic harm and permitted them to function in time of chaos.

So it was that Officer Tanti could not tell Officer Coyne that he had not liked seeing the two bloody corpses the day before. He could not explain that he had felt pain over the fact that two innocent children no longer had a mother.

Tanti simply sauntered away with a smile on his lips. Without a visible care in the world he entered the muster room where his platoon would be turned out next.

A large wooden partition supported from the ceiling ran the length of the ground floor. It separated the main floor area of the station house from the muster room. On the walls where the officers would be inspected and given their assignments hung posters of assorted felons. Some were wanted by NYPD, others by state and county agencies and some by various federal enforcement units. No one ever gave them a glance.

On the cork bulletin board next to the wanted posters were social announcements. They were about various upcoming parties for retiring members of the service, a baseball game, and the upcoming precinct picnic. Next to that was a memo from one of the precinct's lieutenants informing the members of the command that they shouldn't feed the house cat, Vito, anything but his special canned food. It was bad for his kidneys.

Tanti walked over to the section of the board which held the day tour's roll call. In the Four-Seven Precinct, which put out many dozens of officers on a normal tour of duty, the roll call was several pages long. It was also recently computerized and thus made unintentionally difficult to read.

Tanti looked to see where he was on the sheets and with whom he would work. When he finally found his name he swore under his breath.

"Shit! The homicide from yesterday!"

Because he was the first officer to arrive at the double murder he would have to go down to the morgue and identify the two bodies. The department doesn't run a taxi service for its personnel. Assignments such as going to court, picking up evidence at the police laboratory or identifying homicide victims meant that officers who worked in commands located away from these main offices frequently spent the better part of a day traveling to and from their assignment. The morgue was located on First Avenue and 30th Street in Manhattan and Tanti would have to take the subway there and back.

Tanti considered his options. He would be damned if he'd take the subway all the way into Manhattan on a day that promised to be as warm as this one. With his luck the train probably wouldn't be air-conditioned. And since he would have to travel in uniform he'd be besieged by lost civilians. They would ask him questions about which train to take where, not knowing that he'd be more lost than they were. Besides, there was always the chance he would get "involved." That is, see someone commit some petty criminal offense that would require him to make an arrest. If that happened in Manhattan, he could be stuck in court for the next twenty-four hours.

He decided he had no option but to take his own car. When in uniform officers were prohibited from traveling in their private autos, but it was done all the time. What annoyed Tanti was the fact that he would have to put thirty miles on his personal car, "for the job." As a matter of principle that bothered him. Then inspiration struck. He quickly walked from the muster room to the side stairway and bounded up the steps to the second floor two at a time. From the stairway exit he could see the sign 47 PDU. A large red arrow pointed down the hall. He followed the arrow and entered a fifty-by-thirty-foot room, the precinct's detective unit.

Inside he saw the row of detectives' green metal desks that stood against the wall. Their tops were covered with old newspapers, unwashed coffee cups and assorted blank department forms. Manual typewriters were set out on moveable stands around the room. Some still held snap-out report forms in their platens, the previous typist too lazy to remove them.

A heavy-set black detective in his early forties sat at one of the desks, a newspaper in his hands. He wore what remained of a short cropped Afro, the bald spot on the top of his head taking up most of the space. The black hair was specked with white as was his large moustache and he had a warm and friendly face. His name was Joe Blakemore and he had been born in the United States Virgin Islands.

Blakemore looked up at Tanti. "What's up, Tony?" the jovial man asked with a hint of the lilting singsong accent of the islands.

"Joe, is Jon Grau around?"

"He's due in at eight." Both men glanced up at the office's large round-face wall clock. It showed five minutes to seven.

"Do me a favor. When he gets in ask him if he's going to the morgue. On that double homicide from yesterday. I've got to ID the bodies downtown and I'm looking for a ride."

"No problem, Tony," the big detective said and went back to reading the *Times*.

Tanti hurried down the stairs. Passing the first floor level he continued into the basement where the officers' locker rooms were located.

As with all locker rooms this one had the musty odor of sweaty bodies and clothes worn a day too long. High metal lockers lined the walls and stood in rows in the middle of the room. Tanti walked down the third aisle, past other officers who were busy changing, engaged in chatter about women, ball games, the job, and women.

He knew he was really pushing the clock now. The platoon was due on the floor at 0705 hours. He had been late several times in the last two months and had been told by his sergeant in no uncertain terms that the next time he was late he would "get one," meaning a complaint.

Tanti moved down the row that held his locker. Already perspiration began to trickle from his underarms and he debated whether or not to suffer the discomfort of wearing his bulletproof vest.

Since the adoption of soft-body armor by the department over ten years earlier, it had shown its worth many times over. Designed to protect officers from the relatively low-powered handgun rounds so popular with common street criminals, the design, by necessity, was a compromise.

Much debate had taken place at the highest levels of the department as to the appropriate degree of protection the standard-issue vest should afford its wearer. The problem was, as the protection level increased, the comfort level decreased. Police managers in other agencies, many well intentioned, some simply concerned with their careers, specified protective vests for their personnel that would defeat virtually any handgun caliber. These vests were so bulky, and retained so much body heat, that they were most frequently found hanging in officers' lockers or stored in the trunks of their police cars. The top management of NYPD decided that a vest not worn was the equivalent of no vest at all. Thus the department vest was among the lightest in use by police agencies and consequently was worn by the majority of officers out on patrol. And, because of the number of officers who routinely wore their vests, dozens of lives had been saved.

But today comfort won the argument. Tanti began to throw off his civilian clothes. He dumped them in a heap at the bottom of his locker. Quickly he put on his uniform pants, shirt and shoes. Placing his hat on his head he grabbed his gun belt, nightstick and memo book and ran from the room and up the stairs.

Just as Tanti broke out of the ground-floor doorway he heard a voice call, "Fall in for roll call!" The platoon began to form up in ranks on the muster-room floor. He hurriedly entered the room and took a place in the back row, still fumbling with his uniform equipment.

The sergeant stood with his back against the wood partition and faced the three rows of officers. He was young, about thirty, with short brown hair and sharp features. He had held his rank for four months and was still uncomfortable with the responsibility that came with command. Pointedly he kept his eyes on the roll-call sheets in his hands as the last few belts were buckled and snaps fastened.

He turned to the page where the officers assigned to patrol were listed and started to call off their names.

"Maxwell!"

"Here, sarge."

"Arrest Processing Officer, give the desk officer a hand."

Officer Maxwell left the ranks and disappeared beyond the wooden partition.

"Scanlin!"

"Here."

"Patrol Post Twenty-four."

Tanti only half listened as the roll was called. His thoughts drifted to how he was going to get downtown when finally the sergeant called, "Tanti!"

"Here."

"You're scheduled for the morgue. See the desk when you get back."

"Right, sarge."

Tanti knew that they were always short a few officers for a day tour. Some who were scheduled to work might be out sick or maybe a few of the guys had taken an emergency day off. If the precinct was below minimum manning levels when he got back from downtown, the desk officer would have to assign him a partner and a sector. It would be catch-as-catch-can, he thought. God knows whom he might be stuck riding with.

After the roll was called, specific instructions for the day given, and an inspection conducted, the sergeant called the platoon to attention. In his best supervisor's voice he barked, "Take your posts!"

The room emptied all at once. Those officers assigned to patrol sectors clustered around the end of the big wooden desk where the patrol car keys were being given out. Their partners were busy at the other end, signing out portable radios.

Tanti watched as the midnight tour officers began to enter the station house. Only moments earlier they had looked like walking zombies, dark circles under their eyes. But now, with their one last bit of remaining energy, they mixed with the outgoing platoon in a burst of youthful enthusiasm. The midnight- and day-tour officers roughhoused and yelled and called each other names. The new din put pressure on Tanti's ears.

He ducked off the floor and retraced his steps to the detective squad. He saw that other members of the squad had begun to wander in.

Blakemore had noticed Tanti enter the squad room. Realizing that the uniformed officer might feel ill at ease among people he rarely worked with, Blakemore called out loudly, "Tony, come on in! Grau should be in soon. Help yourself to some coffee."

Tanti waved his hand in thanks and walked over to the little coffee machine in the far corner of the squad room. A small group of detectives was already there, pouring coffee and buttering rolls.

Tanti was acknowledged by the group with a nodding of heads and the offer of an empty cup. He reflected on the difference in atmosphere between the patrol force and the detective bureau.

In patrol, everything was structured and regimented. Once turned out, officers weren't even permitted to remain in the station house without having some genuine function to perform. In the field, they were supervised by a multilayered bureaucracy. Patrol sergeants responded to many of their assignments where they routinely signed memo books to verify the fact that the officers were performing their job. The precinct's Integrity Control Officer, dressed in civilian clothes and driving an unmarked car, also showed up at unexpected moments. He monitored the time it took officers to respond to jobs, also signed memo books and generally supervised the patrol force. Captains from the borough, designated as supervisors of patrol, were out actively seeking minor violations of department rules and dress codes. The greatest sin they found while in the field was an officer not wearing his hat. For that offense, the culprit could receive a command discipline and have several hours of vacation time deducted from the yearly allotment.

Tanti at once became very angry and very determined. Angry with the sudden realization that he had been treated like a child for the last twelve years of his life. And determined that he would get out of the "bag" and find a detail where he wouldn't be harassed until he put his twenty years in and retired from the job.

He helped himself to a cup of coffee.

"Want some milk, Tony?" Harry Purvis asked. At Tanti's nod Purvis picked up the open container of milk that sat next to the coffee machine and handed it over.

Tanti filled a full third of his cup with the white liquid. He really didn't care for coffee, but this was a social event, a morning ritual, and he wanted to be part of it.

As he raised the cup to his lips Tanti saw Grau enter the squad room. The detective, dressed in a blue pinstripe three-piece suit, walked directly to a metal cabinet against the far side wall. Oblivious to Tanti's presence, he picked up a sheet which held the list of the assorted crimes committed in the precinct since he had last been to work and began to read. Since it was from this piece of paper that cases were assigned, Grau wanted to make sure nothing pressing had been made his responsibility since the last evening.

Tanti casually walked over and asked, "Jon, you going downtown today?"

Grau looked up from the sheet he held. "Oh. Hi, Tony. Yeah, I've got to go to the morgue."

"Any chance you giving me a lift? I've got to ID the bodies."

"No problem. When you want to go?"

Tony smiled. "Pal, you got the car. Tell me."

"Good, let's go now. I want to catch the doctor before they cut open the bodies. I'd like to take a look at the slugs still inside them."

Grau tossed the form back where he found it and walked over to a small wood cabinet that hung from a wall in Sergeant Carrol's office. Someone had neatly written the words CAR KEYS in bold black marker pen on its cover. Grau opened the cabinet up and studied the selection of vehicles available. Someone had already taken the new Chevy with the working air conditioner so he settled for a year-old sedan he knew to be reliable. He closed the cabinet door and wrote the auto number, date, time and his destination in the log sitting on the table underneath. From the back of the log he removed the vehicle police plate that corresponded to the car. That would be needed for bridge and tunnel tolls and parking in Manhattan.

The two men left the squad room and walked downstairs. Tanti stopped for a moment by the desk to let the desk officer know he was leaving for the morgue. The lieutenant wordlessly recorded the information in the command log.

The men walked out of the precinct and down the red brick stairs that were falling apart. The squad car was a late-model gray Ford sedan. It looked far older than its true age and was sitting angle parked in one of the spaces reserved for department autos.

Grau unlocked the passenger-side door and then went to the driver's side. He opened it and both men got in at the same time.

Sunday morning in New York City is a good time to travel. With little traffic on the streets the City's truly excellent road system permitted them to get from the North Bronx to First Avenue and 30th Street, Manhattan, in thirty minutes.

Grau parked just off the corner of their destination. They left the squad car and stepped through the entrance of the large low brick building.

An Hispanic-looking man, the Medical Examiner's office receptionist and guard, sat at a desk to one side of the front door. He glanced up from the Sunday comics he was reading.

"Can I help you?" he asked, then saw that one man was in full police uniform and the other held a detective shield in his left hand. Without further comment the guard's head simply bobbed a few times and he went back to his paper. Grau and Tanti walked past the receptionist to the doors leading to the autopsy room below.

As they made their way down the stairs the familiar odor of decaying bodies hit them. Grau gritted his teeth but Tanti paid it no attention.

For Tanti the trip to the morgue had become a diversion from routine police work. He had been here a few times before, always to identify the remains of the victim of a homicide. But today, instead of having to struggle to find his way downtown, he had gotten a ride. Furthermore, he

The Murder of Old Comrades

had enjoyed Grau's company during the trip and now found himself in unusually good spirits.

Grau, on the other hand, had been to the morgue many times in the past. He made it a point on every homicide he caught to view at least part of the autopsy and speak with the doctor who performed it. Grau found that unless he shared information about the case with the person doing the autopsy, the potential for the doctor to overlook some significant bit of physical evidence was very real.

On the other hand, Medical Examiners' doctors were generally used to working in the blind. A body would be assigned him or her and a routine autopsy would be performed. When an investigator took the time to come to the morgue, to communicate the facts of the case to the doctor, Grau found that they would extend themselves in a genuine effort to assist in the investigation.

Yet, no matter how often Grau came down to the morgue, he could never get used to the odor. Often he would catch himself about to gag. Sometimes he tried breathing through his mouth, which he found helped. At other times he had tried both eating and not eating before going to the morgue, but found that neither tactic made much difference.

Grau found this all very embarrassing. Of course the detective would never let anyone around him know of the problem he had. At the autopsy he would become very matter-of-fact. He would pay rapt attention to whatever procedure the doctor was performing and discuss the case with a professional, detached and unemotional air. But the fact was, all the while Grau was there he would be fighting the urge to throw up.

He would watch the people who worked down at the morgue go about their business. They'd shift the carcasses about, dissect them, store the remains. Surrounded by blood and gore. And all the while chatting amiably about this and that, as if they were handling vegetable produce.

The officers silently passed the rows of silver-colored refrigerated lockers that held the dead. They moved along the hallway until they came to a set of swinging doors. Grau pushed them open and they entered the main autopsy room.

The area was large. It had a tile floor with white tile walls. Surgical instruments rested on tables and gurneys, while scales lay out at different parts of the room.

A dozen metal tables, set in rows in the middle of the room, held corpses in various stages of dissection. Assistant Medical Examiners in white smocks labored on three separate bodies with aides assisting them.

Grau saw that the female victim of his double homicide was being worked on. He walked over to the doctor who had just finished cutting her chest open and was now excising the heart from the exposed cavity.

The doctor was Oriental and stood a half foot under Grau's six-foot two-inch height. He had a head of full black hair and a lively sparkle in his dark brown eyes. His white surgical coat remained spotless while he held the woman's heart in his hand and cut slices from it with a scalpel, all the while chanting some incomprehensible medical incantation into a microphone suspended from the ceiling. As Grau watched the man work he wondered how old he was. The doctor had a face that could belong to a man from thirty to fifty years of age.

The two had seen each other many times in the past yet neither knew the other's name. To the Assistant Medical Examiner, Grau was "Detective," and to Grau the man was "Doctor."

"Morning, doctor."

"Hello, detective. These two yours?" There was no hint of an accent in the man's voice. Of course Grau could not know that the doctor was a third-generation American.

"Yeah. As you know, both were shot in the head. I'd like to recover the slugs if possible. I already found one at the scene and it looked kinda strange. I figured there was a chance there were more in the bodies. If so I want to hand carry them over to ballistics."

"No problem."

The doctor placed the heart on a nearby scale and stepped to the end of the table where the woman's head rested. He picked up a long metal rod and began closely examining her scalp. Grau walked over to the doctor and bent down to better watch the process.

The Murder of Old Comrades

"I believe she was shot three times in the head. The man also," Grau said.

Dr. Choo made a little grunting sound. He inserted the rod into one of the wounds in the scalp. After careful probing the doctor mentally calculated how far the bullet had gone into the tissue. He withdrew the rod and placed it in a second bullet entrance hole. The silver metal shaft was pushed into the skull nearly five inches before Dr. Choo was satisfied he had found the correct track.

"They were probably hit with .22s," Grau said.

The doctor nodded. "These entrance wounds seem consistent with that theory. Except of course for the unusually nasty one I noticed on the man."

"Yes. Whatever round caused it sure had plenty of power. But I figured that just maybe they were both hit by that round. We only found one strange casing at the scene but you know how the damn things can bounce around and disappear. And if by chance there are any more of those slugs still inside these two, I'd sure like to get them."

"Okay. Let's see if we can help you."

With a scalpel Dr. Choo deftly cut along the back of the neck of the woman from ear to ear. He then grasped the severed flesh and gently but firmly pulled the back of her scalp over her face, exposing the top of the skull bone.

While this was going on, Officer Tanti quietly watched from a few feet behind Grau. He was pleased just to be present and didn't wish to intrude into the conversation.

The doctor picked up a silver electric drill. Fastened in its bit was an odd-shaped cutting tool, an incomplete circle of metal, the rounded portion containing raised metal teeth. Grau knew what was coming next and tried hard to think of something else.

Dr. Choo turned the machine on and the cutting part of the tool vibrated into a blur. He placed the moving edge against the skull bone and the high-pitched whir changed to a grinding noise. White chips of bone flew off to the side.

The doctor carefully worked the machine around the head, making a complete circle of the skull. When finished he put the tool down and carefully removed the skull cap from the top of the head, exposing the brain underneath.

Carefully he removed the brain from its chamber and placed it on a metal tray. It would have to be weighed and cut open for examination, but that could wait.

He took up the metal rod and sought the path of the third bullet. Grau watched while the doctor inserted the rod into the underside of the skull cavity and worked it deep into the muscle of the victim's neck and beyond. The rod went in about ten inches before the doctor was satisfied it could probe no further.

Leaving the rod in place the doctor palpated an area of left chest muscle about four inches above the woman's breast.

He came around to the side of the corpse and picked up a scalpel. Working from inside the open chest cavity he made an incision. When his hand came out from inside the carcass it held a tiny bloody projectile. Smiling, he presented the detective with the small slug. Grau took it. It was a deformed gray lead .22 bullet. He nodded and handed it back. The doctor made a tiny mark with a small pointed instrument on the base of the bullet. That scratch would have to pass for his initials.

"Detective, I'll have to finish up on the female first before I can dig out any slugs from the male."

"I understand. About how long do you think it will take?" Grau asked.

The doctor looked down at the body for a moment. "Give me a half hour."

"Fine, we'll go for coffee."

Grau and Tanti walked through the doors and up the stairs. Grau took a deep breath as he got to the lobby, relieved for the respite from the foul air below them.

Tanti said, "Let's get a bite. I'm starved."

Grau nodded in agreement and the two set off for a coffee shop. They had to walk up to Thirty-fourth Street and almost all the way to Second Avenue before they found one open for business.

It was a small place with a long counter on one side and banks of red vinyl booths on the other. By unspoken agreement the two men sat at the far booth. Grau faced the front door.

A waitress appeared before the two officers from behind a set of swinging doors. Grau thought her to be about fifty. She was chunky but had a pleasant face. Her white uniform, both men noted, was not overly clean.

"Menus, fellas?"

The offer was declined and two simple breakfasts of scrambled eggs, toast and coffee were ordered by the men. The waitress walked away.

To pass the time Grau made small talk with Tanti. He found out that the officer had been assigned to the Four-Seven precinct for almost the entire twelve years he had been on the job. His only other command had been the Police Academy and that was for the first six months he was on the force. Tanti told him that he had a young child, a girl, and he and his wife lived in a modest home in Putnam County which, because of an influx of several major corporations into his area, was now worth far more than he paid for it.

Grau responded with information about himself. A detective for seventeen years, he had been on the force for over twenty. He had been married once, but that had been more than ten years earlier. The union resulted in two children, both boys, almost grown now. He lived in the Bronx, in the Four-Five Precinct, where his absurdly small apartment rented for an outrageous sum of money.

"What do you think of the case, Tony?" Grau asked, toying with a fork in one hand.

"You don't seem to have much to go on," Tanti replied cautiously, not wanting to say anything foolish.

"Nope. Just a couple of dead bodies and two names. That's the problem with homicide investigations. It's not like robberies or larcenies. There, at least you have witnesses. Most homicides are like this one. The only people who saw what happened are either dead or aren't talking."

"Why are you so interested in that one shell casing and the bullets in the bodies, Jon?" Tanti asked. He noticed that the waitress was giving him a smile.

"Because that bullet and casing were really strange. Some years ago I used to be assigned to the outdoor range, as a firearms instructor. That casing and bullet didn't come from any gun I ever saw before. Now normally I don't get too excited about what kind of gun killed my victims. But my instinct tells me that in this case it's something I should be worried about."

The coffee came. Grau sprinkled his liberally with sugar while Tanti just filled his cup to the brim with milk.

Grau was becoming fidgety sitting in the booth. He was anxious to get any other bullets which the doctor might find and get back to the Bronx. There were still a lot of people to interview, not the least of whom were the relatives of the deceased woman. They might be able to shed some light on the male victim. Grau figured that it was the man and not the woman that the killer was after. She just happened to be there. And as far as Grau knew, no one had yet made an inquiry about the dead man, not even a relative. This he found very strange.

Grau looked at his watch. It was 10 A.M.

"Sit tight, Tony. I'll be right back. I'm going to give the squad a ring."

Tanti nodded and raised the cup of coffee to his lips. Grau saw a pay phone at the other end of the restaurant. He slid from the booth and headed for it.

Tanti looked over his shoulder as the detective walked to the front of the coffee shop. His resolve from earlier in the day hardened further. He thought to himself that he just had to get out of "the bag." And now that he had a goal, he would pursue and win it. Police Officer Anthony Tanti would someday be Detective Anthony Tanti.

Both the food and Grau got to the table at the same time. Grau forked some egg into his mouth and swallowed it with a gulp of hot coffee. Tanti looked at him and waited for some explanation of his hurry. After his second bite of food, Grau said, "Got a call for me at the squad. 'Bout twenty minutes after we left. Some guy with an accent. Wouldn't leave his name or a number but did say he was calling from Brooklyn. He wanted to talk to the detective who was handling the killing of Sergi Gorkin. Said he had important information and would call back at noon. We got plenty of time, but still, I'd rather be back at the squad. Just in case the guy gets antsy and calls early. Let's finish

The Murder of Old Comrades

up and run over to the morgue. Slug or no, we'll say goodbye to the doc and head back."

"No problem," Tanti replied.

Their leisurely meal had now turned into the equivalent of a pie-eating contest as both men gulped their food. Grau picked up the check, gave it a glance and took some bills out of his pocket. He laid them on the counter and, with one last sip of coffee, slid off the padded bench.

Tanti reached for his wallet to share the cost but the detective waved his hand. With a smile Grau said, "Don't worry about it. I'm saving you for the steak dinner." The men left the restaurant and with a determined step walked back to the Medical Examiner's office. Grau offered Tanti the option of waiting upstairs in the lobby while he went down to the morgue to see if any other bullets had been recovered.

Tanti declined and both men went back down to the basement. They could see that the doctor had wasted little time, and had the man well opened up. They also noticed that the female had been sewn back together. Her chest cavity was held in place by thick stitching. The flap of scalp that had been peeled from her head had been carefully put back in its original place and Tanti could see that the grotesque procedure he had witnessed earlier had done nothing to disfigure the face of the victim. An open casket funeral would still be eminently practical.

Dr. Choo nodded to the two officers and with the scalpel he held in his right hand pointed to a nearby tray.

Grau walked over and picked up the slug lying there. He was disappointed to see it was a regular lead .22 like the first one the doctor had found. He quickly explained to the doctor that he had to get back to the squad and thanked him for his help. He and Tanti headed for the stairs and made their way out of the building.

Once in the squad car Grau relaxed a bit. After starting it up, he headed for the FDR drive. He would go north, take the Triborough Bridge to the Deegan and head north again, getting off at 233rd Street. There he would cut across to Laconia Avenue and the Four-Seven Precinct.

"Tony, I could really use a break on this one," he said, more to himself than to his passenger.

Chapter 4

From the airport's seaplane dock the two men watched as a small airplane moved gracefully across the horizon and flew over the dark brick prison buildings that sat on the opposite shore of the lake. The aircraft banked gently and lined up with the narrow runway, its bright red color in sharp contrast to the clear blue sky.

The smaller of the two men, his eyes not leaving the little aircraft as it arched down from the sky, said, "Too hot for me today, Dave. I got no place I want to go to. I'd just as soon leave my plane on the ground and watch."

David Heath smiled and nodded in agreement. It was noon and the temperature was rapidly approaching ninety degrees.

Billy Dieter, dressed in the dark green uniform of a New York State Forest Ranger, looked as most people imagined a ranger should look: sun-browned leather for skin with crow's-feet at the corners of his eyes. A head full of unmanageable brown hair was kept in check by the green regulation baseball cap he wore on his head. On the front of the cap was the insignia of the air arm of the Forest Service, a floatplane crossing an evergreen tree.

Dieter had first come to upstate New York's Orange County fifteen years earlier. He had found it hard to believe the area was only fifty miles from Manhattan. The region was heavily forested and numerous farms dotted the landscape. But now a change had become evident: The area was rapidly becoming a bedroom suburb, not only for the large city but also the burgeoning industrial and business centers that had sprung up around the city's outskirts.

The Murder of Old Comrades

Heath dug an old handkerchief from his pocket, blotting the perspiration from his forehead. He was a larger man than Dieter. Six foot four, with full beard and prominent stomach, he had a happy-go-lucky appearance that belied an inner seriousness.

He wore tan work pants stained from countless home painting chores, a threadbare blue cotton shirt with short sleeves and brown work shoes whose soles were held in place by a generous amount of silver duct tape. Heath didn't look like a sergeant in the New York City Police Department, which was as it should be, since he was assigned to the Public Morals Unit of the department's Organized Crime Control Bureau.

Like the ranger, Heath moved to the area nearly twenty years earlier. What had drawn him to the town was its little airport. It was one of the few remaining country airports left in the New York metropolitan area, and it was only five miles from his home. His forty-year-old Piper J-3 Cub was hangared at Warwick Municipal Airport, from which both men were now watching small planes land and take off. By any standard the field was small. The strip had been donated to the town years earlier by a local benefactor who was interested in preserving general aviation.

The airport had two runways. The main one was paved. It was a narrow twenty feet in width and a short two thousand feet long. Parallel to it ran a grass strip which was used by pilots who flew older aircraft such as the one Heath owned.

The second runway, of sod, cut across the first at an angle. That one was used only when heavy winds favored it.

At the opposite end of the field was a small mountain. At the point where they stood was Wickham Lake. To their south and east ran a ridge of low mountaintops. It formed part of the bowl that was Warwick Valley. A few tall microwave towers jutted up from its highest point. At night the airport was very dark. The hills and ridge surrounding it were all but invisible to anyone intent on making a landing. There were runway lights that could be activated by an incoming pilot but they were of very low intensity and of little help.

Unique to the airport was its "seaplane base." Dieter had built it for the Forest Service floatplane. Although nothing more than a small wood dock and a depression cut in the lake's bank, it served its purpose well. And Dieter was proud that it was listed in the aviation reference books. After all, Warwick Airport was only one of a handful of places within a hundred-mile radius of New York City which had a facility dedicated to seaplane use.

Heath's dog waded in the water next to him. The big, tawny-colored animal, up to his chest in the algae-covered lake, snapped at the surface of the water. He chased his tail and generally acted the clown. Both men smiled at the large dog's antics.

Heath turned away from the show and said, "Billy, give me the story again. I don't quite understand what happened."

"Well, you know the state is always shorthanded. They got one conservation officer to cover this entire county. He's got to enforce all the conservation laws and sometimes he asks me to give him a hand. Like last night. The guy heard that there was some jacklighting going on at the airport, when no one was around."

"Yeah, I've seen plenty of deer droppings around here. The animals aren't too concerned about people anymore."

"Right. So at night some of the locals like to come out in their pickup trucks. They'll sit off the side of the runway with a .22 rifle and when they see a deer, throw a light in its eyes. The deer are dumb and don't move and the boys got themselves some illegal venison."

Dieter paused as a Cessna took to the runway. They watched as the machine slowly started its ground run. Within a few hundred feet the ship became light on its gear. The nose wheel no longer touched the ground and the airplane took flight.

Heath picked up the thread of conversation. "This place is so damn small. Where do you guys hide? To watch what's going on, I mean."

"That's no problem. Look toward the mid portion of the runway. See how it comes to a hump?" Dieter pointed with his finger. "There's a rise in the ground there. We stay all the way at the far end. The state car gets put in the corner. From here you can't even see the spot I'm talking about."

Heath looked at the part of the runway Dieter was describing. He stepped off the dock and climbed onto the upturned bottom of a metal rescue boat that lay near the shore. From atop the rowboat's bottom he could just make out the hiding place over two thousand feet away. A car positioned in the "vee," where the brush alongside the runway met the scrub and brush at its end, would be well hidden.

Heath hopped down off the boat and rejoined Dieter on the shore. The big dog had gotten out of the water to join them. He prepared to shower both with the foul-smelling lake water that saturated his coat.

The two did a little dance away from the animal. The dog mistook their actions for an invitation to play and moved still closer. Firmly but with a tone of affection Heath commanded, "Lie down!"

The big dog fell to the ground with a grunt, rolled on its back and squirmed back and forth in the sweet-smelling grass. He had long ago learned that humans were very difficult animals to understand.

Heath rubbed the dog's belly with the sole of his shoe to ensure he remained on the ground.

"But, Billy, if guys are riding in the back of a pickup, won't they spot you?"

"Dave, first of all you've got to remember that the state car we use is dark green. The damn thing is almost invisible at night. Also, we put an old army blanket over its grill. You'd walk into the thing before you saw it. And second, once we see a bunch of guys in a pickup who are riding around at midnight with no lights on, we grab them. It's not like the city up here. If they got loaded guns and spotlights in the truck, we lock them up. They don't stand a chance in court. They not only wind up with a heavy fine, but they lose the truck, the guns and everything else they came with. Hell, by the time we're through with them, they're lucky if they don't wind up doing time."

Heath shook his head in admiration. "Billy, they don't get that kind of punishment for a homicide in the city."

Dieter shrugged and went on, "So anyway, we're sitting

on the roof of the state car. It was around 10 P.M. There was no moon last night and Norman, he's the conservation officer, was letting me play with the night scope he'd brought along. It's a military surplus job."

Dieter used his hands to describe the size and shape of the light intensification unit.

"I think he lets me fool with it so I'll come along with him. Anyway, looking through the thing turns night into day. Everything looks green, but clear as hell. So I see a car, with no lights, driving on the taxiway and heading to the lake. I poke Norm in the ribs and both of us watch what's going on. There's only one guy in the car and he parks by the seaplane dock. He just sits in the car, like he's waiting for something to happen."

"How long did he stay there?"

"Damn near an hour. We were getting pretty restless about it. Almost decided to pull up to him and ask him what he was doing. But we didn't and that's when I heard the floatplane."

Heath bent down and picked up a piece of long grass. With care he worked it between a gap in his two front teeth.

"Which direction did it come from?" he asked.

Dieter thought a moment. "I'm not real certain, but I think it came in over that ridge, near Mount Peter." Both men turned their heads to that part of the ridge line that was visible over the roofs of the prison buildings. A large microwave tower rose from its spine.

"But anyway, I see this ship come in over the lake. The guy in the car had already gotten out and was standing on the dock. It was hard to tell, but I'm pretty sure he had a flashlight in his hand. Whatever he had he pointed it in the direction of the plane. Musta been a light."

Heath nodded as he visualized the scene.

"The ship flew farther west, then swung around and set up for a landing."

"What kind of plane was it?"

"Now that's real interesting. When I first heard it I figured it to be a DeHavilland Beaver on floats. It had that throaty rumble of a radial engine. But as it got closer, and

I saw it on the water, I knew it was no Beaver. It was a Wilga."

"Never heard of it," Heath said, his arms folded across his chest.

"Dave, the damn thing is made in Poland. Runs a big nine-cylinder radial up front. Funny-looking plane. It's all wings and flying surface. The body is kinda stuck on as an afterthought. I don't think there are a handful in this country. The only reason I knew what the hell it was is because I saw one a couple of years ago up in Canada. A guy there wanted a rough-and-tumble airplane for landing on the Arctic ice. He had the only one I ever saw. Told me he loved the ship. Probably still would have it if he hadn't folded it up trying to get off one snow patch too many."

"This plane, what numbers were on it?"

"Couldn't tell. The ship was painted a dark color. Either the numbers were also a dark color or there were none. The scope doesn't show contrast all that well.

"The plane pulls up to the dock," Dieter continued, "and someone gets out of the passenger side and joins the guy already there. Then the two guys on the dock push the Wilga free and the plane takes off. Just like that. Then they get into the car and head out of the airport. Still no lights. By this time Norman and I are giving them a loose tail."

Dieter used the jargon of law enforcement for a moving surveillance. He enjoyed telling the story to Heath and wanted to sound professional.

"Which way did they go?"

"Well, we followed them out of the airport. They turned south, in the direction of the city. We broke off the tail 'cause we didn't want to take a burn."

Heath sat on the upturned boat bottom, silent for a moment. He watched a tan Stinson come in over the lake and turn from base leg to final. He tried to fit what Dieter had told him into some mold of his previous experience. Narcotics? Possibly. But that's a lot of effort for what only could have been a very small package. Smuggling? What, diamonds? What else would be of sufficient value to make that kind of effort worthwhile and would come in a small package?

Heath had a sudden inspiration: Maybe it wasn't a thing, but a who that was being smuggled in.

"Billy, you get the plate number of the car?" Like a small boy presenting a parent with some newfound prize, Dieter pulled from his shirt pocket a folded piece of paper.

"Sure did." He grinned and handed it over to his friend.

Heath looked at the note. It was a New York plate. "You sure you got the plate right?"

"Well, yeah. We didn't get too close, but like I said, that night scope works good."

The two men moved away from the lake, back toward the main part of the airport. Heath called over his shoulder, "Marmaduke!" and the big dog sprang to life. As the men walked slowly along, the dog ran up and down the runway border, where the cleared area ended and the trees began. He sniffed and marked as he went. The animal loved going for walks at the airport and was very careful to make sure other dogs were aware of the fact that it was his territory.

While Heath walked he wondered whom he might notify about this. When he got to work on Monday he would first call police intelligence. Better yet, he would call the Joint Terrorist Task Force. That unit was made up of department personnel as well as state and federal officers.

He'd sleep on the problem tonight.

They had come to the blacktop taxiway which went from the main airport area to the runways. Heath called to the dog, who ran up to his master, enjoying the attention. Heath didn't want Marmaduke too far from his side now that they were entering the main part of the airport because of the volume of aircraft that moved along the path.

"Billy, let's go over to Neal's hangar. The guys are probably having lunch. Maybe Marmaduke can con them out of some food."

Dieter laughed and they headed for the hangars.

Propkin looked out at the street from his basement-apartment window. Should a person have to live his entire life in such a place, he would have a strange perspective on the world, he mused.

He turned back to sit at the small table in the one-room "safe-house." Several pages torn from a legal pad lay on

The Murder of Old Comrades

it. On one page were the names of the people he was to locate and "neutralize." A line was drawn through the name Gorkin. The other page held notes about these people's living habits, friends and the places they frequented.

Propkin ran the fingers of his right hand through his short hair and studied a map of Brooklyn that lay open before him. He tried to focus on where he would go next but his mind drifted to other things. Foolish things, like family and home and even his pending, well-deserved retirement.

He had been in the business a long time, perhaps a little too long. This assignment, although it had some exotic elements to it, was really quite routine—and going well. It would be a fine end to a solid and honorable career.

Propkin knew he was a dinosaur. With the speed changes took place in his country, people with his talents would be valued far less than when he had first started in his work.

There was no question in Propkin's mind. The salad days of espionage had passed. Now it was time for the dull clerks to gather their innocuous bits of information to fit together a jigsaw puzzle of information for their masters, whomever they might be.

Yes, this would truly be his last mission. Perhaps that is why he had this nagging concern? The only problem so far had been that damn little pistol. Funny, it had never failed him before. Maybe it was getting old. Like him.

Propkin had carefully examined the small German-made pistol the first chance he had after he had arrived at his safe-house. There had been nothing wrong with it that he could see. Still, it had malfunctioned. He was not a gunsmith, so all he could do was carefully take the weapon apart and clean it. He considered not using it on the next person on his list but quickly rejected the idea. The compact flat-sided .22 was silenced. When fired it made a sound like the snapping of a modest-size dry twig. His service pistol, although far more powerful, was also extremely loud.

No, it would never do.

He held his open hand up in front of his face and inspected it. No tremble, rock solid.

"Fool," Propkin chided himself. "For someone with no emotions, you think too much."

Before he had left for the mission, he had been shown some currency of a kind he had never seen before. His superiors were quite adamant about him locating this money, although they wouldn't tell him why.

"How typical," Propkin thought. "Just give me enough information to accomplish the task, not one bit more."

He returned to studying the map.

Chapter 5

On the drive back to the Four-Seven Precinct Tanti asked Grau in the most casual voice he could muster, "Who you going to work this case with?"

Grau, surprised by the question, hesitated a moment before replying. "I haven't really thought about it. Jimmy Barclay, my partner, retired about a month ago. I've been free-lancing ever since." With a smile, he asked, "You got someone in mind?"

"Well, I know it's like pulling teeth, but you think there's any chance of my being able to give you a hand on this?"

Grau knew, as did Tanti, that the Detective Bureau and Patrol Bureau were two different jobs that just happened to get paid by the same boss. It was relatively easy for an officer who worked in patrol to transfer from one precinct to another. Or for a detective to transfer from one squad to another. But to transfer out of one bureau to another, even to be assigned temporarily to another bureau, was another matter entirely.

But Grau was comfortable with Tanti. And he really did need a partner on this case. As the car turned onto the precinct block he reflected how tough it had been for him to get a break and be assigned to the Detective Bureau. The

The Murder of Old Comrades

crazy hours, the dozens of arrests . . . Grau said, "Look, I think it's a great idea. But nobody cares what I think. Tell you what. When we get back to the house, we'll go to the desk and see if you can work with me for the rest of the day. Then we'll hit my boss with the idea and see what he says."

"Well, I guess it's a shot."

Grau parked the squad car and they climbed the precinct steps. The day's humid warmth kept them from hurrying.

Once past the entrance doors they approached the desk. The same lieutenant to whom Tanti had earlier reported his departure to the morgue was still at his post.

A thirty-two year veteran of the force, Lieutenant James Mulcahy was still wrestling with the day tour's computerized roll call. Among his many tasks at the desk was to ensure that all corrections were properly recorded on the twelve sheets of paper that lay before him. It was after 11 A.M. and the job had yet to be completed. What had taken him an hour to accomplish ten years ago now took the better part of his tour. "So much for progress," he mumbled as he slowly corrected the sheets spread out on the desk in front of him.

"Lou?" Tanti used the common contraction for lieutenant.

Mulcahy looked up from his work and eyed them suspiciously. He sensed that the two officers who stood before the desk were about to ask some favor of him.

"Yes?" His tone was noncommittal.

Grau said, "Lieutenant, I'm working a fresh double homicide. Tony was with me on the case yesterday and today we went down to the morgue together. I may have to run to Brooklyn on the case and there isn't anyone up in the squad to go with me. Any chance of my stealing him"—Grau poked a thumb in Tanti's direction—"for the rest of the tour?"

Mulcahy wordlessly looked down at his computerized roll call. He already knew he had all his precinct sectors covered. In fact the radio had been quiet all morning. If he had to assign Tanti to some job it would either be some foot post (which the lieutenant wouldn't give to a senior man anyway) or some make-work inside clerical slot. And he already had three officers working inside this tour.

Mulcahy said, "Okay, he's yours."

"Thanks, boss!" Tanti blurted, unable to restrain the grin on his face.

As they headed for the stairway door Grau stopped Tanti and said, "Tony, change into your civilian clothes and meet me in the squad."

Tanti nodded and Grau made for the squad room at the top of the stairs. Once inside the office Grau noted that Joe Blakemore looked like he hadn't budged since he and Tanti had left earlier. He passed Blakemore with a quick "Hi!" and walked into his boss's office.

Sergeant Hank Carrol sat at his green metal department desk, wading through a stack of DD-5s which, as squad commander, were his job to read and initial. His desk was a jumble of reports, department memos, legal bulletins and personal notes. A plaque on the wall read, "A clean desk is the sign of a sick mind!" The sergeant gave every indication he held to that philosophy.

Normally a detective squad had a lieutenant in charge. But due to a department-wide shortage of lieutenants, Hank Carrol had been running the Four-Seven squad for over four months. The scarcity of bosses hadn't improved and he expected to be at that desk for quite a while longer.

Carrol found the job demanding. If all was going well within the squad and if the unit's crime clearance statistics were running middle-of-the-pack, he would be left alone. But if the squad caught an unusual homicide that generated media attention or if his detectives were not clearing enough cases, then the borough would be on his butt in a second.

Sergeant Carrol reflected, "Do a good job and they ignore you. Have some clown blow away a local burgher during a mugging and the Chief of Bronx Detectives moves in with you."

Carrol had gotten to his present position within the detective bureau in the conventional way. After making sergeant twelve years earlier he had worked as a uniformed patrol supervisor for four years. Because of his ability to handle his subordinates, his captain then assigned him to the precinct's Anti-Crime Unit. These were uniformed personnel who worked in "soft clothes." Not considered detectives, they functioned in a gray area. Their job was to agressively seek out street criminals, particularly violent felony offenders, but not to involve themselves in detailed investigations. As with most anti-crime units, his officers worked closely with the precinct's detective unit. Many a homicide in that particular squad had been solved with information supplied by one of Hank Carrol's Anti-Crime people or one of his officers' unofficial street informants.

The pressure of being squad commander had thinned his gray hair and caused worry lines to form on his forehead. And although he had over twenty years on the job he couldn't retire. Not with one kid in the third year of college and his daughter a high school senior.

"Sarge, got a second?" Grau pulled up a chair.

"Sure, Jon. How's that double of yours coming?"

Grau flipped a hand. "So-so." He paused for a moment. "Listen, I may have to shoot over to Brooklyn. Someone who said he knew my white male called the squad while I was at the 'M.E.' He didn't leave a name or number but said he wants to see me."

Grau chose his next words carefully. "Tony Tanti went with me to the morgue. He was first on the scene yesterday . . ."

"I know, I was there. So come to the point," Carrol interrupted, painfully aware of the amount of paperwork he had yet to deal with that day.

"Look, sarge, I don't have anyone to work this case with. And all the other guys are busy doing their own thing. What I'm asking is, can we steal Tony for a while? The guy is interested in the case, he's been around and we work well together."

Carrol sat back in his swivel chair. With arms folded across his chest, he looked across the room at nothing in particular. He sighed, turned back to Grau and said, "Jon, I like Tony. He's a good cop, and like you said, he's been around a while. But tell me, how do you propose I pull this little coup off?"

"Well, I thought you and the precinct C.O. worked together when you were both cops."

"We were partners in the Three-Two, about fifteen years ago. Except he studied more than I did." Sergeant Carrol smiled as memories of some of the dangerous and crazy adventures he had shared with the other man flooded into his head.

"Look, Jon, it's not that I object to Tony working with you and you know it. But tell me, how the hell am I going to ask an understaffed precinct captain to give me one of his senior and more active officers?"

Grau didn't reply but simply held his ground in front of his boss's desk, hands in pockets.

"Here's what I'll do. Tomorrow I'll go see Willie," Sergeant Carrol said, using the captain's nickname. "Who knows, maybe I can pull it off."

"Thanks, I'll tell Tony," Grau said, already halfway out the door.

Calling after him, the sergeant yelled, "Tell him what, that he's got a snowball's chance in hell of being assigned to the case?"

Chapter 6

Tanti entered the squad room resplendent in his construction clothes ensemble.

Grau groaned and said, "Tony, I should have told you not to overdress."

"Give me a break, Jon. How was I to know I'd be working with the 'big guys' today? I promise to dress sharp next time."

"Listen, tiger, I just spoke with my boss. He's gonna try to con the precinct C.O. into letting you work this case with me. But he didn't sound too confident."

"Well, it was a nice try."

Grau patted Tanti on the back and said, "Look, come

in tomorrow ready to work with me. No guarantee, you understand, but I think Hank Carrol may have just enough clout with your boss to get you assigned here. At least for a while. After that, we'll see. Meanwhile, keep out of his sight. I don't want him seeing you in that outfit."

"Okay, Jon. Tomorrow I'll dress like a pimp."

"Super. Sit tight, I'm going to knock out a couple of fives I owe on some old cases while we wait for that Brooklyn call." Grau headed for the next room and his bulging case folders.

Tanti drifted over to an unoccupied desk. He grabbed hold of a piece of the *Sunday Daily News* from the various sections strewn over its top. Behind him was Joe Blakemore, busily engaged at his typewriter. Two desks to Tanti's front sat Detective Harry Purvis, talking to some guy. As Tanti rummaged through the paper for the funnies he overheard the informal interrogation Purvis was conducting.

From what Tanti could gather, Purvis was investigating the rape and sodomy of two children. The young man sitting at the end of the detective's desk had been the kids' baby-sitter. And judging from Purvis's tone and line of questioning, he was also the prime suspect.

Tanti rightly suspected that there was no physical evidence in the case. So it boiled down to the two children's accusations against the suspect's claim of innocence. Without some sort of admission by the suspect, there would be no case.

Tanti eyed the young man more closely and guessed he was Hispanic. Of thin build and dark complexion, he was no taller than five seven and wore his brown hair in a sort of Afro style. There was a small gold earring in his left ear lobe and his yellow tee shirt had the words Make My Day written on the front. The muzzle of an impossibly big gun was drawn underneath.

Purvis, affecting an I'm-just-one-of-the-boys tone of voice, said, "Sal, look, I'm not angry with you. You know that. It's that fuckin' mother. She's makin' a big deal over bullshit."

Sal sat silently. His mind raced in an attempt to think up something to say that would get him out of this predicament.

Purvis dropped his tone to a conspiratorial whisper. He placed his hand on the young man's arm, looked left, then right, and quietly said, "Listen, to tell you the truth, I fuck my kids too."

Sal's eyes brightened, having just found a kindred soul.

"Hey, Joe," Purvis yelled over to Blakemore, "don't you fuck your kids?"

Blakemore, unmarried and childless, never missed a beat. "Yeah, sometimes I fuck my kids. Everyone does that shit," Blakemore replied as he continued to peck at his typewriter.

Sal, now that he was around people who understood him, felt he knew the best tack to take. "Yeah, sure I fucked 'em. Like you said, what's the big deal?"

"Yeah, right. Screw that dopey bitch," Purvis agreed with enthusiasm. "Let's get your side of the story!" The detective held his pen poised, ready to assist the misunderstood man.

Purvis's eagerness was catching. Sal began to relate the rape of the eight-year-old girl. From time to time Purvis nodded and interjected an encouraging grunt. Then came the sodomy of the ten-year-old boy. Purvis took down the story without interrupting, not batting an eye as Sal described the boy's cries of pain and how they had heightened his own pleasure.

While Tanti listened he couldn't help but wonder if Purvis would be able to make his case stick. Some defense attorney was going to have a field day with the state's attempted admission into evidence of this "voluntary" confession.

The phone rang. Blakemore picked it up. "Four-Seven Detectives, may I help you?" There was a short pause, then, "One moment, sir." Joe cupped the mouthpiece with his hand. "Jon, pick up. It's Brooklyn!"

Grau took up the extension. He glanced at the clock on the wall. It showed ten to twelve. In a matter-of-fact voice, he said, "Detective Grau."

"Yes, you are the detective that is investigating the murder from yesterday? Of Sergi Gorkin?" The voice was heavily accented.

The Murder of Old Comrades

"Yes, sir, I am." Grau knew not to question the anonymous caller. The risk of frightening him off was too great. If something were to come out of the conversation, Grau would have to play the coy seducer.

"I do not wish to become involved with the police for reasons that are difficult to explain, but there are some things you should know."

"Sir . . ." Monotone but firm voice, reassure him, everything is all right, you can trust me, you're safe with me. . . . "I understand your reluctance. I'm simply interested in whatever information you have. I have no desire to involve you in any court proceedings." Grau would have promised the man a trip to the moon if that was what it would take to get him to agree to a meeting.

For a moment there was silence. Grau sensed the caller was thinking, pondering his options. What to do, what to do?

"You promise I will not have to go to court? Even for it to be known that I have talked to you?"

"Sir, there is no advantage to me if others know you've spoken to me. Listen, I really don't feel comfortable discussing this over the phone. Let's meet somewhere and talk."

"All right. But I only wish to speak with you. Please come alone. We'll meet at this restaurant, the Bealka. It is on Brighton Beach Avenue, one block in from Ocean Parkway. Do you know the area?"

"Sure," Grau lied. "I can be there in about an hour. Who should I ask for?"

"Detective, what do you look like?"

Grau described himself and the clothes he was wearing.

"Please, just walk into the restaurant. I'll come to you. Remember, alone."

"I'll see you in an hour, alone." The line went dead.

"Let's go, Tony." Grau grabbed his jacket and hurriedly made for the exit. Tanti got up from his comics and followed his partner, running to catch up.

Chapter 7

Tanti drove them to Brooklyn. For most of the ride Grau sat quietly at his right. Tanti correctly guessed that his new partner was contemplating what questions he should put to the anonymous stranger, and wisely chose not to interrupt Grau's thoughts.

They moved along rapidly on the Belt Parkway. Crossing over a small drawbridge, Tanti looked out the left window. A two-hundred-foot-high grass-covered mound that had once been raw garbage butted up against the ocean shoreline. Filled with the refuse of the city, it had been covered with earth and now mixed the odor of rotting foodstuffs with the sweet smell of salt air. Sea gulls that made the dump their home effortlessly glided alongside the moving traffic, the ever-present sea breeze providing the energy to sustain their flight.

Suddenly Grau came to life. "Tony, the guy said I was to come alone. I don't want to spook him. So when we get to within two blocks of the restaurant you'll hop out of the car and walk the rest of the way. Try to set up on the opposite side of the street. I'll park as close to the place as I can. The way you're dressed, you should be able to blend with the scenery. And listen, keep an eye out for anyone you think might be watching for me. I know this all sounds a little paranoid, but this is a screwy case."

"No problem. What if we're separated? What if he wants you to give him a lift somewhere?"

"The Sixtieth Precinct isn't far from where we're going. Head there. I'll come and get you."

Tanti nodded. The green exit sign ahead read Ocean Parkway. He signaled, got off the highway and at the first light made a left turn onto Ocean Parkway and drove south. Once he had maneuvered onto the service road he found the only place to pull over was in the no-parking zone by a large church. Tanti got out and Grau slid into the driver's seat and drove off.

Tanti casually walked toward Brighton Beach Avenue. He immediately felt a comfortable cool dampness in the air, normal for this part of the city. The ocean was less than a mile away and the smell of the salt air was in pleasant contrast to the harshness of the Bronx.

He strolled along a concrete pedestrian and bicycle promenade that separated the parkway from the service road. Large numbers of people sat on the wooden benches that were imbedded in the concrete of the walkway. Some people took in the sun. A few of the men played chess using the middle of the bench to support their game boards.

The neighborhood was a mix of small apartment complexes and attached two-family homes. He thought the streets were clean, at least by New York City standards. To the south ran an elevated train. The station spanned the parkway and had been constructed as a massive concrete structure, now dirty tan in color. Even though he was a full city block from where it stood, the sound of a train that roared along the tracks made an uncomfortable din. Under the elevated tracks ran Brighton Beach Avenue.

At the avenue Tanti crossed over to the east side of Ocean Parkway. He noticed that many of the stores in the area had signs in their windows in both English and Russian. And many of the adult pedestrians wore eastern European-style clothes. Across the avenue he spotted where Grau had parked the department car. Its ascetic gray color and plain body style made it stand out from other cars in the area. The restaurant was no more than twenty feet down the street from where it sat.

Tanti walked into a small luncheonette referred to as a candy store by Brooklynites. He sat at a counter stool where he could keep an eye on both the front of the restaurant door and the car. Ordering a tuna salad sandwich, he prepared to wait.

Grau had parked close by the Bealka Restaurant. A hand-drawn caricature of a squirrel decorated its small front glass window. He of course did not know that the word bealka in Russian meant squirrel.

Inside he found himself in a small vestibule, beyond which were another set of doors. A heavy-set man dressed in slacks and flowered shirt leaned back against the far wall in a metal and wicker chair. Grau thought he must be employed by the restaurant but the man ignored him as he continued through the next set of doors.

Within the main room the restaurant was appointed as a kind of nightclub. Several dozen wood tables and chairs were set about the room. A raised platform, clearly designed for use by a band but now empty, had been built at the rear. In the middle of the room a large ball of tiny mirrors hung motionless from the ceiling.

Several groups of people, many with children, sat at the various tables. Grau saw that they were families out together for lunch.

A waiter came over to Grau. Recognized by his dress and demeanor as an American, he was politely seated at a corner table for two. Another waiter brought over a glass of water and a menu.

Grau opened the menu and looked around for someone who might be his nervous caller. Everyone appeared normal and at ease. No one seemed inclined to pay undue attention to the well-dressed American who sat by himself.

The door to the big room opened once more. A thin man with intense face and pallid complexion entered. The same waiter who had seated Grau walked over to him. Grau could hear them having a brief conversation in Russian. The two separated, the thin man making directly for the detective's table.

"Detective Grau?"

Grau nodded. Without another word the man sat down at the opposite side of the table, and picked up the menu in front of Grau. A moment later, still without speaking to Grau, he called over a waiter. He spoke a few rapid Russian words then turned to Grau and asked, "Do you know what you would like?"

The man responded to Grau's shrug with more Russian.

The waiter nodded and removed the menu. The man turned back to Grau and said, "I have ordered something for you."

The waiter returned with a basket holding a semicircle of heavy tan-colored bread, a bowl of butter and a bottle of vodka. The man picked up the bottle and poured some of the clear liquid into the two empty water glasses sitting on the table.

The first impression that Grau had of the man was enhanced by closer scrutiny. He looked like a ferret fleeing a hunter. His eyes darted around the room and took in the people at the other tables, none of whom were paying them the slightest attention.

The man's clothing was nondescript. He wore light brown slacks and a long sleeved white shirt open at the neck. The sleeves were rolled up. The stubble on his face told Grau the man hadn't shaved for several days.

Picking up his glass and holding it in the air the man toasted, *"Na zdrovye,"* and gulped down the contents.

Grau sipped some of the vodka from his own glass. He was not as foolish as some who equated masculine honor with the ability to consume huge amounts of liquor. Grau wasn't about to get himself involved in a drinking contest with the stranger.

"The man who was killed yesterday—do you know anything about him, Detective Grau?"

Grau shook his head.

"I knew him well. You might say we sometimes worked together." The man poured himself more vodka.

"Mr. . . . ?" Grau let the word hang there, as a question.

"Charlie, my name is Charlie."

"Charlie, your friend lived around here, yet"—Grau searched for the least threatening word—"the incident happened up in the Bronx. Do you know why?"

"He spent a lot of time up there. It was the house of his girl friend. He bought it for her. And a car and other things. Women can be very expensive."

Grau nodded and gently steered Charlie back to the victim. "Gorkin, how long was he in this country?"

"Eight years. We both arrived from the Soviet Union within a few months of each other."

The waiter came with the food. Bowls of a steaming stew-like dish were put in front of both men. A large cup of sour cream was placed in the middle of the table.

When the waiter was finished and had left, the man continued. "Sergi had told me he was being followed. That was almost three weeks ago. He said he spotted two, maybe three, people on different occasions and at all hours. They followed him when he worked and sometimes when he was near home."

Grau gently asked, "Why would anyone want to follow him?"

"He didn't know and he was very nervous about it."

"Did he go to the police?"

Charlie laughed softly. "He thought they might be the police."

Grau cocked his head to one side and waited for an explanation.

"You see, Detective Grau, Sergi was involved in some, uh, unusual businesses. And his competition at times could be difficult to deal with."

"Organized crime?"

Charlie nodded.

"So you're saying some wise guys killed your friend?"

Charlie put his hand up. "No. That is what's so strange. When Sergi first saw he was being followed he made some inquiries. There are ways to settle disputes without having to resort to shooting people. I've heard some people say such things are bad for business."

Grau recalled the photo in the dead man's wallet and asked, "Did Sergi have any relatives in this country? Maybe a wife or daughter?"

"No. Not in America. Back in the Soviet Union he has a daughter. But they haven't seen each other for over eight years." Charlie smiled a sad smile and said, "I myself left a wife and two sons in my mother country to come here."

Charlie wiped his now-glistening forehead with the sleeve of his shirt. Grau noted the new dark smudge on the white material.

"I can also tell you that during the last week, people have been watching me, too. Following me."

Grau asked, "How well did you know the woman who was with him?"

"Forget her. She had nothing to do with any of this. She was there so she was killed. That's all." Charlie patted his beaded forehead with a paper napkin.

"Only a few weeks before he first believed he was being followed, Sergi approached me with a business deal. He wanted me to do something for him. He told me it would be worth a good deal of money but it might be dangerous."

"What was the deal?"

"He never got to tell me. He said it was very secret and he'd give me the details when the right time came. And then he was killed. Whatever it was he wanted me to do with him, I'm sure it was the reason he is now dead."

Grau sat back in his chair and picked up a hunk of bread. He broke off a small piece and, with great deliberation, began to butter it. He noticed that Charlie, or whatever his name was, had started to fidget. Grau continued his slow buttering.

The detective put the bread in his mouth and stared at the frightened man in front of him. He decided he had been coy enough.

"Charlie, I think you're full of shit."

The other man began to sputter. Grau cut him off with a wave of his hand and continued.

"I think you know exactly why Gorkin was killed. And if you think I'm going to baby-sit you just because you cook up some bullshit fantasy, then you're nuts."

Grau took a small sip of vodka and watched Charlie. The other man's eyes had lowered to the edge of the table. Grau pushed on.

"What do you do for a living, Charlie?" Grau asked softly.

"I'm a printer. I do lithography and such. Mostly specialty work, copies of old masters, that sort of thing."

"And Gorkin, did he work with you?"

Charlie shook his head and with hesitation said, "Not in printing. We did other things together . . ." The last word trailed off.

"Charlie, listen to me. You called me, remember? You want my help, right?"

Grau was rewarded with a slight nod.

"Good. Okay, now listen. Unless you start to tell me the truth, what you and Gorkin were up to, I can't do a thing for you. Makes sense, right? And let's face it. Unless you guys were killing people, whatever it was you two were doing had to be a lot less serious than murder."

"We were going to print some money."

Charlie had spoken the words so softly that at first Grau didn't understand what the man had said.

"Print? Money? Oh, you mean counterfeiting, like say twenty-dollar bills."

Charlie stumbled, "Yes. No. Not exactly. You see, the money wasn't American. You have to understand, when we started it had been all right. But plans changed, and then the trouble came."

"Charlie, what plans? What kind of money? You'd better start at the beginning."

Charlie took a deep breath and was about to speak when the inner door to the restaurant opened. A young man entered, looked around and headed for an empty table. Grau looked over to Charlie, whose eyes were riveted on the new customer. As far as Grau could see, the other man never so much as glanced in their direction.

Charlie started to rise, saying, "We cannot talk now. Later, in a different place."

Grau put out his hand to stop him and said, "Relax. I'm here. No one's going to get to you. If he makes you nervous," nodding in the direction of the stranger, "I'll check that guy out."

Charlie bent across the table and whispered loudly, "Detective, there is more to this than you know. I'll call you soon."

Grau spoke quickly, "Charlie, listen to me. I can protect you."

"Not from the KGB."

Charlie pushed his chair back, and before Grau could catch him, hurried from the restaurant.

Grau looked out from the street door. He saw neither Charlie, who had disappeared among the Sunday shoppers, nor Tanti.

Grau returned to the restaurant for a chat with the man who had spooked Charlie.

Five minutes later Grau again was out on the street. This time he spotted Tanti standing across the street, on the opposite corner. Grau got into the squad car, swung it around, and stopped by Tanti. His partner jumped in.

"Well?" Tanti asked as Grau drove slowly down the block.

"I'm not sure. Did you catch the thin guy in the white shirt that came in after me?"

Tanti nodded.

"Well, that was my boy. We were doing fine until he got frightened off by a customer that just walked in off the street."

"I don't get it."

"Neither do I. After my man took off I went back in and spoke to the guy that gave him the scare. Turned out to be some guy named Ferro, from Bensonhurst. Works in construction and just wanted a little lunch. You could have cut his Brooklynese with a knife."

"So, what next?"

Grau pulled to the side of the road and took out his spiral note pad. He glanced inside and said, "Gorkin's apartment is somewhere near here. Let's see if we can get inside."

Tanti nodded. Grau put the car in drive and started down the block.

Propkin walked along the street. He kept a discreet distance from the man he was following and reflected on what he had observed. His target had had a meet, that was clear enough. Two policemen at least, maybe more that he had not seen. And then, for no reason Propkin could see, the man he had been following had bolted from the restaurant. Maybe all had not gone well, Propkin conjectured.

Nothing in his target's dossier had indicated that the man would have been likely to contact the authorities, certainly nothing that could have been deduced from the subject's past actions. The man was supposed to be nothing more than a frightened little technician, one of the half-dozen that had been sent to America and who now had to be eliminated for the protection of the motherland. What these people were up to put them in a perilous legal position, making it even more unlikely that the target would have gone to the authorities for protection.

Still, Propkin thought, they had all been rather obvious. The American police car had stood out quite clearly. And the poorly dressed officer who was sitting for so long across from the meeting place did not conceal his weapon very well. And then there was his subject, constantly peeking over his shoulder. The man might as well have worn a neon sign, he was so conspicuous to everyone around him.

But why New York City police?, Propkin wondered. Why not American counterintelligence, or perhaps the CIA?

Propkin kept his target in sight as he walked and asked himself, "Am I now being followed? No, I doubt it. The two policemen drove away. But in that, also, they were so obvious. These events disturb me."

His target was wary, Propkin saw. As was his habit he was looking back over his shoulder, checking to see if he was being followed. Looking, but not really seeing.

"Amateurs," Propkin thought. And then it came to him: The man had chosen the American police because he didn't know enough to contact someone who might actually help him.

Propkin smiled as he contemplated his options. His orders had been specific, right down to a timetable. All those targeted in the operation had to be eliminated within a certain number of weeks. And to ensure the success of the job, each of those to be neutralized were to be done on a specific day, the day that there would be the least likelihood of unwanted interference.

Propkin shook his head. Those two policemen had changed things. The plan to eliminate the target tomorrow evening should be changed, and to hell with orders. After all, this was to be his last mission. What could they do to him?

Propkin looked around. It was early afternoon and the streets were crowded with shoppers. Whole families and many of the local area residents were out for a stroll to enjoy the fine weather.

Propkin made an immediate decision. He would eliminate

the man now. It was going against their predetermined plans but there was now no time to confer with Andrapovich. He would have to do what was necessary.

True, he didn't have the small pistol's silencer on him. But he reasoned that the increase in the gun's report would be outweighed by the advantage of surprise. No, they could never suspect he would do such a thing, among all these people. If he waited until later, a trap might be laid for him.

His subject walked only ten meters ahead of Propkin. He could see that although the man still moved rapidly it was with less caution now.

Charlie the Ferret swung his head quickly over his right shoulder. He sighed. No one had been following him since he left the restaurant, of that he was sure. He knew he had to be careful, he lived only half a block away.

The nervous little man made a sharp right turn into his block. A feeling of security came over him. In front of his six-story apartment building, sitting on metal and web lawn chairs, were the usual *yentas*, old women with nothing to do but gossip. There was Mrs. Greenberg, her silver hair tied up in a bun, wearing a black dress that had difficulty containing her substantial bulk. Two other ladies sat with her, Mrs. Plotkin and Mrs. Chemka. They all looked as if they had been cut from the same mold. The three were involved in an intense debate regarding the proper ingredients for potato pancakes.

He was almost to the front door of his apartment house when he slowed his pace. He wished to savor the feeling of safety which came over him as he reached his sanctuary.

Propkin realized he had slightly mistimed his approach as the other man disappeared around the corner. He hurried onto the subject's street. As he cleared the building line it became clear that the man would reach his home before he could get to him. Propkin decided to use a simple trick.

"Mikael, kak ti?" Michael, how are you? Propkin called to the Ferret by his true name. There was a smile on Propkin's face as he waved his hand in greeting.

Mikael looked back toward the friendly voice. He stopped and returned the smile. Where do I know him from? he thought, as Propkin confidently strode up to him, still smiling.

Officer Irene Rivera drove slowly down Brighton Beach Avenue. Her partner, Frank Ingrim, fiddled with the AM radio, searching for a popular music station. They had been assigned only a handful of calls the entire day and both were glad to see this boring tour of duty wind down.

Ingrim found his station and the raucous sound that passes for modern music filled the car.

Rivera made a face and pleaded, "Frank, please, anything but that garbage."

"Irene, we've been listening to your junk all tour. Give me a break, will ya?" Ingrim started to bounce to the rhythm of the music.

Rivera ignored her partner. She knew that to do otherwise would only encourage him. A few moments later her patience paid off as Ingrim began to again fiddle with the radio.

The barrel-chested officer eventually settled on a more reasonable selection. Rivera smiled but withheld comment. A petite five footer to Ingrim's athletic six three, she had long ago learned how to handle him.

Rivera rubbed her back against the car's seat. Her vest was itching her and there was no way to scratch the right spot. Ingrim ignored her gyrations. Near the end of a full tour of duty, his bullet-resistant vest bothered him also, and like his partner, there was no way to relieve the discomfort but to take the vest off. This was impossible at the moment since the vests were concealed under their short-sleeve uniform shirts. Even though the Kevlar material weighed little more than a pound, they severely restricted air circulation. It made wearing them uncomfortable during the summer months. Fortunately for the two officers, the 60th Precinct's closeness to the ocean kept the day's temperature down and helped to make their vests at least tolerable.

Crack! Crack! At first the officers thought the sounds were a couple of firecrackers. Then they heard a woman scream. Then another shot, louder than the first two, reverberated off the concrete building walls. *Pow!*

The Murder of Old Comrades

Rivera jammed on the brakes as people came running from the block ahead of them. The officers saw other people, transfixed, hands to their mouths, staring down the side street.

"Irene!" Ingrim yelled.

"I know! Over there!" She made a sharp right down the narrow street. Ingrim already had his service revolver drawn. He brought the portable radio he held in his other hand to his lips.

Propkin saw the blue-and-white police car turn swiftly into the street. He hovered over the dead man, the small jammed .22 pistol in one hand, his personal sidearm in the other. Quickly he searched for a place to run. The boardwalk was only a block away. Underneath was a maze of concrete columns. With no time to reholster the smaller pistol he tossed the useless .22 handgun away and bolted for the safety of the columns.

Ingrim was out of the police car before Rivera had a chance to stop.

"Frank, Goddammit!" Rivera yelled, helplessly watching her partner as he ran after a man who held a gun in his hand. Spotting the body on the sidewalk, she yelled into her police portable, "Ten-thirteen, man with a gun! In pursuit, Brighton Sixth! Toward the boardwalk!"

She jumped from the car and chased after her partner, service revolver in her hand.

Propkin was in superb physical condition, but the pursuing officer was rapidly catching up to him. He saw that the boardwalk was just ahead and whirled, raised his gun, and with the cool deliberation of the well-trained killer he was, fixed his sights on the chest of his pursuer, now but twenty feet away.

Ingrim saw the gun come up. He raised his own weapon, dropping the portable radio so as to grasp the revolver with both hands. He heard a loud *Pow!* and returned fire, emptying his gun before it had come up to eye level. He didn't feel the impact of the tiny projectile as it penetrated his vest and blew a quarter-size hole in his heart.

Propkin turned and ran. He headed for the massive wooden walkway ahead and then through a rip in the metal fence. Once under the boardwalk, Propkin took advantage of the twists and turns of the supporting beams. He glanced over his shoulder and saw that he was gaining distance from the officer.

Ingrim ignored his empty gun and chased after Propkin. His only thought was to get the man running from him.

All at once Ingrim became confused. He was becoming tired and his legs felt like lead. Weak and light-headed, he had to stop running. The big policeman sensed something was terribly wrong. He sat down on the cool sand, his back against a concrete pillar. His service revolver, now too heavy to hold, fell from his fingers.

"Frank!" Irene bent down by her partner, the man who fled underneath the boardwalk now of no concern. "Frank, what's the matter! Frank!" She raised the portable to her lips and yelled, "Officer shot! Ten-thirteen, under the boardwalk!"

He tried to speak, but his jaw was so heavy and he was so tired, nothing came out. He could hear sirens in the distance. Lots of sirens. But they all seemed so far away. Maybe if he slept a while . . .

All at once Ingrim found himself in a tunnel. He saw a bright light at the very end and began rushing toward it. Faster and faster. Rushing to the light.

"Frank, Frank!" Irene called to her partner as tears of fear and frustration ran down her cheeks. His head had rolled to one side, his eyes half-closed.

Chapter 8

Andrapovich looked up from the *Times* and eyed the 16th Street and Avenue U station sign as the D train lurched into the south Brooklyn stop.

He glanced over his newspaper. Because it was a Sunday afternoon the normally full car held only two other passengers besides him. A middle-aged woman sat at the extreme far right and stared blankly out a window. An old man sat opposite her, his arms wrapped around two brown-paper shopping bags that he held protected in his lap. Andrapovich saw that in the cars at either end of his were also only a handful of other people. He noted with satisfaction that the other passengers didn't appear to be particularly interested in what was going on around them.

With a rush of air the doors slid open. Andrapovich slowly got to his feet and stepped from the train. When just a few feet from the car, he turned around as if to get his bearings. No one else had gotten off.

Rolling the *Times* into a cylinder, he placed it under his arm and casually strolled to the elevated station's stairway and down to street level.

The movement felt good. For the last two hours, except for the few times he had changed trains, he had been sitting on the inhospitably hard plastic seats of various subway cars. The trip had started in Manhattan, less than an hour after he had been informed of the Brooklyn shooting. He had begun by taking a northbound train. Once in the Bronx he changed trains, all the while searching for some sign of an American surveillance team. The journey had taken him into Queens, back to Manhattan and finally to his destination stop.

Now on the street outside the station Andrapovich began to walk. His stroll was in the opposite direction from where the meet with Propkin was to take place. He wandered down side streets lined with small neat homes. Men in old clothes watered neatly trimmed lawns in the coolness of the late afternoon. The smell of steak broiling over hot charcoal reminded him that he hadn't eaten for quite a few hours. And he knew it would be some time before he would have a chance to eat again.

After squaring several blocks he returned to the main avenue. Satisfied he hadn't been followed, Andrapovich strode off directly for the meeting location, a small park. Not far from the block-size green he recognized Propkin seated at a public bench. As he approached him he saw that the man was sharing a bag of popcorn with a small flock of pigeons that had gathered at his feet. Andrapovich sat down next to him.

Propkin tossed a kernel of popcorn several feet away. The birds moved noisily and en masse toward the crumb.

"You would think these birds would be wilder in such a big city," Propkin said and tossed out more food.

"Alexi, what happened?"

"Nothing, really. I eliminated Saminov."

"A day early." Andrapovich unrolled his newspaper, held it as if he were reading, and continued. "And the policeman?"

"Unavoidable. He would have caught me if I hadn't shot him."

A young woman walked by pushing a baby carriage. Once she was out of earshot Andrapovich said, "And you lost your pistol. The Americans will match it with the earlier shooting."

Propkin bristled, "I didn't *lose* it. I threw it away. And what if they do match it? Since when are such things of concern to us?"

Propkin silently tossed the last of the puffy kernels at the birds. Without looking at Andrapovich he said, "Anyway, there was little option. The damn thing malfunctioned again and that policeman was almost on top of me. What would you have had me do, hold on to it for a souvenir?"

Andrapovich took a deep breath and said, "No matter, this changes the situation dramatically. I've decided to pull you out."

Propkin sat up straight and looked directly at the other man. "Ridiculous! After all the effort that went into setting this mission up?"

"I see no other choice. You killed an American police officer."

"So, what of it?"

"You don't understand their system. The police will be looking for you. Inquiries will be made. Who knows, they may find something should they search Saminov's apartment. After all, what we want wasn't in either of Gorkin's places. And once that happens they will start to piece the puzzle together."

"You haven't searched Saminov's place yet?"

"Tell me, when did I have time for such things? Especially since you decided when it was best to eliminate him. You, who are above orders."

Propkin began to speak but Andrapovich cut him off.

"Whatever occurs, I cannot permit one thing to happen, for them to find out of our government's involvement in this matter."

Propkin rolled the now-empty cellophane popcorn bag into a ball, reached over to a waste can and dropped it in.

"I think you are overreacting to the situation. If I remain in place and permit some time to pass, the mission can be continued. Anyway, there is nothing else for us to do, since we still haven't found what I was sent for."

"The mission is my responsibility. I have made the decision. You are to leave as soon as possible," Andrapovich said.

"When?"

"Tonight. The aircraft will arrive at 2300 hours. Get your equipment. I will pick up the car and meet you at the designated location."

Propkin sat with his arms over the back of the bench and watched traffic pass.

"What do you plan to do after I'm back on the ship?"

"Nothing. I hope to let some time go by before taking further action." Andrapovich glanced at his watch. "It's getting late. I'll see you later." He stood up.

Propkin remained seated. "Do you really think you can enjoy the luxury of putting off the completion of this assignment just because there's an added element of danger?"

"That is my concern."

"And me, Yuri Andrapovich. What shall I do, once I'm away from here?"

"Wait for further instructions," Andrapovich said, and added, "except this time obey them."

Before Propkin could reply Andrapovich turned around and walked away.

Tanti sat on the edge of the torn mattress as Grau continued to search Gorkin's single room. He rubbed his hands together in an attempt to rid them of some of the grime picked up during the search of the apartment.

"Jon, we've been at this place for hours. If something we were interested in were here, whoever tore the place apart before we arrived probably already found it."

Grau responded with an absentminded "Hmmm" and continued to systematically go through the pages of a paperback adventure novel. Finishing that one he picked up another and repeated the process. A stack of completed books lay at his feet.

"Tony, how well did you search those clothes?" Grau asked, nodding in the direction of what looked like a multicolored pile of rags.

"I went through every single one. All the pockets are turned inside out, most of them had been ripped open before I even touched them. Nothing. Jon, I'm telling you, we're wasting our time."

Grau tossed the final book at his feet. He took a step back and surveyed the room.

"Tony, just look around you," he said, as he made a sweeping motion with his hand. "Whoever was here before us ripped into every part of this place. Which tells me that since they left nothing untouched we've got a

The Murder of Old Comrades

good shot that they didn't find whatever it was they were after."

Tanti shrugged, unconvinced. Grau stepped over to a small closet, already thoroughly searched by both officers and now empty. Grau started to tap on the sides of its interior walls.

"Jon," Tanti pleaded, "you already did that. Let's get out of here."

Grau ignored his partner and fished out his pocket knife. He pulled up on the linoleum covering of the closet's floor and began to carefully work the knife tip around the slats of the exposed wood boards. As he prodded he said, "Did I ever tell you about when I worked Narco? And where we used to find stuff stashed?"

Before Tanti could reply Grau pushed down on his knife like a miniature lever. Four of the floorboards came loose as one. He removed them from their seat and looked inside the exposed hole.

Silently, Tanti appeared next to him. Inside was empty except for a few scraps of paper.

"See, they got to it already," Tanti said, as Grau reached in and picked up the small white rectangles.

Grau walked over to the single overhead light of the room and held the pieces up to the exposed bulb. He smiled and handed the papers to Tanti.

"Tony, hold one of them up to the light."

Tanti shrugged and held one of the letter-size white sheets up to the ceiling.

"So? There's nothing written on them. They're just blank scraps of paper."

"But what kind of paper are they?"

"Thick?"

Grau shook his head. "Tony, those are pieces of bank note. For Christ's sake, look at the different-colored thread running through them. Feel how heavy the stock is. You think you're gonna walk into a local stationery store and pick up a ream of this stuff?"

"Okay, so what does this stuff tell us?"

"That my man Charlie may not have been full of it. Remember what the guy said about counterfeiting? This fits right in."

Tanti nodded, keeping his reservations to himself. He asked, "Where to now?"

Grau folded the pieces of paper in quarters and put them in his jacket pocket. He replied, "Back to the restaurant. Let's see if we can track down Charlie."

Chapter 9

Kyle Mante first noticed the blip, a primary target, as it entered his radar screen from a southeasterly direction. As was usually the case on a quiet Sunday night his normally pockmarked screen was almost free of air traffic. It was only because the aircraft had come in from the Atlantic Ocean that he had paid it any attention at all.

Most aircraft which the controllers handle in and around the New York Terminal control area are transponder-equipped. This device broadcasts a response to ground signals sent by the controller's equipment. Any aircraft carrying such a unit shows up as a clear and distinct image on the radar screen. Besides presenting the ground controller with a strong radar blip, the pilot of an aircraft so equipped can be assigned a discreet numerical designation, which is also displayed on the controller's radar screen along with the ship's ground speed. Primary targets, aircraft not equipped with a transponder, vary in difficulty of radar detection by their size and location within the radar coverage area.

Mante worked on the second floor of a white nondescript building located near the border of Queens and Long Island. Called "the room" by the men and women who work in the Federal Aviation Air Traffic Control facility, it houses thirty-seven radar screens. These in turn are connected by underground cables to radar dishes at John F. Kennedy International Airport, Newark Airport and Islip Airport.

The people who sit at these screens control the airspace around greater New York City, which for their purposes, is divided up into five sectors: LaGuardia, Newark, Islip, Kennedy and Kennedy/Liberty. The last sector, handled as part of the Kennedy area of responsibility, was where Kyle Mante was working at that moment.

Any aircraft that flew within a forty-five mile radius from the geographic center of Kennedy Airport and at a high enough altitude might be seen on Mante's radar screen.

Mante had noticed similar traffic two days earlier. It had also flown in from the Atlantic, and at about the same time. That ship had also been a primary target, and like the ship he was now tracking, had traveled northward. Slowly it had made its way up the Hudson River. Finally he had lost contact with the blip somewhere above the Tappan Zee Bridge, just north of New York City between Westchester and Rockland counties.

Later that same evening he had noted another primary target, this time moving from north to south. The second blip came onto his screen where he had lost the first target. And that aircraft had followed the reverse route taken by the earlier target, flying off his screen as it headed out over the Atlantic Ocean. Mante had wondered at the time whether the two blips had been the same ship. He eventually came to the conclusion that they were. But during that tour of duty he had been too busy working other traffic to pay the ship much attention. And, anyway, the aircraft hadn't appeared to be doing anything illegal, at least as far as its movement around the terminal control area was concerned. He had pushed the incident from his mind.

Still, Mante reflected, it was a strange direction for a primary target to come from. Certainly, each day at work, he saw dozens of transponder-equipped commercial aircraft fly in from Europe from that direction. But those ships moved very rapidly and they headed toward some specific airport.

Mante looked around the room for his supervisor, Glenn

Cummings. Cummings was bent over the shoulder of a newly hired controller two screens away. Mante called out, "Hey, Glenn, check this out."

Cummings stepped over to Mante's position. A balding forty year old with thick glasses, his thinning hair was combed back to front in a vain attempt to cover his bald pate.

"What's the problem, Kyle?" he asked as he snaked the headset wire connecting him to the supervising controller at the far end of the room around Mante's chair.

"Forty miles to the southeast, primary only, northwest bound. I've seen this guy before. He's coming in off the Atlantic. I saw him a couple of days ago. He flew somewhere upstate New York."

Cummings peered over Mante's shoulder and watched the eighth-inch rectangle move slowly across the screen. Mante continued, "Then later the guy flew back out over the Atlantic. Where the hell could he be going?"

Cummings straightened up, understanding at once that this wasn't a normal contact. Mante was right. There was no place for a light aircraft to fly out of—or back to—when it came from the direction of the Atlantic. Cummings made a decision.

"Okay, Kyle. Tag him. So long as it's quiet out there, follow him. But don't get mesmerized by this guy if it begins to get busy."

"Right, Glenn," Mante said, smiling. He punched some keys on his console. The letters UNK appeared by the unidentified blip. Below the now-tagged target the number 80 showed, indicating the aircraft's ground speed in nautical miles per hour.

The blip continued to move up the river between New York and New Jersey, as it did on the earlier occasion Mante had noticed it. Shortly after it moved beyond the Tappan Zee Bridge, Mante lost contact with it.

He again looked around for Cummings, who was back assisting the trainee. "Glenn, the ship moved off my scope. Her last heading was northwest."

Without taking his eyes from the new man's scope, Cummings responded, "If you see her again, tag her and let me know." Cummings then moved down to another controller who requested assistance.

Forty minutes later Mante saw the target reappear. It came back in exactly the same place it had left Mante's screen. He tagged the blip again and called over to Cummings, who now stood at the opposite end of the room.

"She's back!"

"Watch her, Kyle. If she looks like she's going to head out over the Atlantic, I'll give the Coast Guard a call. We may have a smuggler." Cummings turned back to the controller he was supervising and muttered, "Damned strange."

Mante silently tracked the target until it reached the area just north of Governors Island, close by the Statue of Liberty. For some time it had been obvious to him that the ship was retracing its route and he was becoming restless.

"Glenn, if you're gonna call someone, do it now! She's heading out to sea."

Cummings went over to the area supervisor. He quickly explained the situation. After hearing the story the ranking man picked up a phone and dialed the number for the nearest Coast Guard Air Station, at Floyd Bennett Field in Brooklyn.

From where he sat Mante could see the area supervisor in conversation on the phone. After hanging up, the supervisor spoke with Cummings, who walked back to Mante and said, "Sorry. The Coast Guard told the boss if all we got is a guy flying up and down the Hudson River, they ain't gonna send one of their choppers to go chase him," then started to walk away without waiting for a reply.

Mante called after him, "Contact the PD's Aviation Unit."

Cummings turned back and gave Mante a puzzled look. The young controller continued, "My dad works there. Paul Mante. He's a lieutenant. Just tell him his son . . . look, just let me give him a call. I bet he'll send a ship up."

Cummings nodded. "Go to the phone. I'll watch your screen."

The two men exchanged places and Mante headed for the phone in the corner of the room.

* * *

"Aviation Unit, may I help you?" asked the uniformed officer who picked up the telephone in Operations. The gold wings above his silver police shield identified him as a pilot. "Oh, hi, Kyle, how you doin'? Your dad? Sure. Hang on."

The officer placed the receiver down by the telephone, walked through a narrow hallway and into an adjoining room. Half a dozen department pilots and mechanics sat around a large wood table. A few read aviation magazines, two drank coffee and talked and several watched the evening news on television. The officer stepped over to a lanky pilot with short chestnut hair who wore a single gold bar on each of his collars. "Lou, your son's on the line. In the Operations office."

"Thanks." Lieutenant Paul Mante got up, took one last sip of his tepid tea and followed the officer back through the corridor.

He picked up the phone receiver from the desk and said, "Lieutenant Mante."

He smiled on hearing his son's voice. "Hello, Kyle, how're you doing?"

Mante's son quickly explained the situation and the need for quick action. The aircraft was now past the Verrazano Bridge and heading out to sea.

"What frequency you on?" Lieutenant Mante scribbled a number on a piece of scrap paper.

"Okay. Give us five minutes and keep track of the ship." Mante slammed down the phone, and as he moved through the narrow corridor, commanded, "Get the 222 up!" Entering the pilot's room, he ordered, "Mike, you're pilot. Nick, you'll handle the FLIR. I'm going also."

The group of relaxed pilots and mechanics jumped from their chairs and ran for the metal door which lead to the adjacent hangar. Mante and the two men he ordered on the mission grabbed their life jackets and headsets, putting the equipment on as they headed for the ship.

Mante stepped into the fifty-year-old labyrinth of a hangar and saw that his men needed no additional direction. Under the eerie glow of a dozen ceiling-high mercury-vapor lights the chocks were removed from the wheels of the dolly that held the big blue-and-white, twin-engined Bell helicopter. Other ships surrounded the 222, including single-engine Bell JetRangers, military surplus Hueys and monster-size Bell 412s, each on its own wheeled platform. The 222 that Mante ordered for the mission was the fastest and sleekest helicopter the department had, capable of speeds in excess of 150 miles per hour.

Trucks were brought to life and orders were shouted among the men as one of the vehicles was backed up to hook onto the ship's dolly and another to the wheeled auxiliary power unit, its small engine already running. The compact unit screamed in protest, ready to energize the electricity-thirsty starter motors of the 222.

Two officers fought with the hangar's manually operated doors. One used a large pry bar to start the massive half-century-old rusted hulk along its track, while the other pushed with his shoulder along its edge. A third man ran over to help and the doors groaned open.

A mechanic, dressed in a blue jump suit, ran up to Mante and asked, "Lieutenant, do you want the ship brought out to the flight line?"

"No time. We'll take off right next to the hangar."

A small wheeled tug was hooked up and slowly pulled the large craft seventy-five feet away from the building. The officer who drove hopped out of the vehicle's cab, rechocked the dolly's wheels, unhooked from the ship and moved the tug clear of the area. The helicopter's nose had been positioned into the wind and faced to the southwest, the same direction the target she would search for flew in.

The officer Mante had assigned as pilot in command jumped onto the wood dolly and yanked out the engine inlet covers. He tossed the dirty orange-colored puffs into the ship's cabin. His yellow life jacket flapped gently in the evening breeze, forcing him to pause for a moment and secure its bottom strap. This done, he entered the cockpit and took the right-hand seat. Mante swung his thin frame into the copilot's seat and buckled on his safety harness. Both men adjusted their foot pedals and visually checked the dozens of gauges in front of them. Everything read in the green and normal.

Mante glanced over his shoulder, making sure Nick Steffins had taken his place by the Forward Looking Infra Red screen. The FLIR would enable them to see in the dark as the device was sensitive to the normally invisible infrared spectrum of light waves.

Abruptly the instrument panel glowed brightly as a mechanic plugged the APU into the side of the ship. Mike Casson, the pilot, adjusted his bulbous green headset and rechecked the gauges one last time. He looked to the right, then the left. Seeing that the rotor blades were free and all personnel were away from the ship, he yelled, "CLEAR!" and pushed the automatic start button. The whine of the large electric motor overhead could be heard as power flowed from the APU into the ship's starter. Once he saw the big blades begin to rotate he turned his attention to the instrument gauges. When the gauge indicating engine speed showed the correct value he introduced fuel into the system. A dull roar blotted out the noise of the smaller electric motor as jet fuel entered the first of the two big turbine engines and the machine came to life.

The men inside the ship began to rock as four hundred pounds of rotor blades picked up speed. A series of warning lights flashed on the glare shield. Loud emergency alarms raucously sounded as the ship's safety systems warned of low rotor and engine RPM. Once the blades came up to speed, the lights and sounds automatically went out, assuring Casson that the safety system was in order.

He brought the second engine to life. Inside the cabin the crew could smell the distinctive odor of jet fuel exhaust. Casson checked around the ship to make sure the area was clear then looked at the gauges one last time. He felt a thrill as his hand tightened on the power lever at his side and the helicopter roared its readiness to fly.

He looked out the right window. "Clear right!"

Mante looked out his window and called, "Clear left!"

Casson gently pulled up on the stick at his left, the collective. The ship lightened on its skids. With an added fraction of an inch of additional upward pressure on the control, the pilot had over seven thousand pounds of aluminum, fuel and men hovering six inches from the surface of the dolly.

Keeping the ship's nose pointed forward he increased the power to her engines. The big ship first lumbered ahead, then leapt into the night air. A moment later they were cutting through the sky at 160 miles per hour, five hundred feet above the surface of the water.

Casson pressed the radio switch on the joy stick.

"Kennedy, PD Eleven."

"PD Eleven, go."

"PD Eleven off Floyd Bennett, squawking zero three zero zero. We would like to take her clear to the west."

"PD Eleven, keep your squawk. Cleared as requested."

"PD Eleven, Roger."

Casson turned to Mante and asked, "What do we have?"

"I'm not sure. An unidentified was picked up by New York Approach. They've tracked her before. She flies out over the Atlantic where there's no place to go. They asked if we'd find out what's the story. Sounds like some sort of dope-running operation to me, but that's only a guess."

Mante looked over his right shoulder. "Nick, you'll be looking for a light aircraft. Stand by and I'll see if New York can give us some directions."

Steffins threw a thumbs up at the lieutenant and continued readying his equipment.

Mante dialed in a frequency on his aviation radio and activated the transmit switch.

"New York Approach, PD Eleven."

"PD Eleven, go ahead." Mante recognized Kyle's voice.

"New York, you got us on your screen yet?"

"PD Eleven, squawk five four zero zero and ident."

Mante turned the knobs on the ship's transponder to the requested numbers and pushed in the button which would broadcast a powerful signal to the ground station and identify his transmission.

"Okay, PD Eleven, we have you at about ten miles south of the Verrazano Bridge. Your target is approximately twenty-five miles from your position, on a magnetic heading of about 140 degrees."

"Roger, Approach, PD Eleven is turning to a heading of one four zero." Mante nodded to the pilot and the ship banked gently to the new direction. He quietly added, "Mike, give me full continuous power."

Casson brought both turbines up to nearly 100 percent power. He stopped the increase just as the ship's airspeed approached the red Never Exceed line on the airspeed indicator.

Mante looked over his shoulder at Steffins. "Anything on the FLIR yet?"

"No, boss, she's still too far away. But you'll be the first to know when I got something."

The radio came alive. "PD Eleven is twenty-five miles from the bridge and within twenty miles of the target and closing."

"PD Eleven, Roger. Approach, what speed is the target indicating?"

"She's showing eighty knots on the screen, PD Eleven. You're showing one five zero knots."

"Roger. By the way, Ground, are there any other targets in our vicinity?"

"Negative, PD Eleven."

Mante quietly said to Casson, "Mike, kill all the outside lights."

Casson, without any comment, reached overhead and flicked off the ship's strobe and outside running lights.

Mante asked the pilot, "Any chance for more speed?"

"Only if you want retreating blade stall, Lieutenant."

"No, thanks, Mike, I want to get home tonight."

"By the way, just for the record, at this rate of speed we're burning up fuel like we got a hole in the fuel tank."

"Yeah, I know. Keep an eye on the fuel gauge. I figure when we catch up to the target, we'll be able to slow down enough so we won't have a fuel consumption problem."

Steffins tapped Mante on the shoulder. "Lou, I got something."

Mante looked at the FLIR screen. A tiny dot glowed at its center.

The aviation radio came to life with, "PD Eleven is now ten miles from the target, closing fast."

"PD Eleven," Mante transmitted, acknowledging the information.

The big ship closed on the light plane at almost one hundred miles per hour. The image Steffins watched on the FLIR screen continued to increase in size. Warmer parts of the target ship showed as bright green while those parts farthest from the engine were in darker shades of the same color. The variations reflected the intensity of heat as translated into infrared light waves picked up by the FLIR. Soon the image on the screen showed up clearly as the outline of a floatplane, her big pontoons less distinct than the rest of the ship, but clearly visible nonetheless.

"Lieutenant," Steffins said, "we got a seaplane in front of us."

Mante nodded. To Steffins he said, "Of course. That's why she's flying so slow. And out over the water. Nick, keep an eye out for some sort of a large boat."

"Right, Lou," Steffins replied, the light from the FLIR casting an eerie green hue over his face.

"PD Eleven, New York Approach. You are now three miles from the target and closing." Mante stared intently out the window. He could see nothing but a black void ahead of him.

"Mike, our friend isn't running any external night lighting. Watch your ass."

"That custom seems to be catching on," Casson responded sarcastically.

Mante smiled at the wisecrack. He tripped the transmit switch and broadcast, "Roger, Approach, we're going to fall in trail and maintain this distance."

Casson automatically reduced power to the helicopter's engines. As the airspeed bled off, the indicator unwound from near the redline to just over the eighty-knot mark.

"PD Eleven, New York. Be advised we have lost the primary target on our screens. You're still with us but you'll be off the screen shortly."

"Thanks, New York. We'll give you a shout when we get back."

"Okay, Dad."

Mante smiled at the unauthorized transmission.

Steffins called from behind him, "Lieutenant, the target has started to lose altitude. It looks like it's flying only a few feet above the water."

"Mike, how low do you want to take her?" Mante asked the pilot. Although Casson held the rank of police officer Mante had assigned him as pilot in command of the ship. The safety and proper operation of an aircraft was by law and tradition ultimately the pilot's responsibility. As a fellow pilot, Mante obeyed the code.

Casson replied, "I'll take her down to one hundred feet above the water. Set your radar altimeter."

Mante and Casson set the low-altitude alert dial on their respective radar altimeters at one hundred feet. If the ship descended lower than that, a warning tone would automatically sound.

Mante knew that this was pure instrument flying and required intense concentration. He and Casson would be taking turns at the controls.

For the next hour the two ships flew as if in formation. Steffins had warned the pilots when he saw surface ships come into view on the FLIR screen, but the seaplane had continued to drone on. Mante was now becoming concerned over their fuel supply.

The 222 carried enough jet fuel for almost four hours of flight, but they were now well out over the Atlantic and every minute heading farther away from land. If there was a problem with the machine the chances of their survival in the chilly water below ranged from zero to nil.

"Mike, I'm giving it another fifteen minutes. If the floatplane keeps on going, we'll turn around."

"No problem, lieutenant. The fuel gauges still show over half tanks. As long as we don't get crazy with the power we should be all right."

Steffins tapped Mante on the shoulder. "Lou, the seaplane is slowing down."

Casson reduced power immediately.

Mante looked over his shoulder and watched as Steffins' face turned light green from the reflection of the FLIR screen. Steffins said, "There's a ship in the water. The floatplane's landing next to her."

All Mante could see out the front window was blackness. "Mike, you got a visual?"

"Nothing." Casson had slowed the helicopter to less than fifty knots. He began a shallow turn to keep them away from the target and its mother ship.

"Mike, take her up to five thousand feet. I don't want anyone on the ship below to hear us."

The nose of their ship angled up gently as Casson complied with the order.

On Steffins' FLIR the scene below could be clearly read. The floatplane had touched down on the ocean and was coming up alongside a large vessel. Within a few minutes, while the 222 flew in high orbit around the two craft below them, the single-engine plane was hoisted aboard the trawler.

"I've seen enough. Mike, let's get out of here. We'll give Special Operations Division a call when we land."

Casson brought the helicopter around to a heading of 325 degrees.

"How's the fuel gauge read, Mike?"

"Lieutenant, since I'm an optimist, she reads half full."

"Okay, optimist. Take us home."

Chapter 10

Early Monday morning Tanti showed up at the Four-Seven Squad resplendent in brown polyester pants, light gray jacket and nondescript tie. He and Grau immediately went in to see Sergeant Carrol and to remind him of his promise to speak with the precinct commanding officer. The sergeant, a man of his word, immediately went downstairs to see the captain. He returned to the squad room fifteen minutes later.

The captain, Carrol related, would have been delighted to assign Tanti temporarily to the squad for Grau's case. Except, as the sergeant had predicted the day before, he was short of manpower. The captain, Carrol said, informed him that recently the precinct had found itself seriously short of officers, particularly during the critical high-crime period, the evening and early morning hours.

Carrol told them that the captain hadn't completely closed out the possibility of Tanti's being assigned to the case. If things were quiet (as they had been Sunday) and a man could be spared, then they could have the officer.

Thus Grau now found himself working the case alone once more, moving along FDR Drive in the direction of the Police Ballistics Unit. To top off the morning's bad news, the radio announcer told of an officer shot and killed the day before in Brooklyn. Listening to the scanty information the broadcast provided, Grau understood that the officer and his partner had apparently stumbled onto a homicide on the street. From the description of the incident it sounded to Grau as if the shooting had taken place only a few blocks from where he and the strange Russian had met and where he and Tanti had searched Gorkin's apartment.

Grau couldn't help but mull over what he and Tanti had found in Gorkin's small apartment the day before. Clearly Gorkin's dwelling had received the same treatment as the place up in the Bronx. Someone had looked very hard for something. And if Grau was right, they hadn't found what they were after. Grau figured that if he could find out what that something was, he knew he'd be a lot closer to solving the case.

He and his partner had gone back to the restaurant after finishing up the search of Gorkin's apartment. Nobody knew anything. The waiter who had served Charlie and him would barely admit even doing that much. They were spooked all right. Why, Grau had no idea. But he'd have to go back to Brooklyn and try to track down his one main lead.

Grau signaled and turned off the drive at the Twenty-third Street exit. The Ballistics Unit was on Twentieth Street, between Second and Third Avenues in the Police Academy Building. Though he was still quite a few blocks away from the place Grau had already begun to look for someplace to park. Spaces around the academy building were at a premium and he wasn't about to pass up any unoccupied spot.

On Twenty-first Street he saw an open parking meter. He pulled his squad car into the space and tossed his department identification plate in the window. Locking and slamming the door, Grau looked up at the sky. He noted a change in the weather. The air had become much cooler than it had been over the last few days. Overhead all he could see was a gray overcast, the vanguard of a cold front moving into the area. Grau preferred the coolness that came with the overcast to the heat of early summer that had made working in the city so uncomfortable during the last week.

He moved quickly along the four blocks to the academy. As he walked he ran through his mind the things he wanted to accomplish that day. First he had to take the strange shell and spent bullet to ballistics. Hopefully there they would be identified and perhaps give him some clue as to the shooter's background. Next he wanted to drive up to Yonkers, to meet with the relatives of Judith Bartlett. That information would determine where he would go from there.

Grau knew this case was not going well. The rule of thumb used by experienced homicide investigators was: If you didn't come up with some clue as to whom the killer might be within the first twenty-four to forty-eight hours, the case was going to be a problem. Grau had no witnesses, not unusual in a homicide case, but he'd also had no anonymous phone callers whispering a nickname. So he had absolutely no leads as to who pulled the trigger. Worse yet, even after the interview he had with that bizarre character the other day, he still had only a vague theory revolving around counterfeit currency as to why the trigger was pulled. The case was showing every indication of being a mystery, as detectives referred to a case that would remain unsolved.

Grau waited to cross Second Avenue at Twentieth Street. The heavy volume of cars and city buses belching blue smoke blocked his way. With the green Walk signal he darted across the avenue. He headed along the north side of Twentieth Street until he came to the New York City Police Academy. The building was large. Eight stories high and constructed of marble and brick, it took up the entire middle of the block. On the street level, at the building line, was a glass-enclosed security booth. Beyond that was an open area called the muster deck. The rest of the structure rose above this space which was designed to protect anyone standing beneath it from the elements. Here was where the department's recruits fell in for their daily roll call, called to attention by academy sergeants.

Past the open area of the muster deck stood a wall of glass. A door at one end allowed people to enter and leave the building while under the watchful eyes of officers assigned to security duty.

Grau held out his shield and identification card for the officer in the first booth. He kept the worn black leather case out, walked past the muster deck and entered the building proper. Again he displayed his identification to the security personnel at the door.

Once inside he took an elevator to the eighth floor. On that floor was not only the Ballistics Unit but also the other scientific forensic units which the department's investigators now depended upon so heavily. Years ago a detective was measured by the quality of his informants and on how readily he could secure confessions from the criminals he came in contact with. But court rulings over the last twenty years had negated much of the value of such things. And now the only viable legal replacement for those resources was to be found in the forensic sciences.

He stepped out of the car and walked into a small steel mesh enclosure, designed to keep unauthorized personnel off the floor. The cage was approximately twelve by twenty feet in size, with an electrically operated door at one end. Grau raised his police identification for the receptionist seated behind a counter to his right, who buzzed him through the locked metal door.

The white-smocked man who let him pass was small and dark-skinned. He asked, "Where to, detective?"

"Ballistics," Grau replied, noting the soft Indian accent. Before the man could direct Grau to fill out the captions in the sign-in book, the task was completed. Grau had been to the eighth floor many times before.

He walked down the hall to the left and headed for the Ballistics Unit. Along the way he looked at the array of exotic handguns, shotguns and submachine guns which were displayed in the unit's window. Some of the firearms he saw were of museum quality and scarcity. But here they were nothing more then interesting and necessary samples of the types of weapons that New York City police officers removed from the streets on a regular, daily basis.

Entering the front door, Grau came upon yet another sign-in log. He finished that entry and walked into the main room of the unit.

It was a large office, with desks crammed in most of the available space. The detectives who sat at them were busily involved in their various specialized tasks. One man held a dark-colored Colt government model 1911 .45-caliber pistol under a magnifying glass, attempting to read its worn serial number. Another detective—young, with red hair—was examining a MAC-11 submachine gun and recording the headstamp information on twenty assorted .380 ACP cartridges that had been seized with the weapon.

Seated at an old wooden desk in the middle of the room was a large heavy-set detective. Older than the other detectives, he wore his tie loose around his neck and the sleeves of his shirt were rolled up tightly, high above his elbows. White hair exploded from the man's head and his cheeks were the color of a holiday calendar Santa Claus.

Grau walked directly to the senior officer and loudly said, "Ray, how you doing!"

Detective Raymond Adleman looked up from his work and smiled on seeing Grau, extending his hand.

The two men had first met when Grau was a young detective and Adleman had only been assigned to Ballistics for a few years. Now Adleman had over twenty of his thirty-six years with the Ballistics Unit. Within three years the detective would have to leave the department, since he would reach the mandatory retirement age of sixty-two.

Ray Adleman had become something of a legend within the Ballistics Unit. His co-workers would comment to one another that he had a mind like a sponge. Every esoteric weapon, cartridge or bit of ballistic trivia seemed to be at his mental fingertips.

A game had evolved over the years within the unit. One of the detectives would throw a question at Adleman and the senior member of the unit would attempt to come up with the answer. He would sit back in his ancient, creaking, wood swivel chair. With his short pudgy fingers intertwined and resting on his considerable stomach, his thick white eyebrows would furrow as Adleman gave the appearance of great thought and concentration. Then, as if inspiration had just struck, his eyebrows would shoot up, the chair would come up straight and the forefinger of his right hand would point to the ceiling. Adleman had the answer again! The men in the squad would moan and groan and plot ever more intricate conundrums to stump the master. And on those occasions when a question did not elicit the correct response, the squad broke out in pandemonium. Poor Adleman would hear about his failure for days.

Grau removed two plastic packets from his jacket pocket. He handed them to Adleman and explained the case and how he came upon the proffered evidence.

The older detective examined the unusual shell case first. Speaking more to himself than Grau, he said, "Might be a .22 JGR. Except the headstamp is wrong." He took a small flashlight from his drawer and shone its light down the mouth of the cartridge. "Wrong primer, too. European Berdan, not our Boxer."

"I don't understand, Ray."

"Here, look." Adleman again shone the light down the mouth of the case. "See the two holes?"

"Yeah, so?" Grau said, watching Adleman.

"Well, that means the case is of European manufacture. The two holes are vents, to permit the hot primer gases to escape into the case and ignite the gunpowder. An American shell would have only one hole down there."

Grau continued to scrutinize the older man. Adleman removed the small pointed projectile and held it in his left hand. His right rummaged through the desk drawer and retrieved a micrometer. He placed the slug in the jaws of the measuring device and with his thumb and forefinger deftly twirled the micrometer's knurled knob. He bent over the table lamp and read the numbers.

"Jon, the caliber of this bullet is less than a .22. It mikes out at .215 inches in diameter."

"Okay, Ray, so how many guns come in that caliber?"

Adleman sat back in his chair. His eyebrows furrowed, this time in sincere concentration.

"Jon, the diameter of the bullet is about 5 mm."

"Great, how many 5mm guns are there in the world?"

"Not many. But the problem is, none of them are what you have here."

Grau looked at Adleman without responding. In all the years he had worked with him he had never received such a vague response from the man.

"Jon, I haven't the faintest idea what cartridge or bullet these are, or what gun they came from. They're the damndest things I've ever seen."

Adleman reached up over his desk and pulled out a large book, *Jane's Infantry Weapons—1981-82*. Placing it on his cluttered desk, he opened it up and thumbed through the pages. He stopped in the ammunition identification section.

"Jon, see here," Adleman pointed with his chubby finger. "These are the headstamps that various governments put on the backs of their military cartridges. By the markings on your case, it appears to be eastern European."

Grau simply nodded. His mind went back to the meeting the day before, with the man who called himself Charlie.

Grau reflected on their conversation, particularly on the part where Charlie said that he and Gorkin had been followed. He wondered if Charlie really knew what he was talking about and if this strange cartridge helped make any sense out of the puzzle.

"Listen, Jon, I'm going to have to make a bunch of phone calls on this one. I'll give it top priority. Promise. I'm damned curious about what the hell this thing is myself."

"Okay, Ray. I'll call you later from the squad."

The men shook hands and Grau left the room. Adleman sat back in his chair and looked at the overflowing bookshelves around him. Hundreds of texts, on every conceivable aspect of firearms identification, were on those shelves. He had read every one and knew full well that the shell casing and bullet lying on his desk were not mentioned in any of them.

He picked up the slug again. On a hunch, he took a small horseshoe-shaped magnet from out of the chaos that was his desk drawer and put it to the projectile. The little bullet clung to the magnet.

"This ain't copper," he said softly.

Unless there was a steel insert imbedded inside, or the

bullet's jacket was made of steel, the magnet should not have attracted the slug. Adleman knew that only one country manufactured such a complex round for general issue, the Soviet Union. But the Soviet's round, although of the same caliber, was of a much longer length, and was designed for use in their assault rifles.

Adleman picked up the *Jane's* again and thumbed through the big book. He found the section he was seeking. It told him what he already knew. The Soviets were changing over from a 7.62-mm-caliber assault rifle round to a new 5.45-mm-caliber rifle round. The new bullet was of compound construction: steel at its base, with a lead insert near the tip, then covered with a mild steel jacket. The diameter and construction of the cartridge before him and the Soviet one described in *Jane's* were the same. The problem was, the little slug was far too light to be one of the new rounds, and the casing was very small compared to the larger assault-rifle cartridge described in the book.

As Adleman pondered his mystery two uniformed officers entered the office. Both were young and, from their manner, it was apparent they had never been to the unit before. Another detective tended to them as Adleman thumbed through his Rolodex file, searching for someone to contact regarding the strange round.

The two officers engaged in loud conversation with the other detective, a clear sign that they wished the entire office to be aware of who they were and what mission they were on.

Distracted for a moment, Adleman looked up. The officers wore the brass collar insignia of the Sixtieth Precinct.

The taller of the two men said, "Poor Frank never had a chance. That son of a bitch that shot him drilled him through the heart." Waiting for the proper timing, the young officer continued, "Let me tell you, when we find out who that motha is, he's dead meat!"

Adleman stood up and could see that the officers were surrendering a small pistol and some spent rounds and bullets to the intake detective.

As the Ballistics Unit specialist wrote up the new material he softly said, "Funny-looking little shell case."

The Murder of Old Comrades

"Hank, what do you have there?" Adleman asked the detective involved with the new evidence.

"Sec, Ray, let me log this stuff in," Hank answered, as he busily filled out the necessary forms which were required to be completed in order to maintain the legal chain of custody of the evidence.

It was normal procedure for officers to be assigned to bring weapons, spent projectiles and cartridge casings to the Ballistics Unit. Sometimes, if the case was routine, it would take a day or so for the evidence to be delivered. For an important case—and no case was more important to the department than the killing of one of its own—the relevant material was hand carried directly over from the crime scene and/or the autopsy room.

Finished, Hank walked over to Adleman's desk and handed the older detective what the officers had brought. There was a small black metal .22 pistol. It was smeared with white powder, a sure sign someone from the Crime Scene Unit had dusted it for prints. The scratch marks on its slide showed where the gun had rubbed against concrete when dropped. There were also four plastic bags. One contained some spent .22 shell casings. Another a badly deformed .22 lead bullet. The marking on that bag showed it had come direct from the morgue. The last two held a tiny pointed bullet, also direct from the autopsy room, and an unusual-looking spent cartridge case.

Adleman opened the last plastic bag, took out the small bottlenecked shell casing and examined its rear. There was an indentation of two stars astride the primer, and the numbers 270 and 79 above and below it. He picked up the casing Grau had left him and looked at the back of that case, at the same stars and identical numbers.

Adleman put the two casings down and took up the tiny bullet just handed him by Hank. He used the magnet as before, and with the same results.

He put the evidence down in front of him. The other detective had remained by his side, not understanding why this usually garrulous man sat motionless and silently stared at the collection of spent casings and bullets lying on his desk.

Quietly, almost in a whisper, Adleman said, "Hank, let's go to the microscopes."

Adleman, with considerable physical effort, moved his bulk from out of his chair. He picked up the bags of spent casings and projectiles, careful not to mix the evidence from the two different cases.

Walking to a rear room with Hank, he sat down at one of the large ballistic comparison microscopes. With the skill and manual deftness that comes from thousands of repetitions of the same act, he imbedded the shell from Grau's homicide in a plasticine material which was held supported under the lens. He next took the plastic container from the second shooting, removed the spent casing from it and did the same.

Satisfied, he bent over the eyepiece. His right hand's thumb and forefinger turned a small knob that controlled the rotational movement of one shell. The image he saw was that of the two case heads, optically split in half, so that they could be compared, one to the other.

In a moment he raised his head from the eyepiece.

"Hank, please tell me what you see."

Still mystified by Adleman's strange behavior, the other man bent over and looked through the lens.

"The casings, they came from the same gun," he said matter-of-factly and raised his head from the eyepiece, not realizing the import of what he had seen.

"Hank, the two casings came from two double homicides a day apart. Whoever killed that man and the young officer yesterday in Brooklyn was also involved in the murder of two people in the Bronx the day before."

Hank whistled softly, now realizing what Adleman was implying. The shooting of the officer yesterday was not an isolated, random tragedy. Whoever shot that police officer had committed a total of four homicides within two days. And the killer was still somewhere on the streets of the city.

Chapter 11

When Dave Heath walked into the police department's Bronx Public Morals Office on Monday morning the first thing he had intended to do was make several calls about the strange story told to him by Billy Dieter.

But he was delayed by a more pressing matter. One of his officers had become involved in an off-duty incident during that day's early morning hours. The story, as far as Heath understood, involved a bar, too much alcohol, a woman, and another man. The mix of all these elements resulted in the suspension of his officer for punching out the man, who wound up occupying a bed in a local hospital.

Knowing how the department viewed this type of extra-curricular activity, Heath figured that the officer would count himself lucky if all the punishment he received was a suspension, thirty days' loss of vacation time and a year's probation.

It wasn't until nearly noon that he was able to get around to dealing with what Dieter had told him. He patted his shirt pocket and felt for the piece of paper with the car license plate number that his friend had handed him the day before. The paper made a crinkle sound as Heath removed it from his pocket. Leaving his office he walked two flights down, to the precinct's computer terminals. A lone officer sat by the blank green screens and thumbed through the day's newspaper.

"Officer, do me a favor and run this plate," Heath said, then added, "for the registered owner."

Without saying a word the young cop took the scrap of paper, glanced at it, then punched some numbers into the console. A moment later a name and address flashed on the screen, along with the information that the vehicle was not wanted by either New York State authorities or law-enforcement officers anywhere in the country.

"Give me a hard copy, will ya?"

The young officer pushed a button and the printer, which sat off to the side of the console, came to life noisily. When the machine stopped Heath reached over and ripped the sheet from the roller.

"Thanks," he said absentmindedly and walked off with the paper. He read the name and address:

> ANDREW PINKIN
> 178 WEST 205 STREET, APT. 7B
> NEW YORK, NEW YORK

Had the address been from upstate New York he had already made up his mind to forget the whole matter. Heath figured in that case whatever was going down wouldn't be a city problem. But with a city address he thought, "What the hell," and returned to his office to make the belated phone calls.

Once back at his desk he tried to rehearse how he might explain the reason for his call. Should he tell how Billy Dieter happened to be at the airport when the floatplane landed? What was so sinister about a man being let out of an aircraft at an airport and then being driven away by another man? The lack of lights? The late hour?

Sighing the sigh of a man who suspected that he was about to embarrass himself, Heath picked up the telephone and began to dial.

He made two phone calls. The first was to the Joint Terrorist Task Force. The agent who took down the information was polite enough, but Heath sensed the man was humoring him. The second call was to Police Intelligence in lower Manhattan. He was handed off from one person to another until he managed to convince a detective to take down the information. The man to whom he eventually related the story recorded all the facts and thanked him for his interest.

As with the first call, when Heath hung up the telephone

he felt foolish, even though the detective from Intel had even asked him a few questions about the incident. Which was more than the guy over at the Task Force did, Heath reflected.

He was tempted to make a few more calls but couldn't think of anyone else who might be interested in the information. Heath went back to his pile of paperwork and pushed the incident from his mind.

Adleman still had to figure out what caliber and type of gun the strange bullets had been shot out of. Both the slugs had matched. Examination under the forensic microscope proved beyond a doubt they came out of the same barrel. The striations on the two bullets had lined up perfectly. He figured the good engraving of the rifling was probably due to the hardness of the bullet jackets and the lack of deformation of the projectiles. And as he had expected, all the .22 shells had also been fired from the same gun, the one brought in by the cops from the Sixtieth Precinct.

Now calls were beginning to come in from downtown on the case. So far his boss had been able to field them, but sooner or later someone was going to ask him what slug managed to get through a department vest. Adleman figured he needed an answer, and the sooner the better.

With both elbows resting on top of his desk, and the telephone receiver cradled in the crook of his neck, he dialed a number. After a few rings the other end picked up. A woman's voice said, "Firearms and Tactics Section. May I help you?"

"Research and Development. Sergeant Wilkes, please."

"One moment, I'll switch you."

Adleman waited impatiently, absentmindedly toying with a thumb-size 45/70 cartridge from among the collection of shells he kept on his desk. Studying the nearly hundred-year-old round, he noticed that the lead bullet was oxidizing into a white powder. He rummaged through his drawer for gun oil, intending to put a protective coating on the bullet, when a voice came on the line.

"Sergeant Wilkes, can I help you?"

Wilkes was Adleman's counterpart at the department's

firearms training and testing facility. The two men conferred frequently, each depending on the vast amount of information the other man possessed in the field of weaponry.

"Dick, this is Ray."

"Hey, what's going on? You coming up here to shoot the outdoor cycle?" Wilkes asked.

The cycle referred to was the biannual firearms qualification all members of the service were required to attend.

"Hell no! Give me a break. I just finished shooting my indoor cycle. Listen, I have a little problem. I got a couple of slugs and shell casings that I can't identify. I thought maybe you could help."

"Ray Adleman not being able to ID a cartridge case! Must be a real winner. Okay, Ray, I'm listening."

"Dick, the casings and slugs come from two double homicides. One of the DOAs was the cop that bought it in Brooklyn on Sunday." Adleman heard Wilkes softly whistle in surprise. He continued. "The casings are bottlenecked. Their headstamp looks to me to be eastern European. I miked the length of the cases. They're about eighteen millimeters long. The projectile diameter looks somewhere around five millimeters. Maybe twenty-one or twenty-two caliber. The bullets have jackets of steel and they're pointed, like little spitzer-shaped rifle slugs."

Dick Wilkes hesitated a moment, then said, "Ray, I think I know what you got. It's a Soviet round. Pretty new really, only been around for the last few years. I never saw one up close, just pictures. It's identified as their 5.45 by 18-millimeter round. Used in the PSM pistol, a compact Russian semiautomatic."

"Dick, where did you learn about her? I've looked everywhere."

"It's in the latest *Jane's*."

"Wouldn't you know it, our *Jane's* is five years out of date! Dick, send me a copy of what your book says, will ya?"

"You got it. I'll have our mailman drop it off at your squad today."

"Thanks."

After Adleman finished with Wilkes, he telephoned the

Four-Seven squad and asked for Grau. When told the detective was out in the field he settled on giving Sergeant Carrol the new information.

Once that was done he called the Six-Oh Detective Squad. He had more luck there and was able to relay what he learned to the detective catching the case.

Each in turn thanked him, and after hanging up, he knew they made their own phone calls to their respective bosses.

Strange, he thought, after speaking to the investigator from the Brooklyn squad. I'm always the middleman. They come here in a huff and ask, *What do I got, what do I got?* I give 'em the answer and it's like they were smoke. Until the next mystery they bring me. Adleman shook his head, smiled and picked up the old cartridge on the desk, gently spreading a thin coat of oil on the white lead bullet.

It was just past noon when Grau got back to the Four-seven Squad. Joe Blakemore greeted him with a "Get your butt into the boss's office," and a thumb pointing in the right direction.

As he entered Hank Carrol's room, Grau asked himself how he had screwed up. The sergeant sat behind his desk talking on the phone. He waved for Grau to take a seat.

"Right, chief, that's what the boys in ballistics say. Looks like we have four dead bodies from the same two guns."

Cupping the mouthpiece with his right palm, the sergeant said, "Your killer did the cop yesterday. I got the Chief of Bronx Detectives on the line."

Grau stood quietly by the desk, digesting the information.

"Chief, Grau just walked in. I'll let him know what's up and get back to you if anything develops."

Carrol replaced the receiver on the cradle and sat back in his chair, a cellophane-wrapped cigar in his hand. He collected his thoughts while freeing the recalcitrant smoke.

"Jon, Ray Adleman called about twenty minutes ago looking for you. It seems that after you left Ballistics a couple of kids came in from the Six-oh Precinct. They were delivering some evidence from yesterday afternoon's double homicide. The one down by Coney Island. It seems that the cartridge case you delivered today matches one of those found at the Brooklyn killings. Ballistics is working on matching the bullets now, but according to Adleman, that's not even an issue. The same gun was used in both sets of double murders."

Grau's routine investigation was now taking on a totally different complexion. Significant among his new problems would be downtown's interest in the case and the resulting interference in the investigation.

"How we going to work this, boss?"

"The chief wants to meet with you for a solid briefing on what you've got so far. Get all your papers together and make sure you're up to date on your fives. Oh, and I cleared it with the chief. If you want, you can bring Tony in on this. The chief said that the rule book is being thrown out the window until this case is solved."

Grau rose from his chair and said, "I'll go down to the desk and have them give Tony a ten-two. By the way, do we know who's working the case from the Brooklyn end? I really ought to talk to that guy as soon as possible."

"Don't know. But you're right. I'll call the Sixtieth's PDU boss and break the ice."

Grau nodded and headed for the stairs.

"Oh, Jon. One last thing."

Grau stopped and turned around.

"According to Adleman, that slug came from some screwball Soviet pistol."

Grau stood quietly for a moment, shook his head and turned once more for the stairs.

Chief Peter Kinney, thirty-year veteran of the department and head of its Special Operations Division, reread for the fourth time the puzzling series of reports which lay on his desk.

The Aviation Unit had reported the tracking and following of a seaplane. Apparently it came from somewhere in upstate New York and flew almost two hundred miles out into the Atlantic, where the ship was seen landing alongside an unidentified freighter. That was strange.

Picking up another report, this time from the Chief of Detectives' office, he read about four people being murdered within forty-eight hours. Three of them with a bizarre weapon, a handgun that should only be in the hands of Soviet security forces.

Finally, he thumbed through the short blurb he had received from Intelligence. The day before the Aviation Unit's incident and the Brooklyn shooting there was the quiet night-landing of a Polish-manufactured seaplane on a small upstate lake, with the ship's passenger being met by someone already waiting on the ground.

The chief stood up and walked around his big wood desk. He looked out of the office window, onto Flushing Meadow Park. A big chunk of New York City real estate in the borough of Queens, it was home to Shea Stadium, the decaying remnants of the 1964 World's Fair, a museum, lots of grass and trees and the headquarters of the New York City Police Department's Special Operations Division.

SOD, as it's referred to by members of the service, is a unique and vital unit within the department. It contained the most highly trained, best-equipped personnel the department had. Among the subunits within SOD are the Mounted Unit, Harbor, the Aviation Unit and the Emergency Services Unit.

If Mounted, Harbor and Aviation hold personnel who are specialists by the nature of their work, the Emergency Services Unit is manned by officers who pride themselves on being generalists. Its members were trained to handle situations that might range from a stuck elevator to a heavily armed terrorist.

Someone once published a story about the unit in a national magazine. The writer had been shown all the specialized equipment the emergency trucks held—everything from rowboats for water rescue, to emergency medical and rescue gear, through high-powered rifles and submachine guns. He reported that there was a major difference between the department's ESU (pronounced by its members as if it were one word) and other police agencies' Special Weapons and Tactics Teams: If a SWAT unit arrives at a scene the only thing they can do is kill you; when ESU shows up they can also save your life.

The SOD headquarters building is set back from most of

the park's traffic. Housed in a sprawling single-story complex of permanent and temporary structures, its modest appearance masks the importance of the location.

Chief Kinney looked the part he played in the department. A tough veteran of the street, he had made it up the ranks the hard way. No soft desk jobs at One Police Plaza for him.

A decorated veteran of Korea, his six-foot frame was as lean and trim as when he was a kid out of boot camp. The crew cut he wore defied current hairstyles and his craggy face and cool gray eyes would have served well on a military recruitment poster.

From his office window he saw a small dot in the sky coming in low from the direction of the stadium. Soon the dot turned into a blue-and-white helicopter, a department Bell JetRanger, the *whup-whup* sound of her blades becoming louder as the ship neared.

The aircraft began a descent into an open space adjacent to SOD headquarters. The pilot deftly worked the ship in over the landing area's trees and settled down gently on the soft grass. The officer sitting in the copilot's seat got out, an envelope in his hand, and made for the headquarters' front door.

The chief smiled and thought, "Those silly bastards will come up with any excuse to fly."

The helicopter gave him an idea. He turned around and hit the intercom button on his desk. A voice came on.

"Yes, Chief?" It was Neal Thompson, a veteran ESU cop. When not acting as Kinney's receptionist, he might be found scaling one of the city bridges rescuing an attempted suicide or, submachine gun in hand, kicking in heavily fortified drug dealers' doors and making the inhabitants an offer they couldn't refuse.

"Have Inspector Himmel come into my office."

"Yes, sir."

Thirty seconds later, Deputy Inspector George Himmel, commanding officer of Emergency Services, walked into Kinney's office.

"Sit down, George." The chief pointed to a wood chair opposite his desk. He stepped away from the window and retook his own seat. Himmel sat down on the edge of the chair, his hands resting flat on his legs. Silently he watched his boss. He knew from past experience that anything could come from this kind of an impromptu summons.

"George, something's going on. I don't know what it is, but my gut tells me it isn't good." Kinney relayed to Himmel all the information he had just digested from the reports on his desk.

"What do you think?"

The inspector chose his words carefully. "Let's look it over for a second and see what we really know. Fact number one," Himmel raised his thumb. "There are four dead people. Two of the four are former Soviet citizens who have been in this country for a number of years. Two," another finger went up. "Three of the four were shot with a gun which happens to be a weapon known to be used only by Soviet security people."

Kinney nodded and smiled. "Keep going, George."

"A floatplane, coming from somewhere out over the Atlantic Ocean, makes a midnight drop of some guy in upstate New York. The plane is an eastern bloc aircraft. It returns a couple of days later, again around midnight, follows the same route in and out of the area and eventually lands nearly two hundred miles out in the ocean, picked out of the water by a large ship."

"So, George, tell me what we've got."

"I don't know. But it could be political dynamite. From the raw facts it looks like there's a real good chance someone from the Soviet government is whacking out American citizens and Russian émigrés on American soil, for reasons unknown. Have you spoken with any of the detectives that caught the four homicides yet?"

Himmel leaned back in his chair. "No, not yet. But you've got a good point. We're going to have to work closely with the bureau on this one."

Kinney rubbed his chin, then said, "We could use some more information. One good place to start would be where that seaplane landed, in upstate New York. Maybe we should have someone speak to the guy that spotted it. How about if I have one of our ships fly up there along with one of the investigating detectives. Let's talk to the source of the information and get a look at the layout. We might learn something."

"Okay, that makes sense." The chief suddenly grinned at his subordinate. "What's the matter with you, George, don't you believe in *glasnost?*"

"Sure, chief. I also believe in the tooth fairy."

Chief Kinney smiled and nodded. "Well, I agree with your assessment. We could have a political hot potato on our hands. So while your guys are out snoopin' and poopin', I'm gonna give the Chief of Department a call. He's an old SOD man. My gut tells me to keep the politicians out of it for a while. I'll need his help on that end. If there is Soviet involvement in this, sure as God made little apples, the feds are gonna come in and try to run the show. If we're not careful it'll look like a damn Chinese fire drill."

Gräu hadn't intended to return to the house where the investigation had started, 1157 Goodwinn Street. Actually, once he had left the Chief of Bronx Detectives' office, he just drove around, trying to figure out new angles to work his case. He knew the next day he would be too busy for the luxury of a slow drive. First he had a meeting set up with another strange caller from Brooklyn. Except, unlike Charlie, this guy wasn't afraid of giving his name, Nick Gross. And Grau had been told by the chief that he was to interview some forest ranger in upstate New York. The chief seemed to think there might be some connection to his case. How that could be Grau had no idea. He'd decided to send Tanti on that jaunt. The chief had also given the okay for the officer to be assigned to Grau as his partner, and although Tanti was off duty today, Grau had already spoken to him to explain what they would be doing tomorrow.

So, as he drove along the streets of his precinct, he suddenly realized he was right in front of the place where it had all begun.

The house was in the northeast part of the precinct, in a transition zone between a good and bad neighborhood. Grau pulled to the curb and stepped from the squad car. He looked the place over. It was a two-story tan wood-and-brick house, sitting mid block on a street of similar-size single-family homes. A new For Sale sign had been stuck in the middle of the obligatory patch of grass out front.

He smiled. Just the sort of place that a realtor might bring a young lower middle-class couple to see. Grau wondered how the subject of the former owner's demise would be handled.

The small lawn was fenced in with chicken wire. He walked over to its edge. Clearly no one had mowed it for the past several weeks. Judith Bartlett, he decided, had been less than neat.

Some of the children's toys still lay scattered about the yard. A red fire truck lay on its side, one of its wheels bent inward. A deflated basketball sat near the yard's edge and small plastic dolls were arranged around a tiny tea set.

The two youngsters had been sent to live with their grandmother in Yonkers, Grau knew. He shrugged. Life could deal a lousy hand sometimes.

He walked around the house, trying to get a feel of the place where two people he really didn't know had died.

He ran his fingers along the wood side. It was in basically sound condition, he figured. Still, someone who cared about such things might have had it repainted a couple of years earlier. He also noted a few loose boards as he strolled. A hammer and a couple of nails would take care of them.

To one side was a shared driveway. In the rear, taking up what would have been a backyard, stood a wood garage. It was in somewhat worse condition than the main structure. The articulating front door was off its track, stuck between open and closed. Some windows were broken and several gaps could be seen running along the wood slats on the side. Inside the garage, instead of a car, were stored pieces of old furniture, a yellowed mattress and a number of cardboard boxes. In them were all the things no one knew what to do with, they being too valuable to throw away yet not worth using.

Grau bent low and stepped into the structure. It was late afternoon and although the summer sun was still high, inside the garage it was dark. He wrinkled his nose at the musty smell and took out his small flashlight.

The house had been searched thoroughly, both by Grau's

squad members and whoever had murdered Sergi Gorkin and Judith Bartlett. But no one had bothered to look inside the garage, the undisturbed dust on its floor attested to that.

Grau started with the mattress. He cleared one corner of the garage and pulled the damp mildewed lump from its resting-place against the wall. With his small pocketknife he probed and cut into the material, finding nothing but a few layers of foam rubber.

He dropped his burden and started on an old bureau. It was empty inside except for some closed wood drawers. Pulling on them one by one revealed them to be frozen shut, warped out of shape. Grau spotted an ancient rusted crowbar hanging from a rafter. He reached over and dug its claw end into the top drawer. The wood splintered to reveal an empty space. Each slot in turn was pried open with the same result.

Grau looked at his watch. It was already half an hour after the end of his tour. He eyed the remaining cardboard boxes.

What the hell, he thought, as he grabbed hold of the top one. It would be unlikely that he'd ever get another chance to check this stuff out.

The box's top wasn't even sealed, just held in place by the interweaving of the four flaps. He pulled them apart and looked inside. It was full of men's clothes, a pair of shoes, some shirts and slacks. From their size and style Grau knew they had belonged to Gorkin.

Between the clothes was a neatly folded up sheet of newspaper. Grau pulled it out and played his light on it.

The page had been cut from a copy of *The Wall Street Journal*. It was dated six months earlier. There were several articles on the page. One discussed American business's possible response to Japanese trade restrictions. Another was on the upcoming merger of two large retail food chains.

Grau was about to toss the sheet away when he noticed the underlining of some words in pencil. That article's headline spoke of a new European currency, the underlined words were the date it was expected to be released for general tender and the current market value of the money in dollars. According to what Grau read the money was to be used for legal tender throughout the Common Market Countries. The article indicated the money would be released within the next few months, which Grau quickly calculated to mean around the end of the current summer.

He held the paper in his hand for a moment and debated whether to keep it or toss it away. Finally, he shrugged, folded it up and put it in his pocket.

Chapter 12

"How long you been doing this?" Tanti asked Mike Casson, as he watched the East River move underneath the small JetRanger helicopter. All the while Casson's fingers manipulated the ship's joy stick, gently and smoothly working the control.

"Oh, I guess I've been in aviation for about eight years. I've got about two thousand hours in the air in these things."

"Is that a lot?"

"Yeah," Casson said, "that's a lot. Tell me, Tony, what do you think of this floatplane business?"

"You mean us flying up to where it was spotted landing? Great! I've never been in a little airplane before."

"Helicopter," Casson corrected. "No, I mean about the whole deal. You think we're gonna accomplish anything?"

Tanti shrugged. "I dunno. Jon, he's my partner, is out interviewing some guy from Brighton Beach. Since that's only a couple of miles from the Aviation Unit, it makes sense for you and me to take a look upstate while he's doing that. I mean, you never know what you're gonna find out unless you speak with the guys involved, right? And we're sort of killing two birds with one stone."

"I guess. Hey, would you like to try your hand at flying this bird? I'll stay with you."

Tanti said, "Okay, tell me what to do."

"See the stick between your legs?"

"Sure," Tanti said, looking down at the black plastic grip and the assorted red buttons that stuck out of it.

"Now, gently take the stick and try to keep her straight and level. I'll work all the other controls, so don't you worry about them."

Tanti took hold of the control. Casson said, "You got it."

Instantly the ship began to bob and weave. Tanti would no sooner move the control one way in an attempt to bring her about, then she would swing wildly around and force him to throw the control stick to the far opposite side.

Casson grinned and said, "Tony, lock your arm in place so she'll stop oscillating."

Tanti froze his arm. The violent twitchiness stopped and he found himself in a gentle bank to the right.

Casson helped him straighten the ship out, demonstrating how anticipation of movement along with a soft touch on the stick was needed to control the sensitive machine. Tanti listened attentively and in a few minutes was doing a passable job of keeping the helicopter in the air.

The city quickly gave way to suburban sprawl, which in turn disintegrated before a series of small mountain ranges.

Casson was unaware that they were following the same path taken by the Wilga several nights earlier. As they passed to the right of the microwave tower atop the ridge overlooking Warwick Valley, they could see below them the lake and the small airport at its banks.

"Tony, I got it," Casson said. He took back the control stick and slowed the ship. He maneuvered the helicopter in the same pattern as would any pilot flying a fixed-wing plane who intended to land at the small airport.

Changing the frequency on the aviation radio, Casson transmitted, "Warwick Unicom, New York City Police Helicopter Number One. What's your active runway?"

"Warwick's active is two one. Twenty-one at Warwick," came the reply.

Casson announced his intention to land and swung the ship around. He aimed for a small medevac helipad near the open center of the airport. Tanti watched as the helicopter's nose came up slightly, and at the same moment the aircraft began to lose altitude. With the ship rapidly approaching the ground Tanti heard the increased whine of the engine as Casson added power until, just a few feet from the concrete pad, the helicopter stopped its descent and came to a hover.

Casson then slowly moved the JetRanger toward an open grassy area clear of parked aircraft and away from possible conflict with landing traffic.

Tanti could see the main hangar area several hundred yards down the taxiway. Rows of small aircraft stood between them and that section of the airport. Casson's maneuvering took them away from the other ships.

"Mike, how come you don't park her over there?" Tanti asked and pointed to the buildings.

"No good, Tony. The rotor wash would bounce the hell out of all those light planes. It would piss everybody off. Not a good way to start off introducing ourselves."

Casson gently set the ship down on the grass and reduced the engine power to idle. "It takes two minutes to cool her down, Tony," he said, as he reached over and started an electronic clock on the instrument panel.

Tanti smiled. "I guess it's only in the movies that you can hop in and out of these things like you would a Chevy."

Casson laughed. "Pal, you pick things up real quick!"

By the end of the cool-down period, a small group of people had walked up to the ship.

Casson commented, "The guy in the green uniform has got to be Dieter."

Tanti nodded in agreement. Besides the man they wanted to speak with, there were three other people: a white-haired gentleman in work clothes and an old baseball cap; a younger man, also casually dressed in tan slacks and work shoes; and a brown-haired woman, shorter than the men, wearing a dark blue zipper-front jacket and large green aviator glasses.

Casson reached overhead, about to flick off the ship's electrical power. Holding onto the switch for an extra moment, he said, "Tony, we have to get Dieter away from this crew or we won't be able to talk to him."

"Gotcha. I'll work on it."

Casson flipped the switch and the headsets went dead. He twisted slightly to his left, reached around with his right hand and pushed in the safety button on the throttle lock. With a flick of his wrist he turned the throttle to the off position. The noise of the engine stopped. Only the sound of the swishing rotor blades as they turned above them remained. Casson waited until their speed was low enough, then pulled the brake lever above his head. The now slow-moving blades shuddered to a complete stop.

As they stepped out of the craft, Tanti smiled and said, "Hi," to their impromptu welcoming party.

Billy Dieter broke from the curious pack and walked up to Tanti. "Hi. I'm Billy Dieter," he said, offering his hand to Tanti. He added, "Dave Heath's friend."

"Right," Tanti said and nodded in the direction of Casson, who was now in conversation with the other members of the party. "I'm Tony Tanti and that's Mike Casson. Any chance of us getting you off alone?"

"Sure," Dieter replied. He walked away from Tanti and back to the group of local pilots who had begun to walk around the helicopter to better examine it. Stepping up to Casson, Tanti could hear him explain to the group about the medical evacuation plan that the two officers were there to speak to Dieter about.

"Officer Casson," Dieter extended his hand. "Billy Dieter."

Casson looked over at Tanti who stood by the nose of the ship. Tanti's head moved with an almost imperceptible flick in the direction away from the group. Casson spoke to the small gathering. "Well, listen, maybe we'll catch you guys later. After we speak with Billy."

The man in the cap turned to the others and in a good-natured tone said, "Let's go, folks, and let these guys work." There was a slight foreign accent to his voice. Tanti suspected he might be German.

The two officers and Dieter walked away from the ship. Casson asked, "Where can we talk?"

"If you want privacy, let's head for the lake."

"Okay," Casson replied.

The men strolled along the edge of the grass runway. Ahead of them lay the water, the breeze at their backs rippling the surface of the lake. At the edge of the water stood a small windsock, no higher than a man's chest. It flapped gently in the wind.

As they approached the shoreline Dieter motioned for them to follow him onto the seaplane dock. Casson and Tanti did so, and the wood platform rocked from side to side in protest of the weight.

Dieter, hands in his pockets, faced the two men and said, "I spoke with Dave Heath this morning. He tells me you people are interested in what I saw here last Friday night."

Casson removed his cap and ran his fingers through his hair. "Yeah, we thought it was kind of strange. Could you tell us what happened, just like you told Dave?"

Dieter again related the story of the seaplane's arrival, the dropping off of the man, and the ship's departure. He also mentioned his loose surveillance and his jotting down of the license number of the car.

"No one told my partner or me about a plate number," Tanti said. "Mike, did you hear anything about that?"

Casson shook his head. "Billy, you got the number with you?"

"No. I gave it to Dave."

"Don't worry about it," Tanti said. "Mike and I'll just give Dave a call when we get back to the city."

"Billy, what kind of lights was the floatplane showing?" Casson asked.

"Well, when I first saw it, it had on standard night lighting, but no strobes or rotating beacons. And just before it touched down on the water it put those out."

Dieter stopped for a moment, biting his lower lip in thought. "And when it took off, I don't think it put its lights back on at all."

Casson looked out over the lake. He let his mind go

back to the other evening, to the black windscreen of the helicopter, as his eyes searched in vain for some image of the floatplane the FLIR said was out there. A ship flying without lights through the dark night sky . . .

Tanti looked at Casson and said, "Anything else we need to know, Mike?"

"Nope. Billy, you've been real helpful," Casson said. The three started off the dock. "By the way," Casson added, "are you planning to do any more surveillance work out here? With the conservation officer?"

"Sure."

"Do me a favor and let us know if you see our friend again. And like you did last time, don't let him know you're here."

"No problem."

The trio headed back to the ship.

Propkin looked out over the Atlantic, the gentle surging of the trawler giving a pleasant sensation underfoot. He glanced at his watch and wondered what was happening on the mainland. Four hours earlier he had sent a coded message to the New York Soviet Mission, marked for Andrapovich's eyes only, asking what the status of his mission was. It had been the second message he had sent in two days. And in neither case had a reply been forthcoming.

Propkin cursed under his breath. That son-of-a-bitch incompetent on the mainland was going to screw this up good. Andrapovich knew how important the completion of this job was. And he certainly knew how tight their time schedule was. How the hell could he expect to eliminate all those people, and what was far more important, find what they were looking for, and do this without a person of Propkin's experience being there?

Well, Propkin thought, he had friends. Some in very high places. If that idiot Andrapovich didn't want to bother responding to Propkin's messages, maybe he'd respond sooner to something sent from Moscow? Perhaps from someone inside the Politburo. Or maybe from a high-ranking KGB deputy.

Propkin began to stalk back and forth on the trawler's

The Murder of Old Comrades

deck. He tried to control his anger and think through this problem, to place himself in Andrapovich's head.

A deckhand walked nearby. Propkin glared at the hapless sailor and the man scurried off.

That little show of arrogance and power relaxed Propkin. He took in a breath of air and reflected on Andrapovich's options.

The other man could try and use some of his in-house people to complete the mission. But as far as Propkin knew there was no one with either his experience or anonymity who would be suitable for the work.

Andrapovich could, of course, request another agent be sent over. But the delay would be unacceptable. It would entail a long briefing, travel to America, and a successful insertion. There simply wasn't enough time.

Or, Propkin mused, Andrapovich could try to stall, to blame his failure on Propkin, the perfect martinet's choice. Do nothing and blame someone else. How else could a person of such puny abilities have gotten to Andrapovich's position in the government?

But the real question was, how should Propkin deal with the situation? Maybe a cable to Moscow was premature. But without knowing what was happening on the mainland it would be extremely difficult to determine when to play such a card.

He sighed. He had been in situations similar to this in the past. Perhaps he would do as he did then. Let some time pass and try to feel around for whatever information he could gather. Except this time he was sitting on a boat, hundreds of kilometers from land, moving around in big circles and out of touch with everything.

He spat over the railing and reflected that he was glad this was to be his last time out in the field.

Chapter 13

Grau glanced at his watch as he drove away from Floyd Bennett Field. It was already 11 A.M. He'd have to hurry to be on time for the meeting with his new contact. Just before Tanti and he had left the Four-Seven Squad for the Aviation Unit, a call had come in. It was a man with an accent, although not as pronounced as Charlie's had been.

Funny, Grau thought, even though he now knew Saminov's real name, the poor bastard would always be just Charlie to him. After Sergeant Carrol had told him what Adleman had reported about the matching slugs, for a few minutes Grau had difficulty believing his ears. Certainly, he calculated, it had been no more than five minutes after he last saw the other man that the murderer of Gorkin had killed Charlie. Grau knew that as well as he knew anything. And what hurt most was his inner certainty that the killer had been watching him, and most likely Tanti as well. And that both he and his partner had never even guessed he was around.

This new caller had asked specifically for Grau, and when the detective came on the line, had said his name was Nick Gross. He said he was calling from Brooklyn and that he wanted to talk to someone about the two Russians who had recently been killed. That statement immediately got Grau's attention, since only cops were supposed to know that the Bronx and Brooklyn murders were connected.

So he and Tanti decided that his partner would fly upstate alone. The meeting with Gross took precedence over what, at any rate, Grau considered to be a highly speculative journey. And even though the detective would have enjoyed going on the trip (never having been in a helicopter), the experience would have to wait.

He took the Belt Parkway to the Ocean Parkway exit and made his way to Brighton Beach Avenue. The gray Ford was air-conditioned, but the cool humidity of the shore area permitted Grau to drive with his window open and his arm resting on the doorsill.

He drove under the elevated train and looked carefully at the small street signs. Finally he came up to Brighton Third and turned into the block. The boardwalk lay straight ahead, just down the narrow street. Grau parked the car and began to walk toward the raised wood structure.

Now that he was off Brighton Beach Avenue proper, with its multitude of little shops with their Russian-sounding names and storefront signs printed in both English and Cyrillic, the makeup of the neighborhood changed. It became one of small apartment houses. Most were thirty to forty years old and held perhaps twenty families each. Grau walked along the street and took in the flavor of his surroundings. People on the street chatted among themselves in both Russian and English. Groups of children played along the sidewalk, some of them also speaking in Russian as they ran about.

Grau moved up the steps to the boardwalk, which rose on concrete pillars ten feet above the sand. The structure was huge. He guessed it to be about a hundred feet wide. And when he stopped for a moment at the top step and looked to his left and right, he saw that the expanse of wood stretched farther than he could see.

A number of people leaned on the gray aluminum railing that ran along the edge of the walkway. Beyond them lay a wide expanse of tan sand and the Atlantic Ocean. Other people sat at the benches which were fastened to the heavy gray wood at regular intervals along both edges of the walkway. And still others simply strolled up and back on the wood roadway. He saw that although there were quite a few older pedestrians about, there was also a fair share of children and teenage couples.

Grau casually walked over to the railing. With no buildings to block his view he could see the clear blue sky, full of cotton-ball clouds, extending out to the horizon. The scene was in sharp contrast to his normal world. He smiled when he realized that he had spent his entire life in New York City and had never before been to the beach at Coney Island.

The sand, like the boardwalk, ran for miles to either side of where he stood. White-topped waves sounded pleasantly in his ears as they crashed against the shore.

He sat down at an empty bench, put his feet up on the railing and leaned back. The sensation of the cool sea breeze and warm sun on his face relaxed him. He closed his eyes and let his mind wander to other things beside quadruple homicides and unsolved mysteries. He thought of green fields and how he and his dad used to walk them in upstate New York, during those special days in the summer when the family was on vacation. How they would try their hand at freshwater fishing. His father would bait their hooks with white bread mixed with yellow American cheese. The biggest fish they ever caught had been a tiny Sunny.

Grau felt the pressure of someone taking a seat on the other end of the six-foot-long bench. He opened his eyes. To his right sat a casually dressed middle-aged man. About Grau's height, the man had a noticeable paunch and his long salt-and-pepper hair tumbled about his head, unruly in the strong breeze. The stranger sat back, his arms over the backrest of the seat, and looked out to the sea.

Without turning his head toward Grau, he said, "You're prompt. That's good."

Grau recognized the voice as that of the man on the telephone. Not with the coarse accent that Saminov had, just normal English with a slightly deeper inflection on certain consonants, a gentle rolling of the R's.

The man extended his hand.

"Gross, Nick Gross. How are you, Mr. Grau?"

Grau took his hand. "Mr. Gross," the man had a powerful grip, "you picked a nice place to talk."

Gross settled back on the bench, head tilted back, eyes squinting in the bright sun. "Yeah, I like it here. America, I mean." Laughing, he added, "The city stinks!"

Grau sensed that to be coy with the man would be a mistake. He took a deep breath and jumped right into it.

The Murder of Old Comrades

"Mr. Gross, for starters, who are you? What was with the guy they whacked out here the other day? And just in general, what the hell is going on?"

"Call me Nick." Gross took a pack of cigarettes from his shirt pocket and offered one to Grau, who declined with a wave of his hand. Gross tapped the pack on the bench seat and with a deft flick of his wrist produced a cigarette. With hands cupped around its end he lit it.

Gross exhaled a thin stream of gray smoke and continued, "It's complicated. First you should understand the two Russians who were killed over the last week were both bums. They were bums in Russia, and unlike what they say about wines, these two didn't improve with age." Gross took another drag on his smoke and went on, "I've been talking to some of the other people in the area. It seems that these two guys got into bed with American organized crime. They, or at least Gorkin, were making a bundle in stolen fuel oil and gasoline around here."

"And the other man, Charlie . . ."

"Saminov, Michael Saminov," Gross corrected.

"Yeah, Saminov."

"He worked more as a 'gofer' for Gorkin. And when he wasn't doing that he ran numbers, did little odds and ends for other crooks around the area. A real loser. The problem is, the people around here can't figure why those two clowns were murdered. And now there's a heavy rumor that the Soviet government somehow is involved in the killings."

"Why the hell would the Soviets care what these two were up to?"

"Right. The Soviet government couldn't care less about what they were doing to make a living around here. So it stands to reason that if the Soviets did in those two guys, it was because the Soviet government figured they needed them dead."

"When I spoke to Saminov, he tried to tell me that Gorkin wanted him to do something important for him. But before Saminov found out what, Gorkin was dead. And Saminov told me that both he and Gorkin had been followed during the last couple of weeks."

A fifty-foot ship cut through the water several hundred

yards offshore, heading out to sea. Both men silently followed its progress for a moment, then Gross said, "Listen, I know it sounds crazy, and maybe it is. And I can't explain why, but some silly bastard in Moscow must have gotten a bug up his behind, 'cause that looks like the only explanation for what's going on."

Grau shook his head. It seemed everyone was out to make a couple of murders into an international incident. He asked, "How are you involved in all this?"

"First it's important for you to understand that I've been in this country for over twenty years. I'm a legitimate businessman, an American citizen. The vast majority of people around here are like me. We got out of a lousy situation and came to what's still the most free country on the planet. A little hard work and you get right into the system. That's a pretty good deal and we know it. But now a lot of these people are worried. That's why I was asked to speak to you."

Gross dropped his cigarette to the wood-beam floor and squashed it out with the toe of his shoe. He went on, "Mr. Grau, we came six thousand miles to get away from those bastards and we don't like them screwing around in our backyard, if that's in fact what they're doing. We don't want those people to think they can come over here and start pushing us around. This isn't Moscow and if those jerks think they can put pressure on people around here, for whatever reason, they're gonna get themselves hurt."

Gross spoke in a firm, controlled voice. Grau sensed no false bravado, simply a man who stated the facts.

"Nick, for whatever reason the two guys were killed, whoever did it was playing hardball. Remember, they also killed a cop."

"We know we're not dealing with kids. That's one reason why I met you out here. I'm not afraid of the bastards, but I'm not stupid either. You should remember one thing, Mr. Grau. Many of the people who came from the Soviet Union had already served in the army. They toughen you up real quick there. We also have some friends around here who are former Israeli commandos. They don't care for the Soviets all that much either. If there's a problem they'll be more than willing to give us a hand."

"Nick, let's be logical about the whole thing. The United States and the Soviets haven't gotten along this well since the Second World War. Why the hell would they want to screw up what promises to be a relationship beneficial to both sides? Especially now, when the head guy there wants to make nice-nice."

"Mr. Grau, the people around here have asked themselves the same question."

Gross ran his fingers through his unruly hair and leaned forward. "Listen, you native-Americans think that just because the Soviet Union is a totalitarian country, one guy runs the show. Well, let me set you straight. There's all kinds of power plays going on there. You look at the leader and see a slick Commie. Maybe some hard liner in the Kremlin looks at the guy and figures the opposite, that the guy isn't so slick, and in fact is screwing up the works."

"So, they're trying for a coup?"

"No, no. You miss the point. The country is bogged down in an impossible bureaucratic system. Always has been, always will be. That's why maybe whoever is trying to pull this stunt off just wants to embarrass the head of government. They realize that if *glasnost* gets out of hand they'll have a hell of a time keeping the lid on." Gross smiled. "Hell, they might even have to start letting people come and go as they please. Outrageous idea! So, get rid of the current power structure and you get rid of *glasnost*. Then, business as usual."

"Nick, here's what I think," Grau stared at Gross. "Let's say the Soviet government had something to do with the killings. There might have been a reason, a real important one, that they would let one of their agents cowboy out a bunch of people. Maybe they got all they came for, maybe not. But they fucked it up, royally, and now they're in the wind."

"Could be you're right. If it was just a bad call on the part of some middle-level bureaucrat, sure, they'd fold up their tent and go home. But if you're wrong, and I think you are, you'll know soon enough. Because if what they really wanted was to stir the pot—like, say, in order to keep some of their former citizens in line—they'll have to keep on killing people." Gross smiled. "Either way, it still leaves you with a bunch of unsolved homicides, Mr. Policeman."

Grau then looked out to sea, saying softly, "Yeah, that it does."

Grau stood up and sat on the metal railing, facing Gross. He couldn't tell Gross very much of what he knew, particularly about the strange gun and the counterfeit angle. Still, Grau decided to voice aloud one of the options he'd been considering.

"Maybe I should stir the pot a little myself. A lot of crap has happened real quick. And most of it doesn't quite compute. It might be interesting if I went to the Soviet Mission in the city and spoke to somebody there about all this. What do you say, Nick?"

"I think you're nuts." Gross rose from his seat and stood next to Grau. "I think you're messing with something you really don't understand."

"Could be you're right, but I'm gonna do it anyway. Mind if I call you afterwards? Just to let you know if I accomplished anything?"

Gross smiled. "That's another way of saying you want to use my people like chum. Fishing bait."

Grau started to object but Gross cut him off with a wave of his hand.

"Yeah, you can call me. I'll let you know if you turned the heat up around here." He took a piece of paper from his pocket and wrote down some numbers. He handed the slip to Grau. "I'm not personally worried about these guys. At least I don't think they're that interested in me. So let's you and me keep in touch."

Grau nodded, shook hands with Gross and watched as the man walked away, mixing with the other strollers. He knew what Gross had said was right, that he was using Gross and his people as bait. Grau figured that if there was to be any chance of solving this case then somebody else was probably going to have to get hurt.

Grau looked at his watch. There was still plenty of time until he had to return to Floyd Bennett Field to pick up Tanti. And, anyway, he had to run into the Six-Oh Precinct in twenty minutes to talk with the detective that caught the Saminov and Ingrim killings.

The Murder of Old Comrades

He retook his seat, leaned back, closed his eyes and reflected on green fields and fishing.

Behind Grau, a young couple, arm in arm, walked along the boardwalk. The woman pushed a stroller with a small child in it. A couple of teenagers ran along the wooden walkway and tossed a football between them as they went.

Two benches down from Grau another young couple sat, looking into each other's eyes, seemingly oblivious to everything around them. As the young man stroked the shoulder-length hair of the girl, he spoke to her softly in Russian, "Gross separated from the American. But first he handed the American a note."

The girl smiled, rubbed her cheek on the young man's hand, and said, "Leave Gross. We can pick up on him anytime. We'll stay with the American and see who the new fish in the game is."

"As you wish, comrade."

Chapter 14

Grau leaned against an auxiliary power unit and watched from the flight line as the speck in the sky over Coney Island changed into a helicopter. The small ship flew overhead and circled the field. Finally it turned into the wind and, making its distinctive *whup-whup* sound, descended to a hover a hundred feet away. The helicopter air-taxied to its wheeled dolly and with an abrupt squat settled onto the wood.

Grau impatiently looked on, unaware of the need for the two-minute cool down. Finally the muted roar of the ship's jet engine died out, replaced first by the whooshing sound of the turning rotors, then with silence as the pilot activated the brake and brought the blades to a halt.

Tanti, still unsure of himself in the machine, opened his door and groped his way onto the landing platform. On seeing Grau, he waved and grinned broadly. Casson got out from his side of the helicopter and tied down the rotor blade, then both men jumped from the dolly to the concrete below.

"Jon, say hello to Mike Casson. He's the pilot."

"No shit, Tony, I thought *you* flew the thing," Grau said and extended his hand to Casson.

As the three men started for the hangar Grau asked his partner, "Well, how was the flight?"

Tanti exploded with a verbal barrage, in an attempt to relate to Grau all his new experiences during the last several hours. Grau cut him short. "But did you guys learn anything of value?"

The trio stopped just outside the hangar's gray door. Casson said, "Sort of. I'm now just about positive that the aircraft we chased last week was the same as the one that landed upstate a few days earlier. We also found a couple of good spots to land a welcoming party and maybe even a helicopter or two, *if* the floatplane should decide to come back, that is."

"Yeah, Jon. Mike let me fly the helicopter. Even when we were looking for a spot to hide the 412."

Grau looked at Tanti. "What the hell are you talking about, Mr. Lindbergh, the 412?"

They entered the hangar and Casson pointed to the large helicopter in the middle of the cavernous space. "That's a 412. Since it carries more than any of our other ships, my guess is we'll use her, or maybe her sister, if the shit hits the fan."

Once inside the pilots' sitting room Casson removed his gear and said, "You guys want some coffee?" He received two "Okays" in response. Several other pilots were seated at the big wood table, reading and drinking coffee. Casson asked the closest one, "Where's the boss?"

Without looking up from his *News,* the other man answered, "In Ops, I guess."

Just then Lieutenant Mante walked into the room, eyed

The Murder of Old Comrades

the returned duo and Grau, and motioned the three to take seats.

"Well?"

Casson began, "That's our floatplane all right. Took off from the lake without lights. Also, we found several open areas where we can park our ships if we have to."

Tanti stirred his mug of coffee and added, "We also came up with some good places to hide a bunch of men. That ranger was pretty helpful."

"Okay, Mike, give ESU a call and tell them about the layout of the place. I'll speak to the chief and see what he wants us to do next."

Grau asked, "Where are you guys gonna go from here? I mean, in order to lay a trap for the floatplane."

Mante answered. "We have to figure some way to set up for this guy, without wasting an outrageous amount of manpower. I have some ideas on that, but they have to be worked on. Anyway, it depends on the high-ranking bosses. Right now, it's a pretty hot issue. A week from now, who knows? They'll probably have some other catastrophe on their minds."

"Hey, Jon," Tanti said, turning to Grau, "anybody tell you about a plate number that they have on the car that did the pickup?"

"No. Who got it?"

Casson offered, "The ranger said that the cop who called in the original info has it."

Mante broke in, "I read the original report at SOD. The guy is a sergeant at Bronx Public Morals. David Heath, I think his name is."

Grau turned to Tanti. "I want that number." Then to Mante, he said, "Boss, can I use your telephone?"

Mante replied with a flick of his head in the direction of the phones in the flight planning room. Grau was on his feet and down the corridor in an instant.

Chapter 15

"What kind of a name is Pinkin?" Tanti asked Grau as they drove along the parkway to Manhattan.

"I'm not sure. But my guess is it started out as a long Russian name that somebody decided to shorten."

"What else did Heath say?"

"Not much that we didn't already know. Except that this guy Pinkin is clean. Never took a collar. His car doesn't even have a summons on it." Grau slowed up as they came to the toll booth by the Brooklyn Battery Tunnel, showed the police identification plate and was waved on by the toll taker.

Tanti rolled up his window to keep out the tunnel fumes and asked, "Tell me, what did the new Russian have to say?"

Grau told his partner about his meeting with Gross.

Tanti nodded and reflected on what had been said. As the car exited the tunnel he put his hand up to his face to protect his eyes from the glare of the sun. He inquired, "And at the detective squad?"

"Not much. Marion Kaiser caught the case. You know her?"

"Nope."

"Well, she's a sharp cookie. I worked with her in Manhattan, about five years ago, on a serial killer case. She's been in the bureau almost as long as I have."

"So?"

"So, she's been digging around. But Marion tells me the newly arrived Russians are tough nuts to crack. Nobody knows nothing about anything. And it doesn't help any that neither of these two guys have any relatives here. Anyway, I gave her what we got on Gorkin."

"Sounds familiar. Like your waiters back in the restaurant."

Grau nodded and continued to work his way through the midday traffic.

"By the way, I'm hungry," Tanti said.

"Okay. After we finish up with Pinkin we'll get some Chinese food."

Tanti screwed up his face in distaste. "I'm not eating any of that shit."

Grau shook his head. "What's the matter with Oriental cooking? Don't you know that in the opinion of some of the finest gourmets in the world, that cuisine ranks among the most sophisticated?"

"It's rat meat."

"Fine. What would you like for lunch, Mr. Meat and Potatoes?"

"A hamburger. Or a hot dog." Tanti reflected a moment, "Maybe some pizza."

"You're some fuckin' date."

Grau continued to head north, on what was left of the torn-down West Side Highway, and pulled off at Dyckman Street, the northernmost exit in Manhattan. He worked his way still farther north along Broadway and turned right on 205th Street.

As they traveled along, searching for the right building, they passed numerous apartment houses. Most were under five stories high—a size that, by city ordinance, avoided the necessity and thus the cost of installing elevators. Their ground-floor levels were taken up by small neighborhood stores.

They could see it was a working-class neighborhood. Like much of the city the locale seemed unable to make up its mind whether it was going to turn into a slum or become gentrified, a term used when enough mildly affluent middle class chose to brave an area within the inner city for its conveniences and proximity to work, rather than strike out for the safer and more human-scale suburbs.

Grau and Tanti left the parked car and headed for Pinkin's building. It was a four-story walk-up, of red brick. It had been built soon after the end of World War II, just before the city's Socialist rent laws put landlords and tenants at each other's throats and created the current lopsided housing situation—unique to New York City—that the law had been designed to prevent.

Inside the building Grau found the tenant directory. It was built flush into the wall above the polished brass mailboxes. He was a bit surprised when, by apartment number 7B, the name Pinkin appeared.

They walked through the first floor hallway and saw that the apartments were lettered 1A to 7A. Pinkin's apartment would be on the second floor. Grau and Tanti silently made for the top of the marble stairs. The strong sweet smell of pine-scented disinfectant surrounded them.

Grau got to the door first. He knocked. A moment later the shuffle of feet could be heard, then the noise of the door's inner eyepiece opening. Finally, a muffled voice asked, "Who's there?"

"Police," Grau said, holding his shield and identification card in front of the little glass hole. "We'd like to talk to you for a second."

An inner chain rattled as the hand attached to the voice inside slid it from its slot. Some ratchet sounds could be heard as the door's three front locks were undone, one at a time. The door opened a few inches and the face of a balding, thirty-five-year-old man looked out at the two officers.

"What do you want?" he said.

It was a New York voice. Blue-collar perhaps, certainly not that of a well-educated person. And, had Grau not been consciously seeking the accent, it would have gone unnoticed. The man, Grau knew, was Russian.

"Mr. Pinkin?"

A moment's hesitation, then, "Yes?"

"May we come in? We'd like to talk to you about something," Grau said, still holding his shield and identification card at eye level.

The door opened to a narrow dimly lit hallway. Grau and Tanti stepped inside and continued past Pinkin to the inner apartment. Except for some dime-store pictures on the walls and a few pieces of inexpensive furniture, the residence seemed somehow empty. A woman sat in the sparsely furnished living room and played with a small child. She was not yet thirty, attractive, with long black hair and dark complexion. Seeing the two men, she brightly said, "Hi."

Pinkin came up from behind and indicated the way to the kitchen. Grau and Tanti again led the way and took seats on thinly padded metal chairs around a cheap yellow Formica-topped table. Like the rest of the apartment, the small room was clean but Spartan.

Tanti sat back and let Grau do the talking.

"Mr. Pinkin, my name is Detective Grau. This is my partner, Officer Tanti. Do you own a car with this registration number?" He pushed his note pad over to Pinkin. On the top line was written the license number given to him by Sergeant Heath. Pinkin looked at the pad. His left hand held on to the edge of the table as he sought to control his voice.

"It may be my number. I'd have to look at the registration. What's this about?"

"Well, to be honest, Mr. Pinkin, I kind of suspect we have a mix-up here," Grau said, smiling. "Some guy did a stickup a couple of weeks ago. When he took off, someone got his license plate. Problem is, the guy who did the robbery was Black." Grau laughed lightly. "So, I got to think that the fellow who got the plate got the wrong number. But you see, the guy who did the stickup shot someone, so we've got to check it out. You understand?"

"Sure," Pinkin said. He reached into his back pocket and took out his wallet, rummaged through it and removed a vehicle registration, handing it over to Grau.

"Yeah, that's the plate number all right. But your car is dark blue. The one we want is red." Grau nonchalantly tossed the registration back on the table.

"Nice place you got here," Tanti said. "Hard to find apartments in the city these days."

"Yeah. I've had this one for a while," Pinkin responded, somewhat more relaxed than before. "Rent's not too bad."

"Come on, Tony, we've taken up enough of this guy's time," Grau said, and started to get up from his chair.

"Yeah," Tanti responded. Then, snapping his fingers, he said, "But don't forget what the boss told us before we left the squad. Remember? About checking out the car? He's gonna be pissed if we don't at least take a look at it."

Grau sighed. "You're right. The guy's a real prick." Looking at Pinkin he continued, "And if we don't see the car, he'll say something stupid. Like maybe it had been painted over, you know. Listen, I hate to bust your balls, but just take us to the car so we can say we saw it. Then we'll get outta your hair."

Pinkin nodded and got up, leading them out to the hallway. As he passed the living room, he said, "Maria, I'll be right back." The woman smiled and continued playing with the child.

As they walked down the stairs, Pinkin asked, "Where did the robbery take place?"

"The Bronx," Grau said. "A couple of weeks ago. Some clown hit a bodega. He got diddly squat. If he hadn't shot someone the case would have been closed out the day after it happened."

Pinkin grunted. Outside the apartment building the bright sun hurt their eyes. Grau and Tanti followed Pinkin to the end of the street, across Broadway and to an indoor garage in the middle of the block. A lone attendant sat on a rickety stool, reading a racing sheet. Pinkin walked up to him and asked, "Which space is my car in? Name's Pinkin."

The attendant looked at a sheet of paper attached to a clipboard tacked up on the wall. He said, "Eighty-seven," then went back to his reading.

Pinkin led the two men deep inside the garage. First they walked in one direction, then realized the numbers were wrong and headed off to another. Finally, they came to stall eighty-seven. Parked there was a late-model American car. Grau asked Pinkin, "Got the keys?"

"Oh, damn. I left them upstairs."

Grau looked through the driver's window. The interior was spotless. There were less than five thousand miles showing on the odometer.

"Well, I guess we did our duty," Grau said to Tanti. "Sorry to have bothered you, Mr. Pinkin."

"No problem, officer."

They started to head for the street opening when Tanti

said, "That's a real pretty car. You ought to see the bomb I drive."

"Yeah," Grau said, "my partner's car is an embarrassment. Hey, Tony, why don't you get one like Mr. Pinkin has?"

Tanti smiled and said, "That's not a bad idea. Mr. Pinkin, what does a car like that go for?"

A look of confusion came over Pinkin's face. He stuttered, "Uh, I forget. I got a good deal. You know. End-of-year sale."

"Yeah, good idea. I'll pick up a leftover."

The three men stood on the sidewalk.

"Well, Mr. Pinkin, sorry to have bothered you," Grau said, and shook the man's hand. He turned to Tanti and said, "Come on, partner. I haven't had lunch yet," and pointed at a pizza place across the street.

Pinkin nodded good-bye and headed off in the direction of his home. Grau and Tanti stepped across the street and ordered a slice of pizza each, watching the man disappear.

"Well, what do you think, Tony?" Grau asked, blowing on his steaming slice of pie.

"He's wrong. That car in the garage got to go for around twenty thou. It's not in his class. Hell, he didn't even know where the damn thing was parked."

"Screw the car," Grau replied. "What do you think indoor garage space goes for in Manhattan? Even around here."

Tanti nodded and asked, "What next?"

"We finish our food and then have a little talk with that attendant."

Pinkin walked quickly down Broadway. Just as he got to the corner a city bus came to a stop. He jumped aboard, paid the fare and took a seat at the rear.

Twisting around on the plastic bench he stared out the back window and searched for anyone that might be following him.

At 155th Street he got off, walked crosstown to St. Nicholas Avenue and boarded a northbound bus. Again he took the rearmost seat and looked for anyone that might be following. When the bus came to 170th Street he got off and started searching for a pay telephone. The first two he found didn't work. The third took his quarter. At the dial tone he punched in the number he had memorized for just such a situation. Another tone sounded. It indicated the automatic pager service was ready to receive the telephone number of the phone he was at. He punched that number in, then depressed the hook switch, keeping it down while he held the telephone receiver to his ear. It gave the appearance to passersby that the phone was still in use.

Pinkin rested his throbbing head against the cool glass of the booth. A minute went by, then two. He shook when the ring finally sounded.

"Hello," a voice said.

"Hello, is Max home?"

"Sorry. There's no Max here."

Pinkin replaced the receiver on its hook and glanced at his watch. From that moment he had two hours to be at the meeting spot.

Chapter 16

The attendant hadn't moved from his stool. Barely taking his eyes from the scratch sheet, he asked the two men who stood before him, "What's the name?" and absentmindedly reached for the clipboard attached to the wall.

Grau's gold detective shield got his attention as it was thrust between the paper and the man's eyes.

"Oh. Yeah," he said, sitting upright. "What can I do for youse guys?"

"Relax," Grau replied. "Nothing heavy. Tell me, how many cars you have in this place?"

"I dunno. A hundred. Maybe a couple more."

"Can't you tell exactly, by the number of spots you have assigned?" Tanti asked.

"Nah. That's only for the monthly customers. I got plenty of people who come in only for a couple of days. Some for a week or two. So it depends, see?"

"How many monthly customers you got?" Grau asked.

"Hey guys, listen, I only work here. Maybe you should talk to my boss?"

"Relax," Tanti said, patting the man on the arm. "We got no beef with you."

"What is it? Drugs?" the man asked softly, glancing about for any witnesses to the conversation.

Grau looked at Tanti and said, "I told you we'd never fool this guy." He turned back to the attendant and continued, "Listen, anything we talk about here is between us, right?"

"Sure, sure," the attendant said, standing now with his back to the street. "Listen, let me tell you. It's the Dominicans and the Cubans. They're all over the place. I got dozens of 'em, right here in this garage." He paused for a moment, then said, "And, they're lousy tippers."

Grau moved closer to the man. "Tell me, uh? . . ."

"Fred. Name's Fred."

"Fred, how do you work the system here? Do you get the cars for the owners?"

Fred shrugged. "It depends. If they got their own spot, no. If they're like, transient, here a couple a days or a week only, yeah. 'Cause those short-time people always wind up hittin' other people's cars, if you know what I mean?"

"Fred, if I asked you about a couple of guys, it would be between us, right?" Grau asked.

"Of course!" Fred replied.

"Do me a favor and hand me the roster," Grau said and pointed to the grease-smeared clipboard. Taking it from Fred, he read off three sets of numbers, permitting Fred to go into great detail about each vehicle's owner. Grau and Tanti nodded gravely, giving the appearance of hanging on his every word. Then Grau asked about spot eighty-seven.

"Oh, that guy," Fred said, making a face. "Yeah, he's a funny duck. I can't help you much on that one."

Tanti asked, nonchalantly, "How come?"

" 'Cause one guy pays for the spot and another guy uses the car. And not much, either."

"That's weird," Grau offered. "Who pays for it?"

"Some guy." Fred put out his hand for the board, taking it from Grau. "Pinkin. Right here by the number, see?" he said, and pointed to the block marked eighty-seven. "Once a month the guy comes in and gives me the two-fifty. Must be Pinkin, 'cause it's his spot."

"How much was that?" Tanti asked.

"Two hundred and fifty bucks, the monthly rate. Let me tell ya, that's not bad. Try a little farther south. And in midtown, ha! Anyway, the way they rip off car radios in this city it's probably cheaper than parking on the streets."

"Interesting, Fred." Grau said, "You sure this guy, what's his name, Pinkin, never takes the car out?"

Fred shrugged. "Well, I work here six days a week, twelve hours a day. Noon to midnight shift. I never saw the guy that pays take the car out. Other times," he shrugged again, "I can't help ya."

"And the other guy, what's his name?" Tanti asked.

"I dunno. He walks in and says 'Pinkin' and keeps on going. He don't say nothin' more to me. Hell," Fred scratched the back of his head, "I don't think I'd even recognize the guy. Maybe he's really Pinkin."

Tanti thought for a moment. "But, Fred, doesn't the guy ask where the car is parked?"

"I told you, long-term customers' spots never change."

Grau asked, "This guy. Is he a dark-skinned Spanish guy, with slicked-down black hair and a load of gold chains around his neck?"

Fred shook his head. "Nah. Those two guys are white."

Grau looked gravely at Tanti and both men shook their heads, Grau saying softly, "That's not our man."

Tanti picked up the clipboard now lying on the stool and pointed out several more sets of numbers. The two investigators permitted the attendant to go on about those people. Finally, Grau said, "Fred, let me tell you, you've been a big help." Putting his finger to his lips, Grau looked around and said, "Remember, this is just between us."

Fred nodded and winked.

* * *

The Murder of Old Comrades

Pinkin traveled exactly as he had been trained. Carefully watching for someone trailing him, he took a series of trains on a roundabout and meandering ride through the city.

The trip eventually took him back into lower Manhattan. Staring out the window, he could see the sign for the Christopher Street–Sheridan Square station come into view as the train pulled into the terminal. He glanced at his watch, smiled thinly and stepped from the car. His timing had been excellent. Now it was only a ten-minute walk to the meet location.

Slowly he headed for the station stairs, all the while looking about cautiously. Once at the top he started down Christopher Street and made for the west side and the abandoned piers that jutted into the Hudson River.

As he walked down the narrow streets with their small attached brick homes, he thought about how he had come to be in this predicament. It had been eight years since he had left the Soviet Union. They had made him an offer which gave him few options. Five years at hard labor for black-market offenses, or work for them. They had put it to him that simply.

And, in truth, it hadn't been bad. Once he had agreed to work for the KGB, it was arranged for him to emigrate to the United States. He had been put in touch with the normal agencies that dealt with Russians coming to America. Everything had been as if they had never spoken to him. The agency got him a job and his first place to live. Thus, he fit in with thousands of other Russians who had emigrated to the States, even going so far as to shorten and Americanize his last name. Soon he became just another anonymous face in the city.

Then, three years after he arrived, came the first meeting on the street. The man had called to Pinkin by his correct name, Pinkovsky, and reminded him who he really worked for, and why he was here.

First, Max (of course, Pinkin knew that wasn't the man's real name) had him buy some American military surplus clothes at a local army-navy store: a field jacket and a few sets of camouflage fatigues. He did it, feeling as he carried the bundle of clothes back to Max, as if he held a bomb under his arm.

Max took the clothes and the bill from the store. In turn he gave back the precise amount spent and had Pinkin sign a receipt for the money.

This pattern went on for over a year. Max would send him on seemingly pointless errands. If money was involved, he had to bring Max a receipt in order to be reimbursed. To an American, Pinkin thought, this would have seemed strange. But, to a former citizen of the Soviet Union, anything else would have been bizarre. His native land had the art of bureaucracy down to a science. Its cumbersome requirements held even for their intelligence people who worked in the field.

Pinkin had noted that about two years ago the pattern began to change. The errands he was assigned became somewhat more apparent in their purpose. On some occasions he had to pick up packages from strange men at unusual hours of the day, ultimately to deliver them to Max. And then, finally, the car.

One day, while at home, he received a call from Max. It was the same code as always. First, "Hello?" then "Hello, is Max home?" and, finally, "Sorry. There's no Max here."

The words had no meaning, except that whoever initiated the call wished for a meeting, in exactly two hours, at the current predetermined location. As usual Max had been there, waiting. Max told him, "Buy a car," and gave him a piece of paper, with exactly what kind of car to get and how much to spend. He had asked Max how he would pay for it. There certainly wasn't enough money in his bank account for that kind of expense. Max had said, "Don't worry. When the time comes, I'll give you the cash."

And he did. Over twenty thousand dollars. Pinkin had never held that much money before. On the train to the car dealer he kept feeling his pocket for the wad of money, fearful that, as if by some magic, it would be gone when he got there.

For the last eight months, since just before the baby was born, all he had to do for Max was to pay the garage people. And once he had to have the car's oil changed. That was all, for the last eight months. Pinkin had begun to relax.

At first, when he did the things he was told to do, he had found it exciting. Then, after a while, it had become

The Murder of Old Comrades

boring and tedious, eating into his private life. Finally, after he had thought about the ramifications of his actions, it became frightening.

For Pinkin knew the inevitable would happen. He had been doing terrible things, he was sure, illegal things. When the American authorities found out about his actions, as he knew they would, he would be sent to prison. What of his young wife and baby? They would probably even send him back to the Soviet Union, after he got out of jail. Then what would he do?

A few times, before the car, he had attempted to broach the subject to Max of no longer being involved in any of this. But when he tried to get the words to come out, his tongue would freeze up, his jaw muscles would lock. Deep down inside he suspected that if he ever mentioned that thought to Max, jail would be the least of his troubles.

The sound of trucks as they rumbled along the makeshift West Side Highway brought Pinkin back to reality. He moved northward, to a street corner with a traffic light that allowed people to cross the highway. Once on the other side, he moved quickly to a large abandoned warehouse which jutted out over the Hudson River. He passed other men who were in the area for a different reason. They were, in fact, the primary rationale for the choice of the location. Their furtive lifestyle permitted Pinkin and Max anonymous meetings, even among large numbers of strangers.

Pinkin stepped up to the dilapidated warehouse. The windows that ran along its side had long ago been broken by vandals and the front of the building was all but caved in, whether at the hands of people or simply the result of neglect—he could not tell. Walking carefully along the narrow path between the warehouse and the edge of the pier it rested on, Pinkin headed to its end, which jutted out onto the brown river. He wrinkled his nose at the fetid odor which rose from below, unaware that the most cosmopolitan city in the country dumped over two hundred million gallons of untreated sewage into the water that surrounded it every day.

As he neared his objective he saw Max, backlit by the late day's sun. The man whom he knew as Max, Yuri Andrapovich, spoke first.

"Why the meeting, Andrew?"

"Two policemen came to my apartment today, Max. They asked me about the car."

Max leaned casually against the wall.

"So?"

"So?" Pinkin replied, raising his voice. "So they wanted me to take them to see it. They said it had been involved in a robbery, several weeks ago."

Max smiled and asked softly, "What did you do?"

"I showed it to them. What else could I do?"

"Tell them to go away, for one," Andrapovich responded, then waved his hand and said, "But it's of no matter."

Pinkin began to sputter in anger, when Max asked, "Do you remember their names?"

"One was called Grau. I think the other was named Tanti."

Max nodded and quietly said, "Yes, Mr. Grau again."

"Max," Pinkin said sharply, "what will I do now?"

"Nothing. Just go home and forget it. I'll handle the problem."

"What do you mean, 'forget it'?" Pinkin exploded. All at once his fear of Andrapovich was lost in his release of years of pent-up anxiety. He shouted, "You have me doing all your dirty little jobs, and when the police finally come, you want I should just pretend it's all right?"

Andrapovich tried to calm Pinkin down, but Pinkin grabbed Andrapovich by the collar and went on, virtually out of control.

"I've had it with all this crazy business, Max. I'm through!"

"All right, relax. We'll work this out," Andrapovich said, removing Pinkin's hands from his shirt.

The sun now sat on the horizon, hidden by the buildings arrayed along the New Jersey shore. Its light caused a twilight effect around them and made the surrounding shadows deepen.

Andrapovich patted Pinkin on the shoulder and said, "I've always handled problems in the past and I'll take care of this one. Do you understand?"

The Murder of Old Comrades

Pinkin was drained from his outburst. Almost in a whimper he pleaded, "I want out. That's all, Max, I want out. I promise you, no one will know anything that we've done together. What do you say?"

Andrapovich looked around for a moment, then turned back to Pinkin, smiled, and said, "Okay. I'll take care of it. You've done your share."

Pinkin sighed, saying, "Thanks, Max. You won't have to worry about me, I promise."

Andrapovich, with a deprecating laugh, said, "Don't even think about it. I'm not concerned." Nodding toward the direction of the street, he said, "Let's head back, before we break our necks in the dark."

Pinkin didn't reply, but turned and started off for the street, drained of emotion. Although the tops of some of the taller buildings in the city still caught a glint of dying sun, where they walked was almost completely dark. Pinkin had to tread carefully lest he lose his footing among the debris strewn around the pier. He could hear Max close behind, also carefully threading his way through the maze of discarded plumbing and bricks.

The eighteen-inch piece of lead pipe landed with a dull thud against Pinkin's skull. In moments, the body lay face down amid the rubble. Andrapovich struck the head, again and again, feeling warm blood splatter against his face with each impact. By the fifth blow, pink-gray brain matter oozed from the pulp that had been Pinkin's head.

Holding the pipe in his right hand, Andrapovich bent down and placed his fingers on the side of Pinkin's neck. Satisfied no life remained, he tossed the pipe into the black water below. It made a little splash on impact. He then rolled the body over to the edge of the pier, took one last look around, and gave a final push. The splash was louder this time.

Andrapovich stood up and removed a handkerchief from his back pocket, trying to clean himself off as best he could. He stared at the invisible water and quietly said, "Andrew, I was never concerned. I told you I know how to handle such matters."

Slowly he made his way off the pier.

Chapter 17

Grau sat at his desk in the Four-Seven Squad room and tried to piece together his crazy case. His swivel chair squealed in protest as he leaned back to glance at the big round-faced clock that hung on the wall opposite him. It told him he had a half hour to go before his end of tour. He rubbed the knuckles of his hands into his eyes until they hurt and went through the facts of his homicide one more time. He ticked off the spider web of connections linking four dead people, some strange Russian and a car he couldn't afford, parked in a spot the guy didn't even remember, and a crazy floatplane.

And of course there was that piece of heavy-weight paper. He'd toyed with it for a half hour. It now sat on his desk like an itch he couldn't scratch. Deep inside something told him it was an important part of the puzzle. Except that it didn't add up.

Next to the paper lay a yellow pad filled with notes. At its top was the name PINKIN in capital letters. He glanced down at it. That had been a royal waste of time. He and Tanti must have made twenty phone calls that afternoon, trying to get some background on that guy. A total dead end. Tanti had finally joked that "Pinkin must have been a Russian Boy Scout," he was so wholesome.

The whole thing simply didn't jell for Grau. He had dealt with multiple murders, cult murders, infanticide, even serial killers. But this case didn't fit any pattern he knew, and it was getting to him.

Some detectives, even some good ones, could leave their work in the office. But not Grau. He would stew over his unsolved cases, sometimes even waking in the middle of the night with a new inspiration.

When he had initially begun work in a homicide squad, the first murder he had caught was that of a sixty-five-year-old woman, pushed into her apartment and stabbed to death. Grau had tried every angle. On the theory that it was a daytime burglary-gone-bad, he had reviewed all the burglary patterns in the general area for the previous six months prior to the homicide. The local bookmaker was visited and not-so-subtle pressure brought to bear in search of a name, a nickname, anything. Hundreds of hours of diligent investigative work produced not one hint as to who the killer might have been.

He remembered during that case, how he had paced around in the homicide squad office, trying to think up some new angle to pursue. A veteran detective, and a damned good one at that, had looked up from his newspaper at the young Grau moving nervously back and forth.

The older man asked, "Hey, Jon, did you do it?"

Grau had been startled by the question. Instinctively, he responded, "Of course not!"

"Then you got nothing to worry about," the other man advised, and went back to reading the *News*.

And for years after, when Grau would chance on someone arrested from around that neighborhood, he would ask about that case, offering the criminal a game of Let's Make a Deal in exchange for information. But that murder, his first case, had remained unsolved. And it still bothered him.

Deciding he had had enough for one day, he put all the papers strewn about his desk back in his large maroon-colored homicide case folder and tied it closed.

Harry Purvis sat two desks away from Grau. Grau watched as Purvis laboriously pecked at the keys of an old gray manual typewriter. For no reason he could explain, Grau felt a sudden sensation of emptiness come on him, as if something important in his life had been neglected during the last few weeks. He picked up his phone and dialed the number for Montefiore Hospital Emergency Room. A woman answered and Grau said, "Social workers, please."

"One moment and I'll transfer you." There was a click on the line, then, "Mr. Crimmins, may I help you?"

"Julia Murphy, please."

"Sure." Grau heard the man call Julia's name.

"Julia Murphy. Can I help you?"

"That depends. Wanna screw?"

Murphy laughed. "You really know how to sweet-talk a girl, don't you?"

"Hey, what do you want? I'm a Neanderthal cop!"

"I take it I'm being propositioned."

"No shit!"

"Well, I may be easy, but I ain't cheap. It's gonna cost you dinner."

"Baby, it's never free. I'll pick you up in front of the E.R., around five."

"I'll be there. Bye."

"So long." Grau picked up his case folder and stepped over to the metal cabinet against the wall. He slid open one of the drawers and crammed his folder in its place among the dozens of other open homicide cases.

The team relieving Grau's was just starting to come through the door. Tanti had already taken off and Harry Purvis was still at his typewriter, concocting the fiction needed to close out some bullshit case. Over by the coffee machine in the far corner of the room Joe Blakemore and Clarence Bradford talked and laughed.

Too tired to think anymore about his work, and looking for a diversion, Grau walked over to them.

"What's up?"

"Hi, Jon," Clarence said. "We were just talking about some of the screwy things the new cops are doing."

Blakemore said, "Today, Pat Sweeny—he was the day tour's patrol sergeant—told me a story about one of his female officers. This lady wasn't known for her intellectual abilities from the start, having pulled a couple of major boners when she first came to the precinct. Anyway, she's standing with the rest of the platoon when Sweeny is calling the roll. She hears her steady partner's name and then the name of someone she doesn't recognize who's been assigned to work with him. After roll call she storms up to the sergeant and goes bananas. Threatens to put in a grievance, call the Police Women's Association, that kind of stuff, because they got someone else to work with her partner.

First, the sergeant tells her to calm down and explain the problem. She keeps going on about how they had no right to switch her from her regular partner. The sergeant asks her what she's talking about since she was still working with her regular partner. The name he called was hers, at least, it was hers since she got married the day before."

Grau shook his head and walked away from the two men, smiling.

A few minutes after 4 P.M., Grau signed out and left the precinct. He hopped into his two-year-old red Chevy, headed south to Gun Hill Road, and made a right. Eventually he turned into the street where the sprawling Montefiore Hospital complex stood. Seeing an open space opposite the red awning with Emergency Room in large white letters written on it, he parked and shut the engine. His watch told him it was twenty minutes to five. He knew Julia would still be busy so he decided to just relax and watch the scenery.

An orange-and-white city ambulance pulled up to the front of the E.R. Grau watched two EMTs get out of the cab and open the back doors. They leaned inside and pulled a stretcher from the rear. A middle-aged woman in a light pink dress also came out. She stayed with the stretcher and held the hand of whoever was lying there. They all disappeared through the swinging glass entrance doors.

Grau thought back to the first time he had seen Julia at the hospital. He had walked into the E.R. looking for a shooting victim—one of two, and the survivor. For a homicide detective, that was the equivalent of winning the lottery, since in the majority of such cases, the victims could only be interviewed on the autopsy slab.

The injured man was being worked on by the medical staff, so Grau had sought out and found some of his relatives. They were being interviewed by a hospital social worker. Grau had walked over and waited patiently off to the side, watching the woman work. She was about five foot four, pleasantly proportioned, with shoulder-length brown hair and a pretty face.

That had been almost ten years earlier. Julia had just started working for the hospital, fresh out of New York

University graduate school, where she had been awarded a Masters of Social Work degree.

A red light flashed by Grau and took him from his daydream. A marked department radio car had flown by, lights only, no siren, and made a sharp turn at the corner.

Grau decided that he was bored sitting alone in the car. He got out and headed for the emergency room door. Outside stood a hospital guard in dark blue uniform. Grau showed the man his shield and, with a nod, was allowed through. He walked past a second set of swinging glass doors and into the E.R. waiting area. Several dozen people sat around on hard wood chairs. Some read magazines, others talked, a few slept. Off in the corner of the room a TV was set up high on the wall, bolted in place. A number of children and some adults watched whatever was on the screen.

Grau made a right turn through wooden doors that had the words, NO UNAUTHORIZED PERSONNEL stenciled in red on them and walked into the E.R. proper.

The room was quite deep and a bustle of activity. Along its sides, green curtains were used to partition off the various cubicles where patients were tended to. Because of crowding, some people had to remain outside the screened areas. A few sat about in wheelchairs, others lay on stretchers. All waited their turn to be looked at by the harried medical staff.

Twenty feet from the E.R. entrance was a desk where several nurses sat. In front of the desk, Grau saw a young woman dressed in street clothes, talking with one of the nurses. He walked up to her.

"Hi, Cynthia. Seen Julia around?"

"Hello, Jon," the woman smiled. "No. At least I haven't seen her down here recently. She might be up in renal. Hang on."

Cynthia reached over the desk and picked up a telephone. She dialed a few numbers, then asked for Julia. While she spoke, Grau spotted Julia Murphy, dressed in a tweed skirt and a gray silk blouse, coming toward them from the opposite end of the room. He tapped Cynthia on the shoulder and nodded in Murphy's direction, mouthing the word "Thanks."

As Murphy walked up to Grau, he thought she looked tired. Her normally neat hair was bedraggled and there were dark smudges under her brown eyes. He smiled, saying, "Hard day at the office, toots?"

"Yup," she said, returning, his smile. "Follow me."

Grau fell in trail behind Murphy and eyed the sexy sway of her attractive rear end. The wounded of the Bronx ignored them as they made their way out of the emergency room and to a small corridor adjacent to the reception area. Murphy pulled a key from her pocket and let them into the tiny office used by the hospital's social work staff. She closed the door behind them. With her back to Grau she picked up her purse and a plastic shopping bag from one of the two small desks that completely took up the available space in the office. The jangling he heard from inside the bag was probably cans of cat food.

He put his hands on her shoulders, bent down and ran his tongue down the nape of her neck. She squealed in delight, turned and put her arms around Grau, placing her head on his chest. They stayed that way for a few moments until she raised her head and kissed Grau warmly on the lips as he hugged her.

Parting, Grau said, "Okay, kid. Let's blow this joint." She laughed and opened the little office's door.

Once inside the car, Grau turned to Murphy and asked, "Where to?"

"Feed me," she said, putting her hand on Grau's leg as he pulled the car from the curb.

They drove to the East Village, which was fortunately opposite to the city's evening flow of rush-hour traffic. Once off FDR Drive at Fifteenth Street, Grau headed for Second Avenue, with its potpourri of restaurants. He made the left-hand turn to go south, more interested in finding parking than a specific place to eat. Any possible kind of restaurant they might be interested in was situated well within walking distance. It was a place to park that had become scarce in the Village, particularly in the last few years since the more affluent and trendy New Yorkers discovered the area.

Once in possession of a legal space on St. Marks Place

off Second Avenue they decided on a nearby Japanese restaurant.

The streets were already crowded with the wide mix of people that were normally seen in the area. Grau motioned to Murphy when he spied a particularly unique threesome walking toward them. The woman between the two men had pink and purple hair, black fishnet stockings, black shoes that appeared to be turn-of-the-century vintage and a cut-off black leather jacket. One of the men had yellow hair, worn in spikes so that his head reminded Grau of a World War One sea mine. Around his neck dangled at least two pounds of costume jewelry and every finger on both hands held a minimum of two rings. The third part of the trio wore brown construction shoes, an ancient gray business suit with thin lapels, a formal white shirt open at the neck, a large gold earring in his left ear and red cheek rouge.

Grau grabbed Murphy around the waist, pinched her side and, as he tilted his head in the direction of gray suit, asked, "Wanna date?"

"If you don't get some food in me, I may be looking."

Although it was still early, when they walked up to the restaurant Grau could see through the front window that most of the tables were taken. Once inside, a petite Oriental woman in white shirt and black slacks approached them and asked if they wanted the sushi bar or a table. Grau indicated the latter and they were led to a small corner table for two.

Grau was glad to have the privacy. Without bothering to open the menu he ordered two sashimi dinners, as well as two orders of saki. The woman left and Grau eased back in his chair and reached his hand out to the middle of the table just as Murphy did the same. Their hands clasped.

"So, Florence Nightingale, how was your day?"

"Sucky," Murphy said, and smiled weakly.

"What now?"

"Oh, nothing special. I was up at renal all day. Kidney patients, you know. I guess I got a little depressed."

"A little depressed? I was gonna ask whether you were gonna use gas, or wanted to borrow my gun."

Murphy laughed. Their hand clasp broke as the waitress

returned with a pair of small porcelain cups and two white china bottles of warm saki. Grau poured some of the clear liquid in each of their cups. He raised his to his lips and drank some of the pleasant-tasting wine, savoring its peculiarly attractive flavor.

"What's happening with your homicide?" Murphy asked, unwrapping the protective paper from around her chopsticks.

"It's getting kind of crazy. In fact, I've never been involved in any investigation that's so bizarre," Grau said, as he toyed with his small cup.

Grau paused while the waitress placed salad and soup at their table. Murphy immediately started on her bowl. Between spoonfuls, she asked, "How's your new partner doing?"

"Tony? He's doing fine, really enjoying the work. While I interviewed my new informant in Brooklyn the other day, Tony went upstate in a department helicopter to where we think my shooter landed. He and the pilot nosed around and spoke with a forest service ranger up there who saw the floatplane come in. And he found out that the guy had managed to get the plate of the car that the passenger drove off in." Grau started on his soup. "Anyway, he got a big kick out of the trip."

"Who owns the car the plate comes back to?" Murphy asked. She pushed her empty bowl away and replaced it with the dish of salad.

"Some guy in upper Manhattan. Tony and I checked him out today. He's not right either." Grau stopped talking while the waitress put the heavy wood boards of sashimi in front of them. Finely cut slices of raw fish, dark red tuna, pale yellow whitetail, and translucent flounder, sat on pure white balls of rice. He picked up the bottle of soy sauce and poured some of the dark liquid in a small bowl by Murphy's board, then poured some in his own. Using his chopsticks, he took from his board a bit of green horseradish paste called wasabi and mixed it with the sauce to prepare the dip for the raw fish.

Grau continued, "Naturally I ran the guy's name and DOB for a record. He's clean. The thing is, this guy can't afford the kind of car registered to him. Hell, he can't afford the parking garage fee, if my guess is right."

"So," Murphy asked, "who's picking up the tab?"

"Who and why?" Grau responded. "I wish I knew."

For a while both silently worked on their dinner, then Grau put down his chopsticks and said, "Julia, the way I see it, this case can go two ways. If whoever is responsible for the situation is smart, they'll recognize they've screwed up and get the hell out of here. At least for a while." He again stopped and picked up a piece of raw tuna, dipped it in the soy-wasabi mix, and put it in his mouth.

"Or?" Murphy asked, looking over the table at Grau, a piece of white octopus held suspended in her chopsticks.

"Or? Well, my best guess is, if it's a political problem that they've screwed up and they have to make it better before somebody back home lops off heads, they'll have to try again. Which means the killer will go back to work. Which means I'll get a crack at nailing the SOB. Anyway I've made a new contact, a guy named Gross. And I think I figured out a way to get the Russians excited enough to do something stupid."

"Who's Gross? And what are you going to do?"

"He's a Russian emigrant. He lives near Little Odessa, the Russian section down in lower Brooklyn. I don't think he's directly involved in what's going on, but he's street wise. Just maybe some little bird will sing the right song to him. And he'll sing it to me. Especially after I give a call to the Soviet Mission and feed them a line of bull that I've been working on." Grau took a sip of saki and said softly, "That should perk things up a bit."

"So who does this fellow Gross think the killer is?"

Grau thought a moment before answering. He had already said more to Julia than he should have about the investigation. Not that he doubted her, it was just bad policy to speak about sensitive things to people who had no real reason to know about them.

"He doesn't really know. Listen, enough of this crap. Let's eat."

After dinner and several more bottles of saki the two walked around the East Village. Although the sun had another hour to go before it would disappear below the horizon the man-made mountains of the city kept them in shadow as they window-shopped along the Avenues. A light breeze blew, making the seventy-degree air feel cooler than it was.

Murphy insisted on stopping at a large bookstore to search for some arcane text on astrology, a subject that Grau hadn't the least interest in. As she browsed for her book, Grau thumbed through a large work titled *Weapons of the World*. This was much to Murphy's displeasure, which she showed with a barely perceptible raising of her eyebrows. Her distaste for firearms amused him, and he put the big book down and walked over to where she was looking for her astrology text, her back now to him.

"So?" he said, checking to make sure no one was watching as he pinched her behind. She leaned the back of her head on his chest and said, "Let me guess. Your place or mine?"

"Yours, it's closer."

She put the book she held back on the shelf it came from and they left the store, walked to the car and drove to Murphy's apartment, on First Avenue and Eighteenth Street.

Grau followed the horseshoe-shaped street that made its way through her apartment complex and parked at the first available spot. They walked the block to her building, past the heavy metal entrance front and took the elevator to the fourth floor. Murphy unlocked her front door's multiple locks and they entered her small apartment.

Murphy's three cats vied for her attention, demanding to be fed. She put her pocketbook and plastic sack full of cat food on her kitchen table, removed a can from the sack, opened it and took it over to the animals' feeding dishes.

She bent down and began to scoop the foul-smelling food into the three plastic bowls. Grau came up behind her and started to unbutton the rear of her blouse. Despite Murphy's wriggles he managed to unfasten the hook of her bra as well.

She attempted to stand up. With an empty can in one hand and a spoon in the other she tried to make a break for the garbage bag and sink to unload her burden. Grau got to her in mid stride, cupped her breasts in his hands, and gently squeezed her hard nipples. The can and spoon went *clunk* against the wooden countertop.

Turning to face Grau, Murphy went on tiptoes so her lips met his. They walked into her small cluttered bedroom, throwing off their clothes as they went.

They lay together in bed for a long time. Murphy's back was to Grau, his arm folded around her as he stroked her breasts. A golden shaft of light came into the room from the bedroom window, indicating the end of the summer day. She looked up at the radio alarm and saw it was almost 9 P.M.

"Hey, mister. If we don't get up now, we'll never be able to get back to sleep later."

"Screw it, I'm on strike," Grau said and buried his face in her back.

Murphy reached over to the radio and turned it on. A talk show was in progress, but she felt too lazy and indifferent to move the dial. Her head still on her pillow, she said, "Well?" to which he responded with a grunt, in an attempt to put off the inevitable as long as possible.

An advertisement was being broadcast for the Museum of Natural History. In the background they could hear the roaring and growling sounds of the dinosaurs, for the museum's new exhibit on prehistoric animals.

Murphy rolled over to face Grau. She propped herself up on one elbow, bent her fingers into the shape of claws and snarled, "Tyrannosaurus Rex!" Giggling, she plopped back down on the bed, again turning her back to Grau.

Grau, rising to the occasion, growled, "Bronx cop!" leaned over and bit Murphy on her back.

They stayed in bed.

Chapter 18

"Auto one-seven-two, ten-one and acknowledge, K."

Tanti picked up the portable radio lying on the car seat next to him and hit the transmit switch. "One-seven-two, ten-four," he replied, acknowledging Radio Central's command to call the office, then tossed the unit back on the seat between him and Grau.

"Jon, you want to wait till we get back to the squad? It's only ten minutes away."

"No, let's find a telephone." Grau motioned with his head. "There, by the diner." He maneuvered the car into the left-turn lane, the big red-and-white Yonkers Diner sign clearly visible half a block away.

"Well, I guess whatever they got for us at the squad has got to be better than the crap we've managed to accomplish so far today," Tanti said, arms folded across his chest.

Grau pulled the squad car into the diner entrance and responded, "Relax, Tony, that's just the way it is. Judith Bartlett's family wasn't likely to have anything of value for us anyway. But, it was a base and it had to be covered."

"Maybe. But the way they talked, you'd think they hardly even knew her boyfriend's name."

Grau shrugged, killed the engine and opened his door.

"You want to get a cuppa coffee, while I make the call?"

Tanti shook his head and said, "Thanks, I'll just sit tight."

Grau shut the door and walked to the pay phone outside the restaurant. Although the Four-Seven Precinct was only a few miles away, their squad was in the 212 area code and Yonkers was a 914. He made it a collect call.

Purvis accepted and said, "Hey, Jon, the boss is gonna kill you. You know what a pain in the ass collect calls are for him."

"Harry, save it. I'm in Yonkers and I don't have a pocket full of change. What's the ten-one all about?"

"I got a couple of messages for you. First someone from the Chief of Detectives called. Something about a suspicious death in Manhattan yesterday. He wants you to give him a shout as soon as you can."

"Okay. Probably some inspector from One Police Plaza trying to second-guess my investigation. Stick the guy's name and number on my desk. I'll call him when I get in. What's the other message? I got things to do."

"Some civilian called. Said his name was Nick, that you knew him. Said it was important. He wanted to talk to you right away."

"Now that's interesting. Where did he want me to meet him, Harry?"

"Hang on. Let me get the note." Grau could hear paper rustle on the other end and imagined Purvis sifting for the note through the pile of refuse the other detective euphemistically referred to as his desk.

"Here we go. He said you should meet him at Sheepshead Bay, on the other side of the street from Salerno's Clam House, at 1 P.M."

Grau looked at his watch. It was five to twelve.

"Swell. Harry, you wouldn't happen to know where that place is?"

"As a matter of fact, my good man, I looked it up for you. The joint is on Emmons, near Ocean Avenue."

"Harry, I don't care what they say about you, you're all right."

"Hey, Jon, one last thing."

"Yeah?"

"See if you can get Tony to eat some raw clams while you're down there."

"Screw you, Harry."

Grau and Tanti strolled along the walk adjacent to the bay and inspected the fleet of commercial and private fishing boats docked there. On the opposite side of the street were restaurants of various sizes, their signs proclaiming each one's uniqueness, and always concerning seafood.

Grau stopped at one particularly large vessel, a modern fifty-foot gleaming white yacht. The ship glistened in the midday sun.

"How would you like to own this one, Tony?" Grau asked, leaning against the heavily weathered gray metal railing that ran the length of Sheepshead Bay.

Tanti studied the ship, chewing on his second hot dog since they had arrived. With his mouth still busy with lunch, he mumphed, "How much does it cost?" and took a sip from his Tab.

"I don't know. Maybe a hundred thousand or so."

"Think they'd let me stick it in one of the reservoirs up in Putnam County?"

"Sure."

"Okay, I'll take it. Have it delivered on my day off," Tanti said as he looked around for a trash can to toss his empty soda into.

Grau poked Tanti gently in the ribs and said, "There's our man. He's standing near the old trawler."

"Where?" Tanti asked, his eyes searching among the anchored ships.

"He's the big white guy in shirt-sleeves who's leaning on the railing, right by all those fishermen. Except he ain't fishin'," Grau replied.

"Gotcha."

As they approached Gross, Grau noted a look of surprise on the man's face. He appeared somewhat haggard and needed a shave. Grau and Tanti took places on the railing to either side of the man.

"Detective Grau, I'm glad to see you're still prompt." Then, turning to Tanti, he said, "I'm afraid I've never had the pleasure?"

"Nick, this is my partner, Tony Tanti. I didn't think you'd mind another body."

Gross nodded to Tanti and said to Grau, "Normally not. But things have heated up considerably, haven't they?"

"Sorry, Nick, I don't know what you're talking about."

Gross stared at Grau for a moment, then turned to face back to the water. He let out a slight sigh and said, "I'm crushed. I thought you'd be hot to trot after the last murder, two days ago. Don't you cops ever talk to one another?"

To their left, twenty feet away, the surface of the water splashed. One of the fishermen lined up at the railing reeled in a small black porgy.

Tanti looked over to Grau and raised his eyebrows in question.

Grau remembered the note he told Purvis to leave on his desk back at the Four-Seven squad. He wondered if he should have made that call to the Chief of Detectives office before running off to Brooklyn.

"Nick," Grau said, "stop talking in riddles and tell us what happened."

"Somebody killed a Russian émigré guy over on the West Side of lower Manhattan the other day. After he had talked to some cops."

Grau asked softly, "What was his name?"

"Pinkovsky. Been in the country nearly ten years. Word is, he had been working with the KGB. Low-level stuff. You know, he was kind of a gofer."

Tanti said, "Never heard of the guy. How did he die?"

"They bashed his skull in, then threw him in the Hudson."

Tanti continued, "Nick, you're implying the KGB killed the guy? It coulda been a mugging or something, right?"

Gross shook his head. "You two guys are beginning to get to me. I give you facts and you always want to argue."

"Nick," Grau interjected in defense of his partner, "look at it from our end. We can't go running around the city looking for secret agents every time some Russian expatriate catches it in the neck. Who told you the guy worked for the KGB anyway?"

Nick shook his head slowly. "Gimme a break, will ya? They tell me, I tell you. That's the way it is with these things. You know that."

"All right, all right," Grau said, waving his hand. "Tell you what, give me whatever info you have on this guy. I'll run it down."

"You're a real sport, Detective Grau. Like I said, the guy's name was Pinkovsky. At least to his Russian friends.

The name he was going by in this country was Pinkin, and . . ."

"Wait a second," Grau interrupted. "You said Pinkin?"

"Yeah, that's the name," Gross said. He looked first to one officer then the other, noting their exchange of looks and sudden silence. He went on, "I think maybe I shoulda given you his Americanized name first."

Grau studied the other man for a moment, then said, "Nick, tell Tanti and me some more about how the KGB works."

"Hey, buddy, got any spare bait?" the grizzled old man asked the small group of fishermen standing by the railing.

"Sorry, pal."

"Just got enough for me, mate."

As he started to walk on to continue his search the youngest of the three men said, "Here, help yourself," and nodded to the small white cardboard container by his foot.

"Thanks, pal."

The old man bent down and removed one of the writhing red worms. Seeing that the young man paid him no attention, he deftly removed a few more and placed all of them in a discarded styrofoam fast-food hamburger container he kept for the purpose.

The old man took one of the worms and laid it on the concrete walkway. With a battered pocketknife he cut a third of the worm, placed the squirming piece on his hook and dropped it in the water.

"Any luck?" he asked the young man, realizing he wasn't with the others.

"Nope," the young man replied, smiling.

"Maybe you oughta change your bait. Or at least check it. Sometimes you can't tell if they stole it. Know what I mean?"

"Yeah. That's okay," the young man replied and looked past the old man to where Grau, Tanti and Gross were talking. He glanced at his watch and made a mental note of the time.

"Hey!" the old man yelled, "I got a bite!" He began to reel in his line. A small black fish could be seen rising to the surface.

As he brought it over the railing he beamed and turned to the young man. "A couple more and I got dinner. Your worms brought me luck."

The young man nodded and continued to watch the three men, who were now deep in conversation. He reflected that there were many different kinds of fish in the world. The old man had caught his, and he in turn had snared his own. In their own ways, they had both been lucky today.

"But why can't I go, too?" Tanti asked as he pulled the squad car into an open space by the boardwalk parking lot.

"Because I'm trying to low key this thing is why," Grau responded as he fished through his spiral notebook for Saminov's address.

"Look, I talked this over with Marion. She's running down enough leads on her end of the investigation to keep plenty busy. I asked her if she would mind if I tossed the apartment. And there's probably nothing up there anyway. What do you think, I'm holding out on you?"

Tanti didn't answer but instead sulked behind the wheel of the car.

"Twenty minutes and I'll be back. Promise."

Grau got out of the car and stretched. He made for the street and slowly walked the block and a half to Saminov's apartment building. As were all the others on the block, it was a small six-story brick walk-up.

He came up to its metal and glass front door and pushed it open. Inside it was dark and cool. It almost felt like a cave, he reflected, as he searched for the superintendent's apartment number. Finding it he pressed the little black button next to the Slavic sounding name.

A voice asked, "Who?"

"Police."

A moment later the inner entrance was buzzed open. Grau turned left and headed for an apartment door that had just cracked open. The head of an older woman looked out at him.

"Good morning," Grau said, and showed the lady his shield. "Mind if I talk to you for a moment?"

The woman nodded and let him in to the small apartment. Once inside he could smell the strong odor of cooking cabbage. Grau stood with the woman in the narrow hallway, she giving no indication he was invited to go farther.

"Is the super home?"

She shook her head and said in a heavy Russian accent, "No, he is out buying things. What can I do for you?"

"A Mr. Saminov lived in this building, correct?"

The woman nodded.

Grau lied, "I'm the detective investigating the case and I'd like to take a look inside his apartment."

The woman thought for a moment, then said, "Wait one minute." She walked down the hallway and into another room. A moment later she returned with a key on a string. Attached was a tag with the number Seven printed on it.

"Here." She handed it to Grau. "But please bring it back when you finish."

Grau smiled and said, "Certainly," relieved and pleased that she was so cooperative.

Once back in the building's hall he looked around at how the apartments' numbers ran. On the ground floor there was One to Six. Seven would be on the second floor, facing the street.

He took the stairs two at a time. At their top, to his immediate right, was apartment number Seven. He inserted the key and let himself in.

The place was small. There was a modest-size living room, a kitchen, and a single bedroom off to the side. It was basically neat, Grau decided, at least for a man who lived alone.

The detective systematically began to search the residence. He started in the bedroom. The obvious places were searched first. He poked around in dresser drawers and he picked up the bed's mattress to peek underneath. Finding nothing unusual he walked over to the lone closet in the room. He removed all the clothes and neatly lay them on the bed. Grau didn't wish to search each article of clothing. There was no time for that and anyway he didn't even know what he was looking for. He settled for patting the pile down. Feeling nothing hard or out of place Grau turned his attention to the closet itself.

The top shelf held the usual junk: a couple of hats, a scarf and an old Brooklyn yellow pages.

On the floor were three pairs of shoes and some old rubber rain overshoes. From habits Grau developed when he worked in narcotics he pulled everything out and examined the wood flooring underneath. As he did in Gorkin's apartment he tapped lightly around the boards. He stopped when he thought he detected a slight difference in sound.

Grau pulled out his pocketknife and opened the blade. He slowly worked its tip along the seam of the wood and gently pried up. The board came loose. He removed it and with his thin-bodied flashlight examined the small space. Inside was a rectangular-shaped package. He reached in and retrieved it. Underneath was a larger package, wrapped in brown paper like the first. He pulled that out also, noting it was much heavier than the smaller one.

Nothing else was inside. Grau replaced the boards and then took the time to put back everything he had removed from the closet. That done, he sat on the bed to examine what he had found.

He carefully unwrapped the first parcel. Inside he found a small stack of foreign money.

"Son of a bitch," Grau said under his breath, realizing the currency was the same kind as the bill he had found in Gorkin's wallet.

Grau shook his head and put the packet on the bed.

"Mr. Saminov, I do believe you didn't tell me the whole truth," Grau murmured, and picked up the larger package. Whatever it was, it was hard and heavy. Carefully removing the paper cover, he saw some sort of metal printing plates. Etched on their faces were the negative of the front and back of what appeared to be currency.

Looking carefully at the delicately cut surface Grau realized the money in the first package matched what he saw engraved on the plates.

He rewrapped the packages. An old newspaper lay on the dresser top. Grau picked it up and carefully fit the two parcels inside, and folded the paper around it. He experimented tucking it under his arm and was satisfied that a casual observer would not realize anything was concealed within.

Grau headed for the door, wondering who he'd have to see to get some information on what he had found.

Chapter 19

As the department Ford slowly made its way through the late-morning rush-hour traffic, large drops of rain splattered against the car's window. Tanti yawned loudly. It caused Grau, whose closed eyelids and head slumped against the passenger-side window showed all the signs that he was asleep, to do the same.

"What time is it, Tony?" Grau asked, not opening his eyes.

"Nine thirty-seven, sleeping beauty. You still got plenty of time before you have to be at the meeting."

"Good. Wake me when we get there."

"Screw you! If I gotta work on three hours' sleep, nobody naps."

Grau folded his arms across his chest. His head remained against the pane of glass. He grinned and said, "Is this coming from the same cop who only a week or so ago was bustin' a gut to work with the big guys?"

"But jeez, we busted our asses yesterday, trying to track down that Pinkin story. You really think we're dealing with the KGB?"

Grau responded, "Once a guy told me, if it walks like a duck, and it squawks like a duck . . ."

"Then it's gotta be a duck. Thanks for the bird-watching lesson."

Grau smiled.

"Why are you so damned tired? Didn't you go home after we finished last night?"

"Nope. I went to my girl's house."

Tanti sagely nodded. "You swine."

"Yup."

"Where's she from?"

"She works at Montefiore."

"A nurse?" Tanti asked brightly. The promise of a discussion about women perked him up as he moved onto the FDR Drive from the Willis Avenue Bridge.

"No, a social worker."

Tanti screwed his face up in distaste. "A social worker! That's what every cop needs, a girl friend who's a social worker. Liberal as hell, I bet."

"To the left of Lenin," Grau replied, noting Tanti's eyebrows shoot up in surprise.

"Calm down, Mr. Conservative, I'm only kidding. About her political leanings, I mean. Her name is Julia and she's very nice. You'll meet her sooner or later, when we get some time to fuck off."

"Shit!" Tanti said, and braked hard to avoid the stopped car in front of him. "The damned rain must have screwed up the drive again. Look at that traffic. Bet you there's flooding under Gracie Mansion."

"Tony, maybe we'd be better off taking Second Avenue. It's getting pretty close to ten o'clock."

"Okay. I'll get off at the Ninety-sixth Street exit. By the way, who did you clear this meeting with?"

"No one."

Tanti looked over to his partner and said, "Are you nuts? You're gonna have a meeting with a Russian ambassador and you didn't tell anyone about it?" Tanti shook his head. "We'll both be walking a beat in Staten Island before this is over."

"Calm down. First off, the guy's not an ambassador. He's just some consular officer. Probably in charge of toilet paper. Second, Mr. By-the-Book, if I tried to get an okay for this I would have either been told 'No' or someone else would have gone instead of me—like maybe an inspector or a chief, which would have done us no good anyway."

"Is that how come you're so edgy over this dumb meeting?"

Grau was silent for a moment, then said, "I'm not really sure. This meeting with"—Grau took a piece of paper out of his jacket pocket and read—"Consular Officer Yuri

Andrapovich, is a shot in the dark. Look, Tony, let's go through what we have. Four dead bodies, most probably five. That guy Pinkin didn't wind up doing the butterfly stroke in the Hudson 'cause of some mugger. We got some unusual foreign currency and the plates to print them. Plus, of course, that scrap of paper we found in Gorkin's place. Did I mention I dropped that little gem off over at the lab, along with one of the bills I found in Saminov's apartment? My ten to your five says those pieces of paper will match, which will definitely connect Gorkin and Saminov." Grau paused long enough to glance at his steno pad. "And of course we got that floatplane coming and going, along with a guy being driven off in a car with license plates that come back to our newest homicide victim."

Tanti interrupted with, "Well, if it waddles like a duck, and quacks like a duck, then it must be a duck, no?"

"Who's talking about birds?"

Tanti raised his eyes in mock despair. "I mean, like you said, a good chunk of the evidence points to a Soviet connection. Also, you forgot to mention the fact that the last guy that got whacked out was also a Russian. And that he was bumped off right after you and I did our little act with him. So what the hell more do we need?"

"I'm on your side, pal. The problem is, I can't really tie anything together. I don't know who I'm looking for and I have only speculation as to the motive. Even assuming Gross knows enough about what's going on to give me the right scoop. Hey, watch out," Grau said, and pointed to the green-and-white exit sign ahead, "Ninety-sixth is coming up."

Grau could hear the clicking noise of the turn signal Tanti flicked on. The rain outside was coming down more evenly now and the sky looked lead gray. He cursed under his breath for forgetting to bring along his raincoat.

"Anyway, Tony, look what's likely to happen with this case. Two weeks ago the department was ready to storm the beaches. Full steam ahead and all that crap. But since then there's been so little movement that I can sense a backing off on their commitment. I'm convinced, 'cause I've seen it happen before, that if something doesn't break soon the whole case is gonna die a natural death. And I figure if all this evidence you and I have dug up is on the money, that points to a direct link with the Soviet government, and I'm the only one who can throw some shit in the game. I'm betting on the fact that the Soviets don't know what I know, or should I say, how little I know." Grau looked over at Tanti and with a shrug of his shoulders said, "So what's the harm if I lie a little?"

Tanti headed west on Seventy-second Street and stopped at a light by Third Avenue. The windshield wipers continued to beat their tattoo as the light turned green and Tanti moved the car forward with the rest of the slow-moving traffic.

"How did you manage to wangle this meeting so easily anyway?" Tanti asked, as he maneuvered from the right lane to the left.

"Good question. Beats me. I called up the Soviet Mission first thing when I got into the office today. Some woman answered the phone. Told her I wanted to talk to somebody regarding a possible problem that may have involved a criminal act on the part of a Soviet citizen. Hell, I was winging it. Anyway, she put me on to some guy, who put me on to some other guy, who switched me into the guy I told you about. Up to then, none of them seemed to give a rat's ass about me. I say hello to Andrapwhatever, tell him who I am and where I'm from and all of a sudden he's real friendly. Turn here, Tony."

"Right." Tanti turned left onto Lexington Avenue.

"I figured, the best I could hope for was to set up a meeting for next week. Figured they'd want to check me out. After all, all I was was a voice on the phone. But no, he would be delighted to see me at ten, he says." Grau looked at his watch. "Which it will be in three minutes. Shit. I didn't want to be late for this clown."

Tanti drove along Lexington Avenue until Sixty-seventh Street, then made another left turn. "Is this the place?" he asked Grau. Four uniformed policemen stood in front of the large mission near its gray wrought-iron fence. The metal security barrier was built thirty feet away from the entrance to the complex and ran along most of the length of the building line of the large light-colored brick structure.

"Yeah. Pull in to that hydrant on the side of the street

opposite the cops. By the way, smile. I've been told the FBI has the place covered with video."

"I'll try to show my good side," Tanti quipped and parked by the fire pump. "What's the drill, fearless leader?"

"You sit, I go," Grau replied, his hand on the door handle.

"What else the fuck is new," Tanti said.

"Calm down. I can screw this up enough by myself without your help." Grau opened the door a crack. Drops of rain hit his hand. "I don't know how long I'll be, but if it goes past lunch you better call in the cavalry to get me out."

As Grau slid from the car, Tanti yelled after him, "Sure, be a smart ass. But remember, once inside you're on Soviet territory. You think maybe we should start a war on your behalf?"

Grau slammed the door closed and waved good-bye. Tanti watched as his partner trotted up to the four uniformed officers, showed his shield and walked into the building. Tanti turned on the AM radio and waited.

Once past two sets of heavy glass doors, Grau found himself in a tastefully decorated vestibule. A pleasant-looking young woman sat at a small desk and asked, "May I help you?" There wasn't a trace of accent in her voice, Grau noted.

"Yes. I have an appointment with Mr. Andrapovich. Detective Grau."

The woman nodded her head, smiled, and touched an intercom switch on the desk. A female voice, speaking in rapid Russian, came from the little box. The receptionist replied in the same language and flicked off the machine. She said to Grau, "Please walk down the hallway and take the first elevator to your right to the tenth floor. Someone will be waiting to help you when you get there."

Grau said, "Thank you," and wandered off down the hall, found the elevator and pushed the button. A moment later an unsmiling man dressed in a dark gray suit stepped up to the same elevator. When the door opened he got in with Grau, ignoring the detective.

Grau hit ten and the other man touched the button for twelve and took a place at the rear of the car. As the elevator moved up Grau idly speculated on whether the guy was there to baby-sit him to the tenth floor.

The door opened and Grau stepped out. Another woman, older than the first, greeted him. "Detective Grau, this way, please."

She led the way down a thickly carpeted hallway where handsome pieces of furniture sat, mostly chairs and small tables. Large mirrors hung on the walls.

At one of the doors the woman stopped and gently knocked. A voice inside called out in English, "Come in."

The woman opened the door and indicated to Grau he should enter. She remained in the hallway.

"Mr. Grau, won't you have a seat?" Andrapovich said. He stood and motioned to a low couch that rested in front of his large desk.

Grau walked over, shook Andrapovich's offered hand and took the seat. He sank several inches into the soft material and realized that the other man, although certainly several inches shorter than Grau, towered over him from the other side of the desk. Grau smiled inwardly and thought, "The son of a bitch got the power chair."

"Now, how may I help you?" Andrapovich started.

Grau took a deep breath and began, "Well, let me get to the point. Several former Soviet citizens have been murdered over the last few weeks. I have reason to believe their deaths weren't coincidental."

Grau watched the other man as he spoke. First Andrapovich pursed his lips, touching them with the tips of his fingers which formed a tent. As Grau went deeper into his spiel the other man began to fidget. Seeing Andrapovich's discomfort emboldened the detective, and the make-believe story he unfolded became more and more imaginative.

Tanti woke with a start as Grau got back into the car, slamming the door after him. He rubbed his eyes and looked over to his partner, inquiring, "Well, how'd it go?"

"You want the five-cent answer or the ten-dollar answer?" Grau asked, as he wiped the rain from his forehead with a handkerchief.

"Both." Tanti glanced at his watch. "You were in there long enough. Nearly an hour."

"The short answer is, the guy inside said he doesn't know what I'm talking about. It's all bull and an American plot to interfere with our two countries rapprochement. His word, by the way."

Tanti started the car and asked, "Where to?"

"Home, James."

The car pulled away from the curb.

"But on the other hand, he seems to have asked most of the questions. At first I thought he was just trying to figure out where I was coming from. Then he asked about whom I had spoken to regarding this, how deeply the department was investigating the matter, where we planned to go from here. That kinda stuff."

At the corner of First Avenue, Tanti started to signal for a right turn.

"Go straight, Tony. We can pick up the drive from York Avenue."

The sound of the signal stopped and the car headed straight ahead.

"And besides that, he was either lying about something or he was a very nervous guy."

"How do you know?"

"Well, he tried to be cool and leave me with the impression that he had an I-don't-really-give-a-shit-about-this-interview attitude. If you didn't know what to look for you might not have spotted it. But I could tell, when I was laying some of my fantasy on him, he was getting real edgy. Like he had to work on controlling himself."

"I still don't get it, Jon. Be specific," Tanti said, as he noticed an overhead sign attached to the next traffic light which read FDR Drive North. The arrow pointed straight ahead.

"Like when I said I had reason to believe there was Soviet government involvement in the killings, it was like I had said Lenin wore dresses. He started to swallow hard. And he had to hold his hands together to keep them from jumping around."

Tanti entered the FDR and merged with the flow of traffic. He asked, "Did you mention the seaplane or that funny money you found in Saminov's apartment?"

"No way! I left the guy with the impression that all I had I got from sources within the local Russian community. I kept it real vague. The son of a bitch can read anything he likes into my little talk."

"What do you figure he's gonna do?"

Grau smiled. "I just gave him a taste today. He now knows I'm working on whatever it is he's up to, but he's not sure just what I have. My hunch tells me that whatever it is the Soviets want, that money and those plates are in the middle of it."

"So?"

Grau replied softly, "Tony, you ever fish?"

"A little. What's that got to do with this?"

"What you catch depends on the kind of bait you use. I got a couple of different types, and I want to use the best one for the job."

Chapter 20

From his office window Andrapovich looked down at the street below. The two policemen pulled away in their car and started to move down the block. He watched as his two surveillance vehicles fell in behind the Americans. His orders had been for a discreet observation.

He stepped back from the window and headed for his desk, then changed his mind. He began to pace back and forth on the Oriental carpet which took up most of the large office's floor space. It had been a gift from the grateful Afghan people, for the sacrifices Soviet troops had made to ensure the continued "freedom" of that country. Moving over to a metal file cabinet in the corner of the room,

Andrapovich inserted a small brass key into its top lock and pulled open the drawer.

He took out a manila folder, then closed and secured the drawer. Still standing by the cabinet he opened the folder and removed its contents. Slowly he went through each communication, rereading it for the tenth time, searching for some hidden bureaucratic message that he might have missed.

The mission to secure the counterfeit printing plates and any notes made on them had been extremely secret. Among those around him only he and Propkin knew what the situation was. Nor could he recall any previous undertaking he had been involved in that had been so carefully planned. It had been made clear to him from the start that a great deal was dependent on this job's successful outcome. One of the high-ranking ministers that had briefed him on the project, Anatoli Zybof, had even gone so far as to state that the economic future of the Soviet Union hung in the balance.

Andrapovich thought of the expression: For want of a nail the shoe was lost; for want of the shoe the horse was lost, until finally the kingdom was lost. How appropriate. For want of a few pieces of worthless colored paper, a handful of printing plates and the lives of a few traitors, billions of western dollars could be lost.

He glanced at the calendar on the wall. It was mid-July. In another few weeks the announcement of an incredible agreement between the Common Market countries and the Soviet Union would be made—unless word of the counterfeit currency and the plates to print it got out. That point was made very clear by Zybof.

Andrapovich sighed. With the first coded directive to begin the mission it had all seemed clear enough. He had ordered his people to initiate the surveillance of a number of former Soviet "parasites" who were now living in America, the possessors of what he sought. That part had been simple. Shortly after that he was directed to establish a secure area for the picking up of Propkin. His superiors' idea, to use a small floatplane for that part of the project, had been brilliant, Andrapovich reflected. Everything had been so carefully planned, Andrapovich had thought that the scheme was tidy and secure. There were the usual problems, of course. Propkin's silenced pistol had malfunctioned after he had shot Gorkin. But he had the other pistol with him and that solved that. Andrapovich hadn't thought much of it at the time. Perhaps he should have insisted Propkin use a different handgun for the next target. But that wouldn't have changed the major problem: the dead police officer.

It had been an accident. Of that Andrapovich was certain. That damn American policeman had simply gotten in the way. But was it the shooting of the officer that really concerned Andrapovich? No, he had to admit that it was the attitude of Propkin that truly concerned him. *He* was the loose cannon in the equation. A good man, to be sure. But Propkin had been around a long time, and he had become very independent. His premature and unauthorized early termination of Saminov had proven to be a very bad decision. Very bad indeed.

Andrapovich shook his head, another American adage—If anything can go wrong, it will—repeating itself in his mind.

Perhaps, Andrapovich reflected, he should have consulted with his superiors before he did what he did. But at that moment he felt there was no option but to get Propkin out the night immediately after the shooting. And he had had so little time to act.

Even so, his superiors couldn't possibly know, and Propkin certainly didn't sense, how intensely the Americans would feel about such an act. Nor was there any way to predict how much pressure might be brought to bear in the police attempt to solve the case. And this latest meeting with that damn American detective proved him to be correct.

It seemed to Andrapovich that every time he turned around, Grau was there. He was with Saminov just before the shooting. How the American detective had found Pinkin, Andrapovich couldn't even begin to guess. And then there were those meetings with Gross that Grau was seen at. How many more meetings had there been between the two that Andrapovich was not even aware of? And could Gross somehow have led Grau to Pinkin? After all, the expatriate Russian community was still relatively small. And perhaps Pinkin had talked.

Andrapovich reflected on his actions that day and still held to the belief that he had done the correct thing.

The final rendezvous for the pickup of the agent had taken hours of endless driving, to ensure there had been no surveillance of his car. There hadn't even been time to secure the upstate landing area, although he had little doubt about the location's safety.

And that was the end of it he had thought. With the agent safely out of the country there was no way the Americans could connect the deaths to his government. After a few weeks there would be other problems to occupy the minds of the local authorities. And perhaps, when the timing was determined to be suitable, the mission could be resumed. Andrapovich was certain he could still wrap up the matter before the deadline given him by his Moscow superiors.

Except that lying on his desk was an American newspaper, the *Novaya Pravda*. It was printed in Cyrillic, and its headlines proclaimed "Soviet Involvement in Recent Shootings." The circulation of the paper was at most a few thousand. As of yet no English-language paper had picked up on the small ethnic newspaper's speculations.

The article inside was hardly more than conjecture regarding the recent killings. The paper's reputation for rabid anti-Soviet editorializing probably was the reason none of the larger American papers took notice of its contents.

But, Andrapovich thought, as he shook his head and looked at the messages in his hands, someone in Moscow has probably bestowed upon that newspaper far more importance than it deserved. Messages had been flying back and forth between himself at the mission and Zybof in Moscow for days. He tried to explain to the other man why prudence would be the most appropriate course of action to take at the moment, and Zybof's reply was to demand action. The other man spoke of time constraints and his fear that the American newspapers would soon concern themselves with what was going on.

Andrapovich lay the folder down on top of the cabinet and walked over to the window. The wind-driven rain splattered against the pane, making a staccato sound. His mind went over the problem again and again. Why this Moscow hysteria to continue the mission now if it entailed so much risk? Just to eliminate a few uncooperative sleeper agents and pick up some currency and printing plates?

And now this American detective. If the mission had been suspended the policeman's visit would have meant little. But since Andrapovich had been ordered to proceed with the operation some plan to neutralize the man had to be formulated.

Andrapovich idly rubbed his finger against the pane of glass. Kill the American? Pointless. They would simply assign another one. Yet, a new man would have to start his investigation from scratch. Andrapovich shook his head. Too risky. Better yet, eliminate the American's connections, his source of information. That, Andrapovich reflected, made the most sense. Especially since his people knew who that connection was: Nick Gross. Once that job was done he could then concentrate on the conclusion of the original project.

Andrapovich walked over to his desk and pushed the intercom button. A woman answered, "Yes, Comrade Consul?"

"Send in Karpov."

"Yes, Comrade Consul."

"Hey, Jon," Tanti said, as they approached the Triborough Bridge, moving north on the FDR Drive. "You're gonna think I'm nuts, but I believe we got us a tail."

Grau suppressed his natural reflex to turn around to look for himself and asked, "How do you figure?"

"When we first pulled away from the embassy, I saw a dark blue American car with Jersey plates come around the block and fall in behind us. No big deal. But this guy has been half a dozen car lengths to our rear ever since. And I think there's another car with him. They keep trading off on the eyeball. You know, one will fall back a bit while the other takes the lead."

Grau thought for a moment. "Look, Tony, we'll never know for sure if they're following us while we're on the drive. Take the Triborough instead of the Willis. Keep to the speed limit and head for Queens. If they stay with us, take the Van Wyck south."

"Where are we taking them?"

"To Brooklyn, my boy. We'll really get their blood flowing!"

Andrapovich barked "Come in!" in response to the knock on the door. A tall, well-dressed, fair-complexioned man entered the office and stood at attention in front of Andrapovich's desk.

"Yes, Comrade Colonel?"

Andrapovich leaned back in his chair and said, "Stand at ease, Captain Karpov." The man assumed the military position of feet apart and hands behind his back. "Captain, I meant for you to relax, not stand as if on parade. Relax!"

Karpov still stood stiffly. He brought his hands around to his front, uncertain what to do with them. Finally he clasped them together. Andrapovich could see this was not working and quietly said, "Pull up a chair."

Karpov, now seated in front of Andrapovich, sat like a schoolboy in front of his teacher. Propkin would be so much better for this job, Andrapovich mused. But he dare not risk the older agent's unpredictable behavior again. And anyway, Karpov already knew what Gross looked like.

"Captain, how long have you been assigned here?"

"Eight months, Comrade Colonel."

"This is your first overseas assignment. Am I correct?"

"Yes, Comrade Colonel."

"Captain, up to this point you've been assigned mostly to running agents in the New York area. I now have something which is far more important for you to do. It would seem that some of the fleas which we shook from our coats in the Soviet Union are biting us here. You will eliminate one such flea. The one that you had reported on a few days ago, that you saw meet with the two American detectives."

"Understood, Comrade Colonel."

"Well?" Grau asked.

"Well what?"

"Well, are we still being followed?"

"Hell, yes, we're still being followed."

"What d'ya think, I got a score card? Where are they?"

"Behind us."

Grau rubbed his eyes with his hands and said, "Maybe it's me, world. Tony, could you be a little more explicit in your description of their approximate location?"

"Now the big words again! Every time you're pissed off at me you use the big words."

"Tony, where the fuck are they?"

"That's better. They're four and six cars behind us. There's a male-female team in the dark blue Chevy with the Jersey plates. The black Olds, with New York plates, has a young guy driving."

"Thank you."

"You're welcome. Now will you tell me where we're going?"

"Yes. Take the same exit like you did the last time we were in Brooklyn."

"Okay. That'll come up in about another two miles on the Belt Parkway. Then what?"

"I want to lose them around the same neighborhood we were in the last time. But, and this is important, I don't want them to know it was a deliberate shake."

Tanti nodded his head in understanding. "I see what you're up to. You're gonna make them think we're making a meet. And they won't have the foggiest idea who we're meeting with."

"Right, sport."

"Then what?"

"Then I hope they do something stupid. Remember, what we're doing now is just letting them nibble at the bait. I have an idea on how to set the hook real good later. Now watch out, here comes the exit."

Tanti swung off the Belt Parkway and drove south, down Ocean Parkway, the two surveillance cars staying discreetly behind to the extent the lack of midday traffic allowed.

"Tony, get us under the elevated train. The road construction there is brutal. Make a sharp left at the first available corner and about a quarter of the way into the block pull over at a pump. They'll have to either pass us, or at least keep on going along Brighton Beach Avenue. We'll back out and head in the opposite direction."

"Got ya."

The rainswept roadway was virtually deserted. Up ahead the massive tan concrete train station dominated their view. Tanti watched through his rearview mirror while the two vehicles that followed them struggled to keep some distance between themselves and the detective's car without being obvious. Tanti stopped at a red light at Brighton Beach Avenue and signaled for a left turn. Grau made a point of holding up his open note pad as if reading an address.

The light changed to green and Tanti eased into the turn, the two cars behind them in trail. The rough road surface allowed Tanti to slow to a crawl while Grau made a show of opening his window and craning his neck outside, to make it appear he was looking at the street signs.

At the first one-way street to the left, Tanti made the turn. It happened to be the block that Gorkin had lived on. The dark blue car stayed with them, while the black one kept moving along the boulevard. The maneuver, standard practice with a two-car surveillance team, permitted the second car to race up to the next left turn and down the street, to pick up the target vehicle and relieve the other surveillance unit.

Tanti's sudden move into an empty hydrant space caught the blue car by surprise. The car's driver had no option but to keep on going.

"Wait till he gets to the corner, Tony, then back out of here," Grau said, as he pointed to the numbers of the private homes on the block as he spoke, for the benefit of the surveillance team. From the corner of his eye he could see the female of the team. She had turned herself sideways in the seat and had begun to stroke the driver's hair, all the while watching the squad car.

"Now, Tony!"

Tanti put the car in reverse and at a quick but controlled speed moved the car back to the main avenue. He then backed into the lane of traffic and headed for Ocean Parkway.

"Tony, don't head north on Ocean, it's too empty. Make a left and head toward Coney Island. Take the service road and park," Grau said, now sitting sideways in the seat, to watch for the two tail cars.

Tanti made the left and entered the service road, parking a block from Brighton Beach Avenue. He shut the car's engine.

Grau said, "There goes one. He's heading north on Ocean."

"Want me to go?" Tanti asked.

"Hang on. There goes dark blue, heading west on Brighton. Tell you what. These clowns are going to be crisscrossing the area for a while. If we try to get back to the parkway now we could be screwed."

Grau thought silently for a moment. He snapped his fingers and said, "You know, this whole situation gives me an idea."

"So?"

"So when we lose these guys we're gonna go back to headquarters. I want to see a friend in TARU."

"Those are the guys that do heavy surveillance work. What do you have in mind?"

"Tony, you ever have a Nathan's hot dog?"

"Nope."

"Neither have I. We're overdue. Go straight ahead. The place is somewhere on Coney Island."

"Well, that gets my vote. I'm hungry from all this police work."

Karpov thumbed through the dossier on Gross, acutely aware of the silent Andrapovich who sat across the desk from him. As he read the man's history and the recent surveillance reports submitted by himself as well as other New York City-stationed KGB agents, he reflected on the nature of the assignment given him. During his career with the service he had never been called on to kill someone. Of course, as with all agents, that sort of thing was part of his training. But he knew that there was a big difference between working a theoretical exercise or firing a handgun at a paper target on a combat range and looking into a man's eyes and pulling a trigger. Karpov had this nagging doubt, an inner question about his ability to perform to the standard expected, and it troubled him.

His self-contemplation was broken by the ringing of one of the telephones on the desk. it was the line reserved for agents. Andrapovich picked it up.

"Yes?"

He listened for a moment, paused, then said, "I understand. We'll discuss the matter more fully when you get back."

Karpov noted that the man's face had become flushed.

Andrapovich whispered the word "Idiots," and returned the receiver to its cradle. He looked at Karpov.

"I had put a team out, to follow those American policemen that were here today, the ones you reported on. They drove from here to Brooklyn, right in the middle of the nest of troublemakers. Then the teams lost them."

"Comrade Colonel, did our people think they had been observed?"

Andrapovich shrugged. "From the little that they were able to say over the phone, I don't believe they had been. But, we'll have to wait until they get back here for their full debriefing. Comrade Captain, I have a feeling we are running out of time on this matter. There are too many things happening which are beyond my control. And after my conversation with that American detective I sense he is getting too close. It was clear to me that Mr. Grau had left much unsaid. This makes me very uneasy." Andrapovich stared at Karpov.

"Yes, Colonel?" Karpov said, swallowing involuntarily.

Andrapovich tapped on Gross's folder. "You have forty-eight hours to take care of this problem."

"Yes, Comrade Colonel."

Gross opened the apartment door and let the big man inside.

Speaking in Russian, he said, "Anton, come on in. The rest of us were just having some tea."

The man he called Anton greeted the three other guests who sat around a low glass table in the apartment's living room. The man took a seat on the thick couch. He could feel the warmth from the metal samovar on the table as it radiated heat from the tea inside. A glass was passed to him along with a bowl of sugar cubes and a plate of cookies. He helped himself.

There was some small talk, a big man they called Carl told a few jokes, then Gross began.

"Something is going on, gentlemen. I don't know what it is, but it's important enough that four people are dead."

"Five," the youngest man in the group said. "Remember the American policeman?"

Gross nodded. "Five. But that one I'm sure was not intentional. Three Russians I'm positive were murdered because they were Russians."

"Come now. You have no proof of this. At least give us some idea as to why you feel that way?" Carl asked and took a sip of hot tea.

Gross shrugged. "The last man that was killed I believe worked for the KGB. The other two I'm not certain about."

A man at the end of the table asked, "How are you so sure the last one—Pinkovsky was his name, right?—worked for the Soviet government?"

"I sent my wife over to his widow to comfort her. She told Bernice about strange meetings at odd hours her husband had. There were other things, but the bottom line is it's very likely Pinkovsky worked for them."

"I'm surprised the woman would say so much. Especially to a stranger," the youngest man offered.

"She was an American," Gross replied, as if that was all the answer needed.

Carl thought for a moment and said, "All right. So let's suppose that this fellow Pinkovsky was working for the KGB. So what? What does that have to do with us?"

Gross leaned forward and chose his words carefully.

"There are thousands of Russians living around us. Over the last fifteen years the Soviet Union has had an army of people abandon it for this country. I believe it's only a matter of time before they start exploiting this resource. Look at the money available here. The people. So I say we have to protect ourselves from this foreign intrusion."

The youngest man asked, "But what of the American policeman you made contact with? You've spoken to this

Detective Grau quite a few times already. Why not go back to him? Let the police handle the problem."

A white-haired man who sat next to Anton laughed softly and said, "The American police, really now! They can't protect themselves, much less other people. Why do you think vermin such as Gorkin made such an easy living here? By Soviet standards the Americans don't have police. Their enforcement people are so hampered by regulations and restrictions you'd think their rule books were written by some Kremlin bureaucrat. And their jails," the man shook his head in admiration. "If they had such places like that in the Soviet Union they'd use them for annual vacation leave."

The young man started to protest but Gross interrupted him. "Relax, everyone." He turned to the white-haired man and said, "You exaggerate the problem here. But there's enough truth in what you say so that I must agree the local police will be of no help in this matter."

Carl offered, "But, Nick, you still haven't told us what the problem is. Yes, some people have been killed. And maybe one worked for the Soviets. Now what? Who do we fight?"

Gross nodded. "A good point. At the moment we are groping in a fog. But if I am correct then it will be only a matter of time before whoever is responsible for the murders will be back. I suggest it would be less than prudent not to be ready for him."

The white-haired man nodded. "All right. That makes sense. What do you have in mind?"

Gross smiled and started to explain his plan.

Chapter 21

Karpov looked up, the arrival of night having made the overhead street light suddenly come alive. For the tenth time that day Karpov felt for the 9-mm pistol tucked under his left arm. Touching its warm metal form gave him a sense of control, like a child fondling a security blanket.

His stomach growled. Without conscious thought he rubbed it. This was the second day of the surveillance and he had been following Gross since early morning. Late yesterday Andrapovich had made it clear that this was to be the last day of stalking the other man. And because Karpov had found Gross's movements to be unpredictable he had not dared pause to eat. One stop would keep the man inside for an hour, the next two for a moment, the next, another hour.

Initially the agent had planned to eliminate Gross at the man's residence. But the presence of a large family and a seemingly endless stream of neighbors in and around the home spoke against that plan. So Karpov decided it would have to be done on the street.

The problem that Karpov had the day before and one he still faced was that Gross never seemed to frequent even the less busy parts of southern Brooklyn, let alone a deserted street.

Karpov looked about him and tried to get his bearings. The area seemed to be comprised of a mix of mostly small street-level shops and two- and three-story brick buildings. During the time he had followed Gross over the last two days he had been down many of the narrow and twisting tree-lined side streets, and had seen that the neighborhoods were composed mostly of neat single-family homes.

At the start of this day's surveillance he had been forced to leave his car some miles back, near where Gross lived. At the moment, Karpov had no idea where he was. He guessed they were about ten blocks in from where Sheepshead Bay must be, the small harbor incongruous in its location at the southern tip of one of the most populated cities in America.

Gross seemed to do everything on foot or by bus. Karpov was now uncertain whether they were heading back toward Gross's home or moving in the opposite direction. Ultimately, he reflected, it didn't matter. Karpov had decided that he would not have another opportunity, nor find a better time to deal with his target, than on these busy streets. He had waited for evening and the dying of the sun. When Gross leaves this last location, Karpov was going to walk up to him and end the matter, then disappear as best he could into the shadows.

The day's heat radiated from the brick wall he leaned against. Now, with the coming coolness of evening, the warmth felt good as it permeated his body. During the day he had had to move quickly to keep up with Gross and he had become overheated, even though he wore lightweight slacks and a summer jacket. But now, with the onset of night, a cool sea breeze moved against his perspiring face and body, giving him a chill.

Forty-five minutes earlier, Gross had gone into a small street-level lawyer's office. It sat across the way and mid block from where Karpov waited. The front of the office was constructed of a large pane of glass, but from the angle where Karpov stood it wasn't possible for him to see inside. He rubbed his moist palms against his dark gray slacks and took in a deep breath. The smell of salt air was strong. For some reason he didn't understand it made him wish the business was already over.

Karpov tensed on seeing Gross leave the location. The other man walked away from where Karpov stood, staying on the opposite side of the street. The agent sensed that the time was now right for the job to be done.

He moved quickly to the side of the street his target was

on and began to close the distance between them. Gross had come to a corner, his back to the hunter. Without looking around, Gross waited for a moment, and when the road was clear of traffic, crossed to the other side. Karpov took the opportunity to move to within fifty feet of the man. It was as if the whole world was composed only of the two of them. To Karpov, everyone else was a ghost, a transparent thing he need not be concerned with, could not even see.

People moved about on the sidewalk. Karpov ignored them. He sensed rather than saw some youngsters playing stick ball on the street. Cars that passed him made a dull, otherworldly sound, as they moved along the narrow roadway. All that mattered, all that had any significance, was the large form of the man now walking but twenty feet ahead, his white short-sleeve shirt almost luminous against the darkness of night. Without averting his gaze from Gross, like a cat about to pounce on a mouse, Karpov reached into his jacket and firmly grasped the butt of his pistol.

As Gross came up to another corner, Karpov broke the weapon free of its leather holster but kept it concealed under his jacket. His target, now but ten feet away, had turned sharply left down a small street. Karpov broke into a sprint, oblivious to all but his task, oblivious even to the sound of running feet behind him.

He moved quickly around the corner and started to take the weapon from under his coat. It had almost cleared the cloth when a large hand came from behind and grabbed his face. Powerful fingers pinched his nose and mouth shut. The next instant he felt a blade move deeply into his back. And again. And again. The powerful hand around Karpov's mouth keeping his screams to himself.

At the same moment Gross came from out of the shadows and moved to Karpov's front. One of Gross's arms locked onto the gun arm, while his other hand grabbed hold of the pistol. He twisted it against unyielding bone. A single shot rang out, the muzzle of the weapon pointed harmlessly into the air. Karpov didn't even feel his trigger finger snap in two as the pistol was bent back against his hand and taken from his grasp.

The world went dark for Karpov when the razor-sharp blade dug deep into his neck, and his throat was slit, ear to ear.

Gross and the big man moved with deliberation and without panic down the dark street. The body of Karpov lay in a growing pool of blood behind them. Gross passed an open galvanized garbage can. He nonchalantly dropped the dead man's pistol into its wide mouth, the other man tossing into it the five-inch-long dark-metal military dagger.

"Nick," the big man said in a matter-of-fact tone as he looked toward Gross, "your shirt is full of blood."

Without slowing Gross unbuttoned and removed the garment. He eyed the other man and said, "You should tidy up a bit yourself," and handed him his shirt. The big man wiped his arms and hands with it and tossed it into another open waste can as they walked.

Softly, between clenched teeth, Gross said, "Carl, I didn't think that the son of a bitch was going to screw around with us all day!"

"Well, there was no other way of knowing what his intentions were. He might have been assigned just to follow you. I'm not about to kill another man, even a KGB agent, unless he wants to hurt me or my friends."

The two men crossed the street and turned left, now at a more leisurely pace. Both could hear sirens wailing in the distance behind them. Gross, in his slacks and tee shirt, blended in with other area residents similarly dressed.

"Where'd you park the car?" Gross asked, as they crossed another small street. Around them, neighborhood residents sat on the stoops of their small brick homes or relaxed out in front on webbed garden chairs, chatting and enjoying the pleasant summer evening.

"Three more blocks and we'll be there. Let me tell you, it was a pain in the ass to have to run back to the car every time you went into some joint, then have to bring it to your next stop, then hustle back again to where you were so I could follow that KGB bastard."

"Well, what the hell did you expect we would do, take a damn cab after we killed the guy? And how the hell was

I supposed to know he was going to take two days to get up the balls to make his move?"

The jingle of an ice-cream truck bell sounded down the street as the two men crossed over into the next block.

"On the right, Nick," Carl said, and pointed to the dark green compact car that sat mid block.

The men got in, Carl on the driver's side. He started the auto but left it in park, took a deep breath and rolled his head in a circle to relax his muscles. He let the air out of his lungs with a loud sigh.

"Funny thing, Nick. That knife I used I carried all the time I served as an Israeli commando. Never used it once in combat. Still, I'm sorry I had to toss it away."

Gross shrugged. "We all gotta make sacrifices," he said dryly.

"And Nick, I can't believe how stupid that guy was. Two whole days and he never spotted me." He put the car in drive and started off.

Gross thought for a moment before speaking. "Yeah. The guy wasn't all that sharp. What I'm thinking about is, what's gonna happen when his people find out he's dead. It should get real interesting around here."

"You don't think they're gonna take the hint, huh?" Carl said, as he stopped for a red light.

"It'll go against their grain to walk away from this. You know that."

Carl nodded. He pulled the car alongside the curb near Gross's home. Gross put out his hand and the two men shook. Opening the car door a crack, he added, "You did a good night's work, my friend."

"Yes, we did," Carl said with a smile, as Gross got out of the car.

Chapter 22

The small gray commercial van, the head of an enormous housefly attached to its roof, pulled up to the apartment house's awninged entrance. It began to back into the only parking space in the area, vacant because it was next to a fire pump.

The building's maroon-uniformed doorman scurried out from the coolness of the lobby. He waved his hand at the trespasser and called, "Hey, you can't park there!"

The driver, a bearded young man in tan coveralls with the name Squish Exterminators imprinted on the back, didn't reply. He crawled out of the van, a large dark green canister of insecticide in his hand, and locked the door.

The doorman, his white hair frizzled by the heat of the day and the interruption in his routine, yelled, "Hey, you deaf? I said you can't park here."

Tan coveralls headed for the block's corner. Over his shoulder he said, "Relax, pop. I'll be back in five minutes," and disappeared down the avenue.

The doorman yelled after him, "The meter maids are gonna ticket you to death, asshole!"

Grau felt claustrophobic in the van's tight quarters. Detective Pete Mason, the TARU tech man, sat on a small seat in the middle of the darkened compartment. He looked through a periscope at the world outside.

"Jon, I got the camera lined up square on the mission's entrance. Hank did a real nice job of placing us."

The camera was supported by a metal bridge attached to

the periscope. Mason twisted the long lens of the 35-mm Nikon to focus on the front door.

"Yeah. Well, I just hope that doorman doesn't get too nosy."

Mason smiled and said, "He won't. In another minute or so something else will pop up to occupy his mind. I've been in this business for fourteen years and I've yet to take a burn while working in a surveillance van."

While the other detective set up his equipment, Grau took a quick peek from out of the black-curtained side window. The front of the mission was at a slight angle to the van. Anyone entering or leaving the building would be immediately identifiable. Although he knew no one could see inside the almost pitch-black body of the surveillance vehicle he still felt self-conscious and exposed. He retook his seat in the gloom.

As Mason hummed softly, apparently not hampered by the lack of illumination, intent upon his work, Grau looked around him. He had first seen the inside of the van in full light, so that now in the darkness he recognized the shadowy images and forms around him for what they were.

Inside the vehicle was an area of perhaps twelve by eight feet. The center of the space was taken up by the surveillance periscope. The raised fly head on the roof served to hide the small revolving mirror that brought the outside world to the camera.

There were conventional windows on all three sides of the van. They were each covered with matte-black cloth held in place by Velcro. Mason had told him that as long as no light was turned on inside the truck, Grau could look outside without fear of being observed.

The view to the front was blocked off by a large curtain of the same dark material that was used on the smaller windows. By pulling that cloth aside they could both see—and if need be, photograph—in that direction.

Although Grau hadn't looked in the various compartments that lined the inside of the vehicle, and which in most cases served double-duty as makeshift seats, Mason had explained some of their contents. There was night-vision equipment on board which would enable them to view and photograph scenes under the worst possible light conditions. Video cameras (Mason had had to remove one to set up the Nikon) could be attached to the periscope, as could a wide assortment of sophisticated conventional camera lenses.

To Grau's left was a small desk set in the side of the van. It was the unit's communication link. Besides every one of the dozens of frequencies allotted to the New York City Police Department, they could monitor and communicate with aircraft, watercraft and almost any federal agency in the area. A cellular telephone was bolted to the wall frame next to the desk, almost as an afterthought.

They had been in a rush to get to the mission, so Mason had had only a few moments' time to show Grau the other gadgets that were inside. Grau remembered there were controls to activate the outside lights, and one of the many switches worked the windshield wipers. Why, he couldn't guess and felt too foolish to ask.

Grau heard the soft whisper of the Nikon shutter click. He moved back to the window and opened the cloth a crack. Several men had departed the mission and were now on film.

"Jon, you better set yourself up so you're comfortable watching out that window. I don't know what the guy we're really after looks like, remember?"

"Right, Pete."

Grau reached around until he found a small seat and set it up so that he sat positioned with his face only a few inches from the glass. He looked down at the luminous dial of his watch. It was 11 A.M. Like Mason, Grau wore dungarees and an old shirt. And even though the van had its nearly silent air conditioner working, he dabbed beads of perspiration from his forehead. It was going to be a long day.

Joe Blakemore stared intently into the clear plastic face of the electric clock radio. He scratched his head, picked up the radio from its place on top of the metal file cabinet next to his desk, and turned it over in his hand, examining it closely.

Harry Purvis, noting Blakemore's less-than-normal behavior, looked up from his typewriter and asked, "Joe, what the fuck are you doing?"

"Looking for a hole," Blakemore replied, now prying with the point of a pencil at the knobs on the side of the small radio.

Purvis nodded his head and mumbled to no one in particular, "That explains it," and returned to his typing.

Blakemore placed the radio back atop the cabinet and again stared at its face.

"There he is again!" he blurted.

Without taking his eyes from the keys of his typewriter, Purvis asked, "The hole?"

"No. The cockroach that lives in the radio."

"Oh," Purvis said, shaking his head and returning to peck at the keys.

Blakemore watched while the little brown bug once more came to the front of the clockface. Its slender antennae moved sideways as it progressed to just before the sweep of the second hand.

"Harry," Blakemore asked, not moving his eyes from the insect, "why do you suppose this guy lives in our radio? I mean, there's nothing to eat inside, right? And getting in and out must be a bitch."

"Maybe he was born inside and now he can't get out," Purvis offered.

Blakemore turned to Purvis, a look of concern on his face. "You really think so, Harry?" he said, then turned back to watch the roach while it worked its way up from the numeral five to the numeral two on the clockface. "Maybe I should feed him?"

"Good idea," Purvis replied, and silently hoped that Blakemore's gun was unloaded, so that when the men with the straitjacket came there wouldn't be any trouble.

Just as the office began to again settle into a benign silence, Purvis heard a tumult move down the corridor and head toward the squad. As the racket grew nearer he could make out Grau's and Tanti's voices.

"I don't eat anything that's still breathing," Tanti exclaimed as he came through the door.

"They're not breathing. How many times do I have to tell you—hi, Joe, Harry—they're not breathing," Grau answered, fast on the heels of his partner.

"That's what you say. I heard about those places. They

eat live monkey brains with straws. Hey, Joe, would you eat live fish? That's what Jon wanted me to eat, live fish."

"What kind of live fish, Tony?" Blakemore asked, as he tried to stuff a piece of bread crust from his tuna sandwich into a tiny cooling hole on the backside of the radio.

"It's not live fish, dammit, it's raw fish," Grau loudly answered and tossed his brown briefcase on the desk next to Blakemore's. "Didn't anyone besides me ever eat raw fish in this place?"

"Do steamed clams count?" Purvis asked, trying to be helpful.

"See, you're a pervert," Tanti yelled. "I want a new partner."

Purvis looked up at the two men, one eyebrow raised.

Tanti said to Purvis, "We just finished showing some of Jon's monopoly money to this guy in a stamp and coin store . . ."

Grau interrupted with, "A numismatics shop."

"Yeah, like I said, a money store. And I realize we haven't eaten. Lunch. All I wanted was a little lunch. Hamburger. Or maybe a roast beef sandwich. Even egg salad. I don't care. Then this pervert says, 'How about live fish?' "

Grau broke in. "I said sushi. How about some sushi. You'd think I'd said let's eat snot."

"Hey, Joe," Tanti said, heading in the direction of Blakemore, who had just then succeeded in stuffing a substantial bread crumb into the radio, "what do you think about a guy that wants to eat that shit?"

Blakemore, busy with supplying food to his new pet, mumbled something unintelligible in response. Purvis, who had gone back to working on his report, explained, "Don't bother Joe, he's feeding a cockroach."

"Oh, right. Anyway, like I was saying . . ." Tanti stopped in mid-sentence and turned back to Blakemore. "A cockroach?"

At that moment the phone rang. Blakemore picked it up. He spoke for a moment, then cupped the mouthpiece in his hand.

"Jon, it's for you, on line three."

Grau went to his desk, lifted the receiver and punched the glowing button.

"Detective Grau, may I help you?" He listened for a moment, then said, "Hi, Nick." Another pause and then, "Right. About an hour? Sure, there shouldn't be any traffic midday. Same spot? Gotcha."

Grau hung up and looked over to Tanti, who was now involved in examining the squad roach that lived in the clock radio.

"Hey, galloping gourmet, we got to go to Brooklyn. That guy Nick has something for us." Grau grabbed his briefcase and headed for the door.

Tanti reluctantly moved away from the new diversion and caught up with Grau. As the two left the squad room, Purvis and Blakemore could hear Tanti say, "How about a nice Coney Island hot dog? I'll buy."

Tanti finished the second of the two Hershey bars he bought for his lunch and watched Grau walk back to the car from the direction of the boardwalk. He had wanted to accompany his partner to the meeting with Gross, but for some reason, the other man had been specific about seeing Grau alone today.

Tanti had kept the car running for its air-conditioning. The heat of the late July day, even near the shore, required more than open windows for comfort. Seemingly out of nowhere Grau appeared, came up to the passenger side and got in. A rush of warm air followed him.

He sat quietly for a moment, the fingers of his right hand tapping the dashboard.

"Well?" Tanti asked.

"Tony, my boy," Grau said, turning to his partner, "I think we musta' stirred the pot real good the other day."

"What happened?"

"It seems someone made a move on Gross last night."

"No shit? Was he hurt? Did they scare him off?"

Grau laughed softly. "No and no. Gross talked in riddles, but whatever happened yesterday evening, I think he got the better of the deal. Tony, head out to the Sixtieth Precinct. I want to check on an assault or maybe even a homicide from last night."

Tanti flicked the gear lever into drive and started off.

"Well, go on," he said, making a left turn onto Ocean Parkway so as to head south for the precinct.

"Gross said a Russian tried to kill him, but that he got away. He kinda winked when he said that. I figure maybe he hurt the guy. Which is good. Because if the man had to go for medical attention we may be able to ID him. And if he's still out there we can show Gross our array of mission photos. Who knows, we might get lucky."

"And what if we come up with a dead body? Maybe Gross got your man?"

"If we got us a corpse we'll find out plenty quick. Remember that thumbprint they got off the gun my shooter dumped?"

Tanti nodded and looked out his side window to take in the numerous small arcades that lined the streets of Coney Island. Dangling from their fronts were the gaudy cheap prizes that could be won (and almost all were worth less than the cost to play the game) by knocking down some pins or by tossing a small ring onto the neck of a bottle.

Grau interrupted Tanti's sightseeing by saying, "But even if the guy is alive, and we find him, if his print doesn't match the one on the gun then we're still looking for our man."

"Which means?"

"That we still got a lot of work to do. Which reminds me. When we get to the Six-Oh let's call Pete and see if the TARU pictures are ready."

Tanti nodded and turned the car right, past a traffic light in the middle of the island and drove under an elevated train.

"And if we find that the guy did work for the mission, then what?" Tanti asked his partner.

"Then? If he's dead, and the thumbprint shows it's our boy, it's all over for you and me. The politicians get to handle it. Beyond that I couldn't even begin to guess."

Tanti asked, "Did you mention that funny money you found to Gross?"

Grau shook his head. "No. There was no point in my doing that. Even if Gross had some idea what that currency was all about, the man in the numismatic shop already told us it was the genuine article. And that guy said he had only seen pictures of it. Anyway, if the latest guy isn't our man then I have an idea for getting our flying killer back, and the fewer people who know about the money, the better."

As Tanti turned into the precinct's block, he said, "Tell me more."

"He don't look so tough," Tanti said, as he held the photo up to better catch the light from the overhead fluorescent fixture. He quickly thumbed through the remaining dozen color shots of assorted men. They were the photos taken by Pete Mason of various people leaving the Soviet Mission.

He asked, "Who are these other clowns?"

Grau impatiently pressed on the elevator call button for the tenth time. The notoriously slow lift at One Police Plaza was made even slower by the fact that the two detectives had just come from the photo unit and were in the basement of the building.

Grau turned away from the elevator doors, unconsciously bargaining that if he didn't take notice the car would come sooner.

"They're nobody. At least nobody that I'm interested in. I had the tech man shoot a bunch of extra shots for fillers. So when we show our man's picture the background will be the same."

Tanti nodded. "My partner's a pretty smart guy."

The elevator door slid open. As the two walked into the empty car, Grau said, "Now let's head north and see if this was worth all the effort."

Fred the garage attendant gave the appearance that he never left his stool. Except this time, instead of a racing sheet, he had a copy of the *National Enquirer* stuck under his nose.

"Hey, Fred. Remember us?"

Fred peeked up from the paper and with furrowed brow eyed the two detectives. Then, with recognition showing on his face, said, "Oh, sure. How you doing?"

"Fine, just fine," Grau said. "Listen, Fred. Did that fella Pinkin ever come back to get the car?"

Fred screwed up his face and said, "Not for the last

week or so. To get the car, that is. He *did* come in once to pay for the spot."

Grau nodded and pulled the photos from his pocket. "Do me a favor and take a gander at these. Tell me if you recognize any of the people."

Fred looked past the detectives to the street. No one was around. He took the photos and said, "Can't be too careful these days."

Grau watched over the man's shoulder as he went through the pictures. Fred took the top one from the pack, examined it a moment, then put it in the back. He repeated the drill over and over. The fifth photo was the one of Andrapovich leaving the mission. Fred looked at it for a second and placed it to the rear with the others. He went through the twelve photos in less than thirty seconds and silently handed them back to Grau.

Grau sighed and put them in his pocket. "Didn't recognize anyone, huh?"

"Yeah, I did."

Grau, taken aback, asked, "Who?"

"Pinkin. The guy who comes for the car. He's in there." Fred replied, pointing to the pocket that held the photos.

Tanti looked at his partner for a moment then turned to Fred and asked, "Why didn't you say so?"

"Youse guys just wanted to know if I recognized anyone. Well, I did. Don't get sore."

Grau pulled the pictures out once more and held them out to the attendant. "It's okay, Fred, nobody's mad at you. Which one of these people is Pinkin?"

Fred took the pack and went directly to the picture of Andrapovich. He lifted it from the stack and handed it back to Grau. "This here is the guy. Like I said, he came in and paid this time. I ain't seen the other guy for a while."

"Fred," Tanti asked, "when we spoke with you last time you said you probably wouldn't even be able to recognize the guy. How'd you pick him out so quick?"

With a tone of exasperation Fred replied, "Because before you two guys asked about him he was just a customer. But now, when he came in to pay the two-fifty, I paid attention. Anyway, he was the Pinkin that always used to take out the car, except now he's the one who's paying. Stands to reason I'm gonna notice, don't it?''

Grau smiled, pocketed the photos and patted Fred on the shoulder. "You're absolutely right, Fred. It just stands to reason."

Andrapovich spoke harshly into the telephone.

"Captain, that a Soviet citizen was killed by New York hoodlums is an outrage. And then for the American police to ask to speak to his fellow workers and family is an insult! Do your job and catch the criminals that committed the crime. Until then, don't bother me further about this matter!"

Andrapovich slammed the telephone down on its cradle, sat back in his chair and shook his head. He then stood up and walked over to the window. The bright afternoon sun mocked his mood.

When he had been awakened yesterday evening with news of Karpov's death, that had been bad. The call from the police captain a moment ago, wanting to interview Karpov's associates in the mission was not good. But what had been worse was the response to Karpov's death from Moscow. The secure communication he had received early this morning, and which now sat decoded on his desk, dripped with sarcasm. It asked, "Was the task too much trouble for Andrapovich to handle?" and "If he couldn't manage to control a few refugees, we would be pleased to send someone to assist him." As with all the earlier messages he had gotten regarding this operation it was signed, Zybof.

Andrapovich smiled, the tight-lipped smile of a man who knew that his career was on the line, if it wasn't already too late. Andrapovich racked his brain for a way out of the predicament. Perhaps, he reasoned, he could demonstrate to them that he could still control the situation. Clearly he would have to do something that would both repair the damage done to the mission as well as to his professional reputation.

The only person Andrapovich believed had the experience to deal with this kind of a situation sat twiddling his thumbs on an intelligence-gathering fishing trawler two hundred miles out to sea.

Andrapovich shook his head. He dare not recall Propkin. From the agent's last actions and the tone of his communications from the trawler, he considered the man to be more of a liability than an asset. It would make a bad situation worse. No, he would have to come up with some other answer. Perhaps if he could somehow recover those damn plates and that currency it would placate Moscow.

Chapter 23

"Carl, what are you all excited about? You pulled me away from important business." Gross had to raise his voice to be heard over the train just arriving at the aboveground station at Ocean Parkway.

Carl looked past Gross, down the length of the virtually empty platform. It was 2 P.M., and except for a handful of people at the far end, the place was deserted.

"Nick, you know I wouldn't jerk you around just for nothing. Remember that guy that I sometimes do business with? Gromshkov. Dmitri Gromshkov. The printer?"

"Yeah? So?"

"Well, he's leaving."

Gross screwed up his face in disbelief and said, "For this, you pull me away from earning a living?"

"Nick, com'on, I'm not finished. Don't you remember that the guy used to be asshole buddies with Gorkin?"

Gross nodded and not-so-subtly glanced at his watch.

"And he used to hang out with Saminov. Hell, a couple of years ago he and Saminov even worked in the same print shop."

"No shit," Gross responded dryly. "If you may recall, Gromshkov and Gorkin came to America at the same time. And everyone knew Saminov. That hump was like a bad penny. So?"

Carl took a deep breath. "So he came to me this morning, all upset. He tells me people are following him. I mean, the guy was a wreck. He wanted to sell me some foreign currency. For American dollars. He tells me they're worth a lot of money. Or will be very shortly. But for now he'll sell them to me at a discount. Thirty cents on the dollar."

Carl became silent as another train rumbled into the station. After it took on most of the people standing about, it moved off noisily. The big man, seeing that they were alone, fished into his pocket and took out a single bill. He handed it to Gross.

"This is the valuable money? The damn thing looks like it came out of a Monopoly set."

"Nick, will you just shut up and listen. Here, look at this." Carl opened the copy of *The Wall Street Journal* he held under his arm. He quickly thumbed through the pages until he came to the section on foreign exchange rates. He pointed to the currency called ECU.

"See? Right here. The damn things are worth way more than what Gromshkov wanted for them. According to this they're more valuable than the dollar, unit for unit."

Gross folded his arms across his chest. "So there's got to be more to this story, right?"

"Nick, the guy was desperate. He was talking fast and scared. He said that this"—Carl held up the bill—"was what got Gorkin and Saminov killed."

Gross thought silently to himself for a moment. "You tell anyone else about this?"

The other man shook his head.

"Okay. Keep this to yourself. If Gromshkov was right, and Gorkin and Saminov were killed over this money, then you don't want to tell anyone else you got it. Understood?"

"Sure, Nick."

Gross patted the other man on the back and said, "I'll take it from here."

* * *

Grau pulled into the diner's lot and shut the engine. As he and Tanti made for the glass front door he spotted a telephone and said, "Tony, hang on one sec. Let me give the office a call."

Tanti nodded and continued to walk into the restaurant saying, "I'll get us a booth."

Grau made a police call to his detective squad. Since he was within city limits he could, by simply punching in the unit's telephone number plus a four-digit code, eliminate the need to put a quarter in the slot.

Blakemore picked up the phone and said, "Four-Seven Squad, may I help you?"

"Hi, Joe. It's Jon. Anything doing at the squad?"

"Nope. All quiet here. What can I do for you?"

"Nothing really. Any messages for me?"

"Yeah. That friend of yours from Brooklyn called. About a half an hour ago. Said it was important for you to give him a ring. But he made a point of telling me you were supposed to call from a public telephone. Very secret stuff apparently."

"Okay, what's the number?"

Gross nervously looked at his watch as he leaned against the brick wall next to the pay telephone. He wouldn't be able to wait for that detective to call much longer and now wasn't sure what he was going to do with this new information.

The nearby phone jingled softly, muffled by the noise on the street. Gross snatched it up.

"Hello?"

He sighed with relief when Grau answered, and asked, "Where are you calling from?"

Grau told him.

"Good. Listen, I got something to tell you."

Grau slid into the booth opposite Tanti. His partner was already mopping up the last of the ketchup on his plate with a french fried potato.

"So? What took you so long?"

A waitress came over. Before she could speak Grau said, "Just a Tab with lemon, please."

When she walked away he relayed the conversation he'd just had with Gross. Tanti sat quietly and listened, then asked, "What do you think it all means?"

Grau pursed his lips. He began by ticking off the various knowns, one by one.

"We got Gorkin dead. We don't know why. But in his wallet I found this real strange bill. We got Saminov dead. We don't know why, but we do know he had some funny money just like the kind Gorkin had and the plates to counterfeit them. We got this new guy, who's unloading this money and says it caused the death of the first two men. And this guy emigrated to this country with Gorkin, and Gross mentioned that the guy was in the printing business."

"You told me Saminov was also a printer."

"Yeah. That's right! Shit, I forgot all about that."

"So, Jon, it pieces together nicely. Two printers, counterfeit plates and Gorkin as the tie-in. You got a bunch of guys that were going to make funny money."

Grau nodded. "Which someone in the Soviet government is very upset about."

The waitress brought Grau's soft drink and placed the check in the middle of the table. Grau picked up the bill and got up.

"Tony, com'on. If my hunch is right, I have an idea for getting our killer to come out of the closet."

The phone used for routine calls rang. Andrapovich picked it up and barked, "Yes?" He listened for a moment then said, "Yes, I'll take the call."

"Detective Grau, what may I do for you?"

Andrapovich listened silently, then stood up from his chair. He chose his next words carefully.

"Detective, I have no interest in foreign currency. Even if it was found in a former Soviet citizen's residence. And unless the money to be counterfeited is rubles, it is no concern of mine. However, in the spirit of Soviet-American friendship if you would like me to send one of my experts over to you to examine the plates for you, I would be delighted to do so."

Andrapovich wiped his glistening forehead with the back of his hand. "I see. Then good day, Detective Grau."

He retook his seat and slammed his open hand on the top of his desk. Grau has the ECU notes and the printing plates. And that idiot says he doesn't know what they are! Andrapovich reflected that if he didn't know better he'd have thought that call was designed to taunt him.

It could be worse, he reflected. At least now he knew who had the damn plates and currency. Andrapovich smiled. Perhaps this chestnut could still be pulled from the fire.

Grau hung up the pay telephone and turned to his partner.

"I think he bought it."

"Jon, what the hell did you tell him? With all the traffic out here I couldn't understand a word you said."

"I played dumb and innocent. I told him that I had found the ECU notes and the plates to print up more in Saminov's apartment. You could feel the guy's tension after I said that. So at first he plays 'I don't give a shit.' Just like the last time I spoke with him. Only now he offers to help me identify the currency and plates."

"So?"

Grau smiled. "I declined."

Chapter 24

The desk officer, a sergeant, looked up from making his command log entries and eyed the big round-faced clock on the wall. The hands showed it was five minutes to three in the morning. It seemed like it had been an hour earlier when he had last looked at it and it had read twenty to three. He groaned softly and went back to making his entries.

To his left the T.S. Operator, (telephone switchboard operator) nodded out over his phone. Although the New York City Police Department hadn't had a telephone switchboard in any of its precincts for many decades, the designation of the assignment had never been changed.

The sergeant started to say something to the young officer about being more attentive. Then he reflected that he would love to do the same thing and so decided to ignore the infraction.

His main concern was that he'd be able to spot the new duty captain before the duty captain spotted his sleeping T.S. Operator, should the man decide to visit the Four-Seven Precinct. The sergeant had had such a visit two nights earlier and found the guy to be a real ball buster. The captain was the kind of supervisor who would pick on any infraction, no matter how petty, just to get on the sheet.

As he shuffled the papers about on the wide desk in a vain attempt to get them in order for the day-tour desk officer, he spotted an unmarked car as it pulled up to the front of the station house. The sergeant barked, "Clemmins!" to the T.S. Operator.

The rookie officer woke with a start in time to see someone in civilian clothes come up the steps of the precinct. He quickly got busy and started to fill in the fictitious rings that were required to be on his copy of that tour's roll call. They too were a custom from an earlier time, when officers didn't have portable radios and were required to call the switchboard at specified times during their tours. They were to use special police telephones identified by green lights atop the poles they were attached to. These phones had, in a bygone era, been situated around police posts throughout the city.

But, the officer mused, since no one in authority had the intestinal fortitude to remove the ancient regulation from the books, if it was rings they wanted then, rings they would have. He hurriedly scribbled to complete the last of the make-believe time entries before the stranger entered the precinct.

The man in civilian clothes came through the front door and walked confidently up to the desk. He was in his late twenties and in good shape. The sergeant didn't recognize him but decided he was not a likely candidate to be a police captain. Still, you never knew these days. The sergeant silently waited behind the desk for the stranger to tell him his business.

"Kepler, from borough Night Watch," the man said, flashing a gold detective shield in front of the desk officer. "Anyone up in the squad?"

The sergeant relaxed now that he knew there was only a detective in front of him.

"Are you serious? Who the hell would be up there at"—he glanced at the wall clock—"three o'clock in the morning?"

The detective put his shield away and started off toward the doors that lead upstairs. Over his shoulder he called, "No problem. One of the guys left something for me in the squad room."

Before the sergeant could say anything more, the other man had disappeared behind the stairwell door.

The sergeant shrugged and took his seat behind the desk. He had four more hours to go. God, he thought, how he hated midnights.

Just as he had settled into a satisfactory stupor, two uniformed officers came into the precinct. One, holding two brown sacks, headed directly for the lunchroom. His partner came up to the desk and announced, "Nickerson and Watson."

The sergeant nodded and looked over to the T.S. Operator, who reached over and wrote the two names into the interrupted patrol log. It was another log added to the dozen or so logs that made a busy desk officer's life so difficult. Anytime officers came in to or left the precinct it was a required task to fill it out. The job was supposed to be done by the desk officer, but more often than not, custom and necessity left the T.S. Operator to handle such matters.

That last entry reminded the sergeant it was one more thing the duty captain could catch him doing wrong.

He looked over at the T.S. Operator, nodded in the direction of the interrupted patrol log, and asked, "Did you get the name of that detective who went upstairs?" knowing full well the officer hadn't.

"Nope. I'll get it," the young officer replied, and wearily got up from his chair.

He walked up the stairs to the detective squad slowly, hoping that he'd meet the detective on his way down. At the second floor he turned right and headed for the squad room. The lights were on and as he entered he saw the detective rummaging through one of the desks.

He asked, his tired voice sounding more gruff than he intended, "What are you looking for?"

The detective looked up, an expression of surprise in his face. In his hands was a tightly wrapped brown paper package, which he tucked under one arm.

"Nothing. I mean, I got what I was supposed to pick up," he responded, and started for the doorway the officer stood in.

"Well, what's your name?" the officer asked, anxious to get back to his chair and perhaps a catnap.

The detective approached him, his right hand holding tightly to the package under his left arm. The young officer stared at the other man. There was something about him that wasn't quite right, something he couldn't put his finger on. He started to ask another question when the detective lashed out with his right arm, the knife edge of his hand smashing against the side of the officer's neck.

The uniformed officer silently crumbled to the floor. The body twitched for a few moments, made a gurgling sound, then lay still. The other man peeked over the body and down the short hallway. Seeing no one there he adjusted the weighty brown parcel under his arm. He glanced once more at the package, to reassure himself that the words written on its outside read "Saminov apartment."

Satisfied, he hastily walked to the exit.

Chapter 25

Grau and Tanti drove to the small road that led to the Special Operations Division back parking lot. Grau pulled into an available space and killed the engine. The inside of the car quickly turned warm from the ninety-degree humid August air. Grau opened his door and remained seated.

He said to Tanti, "You know, I'm glad they put together this operation, but I can't help but wonder if it was worth getting that young cop killed in the Four-Seven?"

"You on that kick again? Like I said before, how the hell could you know that was likely to happen? You had those phoney Saminov apartment packages planted in half a dozen places. Your desk, your house, my desk, hell, I've already forgotten where the rest are stashed. What were you going to do, put a guard on all of them?"

"Yeah, maybe you're right. But all I wanted to do was prove my point, that it was the plates and money the Soviets were after. I figured once they snatched one of my bogus packages I'd then have enough to go to our bosses and convince them to set something up a whole lot more sophisticated, so we could nail those suckers good. This other thing I hadn't anticipated at all."

Tanti glanced at his watch. They still had a few minutes before the meeting started. He asked, "How'd your get together go with the Chief of Detectives?"

"Real good. Everyone involved in this case from the bureau side was there. Marion Kaiser, her partner and their boss from the Six-Oh, of course, plus another group from Intel. Marion and they were assigned the other part of the operation, the surveillance of the mission and that sort of thing. You and I got this end of it."

"Who got the better deal?" Tanti asked.

"If you mean which team is more likely to come up with our killers, only time will tell."

Just as they got out of their car, the two men watched as a department helicopter settled down to land in the cleared area by the front of the main building. At the controls of the ship they recognized Lieutenant Mante and Mike Casson.

The two detectives moved away from the car and looked around them. Several emergency service trucks were parked nearby, along with several dozen private cars and marked and unmarked department autos.

"Ever been here before?" Tanti asked Grau, as they walked around to the front of the building.

"Nope."

Grau pushed open one of the four front glass doors. They stepped up to a large wooden precinctlike desk. With both their identification cards and shields held up for the desk sergeant to see, Grau started to ask where they were supposed to go. The sergeant stopped him, saying, "Meeting with SOD, right?" They both nodded. The sergeant continued, "Go around to my right, down the hall, make another right and go straight. There's already a bunch of people there. You can't miss it."

Tanti looked over to Grau who shrugged and both made off down the hallway to follow the sergeant's directions.

As they walked Tanti noticed that the units walls were liberally sprinkled with photos of ESU rescues and training exercises. He commented, "This place reminds me of the Aviation Unit. The walls are held up by pictures!"

Making the two right turns as directed they could see a gathering of blue uniforms at the end of the long hallway. As they approached the group Tanti felt conspicuous in his civilian clothes and was glad to see the two pilots from Aviation standing nearby. He took Grau by the arm and led him over to them.

"Hey, what's up, Mike, Lou?" Tanti said, shaking their hands.

Mante eyed the multitude of officers and said, "Let's

find some seats. From the look of this crowd it's gonna be standing room only."

The stark room was set up like a classroom, with folding metal chairs arrayed in rows from front to back. The blackboard at its front and the training posters hung from the walls gave the purpose of the place away. There was space for about two dozen people but from the number of men who stood about Grau guessed there were well over thirty people present. He recognized only two others besides the pilots. Standing up front, in conversation with an older, red-faced heavy-set officer who wore a gold detective's shield on his blue emergency services uniform, were Chief Kinney and Inspector Himmel.

"Hey, Lou," Grau said softly as he leaned over to Mante, "who's the guy up front talking to the chief and inspector?"

Mante smiled. "That's 'Fat Al' Hastings. He runs training for the unit. That guy has forgotten more about tactics and the training of people to do the crazy stuff ESU does than anyone else in this room will ever know. He's got over thirty years in the job, and, big belly or no, he can still rappel out of a helicopter with the best of them!"

Eyeing the uniformed personnel who stood around the room, Grau recognized the distinctive unit patches on the baseball-style caps and shirts that meant that besides Aviation, there were officers from ESU, Harbor and even a couple of men in the tan uniform of the Firearms and Tactics Section present.

Tanti poked Casson in the ribs and asked softly, "Those three guys over on the other side of the room, what unit they in?"

Casson looked at the group and smiled. "Harbor Unit."

"What the hell are they doing here?"

"Beats me. They're probably here as a backup. In case whatever happens happens in the waters around the city. Their boats are tough, steel-hulled ships. They're designed for work around the Hudson and East Rivers. Good for local stuff but too slow to travel for any distance."

Fat Al stood at the front of the room. "Gentlemen, may I have your attention!" From chief to cop the room fell silent as the big man took control.

"Would someone please close the door?"

An ESU cop complied and Fat Al continued.

"Gentlemen, some of you already have an idea why you're here. Most of you don't. Before I go into what this is all about I want every person here to understand the sensitive nature of the operation and the need for absolute security. That means no bullshitting about what we talk about here today—even with the other troops where you work when you get back to your commands. Understood?"

The men began to murmur among themselves. Casson leaned over and whispered in Tanti's ear, "This looks like a hot one!"

Tanti nodded but remained silent.

"All right, everyone, at ease! Here's what we have." The big officer proceeded to lay out for the assembled group the history and events of the last few weeks. He started with the landing of the seaplane and the first four homicides. Then he told about tracking the plane back to the trawler. To Grau and Tanti's surprise, Hastings began to talk about the death of Pinkin and the ID of Karpov. He ended with the murder of the officer at the Forty-Seventh Precinct. There was no mention of the counterfeit plates or the ECU notes.

Grau whispered to Mante, "Who the hell tells Fat Al all this stuff?"

"You'd be amazed what levels in the department that guy has access to," replied Mante.

Hastings continued with his briefing emphasizing their roles in the mission, and discussing the potential for the killer—probably in the seaplane—to return to complete his work.

"So, I've been given the job of coordinating this end of the operation. By the way, it now has the code name Open Arms, because that's how we'd like to greet these guys, if they decide to come back."

A few of the men in the room laughed. Hastings continued his briefing. "As you can all well understand, we're still dealing with a lot of variables we have no control over."

A tall, white-haired ESU sergeant stood up in the middle of the room and asked, "Like what, Al?"

"Well, Pat, for starters we have no guarantee their guy ever left this city. As I explained before, that is why several concurrent operations are being run. And even assuming they're going to bring their guy back the same way we believe they brought him in, we don't know if they're gonna insert their man the same *place* they did the last time. Otherwise, we'd just stake out the little airport they were last spotted at. But you understand, we don't have that kind of manpower. And anyway, for all we know, next time they could drop him off in a boat on Long Island, or along the Jersey shore somewhere. Then he could be picked up by a car and driven in for his next hit."

The same tall sergeant remained on his feet. "Then what do we do?"

"Nothing. We don't have enough resources to cover the whole Eastern seaboard. But still, we're trying to avoid putting all our eggs in one basket. That's why the helicopters are so important to the success of our end of the mission."

An anonymous voice from the middle of the crowd wisecracked, "Looks like a Chinese fire drill is coming off!"

Hastings barked, "Listen up! This is still no pie-in-the-sky operation. We figure that someone went to a lot of trouble to rig up a floatplane inside a fishing trawler. And remember, their landing site, as far as they know, has never been compromised."

A white-shield Harbor Unit officer broke in. "What if they use the floatplane but decide to land somewhere else?"

Fat Al raised his eyes to the ceiling, shook his head and said, "If you guys will shut up and give me a break, I'll explain what's been laid out." The room calmed down and the big officer continued. "As far as there being a possibility that they could land somewhere else, you're absolutely right. But we don't think that's gonna be a major problem. The trick to the success of our mission is as follows: We have the radar people over at Federal Aviation—the guys who first spotted the plane—alerted so that when it returns—if it returns—they'll immediately call the Aviation Unit." Hastings nodded in the direction of Mante and Casson.

"Once the AU is notified they'll fire up two of their ships.

A big twin-engine 412 and the faster 222. The 412 will head out to SOD headquarters and pick up eight ESU guys."

An emergency man raised his hand. Hastings nodded and the officer asked, "We going to be on standby here at headquarters or what? And how long is this thing going to go on?"

"Don't anticipate. No, you won't be standing by at headquarters. Where do you think we'd get the manpower to have a dozen of you clowns sit around on your asses and twiddle your thumbs for a couple of weeks? You'll be performing all your normal duties. If and when the whistle blows you'll rendezvous here. That's why I have three times the number of guys sitting in on this briefing than are needed for the operation. We don't know when it might be going down, so I had to cover all shifts. As far as how long this operation will continue, the people upstairs tell me they will be reviewing it every two weeks. That's the best info I can give you on that end of the deal."

Hastings looked around the room and asked, "Any more questions or may I continue?" The room remained silent.

"Okay. The guys who are going into the 412, once they're notified the operation is on, will have to hustle their butts to get here. Don't worry about your equipment. We'll have enough heavy vests and Mini-14's for everyone, plus some spares."

Tanti asked Casson, "What's a Mini-14?"

Grau overheard the question and answered, "It's an assault rifle. Same caliber as the military's M-16. They're both 5.56 millimeter."

"Oh," Tanti replied.

"Now, the best the guys at Aviation can estimate, if the feds spot that floatplane near the outer edge of their area of radar coverage"—Hastings turned to Mante and Casson—"the ship will be forty plus miles out. Right, fellas?"

Mante replied, "You got it, Al."

"Which will give us about twenty-five minutes to set up at this end. Lou, you want to say something about that?"

"Sure, Al," Mante said.

He stood and faced the group. "Understand, everyone, that the twenty-five minute guestimate is assuming a couple of things: Number one, that the radar operator picks up on the target immediately when it enters the edge of his screen. Number two, that the floatplane's ground speed is around ninety miles an hour."

An ESU officer raised his hand. Mante nodded in his direction.

"Lou, isn't that kinda slow for an airplane?"

Mante smiled. "Well, not really. You have to realize that the ship they're using is, in effect, a flying truck. It was designed as a general purpose work horse. Big, tough, but it'd never win the Kentucky Derby. In still air, with those fat floats under her belly, she's good for around one hundred miles an hour at normal cruise. If there's a breeze on her nose, she'll take a little longer to get here. If there's a wind on her tail, we'll have less time. Since she'll be traveling in a westerly direction, which is the direction the winds in this part of the country generally come out of, I'm assuming they'll be blowing about ten miles an hour on her nose. To be safe you can figure she'll take from an hour to an hour and twenty minutes to make the trip upstate, once she's spotted on radar."

Mante was about to take his seat when Hastings asked, "Lieutenant, would you mind explaining how you plan on deploying the two helicopters?"

Mante remained standing and continued, "Well, once we know the floatplane is in the air, the 412 will be immediately dispatched from Aviation base to pick up those officers assigned to meet her here. She'll probably be shut down once on the ground to wait for orders from Special Operations Division radio, who'll be talking with the 222. The 222 will have already been sent out and hopefully will be on the tail of the floatplane."

Mante stopped for a moment. Seeing there were no immediate questions, he continued, "In other words, the 412 will be the assault craft. As Officer Hastings explained, we still can't be sure where the floatplane is going to wind up."

A voice from the back spoke out. "Who's going in the 222?"

Mante responded, "Just two pilots plus a FLIR operator and one of the investigators working the case."

The same voice asked, "Lieutenant, what do you mean, one of the detectives is coming? Why?"

Hastings took the floor. "Because, Sergeant Chandler, this is a joint SOD/Bureau operation, and that's right from the top."

Some low moans could be heard from the group. Mante broke in and addressed the same sergeant, "And Norm, understand, if he gets to SOD headquarters on time, a detective is also going along on the 412."

Chandler said, "Lou, wait a second. What you're saying is we're gonna have to play nursemaid to some guys from the Bureau. Gimme a break."

Grau and Tanti looked at each other but remained silent.

"These guys"—Mante nodded in the direction of Grau and Tanti—"have busted their humps on this case. It's their collar. They're gonna be in on the action. End of discussion, clear?"

The room remained quiet and Mante went on. "Okay. Once the 222 tells us where the Soviet aircraft is landing, and that the landing is assured, the 412 will move in and put its personnel on the ground. The job of the guys from the 412 is to neutralize anyone they find around the landing area and capture the floatplane." Mante smiled and said, "Piece of cake, right?"

Another voice asked, "What if the guy in the floatplane says, 'Fuck you' and takes off again?"

Mante laughed and replied, "Good question. That depends. If they don't shoot at you, you can't shoot at them. That's the law. If the ship does get airborne again the 412 will try to force it down. By all legal means."

A murmur could be heard in the room. Mante waved his hand and said, "Don't ask me how, 'cause I sure as hell don't know!"

"Thank you, lieutenant," Hastings said. Mante sat down and the big man continued. "By the way, the 222 will also be responsible for pursuing any ground vehicles that might try to get away. Remember, people, it'll have the FLIR equipment on board. So even if a car were to shut off its lights the FLIR would easily pick up its heat signature."

An officer wearing Harbor insignia raised his hand. Hastings nodded in his direction.

"What about us?"

Hastings replied, "We don't know, Sam. If the whole

The Murder of Old Comrades

ball of wax goes down around the waterways of the city we'll sure as hell need Harbor. And maybe even scuba, if something sinks."

"As long as what sinks ain't a helicopter!" Casson whispered loudly into Tanti's ear.

"How do we know the guys at the radar screens are going to stay interested in this?" the tall ESU sergeant asked.

Mante stood up to take the question. "We told them the floatplane is part of a narcotics smuggling operation. Bigtime stuff. We really got the boys all excited. We make it our business to call them at least once an evening, just to say 'Hi!' and remind them what they're supposed to be looking for. They'll do all right."

"Now," Hastings said, "before I get into the specifics of who's doing what and who's going where, has everyone qualified this cycle up at the Outdoor Range with the Heavy Weapons people? This operation could get nasty and we don't want no lawyer Monday morning quarterbacking the department about lack of adequate training if someone gets shot." He glanced over at the officers wearing the tan Firearms Instructors uniforms.

Grau and Tanti noted that no one around them indicated a need for training. Then, as if everyone in the room had the same thought, all eyes were on the two men in civilian clothes.

Hastings asked, "Have either of you two been trained in heavy weapons?"

Grau answered, "I used to be a department Firearms Instructor, so I'm familiar with the guns. But officially I haven't qualified in years. Tony here will also need some training."

Hastings again looked over to the Firearms Instuctors. One of the men responded with, "Al, don't worry about it." Then directing himself to Grau and Tanti, he said, "You two guys just hang out after the meeting. We'll work something out."

"Okay, enough screwing around. Stand by to copy down your assignments!" Hastings barked. To a man, paper appeared and everyone in the room prepared to write.

* * *

Grau turned to Tanti as they stood outside SOD headquarters and watched the departing cars. He said, "Well, partner, what do you think?"

"I don't know. There seems to be a lotta 'ifs' in our part of this operation."

"Yeah. But I can't see many other options. We cover one base, Marion and her crew cover the other. The only other thing we got going for our end is the stakeout of Pinkin's car. Assuming we haven't burned it with our nosing around, and assuming it's the car that'll be used to pick up our killer from the floatplane, same as the last time the guy was dropped off. And, like Hastings said, we can't know for sure where the floatplane might land. If and when it comes back."

Grau waved to Mante and Casson who were preparing to get into their helicopter.

"Tony, does it bother you, your being assigned to wait at the Aviation Unit?"

Tanti hesitated, then said, "No, not really. It is a pain in the butt to get there from where I live. But on the other hand, if anything goes down while I'm on duty I've got a guaranteed front-row seat."

Just then the two Firearms Instructors strolled up to Tanti and Grau. One of the instructors, the taller of the two, who sported a moustache and jet-black hair, said, "Hi. I'm Lenny Francone. This is my partner, Al Ramirez."

Grau and Tanti introduced themselves.

Francone asked, "When do you guys want to come up to the range for training?"

Tanti shrugged. Grau said, "Lenny, I don't think we have any choice on this. As of tonight we're all on standby. I guess it has to be done first thing tomorrow."

"No problem," Francone replied. "Be at Rodman's Neck around 0800. Come to Building Five."

Grau and Tanti gave the thumbs up sign and the two instructors walked off to their car.

"Well, no matter how you cut it, Tony, the next couple of weeks should be interesting."

"No doubt in my mind. By the way," Tanti said, rubbing his stomach, "I'm hungry. How about a hamburger and some fries?"

Chapter 26

Tanti yawned loudly as Grau drove them through the main gate of the Outdoor Range at Rodman's Neck, a fifty-acre peninsula at the eastern edge of the Bronx jutting into Long Island Sound where the majority of firearms training was done for the department.

Grau stopped the car just long enough to identify himself and Tanti to the officer on security duty at the gate, and continued down the narrow road. To their right, the parking lot set aside for officers reporting to the range for the day's training had begun to fill up.

Grau could see that although it was only 7 A.M. the only remaining spaces were well to the back. Instead of turning into the lot he continued straight along the road.

"Hey," Tanti said, his head swiveling about. "Where the hell you taking us?"

"Trust me," Grau replied. He turned left past the old green mess-hall building and followed a wide road which led in the direction of a row of World War Two-vintage temporary metal huts used for much of the unit's training. The muffled sound of revolvers discharging could be heard to their right. Already the first relay of the day was on the line, firing the initial segment of their day's training program. The two men could see a thin white fog of smoke rise from shooters' guns and float above the range overhang, moving with the gentle morning off-shore breeze.

Grau slowly drove past a set of old wooden police horses. Nailed to one, a sign read, DO NOT ENTER-FIREARMS INSTRUCTORS ONLY. Grau ignored it and moved on to find a space in the lot where the range's personnel parked.

"You're gonna get us in trouble," Tanti said, as the two stepped from the car.

"Hey, relax. Remember, I used to work in this place." Grau replied with a wave of his hand, noting that for once his partner's ratty blue jeans and old khaki army shirt fit in with their setting.

"Yeah, I'll keep that in mind when they come out to tar and feather us."

Grau shook his head. "My partner, the wimp. Come on, I'll let you buy me some coffee."

"Thank you."

"Don't mention it."

The two men headed for the old green wood mess hall they had passed earlier. Other officers walked by them, moving to and from the different training areas of the facility. A line of officers stretched fifty feet from the mouth of the building's entrance, queued up to be signed in for the day's training. While they watched, more officers fell in at the rear of the line.

Tanti looked at his watch and said, "Jeez, it's only seven ten. There must be a hundred cops already lined up."

Grau nodded. "Yeah, sometimes they have to handle over three hundred guys a day in this place. And that doesn't count all the specialized training they do. It can get really crazy here."

The two men worked their way past the row of sleepy officers and into the mess hall proper. They could see that from the entrance door to the sign-in room on the other side of the building was another fifty-foot-long line of waiting people. Tanti broke away from Grau and walked up to the food concession counter. He fished out some old dollar bills from his pocket and bought two coffees and some buttered rolls.

Working his way back to Grau, he asked, "Where to?"

Grau took the food and said, "Come on, there's a guy I want you to meet," and led Tanti back outside.

Directly ahead of them, fifty feet away, sat a long white windowless cinder-block building. At one of its narrow ends was a dutch door with a top half of old plexiglass. Tacked to its wood bottom a sign read Gunsmith. Below that was drawn a brace of pistols.

Grau stepped up to the window. He had to crane his neck to see inside, the ancient plexiglass being too scratched and filled with signs and stickers to see through. A heavy-set officer with thick moustache came to the door and perfunctorily put out a weapon repair sheet for Grau to fill in.

"No, no. I'm looking for Kapinsky."

The other officer turned his head over his shoulder and yelled out the man's name. A moment later Grau could see Kapinsky, wearing jeans and a blue work shirt, a silver police officer's shield pinned incongruously on its front, walking from the back of the building.

Grau yelled, "Hey, Ira, you dopey fuck, haven't they caught on to your act yet?"

Kapinsky recognized the voice of his tormenter and replied, "Well, if it isn't that son of a bitch, defective slime," unlocked the door and let Grau and Tanti in.

Grau said, "Tony, this old bastard is Ira Kapinsky, the worst gunsmith the department has."

Kapinsky shook Tanti's hand. Shaking his head in mock commiseration, he asked, "Listen kid, you work with this clown?"

Tanti smiled and nodded his head. Around him in the small crowded room were several other officers dressed like Kapinsky. They were busy at work on the day's batch of defective service and off-duty revolvers that other instructors had discovered during the shooters' check-in.

The walls were filled with assorted weapons in various stages of repair. Benches, which ran along either side of the room, held various gunsmith tools. A lathe was set off to one side.

"Come on, let's go to the back," Kapinsky said, and led the way. As they walked they passed padlocked cages filled with hundreds of assorted firearms. Beyond the cages in a large room were stacks of cased ammunition. Some of the piles reached up to over the height of a man. Other officers stood by a door set into the side of the room and handed out small black cloth bags to the shooter. Each contained sufficient service and target ammunition for the day's training.

At the rear of the room, pressed into the far corner, were two workbenches. Each was surrounded by stacks of blue and tan boxes which contained new revolvers waiting to be tested before issue to the members of the force. One of the blue boxes lay open on Kapinsky's bench, the gun inside partially concealed by a brown protective paper covering.

The men sat down on stools. Tanti pointed to the open box and asked, "Ira, are these the new guns we're getting?"

"Sure are," Kapinsky said. He reached over and removed the dull gray weapon from its box and handed it to Tanti.

"Hey, it's not blued. And there's no hammer spur."

Kapinsky turned to Grau. "Hey, Jon, this kid is some rocket scientist." Looking over to Tanti, he said, "Play your cards right, fella, and maybe we can get you your job back at the car wash."

"Gimme a break," Tanti protested. "Jon, protect me."

Grau laughed and said, "Let me see the gun," taking it from Tanti's hands.

He opened the weapon's cylinder to ensure the gun was unloaded. Grau tried the revolver's action and examined the outside finish of the piece.

"Tony," he said, "these guns are made of stainless steel, that's why they're gray metal and not blued. They don't need any coating for rust protection like regular steel guns do."

Tanti nodded and watched his partner run through a mechanical function check of the weapon. Grau tested the lock up of the cylinder and the freedom of movement of the various parts of the gun.

"And, as you noticed, the gun has no hammer spur. That's because it can't be cocked. Only a long hard pull on the trigger will set her off."

"How come?" Tanti asked.

Kapinsky laughed. "Because of all the dopey cops that put holes in their legs, and their partners' asses, and their uniform lockers is why not!"

"Oh," Tanti replied, thinking about the unreported hole in the precinct bathroom wall that got there one boring midnight tour when he had fiddled with his service revolver while sitting on the john.

"Ira, tell Tony about the telephones," Grau said, as he

stepped over to the bench and returned the revolver to its box.

Kapinsky grinned and said to Tanti, "You know the two public telephone booths? The ones between here and the mess hall?"

"Sure."

"Well, I got the number to the phones. So when it calms down in this place I go over to the gun check-in room up at the front."

"Where we came in?" Tanti asked.

"Right. Anyway, I already put a ladder or something against one of the booths, see?"

"So?"

"So, when I see someone walking by, I dial one of the numbers real quick. The cop picks up the phone and I say, real professional like, 'Hello. Can you confirm that this is the police department's firearms range?' Usually the cop will say, 'yeah,' or 'sure,' or somethin' like that. So then I say, 'Listen, could you do me a favor? The lean meter at our central office is showing a tilt to one of the booths. Is there anything laying against them that you can see?' So the guy will say, 'Yeah, there's a ladder,' and I'll say, 'Oh, great. Could you do me a favor and pull it away from the booth?' "

Tanti looked over to Grau. "This is bullshit, right?"

"Just listen to the story," Grau said, grinning, his back to the workbench.

Kapinsky continued, "The guy will pull the ladder off, and before he can say anything, I'd say, 'You got it! The meter went back to zero!' and I'd thank the guy a bunch and hang up. Let me tell you, you never seen such confused people in all your life after one of my calls!"

"Jon, this man is dangerous," Tanti said. "What else do you guys do for fun around here?"

Kapinsky looked over to Grau. "Should I tell him about the time we 'executed' a guy in here?"

"Nah, we got no more time," Grau said, and glanced at his watch.

Tanti moaned in protest, but Grau said, "Enough of this crap, Tony," and tossed his empty coffee cup into a metal waste basket. "Let's let Ira earn his paycheck and you and me head out to Heavy Weapons, it's ten to eight. Which reminds me, Ira, I forgot where Lenny Francone told us to report. Where the hell do we go?"

"Building Five. They moved the program since you were giving the course. And now they also have guys who know what the hell they're doing."

"Thanks," Grau said, giving Kapinsky the bird.

"Anyway," Kapinsky went on, "you two clowns run along and watch out you don't shoot each other in the rear ends."

Kapinsky saw the two to the front door. Once the pair was outside they walked along a narrow concrete path that led them past half a dozen metal buildings. All were identical in appearance. Each was painted in a silver metallic color, with dark green trim, and sat on a fifty by twenty-five foot concrete slab.

The building with the number 5 painted on the outside was near the end of the row. With a rusty screech Grau opened the dark green metal door. Already inside and seated on metal folding chairs were a number of officers dressed in old civilian clothes. Most were drinking coffee and reading the morning paper. Off to their left was a small office where two tan uniformed instructors were opening cases of ammunition in preparation for the day's shooting. Grau and Tanti immediately recognized them from the SOD briefing the day before.

Grau stuck his head in the office's doorway and said, "Hi. Where do we sign in?"

Francone looked up from making entries in a large black ledger and said, "Oh, hi. Right, the two guys from yesterday. Sign in here." He pointed to another thick ledger book and, while Grau and Tanti filled in the captions, continued speaking. "Since you guys only need training in the Ruger Mini-14 rifle, I've worked it out so that part of the course will be given first thing this morning."

Tanti looked around the little room at the assortment of weapons that lined the inside of the open metal cabinets. He saw pump-action shotguns of various barrel lengths, submachine guns, long- and short-barreled rifles with telescopic sights and other weapons he didn't recognize.

The Murder of Old Comrades

"That's all we're gonna get trained in?" he asked Francone, sounding like a kid in a toy store that had just been told he could only have one.

"That's all we got time to train you in. Give us two weeks and you can qualify with all of them," Ramirez replied.

Grau patted Tanti on the shoulder and said, "Okay, Annie Oakley, let's sit down before you embarrass me some more."

They took seats in the middle row of chairs among the ten other officers in the room. One of them, a woman with short red hair and freckles, was seated in the second row, chatting amiably with a male officer on her left. A few more men wandered in, signed the log, and took seats in the rear.

Francone stepped to the front of the classroom. In his right hand he held a wood-stocked rifle, its barrel painted red. In his left hand he had a number of rifle magazines, which he placed on a table set off to his right.

"Good morning, gentlemen and lady." The woman stuck her tongue out at him and smiled.

"Hey, sarge, that's no way to treat your instructor," he quipped, smiling back.

"My name is Lenny Francone and my partner is Al Ramirez. All of you signed in, right?"

Everyone nodded his or her head.

"Okay. The first weapon we'll be training with today is the Ruger Mini-14 assault rifle. Since there are officers here who are receiving instruction in this weapon for the first time, I'm going to start the session by going over the basics. For the rest, it'll be a good review."

Tanti fidgeted a bit in his seat and looked around. The rest of the officers in the room, including Grau, seemed comfortable and relaxed. It occurred to him that Francone's little speech had been meant solely for his benefit.

Francone continued with his lecture. He demonstrated the basic parts of the firearm, its safe handling and proper functioning. Tanti couldn't believe how much information had to be imparted for something that appeared to be as simple as a rifle. Yet the instructor spoke for several hours, giving the officers only a few ten minute breaks. Lecturing quickly, Francone stopped just long enough to ensure that his students understood each particular point he was explaining.

Finally, after speaking on the fundamentals of marksmanship, Francone stepped from the front of the room. His partner, Ramirez, handed out green and white boxes of ammunition, along with empty twenty-round magazines.

Ramirez took charge of the class. Speaking with a slight Latin accent, he directed everyone to load up their magazines. The officers chatted among themselves as they inspected each round of ammunition for defects, then inserted them into the spring-loaded rectangles of metal.

"Hey, Jon, what do we do from here?" Tanti asked, loading up his third and final twenty-round magazine.

"We go to the range to make some noise," Grau replied, securing his equipment in one of the ubiquitous little black cloth bags that had been issued to him and the rest of the officers.

From the rear of the room Francone spoke up, "Everyone come on up and get a weapon, ear and eye protection."

The legs of the metal chairs grated against the concrete floor as the officers got on their feet and lined up at the rear. Each was given a rifle, which was slung over the officer's shoulder, a pair of plastic goggles and a bulbous set of sound barriers.

Once all the officers were ready, everyone stepped outside. Ramirez and Francone walked to the head of the group. Each of the instructors carried a rifle in the unlikely event one of the student's weapons went out of service. Francone also supported on his shoulder a cardboard box full of other equipment they would need once out at the range.

The band moved out toward the Heavy Weapons range. It was situated near the end of a series of ranges separated by high berms of earth, each designed for a specific training or testing purpose.

Grau and Tanti moved along in the middle of the pack. Tanti found he had to continually adjust the rifle on his shoulder so that it wouldn't slip off. His goggles and sound barriers were held in his left hand, the black bag in the right. The late July day had become warm and he wished he had left his old army field jacket back in the classroom.

The Murder of Old Comrades

Coming up to "Frank" range the officers walked under its overhang, designed to protect the shooters from the weather and muffle the sound of their weapons from others in the area. Francone stepped out beyond the concrete strip called the line. It was that part of the range no one went beyond except under the direction of an instructor. He turned and faced the group.

"Listen up!" he barked. "Place your weapons on the racks in the rear, ground your ammo bags and step up to the line."

The officers did as instructed, putting the rifles in the wooden holders, their muzzles pointed up. That done, the group stepped back to the edge of the concrete strip. Ramirez had already taken two large empty quart-size tin cans, both open at the top, and placed them on the concrete walkway behind Francone. He had filled one of the cans with water from a plastic gallon jug, and remained standing next to it.

Francone, a rifle in his hand, spoke. "I already explained about the high velocity of this gun's bullet and how it gets it effectiveness from speed rather than size. Well, words are one thing, a visual demonstration is another. Al is going to put a coin under the can with the water in it." With that, Ramirez showed the group a nickel he held between his fingers, then bent down and picked up the can of water, placing the coin underneath. He then took the empty can and put it on top of the full one.

Francone put his protective glasses and sound barriers in place, saying, "Everyone, eyes and ears on."

Looking about to make sure the officers had complied and that Ramirez was behind him, Francone took a single rifle round from his pocket. He placed it in the gun's chamber, pulled back on the open bolt, and let it go, permitting it to run home. He shouldered the weapon, aiming for the can filled with water. The rifle cracked and the can burst like a grenade, the empty can on top flying twenty feet into the air.

Ramirez retrieved the bottom can and handed it to Francone, who held it up for the others to see. One of its sides had been split wide open by the force of the impact.

An officer standing on the line called out, "Com'on Lenny, that's just the seam that gave way."

Francone smiled. He turned the can around, to show the side opposite the open gash. Pointing to the line with his finger where the can's edges were sealed, he said, "Nope. We put the seam on the opposite side from where the bullet entered. What you witnessed was the power of hydrostatic shock. And check this out."

Turning the can over so that the bottom was visible to the group, he stepped closer to the officers. They moved in on Francone and could see a perfect negative impression of the face of the nickel that had been placed under the can. A few of the officers whistled, impressed with the demonstration.

"Understand this. The human body is made up of about ninety percent water. What you saw happen to this can is, practically speaking, what happens to a person when they're struck with such a round."

Behind him, while Francone was talking, Ramirez placed a standard gray-colored cinder building block on a small table. Behind it was a paper combat target, depicting a man with a gun. Having finished setting up for the demonstration, Ramirez returned to a place behind the line.

Francone, seeing Ramirez in front of him, said, "Thanks, Al. Okay, anyone here believe they could safely take cover behind a cinder block wall if someone were using one of these babies against you?" None of the officers offered an opinion.

"Well, then, let's find out for sure. Ears and eyes, everyone."

Francone inserted a twenty-round magazine into his weapon and chambered a round. Taking aim on the block, he rapidly fired the weapon. The first few rounds badly pockmarked the gray block's surface. By the fifth and sixth round the heavy piece of building material had begun to come apart. When half the magazine had been fired, the block had disintegrated into numerous small pieces. The paper target behind it was blasted full of bullet holes as well as irregularly shaped gashes made by pieces of the block carried along with the force of the slugs.

After the demonstration, Francone ran the group through

a normal series of training exercises. Besides their firing from various shooting positions, he had the officers shoot while moving forward, the weapons held at their front, across the chest. One- and two-round drills were included, as was the clearing of malfunctions.

Tanti took to the weapon from the start. As the training progressed the gun's initial strangeness quickly gave way to familiarity, then comfort.

Once the range period ended, the shooters policed up the brass. The paper targets were put in empty fifty-five gallon drums, which were used as garbage receptacles. Finished policing the area, the officers slung the weapons over their shoulders and headed back to the classroom.

Grau and Tanti let the group walk ahead of them. Grau asked, "Well, how do you like the rifle?"

"I like it a lot. You once said this is the same caliber our military uses. What do the Russians use?"

Grau thought for a moment. "They use a couple of different calibers. The newest one they have is basically the same as ours. Small bullet, high velocity."

"Well," Tanti said, "if it hits the fan when those guys come back, it could be a real interesting contest."

"Don't sweat the small stuff. Are you set for tomorrow?"

"Sure, six to twos at the Aviation Unit. I'll be able to sleep late every morning," Tanti replied. "How about you?"

"Six to twos at the Four-Seven Squad. At least I'll be able to get some work done while I'm waiting for the call to SOD. If there is a call."

The two men fell in line with the rest of the group, who were busy handing in their rifles to Francone and Ramirez inside Building Five.

"Tony, I don't know how long they're gonna let us keep this kind of a work schedule."

"Well, partner, I sure hope this thing comes off. Or in a couple of weeks I'll be back on patrol," Tanti said, as he handed in his rifle.

Chapter 27

Brysof held an orange over the ship's aluminum rail and dug his thumbnail into the thick skin. The fruit's sweet-smelling liquid dribbled out and fell into the sea below.

The orange had come onto the trawler the night before, when the ship had received its new shipment of supplies. Even though the vessel was within a day's travel of New York Harbor, all their required stores and provisions were delivered by a supply vessel, which purchased the necessary goods while harbored in Bayonne.

Behind Brysof stood neat rows of fishing nets, held in place by lines of rope. The nets had not been removed since they had departed the Soviet Union and he knew they would never feel the touch of seawater. Their purpose, besides keeping up the facade of the vessel being a fishing trawler, was to screen the floatplane hidden underneath their folds from American eyes.

He had just completed his daily inspection of the aircraft, the orange in his hand being his self-bestowed reward for a thorough job. Takeoffs and landings in the corrosive seawater, as well as the ever-present salt air, required constant vigilance on his part to ensure the airplane was ready to go at a moment's notice. Brysof also thought it wise to check the two engine-start air cylinders which were located under the floatplane's flooring. He didn't want to find himself rolling on top of Atlantic Ocean swells, in the middle of the night, with not enough air pressure in them to turn the engine over.

His work finished for the moment, Brysof occupied himself by watching the water below being split apart by the sharp bow of the ship, the white spray fanning out before it. From the corner of his eye he noticed the figure of Propkin, hands in his pockets, walking along the railing toward him. Propkin, Brysof reflected, had been a bit less formal of late, and he suspected it had something to do with the upcoming mission.

With a nod, Propkin placed his arms on the rail next to Brysof and looked out at the open expanse of sea.

"Beautiful day, isn't it, comrade?" Propkin said, without taking his eyes from the ocean.

"Yes, it is," Brysof replied, ever cautious in the presence of the normally taciturn Propkin.

"Do you think we will be fortunate enough to have this kind of weather for our return to the mainland?"

"Probably. I checked with the ship's meteorologist. She informed me we should have a high-pressure system over the area for the next three days. I don't believe weather will be one of the factors we need to be concerned with."

The KGB man turned his head toward the pilot, smiled thinly and asked, "And if not the weather, what then should we concern ourselves with?"

"Speaking frankly?"

"It is the only way."

"I am sure you have spoken with some of the other crew members. Many believe, when we last landed, they heard a helicopter nearby."

"But no one saw a helicopter, Comrade Brysof. And you must agree, on a night as clear as that one was, a ship flying nearby would have been observed."

"Yes. It certainly would have, if it had been running any lighting. But a dark ship, against a dark—clear, yes, but very dark—sky would not have been visible. That's why I had no lights showing on our aircraft."

"All right, comrade. Let us assume for a moment that there was another aircraft in the sky with us. What does that prove? That was over a month ago. We have been running in a big circle on this boat ever since then, yet nothing has come near us out here. You would think if someone were interested in what we were up to, they would have at least come out and taken a look."

"Perhaps," Brysof said, and tossed the husk of his

orange into the sea. "But nonetheless, if that was a helicopter that the crew heard, and if that helicopter was following the floatplane, it could mean we have been badly compromised, and mean a serious problem for us when we fly again."

"I thought you had the route planned in such a way that we would blend in with American aircraft. We flew in a nonrestricted area, you had said." Propkin leaned back against the railing. The conversation's tone and direction began to make Brysof uneasy.

"That is so, Comrade Colonel. There was nothing I did that should have brought attention to us. And, in any case, when we make the next penetration, I plan on remaining only a few feet above the water until we are much deeper into the uncontrolled airspace than when we last flew."

"Well," Propkin said, "it is of no matter. We have our orders. We will follow them. That's the comfortable thing about the work you and I do, Comrade Brysof. We need not burden ourselves with unnecessary concerns. We are given a task and we perform that task. There are no questions of good or evil, safety or danger." Looking at Brysof, he continued, "Don't you agree?"

"I will do what is expected of me, Comrade Colonel. That, you may be sure of."

Propkin stood erect, one hand on the cool metal rail. "Of that, I am certain. You will excuse me?"

Brysof came to attention and said, "Of course, Colonel."

The other man nodded and turned away. He walked along the railing until he came to an opening in the side of the vessel, which he entered. Brysof watched the man disappear into the body of the ship and wondered if it had been a questioning tone he had detected in Propkin's voice.

Propkin came to the gray metal door of his cabin. He grasped a dog leg-shaped lever, pulled down and pushed in, and entered the small room. A single cot lay flat against the bulkhead, held to the metal wall by thick leather straps. A lone metal chair and tiny writing desk were the only other pieces of furniture in the room, which was lit by a single, screen-covered light bulb suspended from the ceiling.

Propkin moved the chair over to the desk and unstrapped the bed, permitting it to fall horizontal to the deck, held in place by chains at its head and foot. He stepped over to the opposite corner of the room where his kit lay and picked up a charcoal-gray knapsack. It was the same one he had carried with him during his initial trip to the mainland. He placed it on the cot.

Moving the chair to the bed, he sat down before it, and used its flat surface as a table. He adjusted the knapsack so that it stood with its wide flap facing him. Unbuckling the strap he turned the flap over so as to expose the inside of the bag. He reached in and removed a compact pistol. It was stored in a nylon shoulder holster along with eight loaded magazines, each in its own pouch. He laid the weapon and magazines on the bed and neatly opened up the webbing of the belt, holster and pouches for his inspection.

Next he removed a compact assault rifle, its folding metal stock nestled flat underneath the weapon's forearm. As with the pistol, there were eight magazines, each held in a dark-colored military web canvas holder. He placed the rifle and its magazines on the part of the bed nearest the wall.

With slow deliberation, Propkin picked up the pistol and removed it from its holster. Releasing the weapon's loaded magazine, he placed it on the bed, then pulled the pistol's slide to the rear. The round in the chamber flew out, bounced once on the thin mattress and came to rest near the headboard.

Once again he went to the knapsack and rummaged inside. This time he removed a small rag and laid it on the bed, as if setting a table with fine linen cloth.

Propkin disassembled the handgun and inspected it. Finding the gun serviceable he reassembled and loaded it. He returned it to its holster and secured it once more in the knapsack.

Turning to the weapon's magazines, he removed each one in turn. He slowly examined their metal outer body for dents and checked the condition of the topmost cartridge. He chose not to remove the rounds for inspection, as he had done that prior to inserting them and knew that they would suffer greater abuse by the unloading and reloading procedure than if he simply left them alone.

Once he had completed that task, he returned the magazines to the knapsack and started on the assault rifle and its magazines, performing the same ritual disassembly and inspection. While Propkin worked he considered the upcoming mission. Certainly there had been a helicopter. Of that he had no doubt. Over 250 kilometers out in the Atlantic Ocean there could be no reason for the sound of a ship such as was heard by the trawler's crew. There was simply no place for that type of craft to go this far out over the water.

He picked up another magazine for examination.

Thus, he must conclude that the mission had been compromised. Perhaps all of Brysof's talk about their route evading the American radar had been so much wishful thinking. Perhaps they had been followed right from the landing point. But conjecture was pointless. The most intelligent course of action to follow now would be to abort the scheduled return and make a penetration some other way.

He returned the magazine to its pouch and picked up another. Well, there was nothing more to be done about it. After all, he was the one who had goaded Zybof into reactivating the mission, much against the advice of Andrapovich. For Propkin to now recommend a delay would make him appear foolish and frightened. And he was neither.

He finished with the last magazine and returned it to its proper place. Satisfied that his tools were in order, he secured them in the knapsack and returned it to its place in the corner of the cabin.

Propkin slipped back to the bed, lay down, and stared at the military-gray ceiling. Examining the shadows made by the glare of the light bulb, he again thought of the helicopter, thought of the alternatives.

He reached over his head, found the light switch and flicked it off. Lying back, he closed his eyes, and reflected that a person with a job such as his shouldn't burden himself with so many thoughts.

Chapter 28

Tanti sat on the wood and metal helicopter dolly and watched the late day's sun slip behind the Manhattan skyline. Fair weather clouds moved gently overhead in the cobalt-blue sky, their undersides a dark gray in contrast to their brilliant cotton-white tops. Fifty feet to his right, an orange wind sock rustled gently from the light sea breeze. Tanti could feel the oncoming coolness of evening, knowing it would soon force him back inside the Aviation Unit's building.

To his left he could see Gary Simms in his ubiquitous blue mechanic's jumpsuit head toward him from the direction of the Aviation hangar. Next to Simms ran the unit mascot, Maggie, an old brown female stray who had wandered into the hangar thirteen years earlier and decided it was home.

Simms sat down next to Tanti. A toothpick jutted from between his teeth. Maggie lay down between the two and looked up expectantly at Tanti, in the hope of receiving some attention.

"When she was younger," Simms said, pointing to the dog with his toothpick, "she'd have jumped right up onto the dolly. But look at her now. She's a little blimp!"

Tanti bent down and scratched the dog behind her ears.

"You know, Gary, I kinda feel like the second man in a solitaire game around here. All I can do is hang out."

Simms smiled. "It could be worse. You could be running around on patrol in the Four-Seven Precinct right now."

"Yeah," Tanti said. He stood up and rubbed his arms against the oncoming chill. Only a glimmer of light remained visible in the distance. Everything around them had turned to shades of gray. "And I figure in about another week, that's exactly what I'll be doing."

Simms got up and the two men started back to the hangar, with Maggie falling in behind.

Glenn Cummings hung up the phone and moved back to the center aisle of the Federal Aviation Air Traffic Control radar room. He walked over to one of the glowing screens and said to the operator, "Tommy, that was Paul Mante. He asked me to keep an extra sharp lookout for that smuggler I told you about. You know, the one that came in off the Atlantic a couple of weeks ago. He would be coming in from your sector."

Tom Gruber looked up at his supervisor and nodded. "Sure, Glenn. But that guy Mante calls us nearly every damn evening and says the same thing."

Cummings patted Gruber on the shoulder. "Well, it must be important or Mante wouldn't keep calling. So keep your eye out for the target."

Gruber turned back to the screen. It showed a dozen different aircraft entering and leaving the New York area. A busier Thursday evening than normal, Gruber thought.

Grau and Bradford stepped down from the stoop of the two-family home where one of Bradford's complainants lived. The people had reported that someone had cracked a front window. It was probably a neighborhood kid playing ball but since a criminal mischief complaint had been made out, the matter had to be investigated. No one had been home, so a note had been left under the front door to call the detective. It was the third note he had left there that week.

Grau looked at his watch.

"Clarence, it's a quarter to nine. How about we get a sandwich and head back to the Squad?"

"Sure, Jon. Nothin' happening tonight anyway," Bradford said, and slipped his steno book in his jacket pocket.

Al Hastings moved about inside the secure equipment room. He had laid out in a neat row the last of the emergency service vests. Next to the dozen vests were an equal number of protective Kevlar helmets, assault rifles and an ample supply of loaded twenty-round magazines.

Hastings checked the list in his hand against the supplies in front of him. Satisfied, he stepped from the room, locked the heavy metal door and pocketed the key. The only other key to that room was secure in Chief Kinney's office. To get it would require authorization from a ranking member of the service.

As he walked back to his office, Hastings passed Sergeant Chandler. A tall, sandy-haired ESU supervisor, Chandler had been with the unit almost five years. This was his night to "stand by" for the operation.

The men stopped for a moment in the hall, Chandler saying, "Al, I thought you worked a day tour."

"I did. But I wanted to make sure everything was set for Open Arms. The guys did a raid today in Manhattan. The silly bastards appropriated half the vests I had stored up for the operation. Took me a hell of a time to get them all back."

Chandler looked at Hastings' bloodshot eyes and said, "Al, go home and relax. We're ready as we'll ever be. I know where the key to the room is. And everyone who's supposed to be in on the operation is in place."

"You're right, sarge," Hastings softly said. "I'll call it a night. But give me a call at home if anything breaks."

"You got it, Al."

As the big man walked away, the sergeant thought, "They sure don't make them like they used to."

Propkin watched as Brysof directed the trawler's crew in the lifting of the floatplane. The camouflage fishing nets had been removed and set to one side, exposing the aircraft. Atop the center section of its wing Propkin could see the four small doughnut-shaped metal lifting rings built into this ship for its special mission. Already secured to them were four sections of chain, held apart by steel spreader bars.

The scene had an otherworldliness to it, Propkin thought. Harsh working lamps intensely lit up the area around the aircraft. Just beyond the reach of the lights it was an impossible black. Brysof had one foot on the Wilga's cowling and the other on top of the wing. He had to hold onto the cable leading down from the trawler's hoist so as to keep himself from falling off.

"Up slow!" he barked. "Easy! Stop!" He bent down to examine the securing fasteners that attached the chain to the ship on one end and to the cable of the hoist on the other, making sure the aircraft would not fall free. The floatplane, now only a few inches above the trawler's deck, gently swayed to and fro with the movement of the man standing on top.

Satisfied with his inspection, Brysof said, "Up!" The hoist's electric motor whined. It raised the plane to a height that would easily clear the ship's railing. Brysof signaled the operator to stop, then shouted, "Over!"

The floatplane and pilot dangled by the invisible wire over the side of the trawler. Once he had assured himself the wing was clear of the vessel, he yelled, "Down!" The aircraft moved from the center of the lit area and down the side of the trawler into the darkness. One of the crew moved the head of a work lamp so that Brysof was illuminated by the glaring white light as the ship settled into the water.

"Stop!" could be heard from below and the hoist went silent. Propkin watched Brysof unfasten the slack chain from the Wilga, which was now rocking gently, free among the light swells of the Atlantic. The pilot held the chains in his hand and ordered the hoist, "Up!"

He held onto the chain until certain it would not strike the plane while being lifted back to the vessel, and in the process perhaps rip off an antenna or smash in the front windshield. When he was satisfied the cable had been raised high enough he let it go, watching it get hoisted aboard the trawler.

A crewman quickly replaced the chain with a wire-mesh bucket. Propkin, knapsack secured to his back, stepped in and sat down. The hoist operator first raised the bucket enough to clear the railing, then lowered it over the side, close to the rearmost section of the Wilga's floats. Brysof stood waiting below. When Propkin got close to the ship Brysof grabbed hold of the bucket, yelled "Stop!" and permitted the other man to get off and work his way along the floats and into the aircraft. As with the chain a moment before, Brysof firmly held onto the bucket while it was pulled back up, until certain it had cleared the plane.

The trawler, now under low power, moved away from the Wilga. Brysof entered the cockpit, threw some switches and the big radial engine coughed to life.

He glanced over at Propkin to ensure that the man had fastened himself into his seat. Then, after checking the ship's gauges one last time, he advanced the throttle. Their mission had begun.

Chapter 29

Gruber sat down by his radar screen, suppressed a burp and opened his belt an extra notch, having just finished dinner with some of the other controllers. He yawned and glanced at the wall clock. It was 10 P.M., which meant he had two hours to go to the end of his shift.

The operator whom Gruber had just relieved briefed him on the aircraft currently in his sector. A so-called "heavy jet," a 747 coming in from Europe, had entered his area and was descending in preparation for a landing at Kennedy. Another ship, a twin-engine corporate turbo prop, was traversing his area at a cruising altitude of twenty-four thousand feet, moving from south to north, headed for Boston's Logan airport. Otherwise, except for some small targets flying within the exclusion, the screen was quiet.

Gruber contacted the heavy jet and handed him off to the Kennedy controllers. Once that was done he sat back in his chair, folded his arms across his chest and casually took in the all-but-blank screen in front of him.

He turned to the controller at the station next to him.

"Bernie, you wanna catch a beer after work?"

The other man, his screen equally quiet, scratched his head and replied, "I don't know, Tommy. The last time I went out with you for a beer, I didn't see my house until the sun came up. The bride was really pissed."

Gruber made a face. "Gimme a break. One lousy beer, that's all. You are pussy whipped, my man."

He turned back to his scope. Little had changed. Then he noticed it—a faint primary target, moving slowly northward just between New York and New Jersey, about fifteen miles south of the Verrazano Narrows Bridge. Gruber adjusted the intensity of the radar echo as best he could, but the target remained barely visible. Her ground speed read eighty-five knots.

"I wonder where the hell she came from?"

"What'd you say?" Bernie asked.

"Oh, nothing. Just a local. Flying low, I guess," Gruber replied, wondering why he hadn't noticed the aircraft earlier.

"So listen," Bernie said, "does anyone else want to go with us?"

"Hang on one second, Bernie," Gruber said.

Gruber quietly watched the target for a few moments. It moved slowly between the two land masses, a barely visible blip on the screen. He looked around for Glenn Cummings, whom he saw was talking with the room supervisor.

Gruber called out, "Hey, Glenn, take a look at this."

Cummings walked over, looked at the screen for a few seconds and asked, "What do you have, Tommy?"

"I don't know. See this guy?" he pointed to the dim target.

"Yeah?"

"He just kinda popped up. I don't know where he came from."

Cummings rubbed his chin. "Where'd you see him first?"

"About five miles farther south. Around here," Gruber said, and indicated a spot just north of Sandy Hook, New Jersey.

Cummings watched as the target passed over the Verrazano Bridge. He said, "I don't know. That might just be the guy Paul Mante wants us to be looking for. The ship sure is slow enough. But I'd hate to send those guys on a wild-goose chase."

Cummings exhaled deeply and made a decision. He said, "I'd rather be safe than sorry. Tag him and stay with him. I'll give Mante a call."

Mante, telephone to his ear, listened for a moment more to Cummings, then said, "Glenn, where's the plane now?" and at the same time looked around for someone to bark orders to. He knew it was imperative to get his helicopters up immediately but discovered that he was alone. "Okay, Glenn, I think this may be our boy. You'll stay with him, right? Good! We'll call you from the air. And thanks."

Mante slammed the phone down and ran back to the briefing room. Half a dozen pilots and mechanics sat around the large wood table, talking among themselves.

He looked around the room and asked, "Where's Mike and Tony?"

A mechanic laconically replied, "In the simulator room. Mike is giving free lessons."

"Get them," Mante snapped. The mechanic quickly got up from his chair and headed down the hall to retrieve the two men.

With the mechanic sent to find Casson and Tanti, Mante announced, "I think our boy may be in the air. The radar people spotted a small slow-moving target near the mouth of the harbor. And a little over an hour ago I received a call that the car the detectives were sitting on had been taken from its garage."

Everyone in the room stood up as Mante continued, "Jeff and Roy, let's go. Gary, call SOD, let them know we're coming." Simms ran to the phone and started punching in the numbers.

Casson and Tanti hustled into the room just as the 412 crew was leaving for their ship. Running to catch up, Casson fell in with Mante and asked, "What's up?"

"Mike," Mante replied without stopping, "I just got a call from TRACON. If it is our guy, the son of a bitch must've been ten feet off the damn deck right up to the Verrazano. And right now he's somewhere right around Manhattan and heading north. We're staying with the original plan, but we gotta move it. The 412 is gonna fly out to SOD headquarters to pick up the ESU cops and wait for further orders, while the 222 follows the floatplane. Jeff, Roy and me in the 412. You, Steve, Nick and Tony in the 222. Now get your ship in the air and find that sucker!"

Casson gave Mante the thumbs-up sign. He looked around for the rest of his crew, glad to see that his copilot, Steve Talt, was out at the line, preparing the 222 for flight. Nick Steffins, assigned as the FLIR operator for Casson's ship, stood by the roaring auxiliary power unit, its heavy black cable already plugged into the 222.

"Tony, you got all your stuff?" Casson asked Tanti, who had remained by his side since they had been called from the simulator room.

"Just have to get the rifles," he said, and ran back into the hangar. Casson broke into a trot and headed out to his helicopter.

Chandler stood outside the open door of SOD headquarters. His heavy-duty emergency service vest was unsecured at the sides to allow the cool evening air to circulate and ease up on the discomfort. Over his right shoulder he slung his assault rifle, empty of its magazine. He started to pace back and forth, anxiously watching for the headlights of the truck carrying the remaining two ESU officers who were slated to be in on the operation. Four men were already inside and suiting up with their equipment.

Chandler saw a car's lights move down the poorly lit road. It drew nearer, passing an overhead street lamp and he recognized it as being only an unmarked department car. Cursing under his breath, he asked himself, "Where the hell are those two guys?"

The unmarked car pulled up at the front of the headquarters building. A man in a dark-blue suit got out and walked up to the sergeant.

"Sarge," the man said, "I'm Grau. Got here as fast as I could."

Chandler looked Grau over. "Who told you to dress like that?"

Before Grau had a chance to explain his orders, that he had been directed to stand by at the squad until called, Chandler said, "Never mind. Go inside and get your equipment. The helicopter will be here in about five minutes."

Grau nodded and disappeared inside the building, passing Neal Thompson who was heading outside.

"Hey, sarge, just got word from Sellers and McKay's unit. They're both on top of the Brooklyn Bridge. They got a jumper. No way you'll see those two. At least for a couple of hours anyway."

"All right. I'll go with the four guys I got. And of course, the detective," he said, shaking his head.

Andrapovich had carefully reconnoitered the area around the small airport and, as during the previous rendezvous with the floatplane, had observed no activity.

He looked at the luminous dial of his watch and calculated that the plane should be arriving within the next forty-five minutes. Earlier that night, when he had been in position for about an hour, Andrapovich had heard some movement behind him, near the center of the runway. He went so far as to unholster his pistol and take cover behind his car. But the noise had turned out to be a small herd of browsing deer. When he put the gun back in its holster he had chastised himself for being so nervous.

Now, he thought, there was nothing to do but enjoy the quiet country night. He raised his eyes to the sky and could see that except for some fair-weather clouds occasionally blocking the stars, the night sky was clear.

Maybe Zybof and Propkin were right after all, Andrapovich thought. Maybe he should have called Propkin back in earlier. Things were a real mess now with another American police officer dead. And for what? A few pieces of sheet metal that that damned detective Grau had intended to be found.

Andrapovich wondered if Grau really knew the importance of what he had, not that it mattered any longer. The detective's fate had been sealed with Zybof's last message. It had been a very clear, direct order, and gave Propkin full operational control over the mission. Well, so be it. In less than an hour Propkin would arrive and both of them would get down to work.

Andrapovich paced back and forth by the edge of the lake, wishing he dared to light up a cigarette.

The 222 sat on its dolly, her large blades whirling as the ship's engines turned over at flight idle. Nick Steffins sat behind the two pilots and watched as his FLIR unit came to life.

Casson tuned the radio to a special nonstandard aviation frequency. Although it would still be an unsecured transmission, they and the radar controllers had decided it was better than staying on the normal channel. He flicked the red transmit switch on the control stick.

"New York Approach, PD Eleven."

"PD Eleven, go."

"Approach, location of target?"

"PD Eleven, your target is moving north, between the George Washington and Tappan Zee Bridges, showing ninety knots ground speed, negative transponder code."

"Roger. PD Eleven getting airborne. Keep us posted."

Casson pulled up on the power lever to his left. The ship lumbered into the air, her true element, and climbed into the night sky. Casson hit the transmit switch for Kennedy and announced his intentions to head northeast.

Once out of Kennedy's and LaGuardia's airspace Casson again contacted New York Approach. They assigned him a discrete transponder code to ease their job of tracking the helicopter.

"Approach, PD Eleven. Where do you show her now?" Casson asked, as the helicopter streaked along at nearly 160 miles per hour, the Tappan Zee Bridge coming up dead ahead.

"Sorry, PD Eleven. The ship's off our screen. We lost her just as she moved north-northwest of the bridge."

"Can you give me an estimate of our distance from the target when she went off your screen?"

The frequency was silent for a moment, then, "Roughly fifteen miles, PD Eleven."

Tanti shifted in his place and tried to get comfortable.

The unfamiliar bulk of the emergency service vest he wore forced him to sit forward, on the edge of the seat. He tripped his intercom switch and asked, "Mike, what are you going to do?"

"I'm gonna find that damn ship," Casson grimly replied. He hit the transmit switch. "Aviation Eleven to Aviation Twelve," he said, using the department call signs for the two ships.

"Twelve. Go ahead, Eleven."

"Aviation Eleven is heading north, just coming over the TZ bridge. We're searching for the target. Recommend you proceed to probable landing location."

"Aviation Twelve, ten-four."

Tanti removed his seat belt, bent down and unlocked the hard-cover gun case he had brought into the ship. Inside were two Mini-14 rifles, with six loaded magazines for each.

From the corner of his eye Casson saw Tanti handling one of the weapons and exclaimed, "Tony, do me a favor and put that damn gun away. The last thing I need is a slug in one of the engines. Or maybe worse."

Tanti shrugged and repacked the rifle, but first removed some of the weapon's magazines and stuffed them into the pockets of his vest.

Andrapovich breathed a sigh of relief when he saw the Wilga's faint lights as it came in low over the ridge. A moment later he heard the distinctive soft rumble of the ship's radial engine, the light breeze at his back having kept the sound away. As the pilot had done on previous night landings, he passed directly over the lake. Andrapovich flashed the safe signal and the aircraft continued onward, to set itself up for a landing.

He looked at his watch. It was after 11 P.M., somewhat later than he had expected. He reflected that the wind on the ship's nose must have slowed it down an bit.

"Eleven to Twelve," Casson transmitted, "we still haven't found the target. Where are you?"

"Twelve is showing ten miles from the LZ. What do you see?"

"Stand by." Casson turned his head in the direction of

Steffins. "Nick, you're the only game in town. What do you got?"

"Not a damn thing," Steffins replied. "All I got on the screen is cold air."

Talt broke in. "Mike, maybe they went someplace else. Maybe we should search farther north. There are reservoirs and lakes . . ."

"No!" Casson replied. "We'll be chasing our tails all night. Either they're gonna be at Warwick or we lost them."

Tanti could feel the tension in the ship mount. Casson spoke to Steffins. "Nick, lower your angle of view."

"But, Mike, I'll get all kinds of ground clutter."

"Dammit," Casson snapped, "do it."

Silently Steffins complied, and adjusted the external infrared receiver to take in everything off their nose and below the horizon. The screen in front of him became a kaleidoscope of green hues, reflecting the presence of homes, cars and living things below.

Just as Steffins started to complain to Casson, he spotted the distinctive outline of the floatplane below and ahead of them.

"Mike, the ship! I got the ship!" Steffins exploded. "Four miles ahead. Real low on the horizon." He stopped for a moment and studied the screen, then said, "Hell, she's heading for the lake. She's gonna land."

Casson transmitted, "Eleven to Twelve, we've got the target. She's set up to land. I repeat, she's set up to land. Why don't you guys hurry on over here?"

"Roger, Eleven. We're three minutes away. Keep us posted."

"Okay, Twelve," Casson replied. "We're going to make a discreet orbit around the LZ and get back to you." Then to Talt, Casson said, "Steve, I'm going to run along the ridge line, just above the valley.

"Nick, let me know what we have down there," Casson added.

"You got it."

Tanti looked out the side window at the darkness below. The only things that were clearly visible were the yellow lights of the prison and their reflections off the lake. The airport, which he knew was there, was just blackness.

"Mike," Steffins said, "the FLIR is showing at least one car near the water's edge. And there's someone by it. And I'm not sure, but I think there are maybe a half dozen other people, standing off to the west side of the airport, about three hundred yards from the water. They may be lying flat on the ground. I can't be certain."

"Damn!" Casson said softly. Hitting the radio button, he transmitted, "Eleven to Twelve."

"Go ahead, Eleven."

"We got a confirmed vehicle plus one person by the edge of the lake. Our FLIR is showing an additional six off to one side, near the western edge of the airport. They may be lying prone on the ground."

For several seconds there was silence. Then the radio came alive with, "Twelve is going to circle around and come in from the rear, drop its load and get airborne again."

Casson replied, "Understood."

Tanti asked, "Mike, what's up?"

"We think there may be a welcoming committee down there. The 412 is going to come in from behind and drop our guys off so they can engage whoever's down there."

Brysof set the floatplane up for its shallow glide to the water. He had extinguished the plane's lights after seeing Andrapovich's signal that the area was safe and now was simply enjoying the sensation of control he always felt when performing this maneuver.

He glanced at his altimeter. It showed he was less than four hundred feet above the ground. He calculated that the floats would be on the water's surface in about three minutes.

Casson dared not let his ship move in closer than one mile from the floatplane, lest the noise of his blades cause whoever was on the ground to scatter and wave off the other ship from landing. Keeping his altitude to one thousand feet over the terrain he shot a look at his airspeed indicator, which showed fifty-five knots.

"Nick, what do we got?" he said, without taking his eyes from the windscreen.

"On the FLIR I've got the floatplane just over the western end of the lake. The ship should be touching down in a few seconds. The car and that one guy are still in place, except the guy must be out on a dock or something."

"And the other six?" Casson asked, knowing that in a moment the 412, with its personnel, would be touching down into a potential trap.

"Mike, I don't know what to make of them. They're all basically in the same spot. A couple moved around a little, but it still looks like some sort of an ambush."

Casson pushed the radio switch.

"Eleven to Twelve, what's your location?"

Mante had swung the 412 in a wide arc, in an attempt to keep several miles' distance from the center of the airport. He maneuvered around until the nose of the helicopter faced that part of the airfield opposite from the lake. He had wanted to wait until the floatplane was down on the water before landing the assault party. But, with a probable ambush down there, before Chandler and his people could fight their way to the aircraft it would take off anyway. Damned if you do, damned if you don't, Mante thought.

He spoke into his headset's mike.

"Stand by, sarge. I'm taking her down." As Mante spoke he lowered the power lever and nosed the ship forward, allowing her to fall like a stone.

Chandler spoke quickly to the ESU officers. "Okay. We don't know who we got down there. Remember, out the door, make some tracks and hit the dirt. Then we work our way toward the lake."

"Sarge?" Grau broke in.

"Listen, like I told you before, you're neither dressed nor trained for this sort of an operation. Stay in the ship and we'll give you a couple of collars when it's all over. And that's final."

Andrapovich stood at the end of the dock and searched for the shadow that would be the Wilga coming in over the

The Murder of Old Comrades

edge of the lake. His summer-weight jacket gently rippled from the light current of air at his back.

A dark blur came in over the trees to his right. With the reflection of the prison's lights off the water he could see the outline of the floatplane, perhaps thirty feet above the surface of the lake.

Behind him, with the next breeze, Andrapovich sensed rather than heard a faint beating sound. He turned his back to the floatplane and faced into the darkness, but could see nothing. The sensation, really a pressure, became stronger with each passing moment until, all at once, it became a sound. There was now no doubt in his mind that he was hearing the blades of a helicopter beating the air.

He whirled back to the lake and saw that the Wilga had just settled into the water. Frantically he turned on his light and waved the beam back and forth, signaling danger.

Mante saw that the helicopter's rate of descent was over a thousand feet per minute. The radar altimeter indicated they were less than five hundred feet over the surface of the charcoal-black airport.

Speaking to his copilot, he said, "Jeff, I can't see a thing down there."

"Neither can I. It's like we're landing on a pool of ink."

"Listen. Keep your eye on the radar altimeter. When it shows one hundred feet, give me landing lights."

The copilot put his fingers around the light control switch. "You know, we'll be sitting ducks if anyone out there wants to take us out."

"You got a better idea?"

"Nope."

"Mike, the floatplane is on the deck," Steffins said, watching the image on his scope. "Wait a sec. She's moving again. The sucker is taking off!"

"Sarge, five seconds!" Mante barked into his headset, as his copilot turned on the landing lights. His eyes became glued to the spot illuminated before him, a section of black macadam runway, surrounded by dark green grass. He pulled power to reduce their rate of descent.

Chandler ordered, "Open the doors!" On either side of the ship her big doors slid to the rear. Chandler pulled his headset off, tossed it to the deck and put on his helmet.

The ship came to a hover two feet above the ground. He yelled, "Go!" Two officers jumped from the left side; the other two, along with Chandler, jumped from the right.

Mante pulled power, the landing light still burning. As the ship picked up speed, his copilot shouted, "Hey, look, those are deer!"

Frozen in the helicopter's intense white lights, the two men could see six statuelike deer, eyes ablaze with reflected light.

Mante hit the transmit button, "Chandler, they're deer. The six prone guys, they're deer."

Once out of the chopper, the ESU team deployed ninety degrees to either side of the ship. Chandler lay prone in the sweet-smelling grass and watched as the 412 moved forward and gained altitude. His head swiveled around, searching for the rest of his team, when he heard his radio transmit.

Rolling to one side, he unbuckled the walkie-talkie and transmitted, "Ten-five that last message?"

Mante's voice came on the air. "Chandler, it's a small herd of deer. The six guys are only deer."

"Damn it," Chandler spat, "we should've waited for the floatplane to land." Getting to his feet he yelled to the team, "Double time to the lake. There's no ambush. They were fuckin' deer."

Chapter 30

Andrapovich stood on the dock and watched the Wilga as it accelerated over the surface of the water. The big helicopter to his rear thundered overhead just as the floatplane broke from the lake's surface and began to climb. He knew there was nothing more he could do for the plane. His duty now was to get away. Zybof's orders had been very clear on that count. Should the mission be compromised there was to be no Soviet connection.

Andrapovich sprinted to his car, jumped in and started the engine. He jerked the lever into drive and stomped on the gas pedal. The car's rear wheels spun noisily on the damp grass, then bit into the slick surface on gaining traction. The car fishtailed away from the lake, almost out of control from too much speed and careened across the uneven grass and dirt surface.

Chandler heard the car start up before he saw it lurch forward. He ran to cut it off but realized he and his men were too far away to intercept it. Bringing his rifle to his shoulder, he softly said, "Fuck the rules," and led the fast-moving car by several lengths. His finger squeezed the gun's trigger. Half a dozen rounds cracked from the muzzle. He saw the car swerve around toward the main hangar area and could only watch helplessly at it drove out of sight.

Brysof swung the Wilga around, moving it away from the rising ridge in front of them. He headed the ship in the opposite direction, to flatter, safer ground.

Propkin reached into the back seat, took hold of his knapsack and removed the rifle and magazines it held, then tossed it back into the rear.

He turned to Brysof, saying, "Can't you get us any higher?"

"No," Brysof replied, swinging the ship around to the left, no more than a hundred feet over the trees. "The damn American helicopter is staying above us."

Propkin unlatched the ship's large plexiglass door, swinging it up and open. It stayed in place by the force of the rushing air.

"Maybe I can convince them to back off!" he shouted, over the din the fast-moving air made. He loosened his seat belt and moved around, putting his back to the front windscreen. Propkin inserted a magazine into the rifle and pulled the slide to the rear, chambering a round. He put the weapon to his left shoulder and leaned out the door.

The massive American helicopter was above them and only a hundred meters to their rear. Carefully he aimed his weapon and began firing, deliberately aiming for the pilot and copilot.

"Mike, the car's out of the airport. But it hasn't gotten to the main road yet," Steffins blurted, eyes fixed to the FLIR screen.

"That son of a bitch isn't losing us," Casson said, and nosed the 222 down until it was only a few hundred feet above the ground. The ship fell in just behind the fast-moving car.

Tanti, a loaded assault rifle firmly in hand, sat tensely in his seat.

"Hey, Mike, something's funny about the car," Steffins said, studying the multihued image before him.

"Nick, give it to me," Casson cried.

"Damn, I'm not sure. I never saw this before. It looks like, well, like something hot is coming out of the front."

Andrapovich looked down at the bright red warning light on the dash. One word was illuminated—HOT—and he could see steam billowing out of the engine compartment.

He clenched his teeth, recalling that he had heard one of

the Americans fire on him as he was fleeing the airport. He had also heard at least three loud slaps, when the slugs struck the car. It was clear that one or more of the bullets had hit the car's radiator.

If only he could get away from this area. Even if he had to abandon the vehicle some distance away it could work out. But no, Andrapovich thought, a couple of lucky shots and now at best he could only hope to travel a few more miles before the car's engine would seize.

The next country road was coming up ahead and Andrapovich saw it was lined with trees. He quickly turned into it, hoping to evade the helicopter roaring overhead by hiding under their cover.

Almost immediately after swinging into the road he felt his car begin to lose power. When it slowed to less than five miles an hour Andrapovich jumped from the moving vehicle and ran for a cornfield to his left.

Mante saw the spider web of cracked plexiglass in front of him before he heard the sound of the bullets ripping into the ship. The little yellow flashes of light which he had seen coming from the side of the floatplane he now knew were small arms fire.

He moved the 412 off to the side of the Wilga, away from the gunfire, and yelled, "Grau, can you give them something to think about?"

Without replying Grau moved to the open right-side doorway. He fastened a seat belt closed, hooked his arm through it, then leaned his head out the door. Raising his rifle he opened fire, emptying the entire magazine in less than three seconds. He replaced it with a fresh magazine, took a deep breath and commanded himself to slow down his pace. He studied the other ship, trying to calculate how far he had to hold in front of her in order to make his rounds count.

The floatplane was doing a jig in the sky. Mante stayed on its tail, in an attempt to keep the helicopter away from the Wilga's right side and safe from gunfire.

The other pilot was damn good, Mante thought, as the floatplane slewed through the air, making a skidding right turn and exposing the 412 to a ferocious wave of rifle fire.

Mante heard some more loud pings as the enemy's gunfire found it mark. With another yellow flash from the Wilga's side a chunk of plexiglass blew out, hitting Mante in the cheek. He reached up and felt the damp numbness of the bleeding gash.

He realized that Grau hadn't fired a shot in several seconds. Mante turned his head and saw the detective down on one knee, holding his left shoulder.

"Grau, you okay?"

"Yeah. Super. That last one nicked me," Grau replied through locked teeth. Then, bringing his gun up, he again opened fire on the other ship.

"Hey, Lieutenant, look!" his copilot shouted, finger pointing to the glowing yellow Chip Detector warning light on the eyebrow of the glare shield. Mante knew he should land immediately. One of the slugs had hit and damaged the transmission of the 412. The mechanism could fail— *should* fail—at any moment. And without a transmission, he would be flying a brick.

Through gritted teeth, Mante said, "We're staying with it. Grau, hit something, dammit!"

Andrapovich ran through the young corn, his low-cut city shoes bogging him down in the soft earth. He could hear the sound of the helicopter as it landed at the edge of the field, then heard the ship's engines roar as it once more took to the air.

Lying down next to one of the rows of corn he held his pistol at the ready. If only he could get past whoever had gotten out of the ship. Once away from the area he could find a telephone booth and arrange to be picked up. Even if the authorities did locate him they would have no way of connecting him to the night's activities.

To his front, Andrapovich could hear the sound of rustling corn stalks. He felt in the darkness to make sure the pistol's safety was off, raised the weapon in the direction of the approaching noise, and waited.

Brysof pulled the Wilga around in a hard right turn, trying to help Propkin get a clear shot at the helicopter. He held the throttle fully forward, but the big American ship easily kept up with the much smaller-engine floatplane.

Brysof kicked hard right rudder on the Wilga and at the same time yanked the stick over to the left, maximizing the exposure of the helicopter for Propkin and allowing him to fire several times.

Then, in an attempt to prevent the Americans from returning fire, he kicked hard left rudder, putting the Wilga into a steep turn.

"Brysof," Propkin yelled, "can't you get us some altitude so we can get over that damn ridge?" and fired several rounds when the helicopter came into range.

"I have enough power for either speed or altitude, but not both," Brysof said, finding himself once more low over the lake.

"Don't you understand," Propkin argued, "we have no choice. Get some altitude and get over the ridge. If the helicopter hits us, so be it!"

"Hang on!" Brysof said, and pulled back on the ship's control stick. The Wilga nosed up at a crazy attitude. Brysof watched the airspeed indicator bleed off to a perilously low reading.

Propkin yelled, "You see, the helicopter had to pull back!"

"Yes, but we make a perfect target now!" Brysof said, holding his breath and lowering the nose of the ship, barely preventing it from stalling. The maneuver left just enough altitude to clear the trees atop the ridge.

As the Wilga's speed began to build up both men heard loud slaps against the aircraft's aluminum skin. The American's bullets were hitting their target.

The man in the helicopter is finding his mark now! Brysof thought.

Another series of loud bangs had Propkin out the door, trying to return fire. Brysof held the ship steady, seeing that they would just make it over the ridge, when another series of loud smacks shook the plane.

Brysof felt a sudden tingle in his back. Just before he slumped over the controls he turned his head in Propkin's direction, to try to warn him that something was terribly wrong. But for Captain Brysof it was now far too late for such things.

The aircraft went into a shallow left turn. Propkin twisted about, intending to tell Brysof to bring the ship around. He barely had time to see the microwave tower as it filled the Wilga's windscreen.

Tanti moved cautiously through the cornfield. Try as he might he found he couldn't avoid stepping on bits of dry vegetation and leaves. Each crackle underfoot made him catch his breath.

Suddenly, to his right, a flash of light illuminated the night sky. He stopped and turned his head in the direction of the ridge. The dull sound of a muffled explosion reached him. In a moment the light faded and once again Tanti was enveloped in darkness.

He shook his head to force his concern for Grau from his thoughts, and continued the hunt. The 222 continued to fly in a pattern above him. The hasty plan they had decided on was for the helicopter to fly overhead and attempt to scare the wanted man out. There was no indication their quickly formed strategy was working.

With his next step a flash of sparks lit up twenty feet in front of Tanti, followed by a series of powerful blows to his chest. Tanti automatically raised the rifle and fired in the direction of the light, emptying his magazine. Diving for cover, he reflexively hit the release button, inserted a fresh magazine and rolled off to one side.

Tanti lay silent in the cool dirt, listening for any noise that might betray the location of the other man. The high collar of his heavy bulletproof vest dug into his neck, but he didn't mind. His fingers probed the front of the vest and he counted three small holes where the other man's pistol bullets lodged in his armor.

Tanti smiled, remembering what Fat Al Hastings had said at the mission briefing when, holding an identical vest in his hand, he quipped, "It would take a lot more than handgun bullets to get through one of these babies."

Tanti dared not move. In his efforts to escape from the gunman's line of fire he had lost his bearing and was uncertain where the other man hid. The beating of the massive blades of the helicopter circling overhead obliterated most other sounds around him, forcing him to depend mainly on his eyes to locate the enemy agent.

He lay silent for several minutes, and could hear the sound of the ship's blades recede to the far left part of the field. From the change in noise he realized the 222 was landing. A few moments later he heard the shouts of Nick Steffins off to his left, out of the ship and working his way into the field.

Tanti yelled, "Nick, stay down! He's over here and he's got a gun!"

The stalks crashed apart and Steffins came to Tanti's side.

"Nick, are you nuts? There's a guy with a gun, twenty feet away from us."

"Relax. I don't think he's a problem anymore," Steffins replied, kneeling down and patting Tanti on the back.

"What do you mean?"

"We were watching you two guys on the FLIR. I could even see the exchange of gunfire. Except, that afterwards, your body color stayed the same. The other guy's colors began to change. Don't you understand? His body is starting to cool off."

Chapter 31

Grau, wearing his blue dress uniform, his left arm in a sling across his chest, had to speak loudly in order to be heard over the happy din. The voices of several dozen officers and their families reverberated off the hard walls outside the main auditorium of One Police Plaza. A few of the smaller children who had managed to free themselves of adult restraint played in the crowded corridor until once again brought under the thumb of parental authority.

"Where are the other guys?" Grau asked Lieutenant Mante, also dressed in sharply pressed blues.

Mante shook his head, smiled and said, "Beats me. Last time I saw them they were fooling around outside, enjoying the August morning."

Grau took his uniform hat off and rubbed the inside band with his fingers. "You know, it's been a long time since I've been in one of these things. It feels kinda strange."

"Especially with that thing you have on," Mante said, pointing to the sling.

Grau put his hat back on and rubbed his left shoulder.

"Yeah. Funny, I have over twenty years on the job and I've never been shot before. Anyway, the department surgeon told me the slug just tore up a little muscle. A couple of more weeks and I'll be fine."

"Good. And after you get your promotion today, to First Grade Detective, you won't have to wear that uniform again for another long while."

At that moment Al Hastings walked out through the heavy wood doors of the auditorium. Moving with some haste, he headed in the direction of the bank of elevators which were off to the side in a nearby hallway. Mante caught his eye and motioned him over.

"Hi, Lou, Jon. Congratulations on your promotions," Hastings said, extending his hand.

Mante put up his hand. "Hey, Al, I'm just getting a medal." He motioned with his thumb to Grau. "This guy is getting the promotion."

The three chuckled, then Mante continued, "Where you off to?"

"Just running an errand for Chief Kinney. Seems he forgot his white gloves upstairs, in the big boss's office. Hey, I heard you finally got your helicopter back to Floyd Bennett."

"Yeah," Mante answered, "and let me tell you, it was a bitch. You know, after the floatplane hit the tower, I put the ship down in an open field. No more than ten seconds after she was on the ground the transmission seized on me. What a racket."

"So what'd you guys do? Put a new one in and fly it back to base?" Grau inquired.

"If it were only that easy. Nope. We had to truck that sucker back to Brooklyn. It took two days to work a flatbed in over that soft ground to the ship, then another day to put her aboard and fasten her down. She's still in the hangar, waiting for the new tranny."

Hastings asked, "What are you guys going to do, rebuild the old one?"

"Nope. It was trashed but good. That little slug really tore it up inside and I didn't help by keeping her in the air."

"How much will a new transmission cost?" Grau asked.

Mante chuckled and replied, "Jon, think in terms of the cost of a real nice house in the suburbs."

"Jon," Hastings said, "I hear they finally found that dead Russian's gun."

'Yeah," Grau replied. "It was pretty rusted on the outside, having lain in the woods for the better part of a week. You'd think it would have been easier to locate, since our guys found it only a couple of yards away from where that agent's body was thrown clear of the ship. But anyway, Ray Adleman made quick work of it. The slugs fired from it were a perfect match with the bullets taken from both my homicides and the ones in Brooklyn."

Mante shrugged. "Jon, I guess that tied up your case nicely."

Grau said. "Yeah, the gun was nice to have. But the guy's thumbprint matched the one we had from the other pistol he used, so there was never any doubt in anyone's mind that we had the right man."

Hastings asked, "Jon, what about that strange money and the printing plates you told me about? You ever figure the connection?"

Grau sighed. "Al, it's the damndest thing. Some State Department guys grabbed hold of that stuff. They told me I never saw it. And have you been reading the newspapers lately? Almost since the night we ran this operation the Soviet Union has been in a state of turmoil. Sounds almost like they're about ready to find themselves in the middle of another revolution. I can't help but wonder if what we did had anything to do with what's going on there."

Hastings shrugged. He excused himself and was soon lost in the crowd. Grau glanced at his watch. It was nearly eleven. The ceremonies were scheduled to start soon.

From down at the end of the hallway, coming from the direction of the building's entrance doors, Grau could see Tanti, in uniform, arm in arm with an attractive young woman. Grau waved. Tanti waved back and he and the woman made their way through the throng to Grau's side.

"Hi, Jon, Lou. Meet my wife, Sandy," Tanti said, introducing the young woman with him. She was several inches shorter than Tanti, with long brown hair and a pretty face and wore a conservative tan suit that showed off her dark complexion nicely.

The two men greeted her in turn, when movement of the people behind them announced that the auditorium had just opened. The milling crowd began to enter.

Grau turned to Tanti and quickly said, "I'll find you after this is over."

Tanti nodded as he and his wife were carried into the large room with the surge of people.

Grau worked his way down the aisle, to the lone row where those officers who were being promoted to First Grade Detective were to sit. He took his place between two other detectives whom he didn't recognize, nodded to them politely and looked around the room.

Sitting a few rows to his front was Mike Casson along with the other pilots and mechanics who had gone on the mission. Behind them were the ESU officers and Sergeant Chandler. Lights flashed as family members of the men came up and snapped their pictures.

A sergeant walked up to the podium, tapped on the microphone to ensure that it worked and asked everyone to take his seat. There was a bustle of activity on either side of the room while the officers' families and friends found their places. Once everyone had settled in, the Police Commissioner, dressed in a dark gray suit, took the floor. Grau's mind drifted while the commissioner began with his speech. Bits of sentences intruded into Grau's reverie, ". . . members of the department met the challenge," and ". . . we will not permit drug traffickers to confront this department, without their risking the ultimate penalty."

"Drug traffickers," Grau thought. "That's what the newspapers said we did, got into a battle over a drug shipment. It must have taken some pressure from Washington to squash this one."

After the speech, the commissioner took his seat on the dais. The Chief of Personnel stepped up to the podium and began calling off the names of those officers who were to receive medals. Row by row, the officers were led to the foot of the stage stairs. As their names were called they stepped up to the stage and marched the twenty-foot distance to the commissioner, saluted, and were presented with their medals.

Promotions were announced next. The Chief of Personnel, reading from a sheet of paper, said, "The following members of the service are promoted from the rank of Police Officer to that of Detective Investigator."

The officers two rows to Grau's front stood up, in preparation for the walk to the stage stairs. Standing fifth from the end Tanti turned his head, catching Grau's eyes. Both men smiled, then Tanti moved off with the others, to receive his gold detective shield.

Chapter 32

Zybof looked at the clock alongside his bed. It was nearly 6 A.M. What the hell, he thought, another night without sleep. But then, with the political restructuring that had been going on inside the government during the last several weeks, things had been very rough. He sat up on the edge of the bed and looked over at the sleeping form of his new secretary. Even that diversion hadn't been able to keep his thoughts still.

He stood up and walked to the bathroom. A sleepy voice called after him, "Anatoli, are you all right?"

"Yes, my dear. I'll be back in a moment."

Zybof splashed some water on his face and brushed his teeth. These young ones can be so demanding, he thought. Finishing up he returned to again sit on the bed. The first ray of sun had just broken over the horizon and he knew it would be futile to try and return to sleep.

A warm soft hand rubbed his back.

"You are worried, Anatoli. Tell me about your problems."

Zybof smiled and patted the pretty young face.

"There is nothing you can do to help, I'm afraid."

"I know, you think I'm just a silly girl with no brains," she pouted.

He smiled at her innocence.

"Not at all. It's just, well, you know what a mess things are in now. The country is up in arms over the state of the economy."

"But surely that's not your fault?"

"Perhaps. But part of my trouble is that I had been involved in a very delicate negotiation with the European Common Market countries, and because some problems came up the deal fell through."

"The Americans are plotting against you?" the young girl asked, as she sat up and began to rub Zybof's shoulders.

Zybof shrugged. "If it were only that simple. No, the problem is that several years ago my bureau started a very secret operation. It had been my plan, and a very good one at that. You see, there was this new Common Market currency called the ECU. Very valuable. So I decided to try to have the money duplicated for the good of the Soviet people."

"That sounds like a fine idea," she purred, nuzzling his neck.

"Yes. It really was. A handful of the bills were given to a group of Soviet forgers that my bureau sent to America."

"Why did you send them there?"

Zybof took a breath and carefully explained, "You see, at that time we did not, could not, have envisioned the current political climate between the East and West. So we planned to produce perfect counterfeits of the ECU ourselves, absolutely the real thing, and slowly insert the money into the European marketplace."

The woman made an *Uh-huh* noise and started to dig her fingers deeply into the tight muscles around Zybof's neck. Her hard nipples rubbed circles in his back. A little more of this and he'd be ready for bed again, Zybof reflected.

The girl softly asked, "But why send the forgers to America? Why not do it here?"

"Because we lacked the fine edge in technology to make truly perfect counterfeits. Only the Americans had the equipment and, to a certain extent, the technical know-how. The forgers were to come back to the Soviet Union after they learned enough, and they were also to smuggle the proper reproduction machines back to their own country. It was just that when the plan was abandoned, so were they. Anyway, since they had shown no desire to return it was decided they might prove useful as sleeper agents, if the need ever arose. So they were left in place."

"But why wasn't the currency taken from them?"

Zybof smiled at her attempts to understand the situation. And he silently hoped that that question wouldn't be asked of him by some of his colleagues in the Soviet government, particularly that swine in Internal Security, Novic.

"You see, it wasn't all that important a few years ago. It was all so theoretical. Who could have know that the ECU would in fact become the standard European currency?"

"So you are retrieving the notes from the forgers now?" she asked.

"Well, yes. Or at least I tried to do that. I was involved in an operation to get back the money and any counterfeit plates my little group of forgers might have fabricated. It seems that our small band that was sent to America decided to go into business for themselves. And all indications were they were planning to produce the ECU for their own personal gain."

The girl pouted and asked, "But Anatoli, why the fuss?

What if these people turn out some counterfeit ECU? What is it to us?"

Zybof shook his head. "Here is the problem. We had been working on a deal to trade our all-but-worthless rubles to the West for their valuable ECU. One for one. That would have been good for us and bad for them."

"Anatoli, why would they be so foolish as to do that?"

Zybof smiled and said, "For peace among nations, that is why, my sweet. So that there would be no hostilities between our countries. So that we could mutually reduce the size of our armies—which, by the way, are costing us a fortune to maintain. Yes, the price of peace in the world was to have been a few billion ECU from the West every year. Which would have been, after all is said and done, only a tiny fraction of their annual worth. Hell, they would have hardly noticed it, with all the money they would have saved by cutting back on their military spending."

The young woman asked, "Are you saying we were going to actually reduce the strength of our armed forces?"

Zybof laughed. "Of course not. Do you seriously think the West would pay us good money if they didn't perceive us as a threat? No, they would simply trade us a few of their precious ECU for our legal tender. And buy with their money a guarantee of world peace and friendship." Zybof sighed. "And when I tell you it would have been worth billions a year to our country I do not exaggerate. But, just when the negotiations were at a critical stage, things fell apart in America. My little operation to neutralize the forgers didn't work out so well. And after the Americans found out what we were up to they let the other European countries know of our money-printing idea. The people from the Common Market we were negotiating with were not pleased. The damn English, who had never been happy with the deal, have backed out. And the Germans are now not far behind."

Zybof turned and kissed his secretary on the lips. She responded warmly.

He reached around and slapped her naked behind.

"Come, it's time to shower and go to work. If there is still an office to go to. Or have you already solved my problems for me?"

"You always tease me, Anatoli."

Zybof laughed, grabbed some clean underwear from his drawer and padded off to the bathroom.

The woman lay back in bed and stared at the ceiling. A faint smile came on her face. It had taken over six weeks but she had finally done it. Comrade Novic would be very pleased with what she had found out.

Poor Anatoli.

ABOUT THE AUTHOR

Prior to his current position as the chief of police for the Wellfleet, Massachusetts Police Department, Richard Rosenthal spent 20 years in the New York City Police Department, from which he retired as a lieutenant. There he carried out a broad range of duties: he was lieutenant/pilot in the 66-officer NYPD Aviation Unit, he taught at the police academy and ran the Heavy Weapons Training and Undercover Weapons Training programs. He was a detective for many years, dealing with homicide, narcotics, armed robbery and other undercover investigations. Before joining the NYPD, he worked for United States Air Force military intelligence as a Russian language specialist involved in intelligence gathering overseas. He is a contributing editor to *Combat Handguns*, among other publications.

THE U.S. ARMY STRIKES BACK!

THE COMMON DEFENSE

A NOVEL OF COUNTERTERRORISM
ED RUGGERO
AUTHOR OF 38 NORTH YANKEE

The explosive novel of the U.S. Army's race to stop the world's most destructive terrorist from carrying out his ultimate mission.

☐ **THE COMMON DEFENSE**
73008-8/$20.00

Available Now in Hardcover from Pocket Books

Simon & Schuster Mail Order Dept.
200 Old Tappan Rd., Old Tappan, N.J. 07675

Please send me the books I have checked above. I am enclosing $_____ (please add 75¢ to cover postage and handling for each order. Please add appropriate local sales tax). Send check or money order–no cash or C.O.D.'s please. Allow up to six weeks for delivery. For purchases over $10.00 you may use VISA/MASTERCARD: card number, expiration date and customer signature must be included.

Name _____

Address _____

City _____ State/Zip _____

VISA Card No. _____ Exp. Date _____

Signature _____ 478

THE CHINA-MAN

A NOVEL OF REVENGE

STEPHEN LEATHER

The Chinaman is a breathtaking novel of nearly unbearable suspense that begins and ends with an explosion of action. Enter the labyrinth of blood, betrayal, and deadly passions in this engrossing and tightly woven thriller of terrorism and revenge.

Coming in May 1992 in Hardcover from Pocket Books